WHAT DOESN'T
KILL YOU

ALSO BY IRIS JOHANSEN

WHAT DOESN'T KILL YOU

IRIS JOHANSEN

**Doubleday Large Print
Home Library Edition**

ST. MARTIN'S PRESS ✥ NEW YORK

WHAT DOESN'T KILL YOU. Copyright © 2012 by Johansen Publishing LLLP. All rights reserved. Printed in the United States of America. For information, address St. Martin's Press, 175 Fifth Avenue, New York, N.Y. 10010.

ISBN 978-1-61793-642-5

Printed in the USA

**This Large Print Book carries the
Seal of Approval of N.A.V.H.**

WHAT DOESN'T
KILL YOU

CHAPTER
1

Sai Tam Island, China

"Where the hell are they?" Venable, deputy director of the CIA, had his binoculars focused on the small cottage in the valley below. "Special Ops were supposed to go in from the rear fifteen minutes ago and take Hu Chang out of there."

"It's a difficult job," Agent Gregory said. "The place is surrounded by mercenaries. You told Special Ops they had to get Hu Chang out alive."

"You're damn right. We have to know how much he told them and what he gave them." Besides the fact that Catherine Ling, who was one of his best agents, would kill

Venable if he allowed it to be bungled. She and Hu Chang had some kind of history. Even Venable wasn't sure exactly what it was. But, dammit, it wasn't Venable's fault that Hu Chang had gotten into this mess, and the CIA was having to pull him out.

Not that he wouldn't have had to go after him anyway if the story Venable's informant had told him was true. A potion that complex and dangerous had never been invented. It probably wasn't true, but why else was Hu Chang down there being tortured to make him talk? Venable couldn't take the chance.

"There they are," Gregory said as he went to the back of the helicopter and threw open the door. "We should be out of here in ten minutes."

Shots.

The door of the cottage flew open and four men in Special Ops gear ran out. And in the middle of the group was a slim, dark-haired man in a torn tunic. Hu Chang.

"*Yes.*" Venable watched as the Special Ops men fired back over their shoulders while they headed for the woods. Men were streaming out of the cottage.

More shots.

Then Hu Chang and the special team had disappeared into the trees.

"They should reach the helicopter in three minutes," Gregory said. "I'll go tell the pilot to be ready to lift off."

Three minutes passed.

Shots.

No Special Ops. No Hu Chang.

Another four minutes.

Venable began to curse.

Justin, the Special Ops commander, burst out of the trees and was climbing the rocks toward the helicopter. "Is he here?" he called. "I told him where you were in case we got separated. I can't find him."

"What?"

"I can't find Hu Chang. When we reached the trees, he slipped away from us. One minute he was there, the next he was gone. He's not here?"

"No, he's not here."

"Then I'll go back for him."

Shots.

More men running from the cottage to the woods.

"No, get your men back to the helicopter.

You're outnumbered. Just lay down protective fire to keep anyone away from the helicopter."

"What about Hu Chang? He was my mission, dammit."

"Evidently he didn't want to be your mission," Venable said. "And I'm not going to lose any of your men because he endangered you by this stupidity. We'll give him ten minutes, then we're out of here."

"They'll surround the area around the helicopter. He won't be able to get through."

"That's his problem. Go get your men."

Pain.

The bullet had entered Hu Chang's side, piercing flesh and muscle. The pain was blunt and brutal.

He fell to his knees as the second bullet tore past his ear. Then he was behind the rocks, crawling toward the helicopter balanced on the side of the cliff.

"Get the hell over here. Stay low. I can't risk anyone else coming out in this sniper cross fire," Venable shouted above the rotors from the doorway of the helicopter. "Special Ops got you out of that shack fifteen minutes ago. You were supposed to stay with them. Where have you been?"

"I had something to do," he called to the CIA agent. "It was important."

"We had a chance of making a clean getaway." Venable was cursing a steady stream. "You led them back to us. You're a complete idiot."

"Not the thing to say to a dying man," Hu Chang gasped as he started to crawl toward the helicopter. Another spate of bullets ricocheted off the rocks ahead of him, but they were high. "You have no sense of suitability, Venable."

"I came after you, didn't I? I waited." He was silent, watching Hu Chang crawl toward him. "Are you dying, Hu Chang?"

"I would not die from a bullet wound. It is ugly and without subtlety. There are so many better ways to kill a man. This kind of weapon is barbaric." He was almost to the helicopter. "But I'm bleeding. Bloodletting has a certain lethal glamour that even has historical significance. I could bear dying of loss of blood."

"I couldn't bear your dying at all. I'd catch hell, so you'd better shape up," Venable said roughly. "Just a few more feet, and we'll be able to pull you into the helicopter. Keep on coming."

"I find it interesting to know how you're going to get the helicopter off this cliff without a bullet through the gas tank once you're in the air?"

"I have an F-16 in the neighborhood. It will assist with ground fire as soon as I call it."

"An F-16 for me? I am honored."

"Honored? You're going to be dead if you don't hurry."

"I don't wish to cause the blood to flow with more alacrity in case I decide I don't want to pass this way. Be patient."

Silence. "I'll be patient. Take your time."

"I'm almost there."

"You *are* here." Venable jumped out of the helicopter and shouted to the CIA agent next to him. "Gregory, grab his other arm. Let's get him in the helicopter."

A spate of bullets sprayed around Venable and the other agent as they bent double and ran the few feet toward Hu Chang.

"Very foolish," Hu Chang said as he was

dragged toward the helicopter. "All you would have had to do was wait."

"Shut up," Venable said. "You've caused me enough trouble."

"You're just angry because of the F-16. I explored the cost of using one of those fighter jets once, and it was far beyond what I expected. I'm certain you'll have problems with your budget department over this extraction. After all, it's not as if I'm a president or a prime minister."

"You're certainly not." A bullet shattered the rock next to Venable, and he muttered a curse. "In!" They threw Hu Chang onto the floor of the helicopter and dove in after him.

"Though I'm far more valuable in my field than a mere politician. It's all a case of perception."

"Let's get out of here, Hank," Venable shouted to the pilot. "They'll be swarming anytime. When you hear the F-16, get out quick." He made the connection to the Air Force captain on the F-16. "We're lifting off. Give us cover for at least four minutes." He turned back to Hu Chang. "Don't you dare die. Do you hear me? Just give me a couple minutes, and I'll be free to take care of you."

"Not necessary." Hu Chang started to unbutton his shirt. "Attend to business."

The helicopter skittered sideways as it lifted, then veered off the cliff. It dropped over a hundred feet before the pilot was able to right it.

Then Hu Chang heard the F-16 above them, spraying the entire cliff with bullets as it swooped down, made a pass, then turned and made another run.

"I wish I could see it," he whispered. "It's most upsetting to be the center of such a major operation and not be able to witness it."

"Well, unless we get out of here before that F-16 leaves us to our own resources, you may do more than witness it." The helicopter veered to the left, then turned north. A moment later, Venable turned to Hu Chang. "I think we're clear."

"That is good." He was fighting dizziness, and Venable's face was no longer sharp, but hazy. "Then I believe I'll accept your help with this small inconvenience. I can't seem to stop the blood, and I've decided that I'm not ready to die. There are still too many goals to reach for a man of my talent."

"I'm glad that I can be of service," Venable said sarcastically as he fell to his knees beside Hu Chang. "I realize that you're condescending to permit—" He broke off as he opened Hu Chang's shirt. "Shit."

"My thought exactly. It's done considerable damage. I do hate bullets. Did I tell you that?"

"You told me." Venable was reaching for the first-aid kit. "Uncivilized."

"Exactly. I won't allow it to kill me, you know. But I do require assistance."

"You'll get it," Venable said grimly. "Now hang on, dammit. I can't let you die. You're not going to get me in hot water with her."

Hu Chang tried to laugh, but it ended in a cough. "I understand your intimidation. I'll do everything I can to prevent that from happening."

"Do that." He got out a gauze pad and began to use pressure. "How did you get yourself into this mess? You should have called me sooner."

"You're CIA. Doesn't CIA know everything?"

"Sure. We're all mind readers." He looked

up at Hu Chang. "This is bad. I'll try to pull you through, but I don't know if I can."

"Just get me somewhere that they can stop the bleeding. I'll take care of the rest."

"Another miracle potion, Hu Chang?"

"Of course." He closed his eyes. "Leave me alone. Don't talk to me. I have to concentrate. Just promise me one thing."

"What?"

"Don't . . . tell her about this. Don't tell Catherine Ling."

Hong Kong

"How is he?" Agent Bill Gregory asked Venable as he came into the apothecary shop. "And why the hell is he here instead of in the hospital? I thought he was a dead man when we got him off that helicopter."

"So did I." Venable lifted his cup of tea to his lips. "But Hu Chang wasn't having it. After we stopped the bleeding, he insisted on being brought home." His gaze wandered around the pristine shop, with its gleaming vials and bottles containing liquids of a hundred different hues and consistencies. "He brought in a neighborhood surgeon he trusted to do the surgery, and he's been swallowing his own concoctions instead of antibiotics." He made a face. "But considering his reputation, he's probably better off with them. Catherine swears he's a genius."

"But definitely illegal," Gregory said dryly. "He has no compunctions about creating exotic poisons as well as lifesaving medicines. I'm surprised the local government hasn't thrown him in jail, or at least closed him down."

"I'm not. In Hong Kong, when you're the best, you occupy a special place in the hierarchy. There's no telling when you might need his services. He's discreet and smart enough to walk a fine line."

Gregory tilted his head. "And have you used his services, Venable?"

He gave him a cool glance. "Do you think I'd answer that question? I walk a fine line, too, and I'm just as discreet as Hu Chang."

"Just curious," Gregory said quickly. "I thought it might help if you had a history with him. Have you started to question him yet?"

"No. He's been sleeping in his bedroom

in the back." His smile was twisted. "He said sleep was necessary for healing. He ordered me to stay out here in the shop and guard him. He assured me it would only be for 9.5 hours—that is exactly how he phrased it—and then we would talk." He checked his watch. "Which is up now." He finished his tea, put the cup back in the saucer, and set both on the elegant carved table beside the chair. "And I'll make my appearance and see what I can find out."

"Good luck." Gregory made a face. "I did everything from threatening him, to offering him a bribe and I wasn't able to find out zilch. That was why the director called you in to take over. You had this territory years ago. Right?"

"Right."

"And you know Hu Chang?"

"I can't claim that distinction. We've had . . . encounters. There's only one person who has a relationship with him."

"Catherine Ling."

He nodded. "Catherine."

"I've never worked with her." His eyes were bright with curiosity. "But I saw her recently when she was in town. She's drop-dead gorgeous. I could—"

"Good description," Venable interrupted. If he had to use Catherine, Gregory should be warned. "She's one of the most beautiful women I've ever met. And definitely the most lethal. Don't make the mistake of annoying her, Gregory."

"I won't." He grimaced. "She's something of a legend in this town. I hadn't been here more than a week, and I began to hear stories. She was born here?"

"No, in Seoul, Korea. Her mother was a half-Korean, half-Russian prostitute and her father an American soldier. Her mother brought Catherine to Hong Kong when she was four and died shortly after. Catherine had to survive on her own from that time on."

"In her mother's profession?"

"No, she was too smart. She found out that information was the most valuable commodity to sell in Hong Kong and made herself an expert. She became the person to go to when you needed to find out anything. We used her whenever we needed info from the time she was fourteen. When she was seventeen, I recruited her for the Company."

"And taught her everything she knows?"

"I helped." He glanced at the bedroom. "But she knows a hell of a lot more than I do about a lot things. She and Hu Chang are very, very close." He turned toward the door. "Wait here, Gregory. Keep watch."

He smiled. "I'm supposed to guard your back?"

"You're damn right. Just because we managed to get Hu Chang away from those bastards is no guarantee they won't try to snatch him again."

"Or kill him."

"But they'd rather have him alive. I don't think he'd have made it to the helicopter without being blown to bits if they'd wanted to kill him."

"They came close." Gregory held up his hand as Venable was about to speak. "I'm not arguing. Remember, I was the one who sent you the report on that leak I'd had from my informant. I know how important Hu Chang could be."

No, he didn't, Venable thought. Gregory hadn't the slightest idea how devastating this info he'd uncovered could be. He was only aware of the top layer. Venable had gone deep, and it was scaring the hell out of him.

Don't let Hu Chang see it. He was clever, and he would take advantage of any weakness. Venable couldn't afford to show that he had any doubts or fears. He turned and strode into Hu Chang's room.

"You are late." Hu Chang was sitting up in bed, and he stared blandly at Venable. "Punctuality is important."

"I'll try to remember," Venable said sarcastically. Damn, Hu Chang looked amazingly well considering the fact that he had wondered if the man was on his deathbed only the day before. There was color in his cheeks, and his dark eyes were bright and alert in his triangular face. He had no idea how old Hu Chang was because he appeared ageless. He was above average height, slim, but muscular with close-cut black hair and an expression that was totally enigmatic. He had heard Catherine tease him about it once. She had told Hu Chang he had seen too many kung fu movies. "Should you be sitting up? Won't you tear your stitches?"

"No. I will not. Another three days, and I will be well."

"I doubt that."

Hu Chang did not smile. "I do not. And

I know my body better than you, Venable."

"I'm sure you do, but there are laws of nature."

"Which can be circumvented also by nature." He inclined his head. "And no one knows how to do that better than I do. I will require you to assign someone to guard me while I sleep for the next two nights. I could just disappear, but I have work to do here in my lab."

"And I'm just supposed to furnish you with your bodyguard?" He shook his head. "Not likely. Not without adequate compensation. We need to make a deal."

"Oh, you didn't rescue me because you thought that I was too brilliant to leave this Earth?" He sighed. "I suspected that when I saw the F-16. I guess you've heard rumors. I don't suppose you'd believe me if I told you they weren't true? Not that I'd lie to you when I'm so grateful for your timely rescue."

"Bullshit."

"No, truly." He tilted his head. "Perhaps I'd be more grateful if I knew you'd done it to save me with no hint of ulterior motive. But I can't fault you. A person who acts selflessly without thinking of a return is rare indeed."

Venable's eyes narrowed on his face. "Like Catherine?"

Hu Chang nodded. "Like Catherine. Though she would deny it. She regards herself as a warrior."

"So do I."

He shrugged. "Yet she is what she is." He met Venable's gaze. "You have not told her?"

"No."

"That is good."

"But I will if you don't tell me who the target is, dammit."

"No, you won't. Because you're still hopeful of getting information out of me." He leaned back on the pallet and closed his eyes. "And that will not happen if you bring Catherine into it. I will just disappear. I'm very good at that."

"You may do it anyway."

"I promise I will not for the next three days. That will allow you to interrogate me and permit me to rest and recover."

"It will take you longer than three days to get well. That's total bullshit."

"We disagree. You may go now. It's time for me to get back to sleep."

Venable was so exasperated he wanted to yank him out of bed and shake him. Great. He'd probably kill him. Hu Chang might think he was on the way to recovery, but he had to be fragile. "Three days." He turned to go. "And we'll talk every day."

"Conversation can be so frustrating. Do you play chess?"

"No, I don't have the patience for it. Checkers."

"Chess. You're a man who uses your mind. You will conquer impatience."

"Let's go back to conversation." He paused. "This is no game to me, Hu Chang. It could cause too many deaths."

"That is why you're CIA. You take such things with great gravity. That's why I trust you to guard me well during the next days." His eyes remained closed. "But do not assign Agent Gregory to do that task. He is too young to realize what a treasure I am. He might be careless . . ."

He was already asleep, Venable thought, as he turned and left the room. He'd gone off in the blink of an eye.

But not without issuing that last order

about not using Gregory. He hadn't been planning on it. Like Hu Chang, Venable was bothered by Gregory's brash self-confidence. He might be smart, and Venable knew he was brave, but he preferred wariness. He'd do most of the duty himself while he tried to persuade Hu Chang to tell him what he needed to know.

Three days . . .

CHAPTER 2

Louisville, Kentucky
1:40 A.M.

"Catherine." Sam O'Neill was sitting in an easy chair in the living room and looked up from his book as she came in the front door. "I wasn't expecting you. How was Peru?"

"Ugly. It took longer than I thought to get the job done. But I managed to hop a ride on an Air Force jet as soon as I was free." She set her duffel down. "How is Luke?"

"Fine." He frowned. "But we should probably talk."

"After I see him, Sam. It's been three weeks." And it had seemed more like a year to Catherine since she'd seen her son.

"Is he asleep?" She started for the stairs. "I know he reads late most of the time."

"I don't know if he's awake or not. We have lessons during the day, and I give him the entire evening to read as a reward. I put no other restrictions on him."

"I know you don't. Smart." She was climbing the stairs. "Otherwise, we'd have a rebellion on our hands. You can't treat him as a child. He's gone through too much. But he's been happy? It's hard to tell when I phone him."

"Your son has not been unhappy." He grinned. "What's not to like with me as a tutor?"

And Catherine was grateful every day that she'd been able to hire Sam in that capacity. An ex-CIA man with the ability to protect Luke as well as teach him was a rare find. "Let me think." She smiled back at him as she reached the top of the steps. "Perhaps just a little trace of arrogance?"

"Luke doesn't mind. He ignores it." He looked back down at his book. "He just regards me as a vessel of information to drain every day."

Catherine paused before Luke's door and took a deep breath. Then she quietly opened his bedroom door. "Luke?" Her voice was soft, tentative, as she stared into the darkness. She knew he sometimes read late into the night, but it was after one in the morning, and, if the room was dark, she should probably wait until morning to see him. It would be the sensible thing to do.

To hell with being sensible. She was hungry to see him, touch him. He knew she wasn't ordinary or sensible, and she thought he was beginning to accept her with all her warts.

"I'm awake, Catherine." He turned on the light on the bedside table. He never called her mother, and she never pushed it. How could she when he had been taken from her when he was only two as an act of revenge against Catherine by a Russian Mafia head? What memories Luke had of her during that early childhood were like dreams with no substance. All the period of his nine years of captivity with Rakovac he had been told every day how the pain he endured was her fault. She was lucky that he had rejected that lie and was willing to give them their chance together. He sat up in bed. "I just finished a book and didn't want to start a new one tonight. I wasn't expecting you. You haven't called me lately."

"I know. I'm sorry." She came across the room and sat down on the chair beside his bed. She wanted to lie down beside him, hug him, hold him. Don't do it. Let it come from him. Someday it would happen. But she could look at him, and, Lord, he was beautiful. His shock of silky black hair that was like her own, his skin that was a little paler than her own golden ivory, and those dark eyes that could glitter with such ferocity and wariness that they made him look far older than his eleven years. But occasionally, lately, she had seen them gleam with humor, and she regarded that as a major victory. In those striped pajamas he looked thin, but she knew he had gained weight since she had rescued him from that bastard, Rakovac. She'd had his tutor, Sam, weigh him regularly, though that procedure was met with extreme impatience. Luke had never been treated like a child, and Catherine had to be careful not to offend that tigerish sense of independence. "It would have been . . . awkward to phone you."

"You mean it would have been danger-ous." Luke tilted his head. "Why don't you say it? I know what you do. Rakovac told me all the time that you had no time for me because you were CIA and that was all you cared about."

Pain rippled through her. "You know that wasn't true."

"No, I didn't. Not for a long while. But then I knew he only wanted to hurt me, and that was probably just another way to do it."

"Actually, he wanted to hurt me." She tried to smile. "You were just the means to an end." A horrible means that had hurt her more than anything else that he could have possibly done. The knowledge that he was hurting her son had been the most excruciating torture. "We've talked about this before. I'd hoped to put it behind us."

"Did you?" He was gazing at her, puz-zled. "But how can that be? It happened, it's with us. I think about it a lot."

Shit.

"Do you? I try not to remember it if I can help it." She paused. "Would you like to talk about it? Are there any questions that you'd like to ask?"

"No, I just think about it." He frowned. "I think about you, Catherine."

"Do you? Should I ask how I'm scoring?"

"Scoring." He was instantly distracted. "That's a sports term."

"That's right." And Luke had never been permitted any sports or play at all, she thought bitterly. He had been raised by a guerilla and a murderer and had learned about death and killing from the time he was a small child. His only salvation had been his books, and when he'd been freed, he'd immersed himself in the printed word and the worlds it brought to him. "Sam said he's teaching you tennis now. Do you like it?"

He nodded. "Better than golf. But it still seems pointless. What difference does it make?"

When you'd grown up being exposed to life-or-death situations, it wasn't strange that Luke couldn't understand the concept of competition for competition's sake. You fought to live. "It never hurts to be exposed to something that might be a challenge." She could see he was about to argue the point, and she prompted, "You said that you were thinking about me."

He was silent, then said slowly, "I . . . think I'm worrying about you."

She stared at him. "You are? Because I'm CIA?"

"Maybe. Though I don't believe that's the reason. CIA is like being a soldier, and no one worries about soldiers. They just do their job. If they're good, they live. If they're not, they die. That's why you have to work hard to be good."

"Is that what you learned from all those guerilla raids you were forced to go on when you were held prisoner in Russia?"

He nodded. "And Sam tells me that you're very good. So I shouldn't worry about you."

"That's very logical. I should add, however, that here in this country we care very much about our soldiers. They're not considered throwaways like the men who fought under Rakovac. Many of those were professionals hired to fight and kill." It was very difficult to strike a balance in explaining things to Luke. His actual experience had been brutal and without any emotion that was not cruel from the time he was two until she had rescued him from Rakovac a short time ago. When he had been given access to books, it had been a stunning eye-opener, but there were times when he regarded history and philosophy in the same light as fairy tales. "That being said, if you shouldn't worry about me, what's the problem?"

"I think I should make sure that you're as good as Sam said." His gaze traveled the room. "You give me a lot . . . food, books. Maybe I should help you."

"And maybe you shouldn't," she said firmly. "You don't owe me anything, Luke. I owe you. That's the way it works. Mothers take care of their children. It's their pleasure and duty."

"Duty." He repeated the word. "I don't understand. Soldiers have duty, and I can see how that would be necessary. But everyone in my books uses that word for so many other things."

"You don't have to understand. Duty can either be forced or a choice. I choose. So stop fretting and just let me do my job. You owe me nothing."

"But what if I choose to . . . fret?" She could see he had been tempted to stop and savor that word, but had resisted it. He was fascinated by the sound and textures of words, particularly ones he considered unusual. "I'm . . . confused. I'll have to decide . . ."

"I won't try to talk you out of it." That would be futile and might make him rebel, the last thing she wanted. "But discuss it with Sam, okay?" She got to her feet and stood looking down at him. "Is that why you've been so quiet lately?"

"Have I been quiet?"

"For a long time before I left on that Peru job."

"And you noticed? Why?"

Because I love you. Because every breath you take is important to me. "Must be my CIA training."

"I notice things about you, too. It's been happening more and more often since we came to live here." He thought about it. "Though maybe a little more when you took me to Hong Kong right after you killed Rakovac. It was very strange there, but you seemed to . . . like it."

"Like it? It's a city, and a city is people. I know a lot of people in Hong Kong."

"Like Hu Chang. He's your friend."

"Yes, and he'd be your friend, too." She paused. "If you'd let him. You were a little standoffish with him. Not that I blame you. Everything must have seemed crazy at that time."

He nodded. "I wanted to do what you wanted me to do, but I couldn't. He was a stranger."

"And you were never allowed to talk to strangers," she said bitterly. "Or to anyone else either."

"I talked to him when he took me down to his lab and showed me how he blended his medicines. That was interesting. He even let me mix up a couple."

"Then you're honored. He's very particular who handles his herbs."

"I could tell. He kept frowning at me."

"That didn't bother you?"

"No, he wasn't angry. I think he was trying to figure me out the way he did those formulas he was working on."

"Did he do it?"

"I don't know. It didn't matter to me. I was just interested in what we were doing. But I don't think Hu Chang actually minded that I didn't talk much to him. He was busy talking to you. Every now and then, he would look at me, and I could see him trying to find something in . . ." He shook his head. "He liked it that I didn't talk. It gave him time."

"I don't know what you mean."

"And it gave me time, too. I was feeling . . . It was strange being with you. I watched you with him. You're different than you are with other people. You're more . . . open. I could see deeper . . . I didn't feel so strange and alone being with you after that."

"Then bless Hu Chang." She smiled as she lightly touched his hand on the bed. Just a fleeting touch, then back away. There had been a time when she'd not been able to touch him at all without his tensing. They were making strides. Every talk, every confidence, every moment they were together was another step forward. Even Luke's mentioning Hu Chang had been progress. Their trip through Hong Kong on their way back to the States had been necessary for Catherine, but it had been a chaotic nightmare for Luke after his incarceration in that solitary house in Russia. It was not surprising that he had withdrawn into himself and been an almost silent observer. He had never mentioned Hong Kong or Hu Chang since arriving in Kentucky. It was odd that he should bring Hu Chang up tonight.

But no more odd than this introspection that seemed to be preying on him lately. Hell, perhaps it was healthy. He was no longer so absorbed in himself and his beloved books but examining the people and the world around him.

"Next time I talk to Hu Chang, I'll tell him that you sent your regards."

He nodded absently. "If he's your friend, I should do that. Sam says it's polite."

"Then I'll go downstairs and commend Sam for teaching you good manners," she said lightly. "I only waved to him when I came in the front door. I wanted to get up here to see you." She turned toward the door. "What about driving down to Atlanta tomorrow to see Eve Duncan and Joe Quinn?"

"Okay. Eve sent me a new book on forensic sculpting last week." He reached over and turned off the lamp. "It was very interesting."

"Then you can thank her in person. I'll call her in the morning." Luke accepted closeness from very few people, and it was important that Catherine urge him gently to leave that self-imposed isolation and encourage those relationships. She opened the door. "Good night, Luke. I'm glad to be home."

Silence. "I'm glad you're home, too, Catherine."

Another step. Not a giant step, but she'd take what she could get. "That's good to hear, Luke."

She closed the door gently behind her.

More than good. It made her think that she was gaining ground and not just standing still.

The smile was still on her lips when she went downstairs to the living room where Sam O'Neill was reading a *National Geographic.*

"He looks great, Sam," she said. "You're taking good care of him."

"You're damn right I am. Not easy." Sam took off his glasses and wiped them. "He's a challenge. But then he's your son. I expected it." He smiled. "And looked forward to it. When I left the Company, I knew I was going to have some serious problems with tamping down the adrenaline when I went back to teaching. With Luke, every day is a unique experience. *He's* unique."

"Unique? I wish every day that he was an ordinary kid who could just enjoy his childhood." She wearily dropped down on the couch. "And he's changing, isn't he? Is it for the better?"

"I'm not sure. It could be."

"That's right. Reassure me." But Sam wasn't going to tell her anything unless he was certain. He was as honest as he was intelligent. "He was looking at me upstairs as if I were a bug under a microscope. Yet I don't believe there was animosity. You're with him every day. Am I lying to myself?"

He shook his head. "He's been asking me questions about you lately. I've been honest with him. I thought that would be what you wanted."

"Of course it is," she said curtly. "After all Luke and I have been through, it would be stupid to pretend I'm some cozy PTA mom. Complete honesty is the only thing that might save us. Besides, that bastard who held him all those years made sure that Luke believed that I was to blame for every beating he gave him."

"You killed Rakovac?"

"With great pleasure and as much pain as I could inflict. Didn't Luke tell you? He wasn't there, but when he asked me, I told him the truth."

"No, Luke doesn't mention Rakovac. He appeared to live totally in the present . . . until recently." He got to his feet. "Do you want coffee? I could use some."

"No, I've had too much already." She followed him into the kitchen. "I don't believe Luke blamed me for Rakovac. How could he? He hated the son of a bitch. He told me he would have killed him himself if he'd gotten the chance. And he would have done it." Her lips tightened grimly. "Eleven years old, and that's what Rakovac made of him. When other kids were in Little League, Luke was being taught to handle weapons and how to survive fighting with a bunch of guerillas. Rakovac wanted to destroy every sign of the lovable kid Luke was before he took him from me. And he kept me informed every step of the way. Luke was beaten and kept isolated, and it's a wonder he was able to survive."

"A miracle," Sam agreed as he spooned

instant coffee into a cup. "And if he hadn't had your genes, it would never have happened. I see traces of you beginning to appear every day."

"Then God help him."

"He did." Sam smiled. "That survival instinct. He gave it to both of you." He poured hot water from the dispenser into the cup. "You do realize that after going through nine years of that hell, Luke could have turned into a monster. I'm sure that's what Rakovac intended by that abuse."

"So do I."

"Instead, Luke only withdrew and immersed himself in books. It was the healthiest thing he could have done. Luke has a fantastic mind and a memory that borders on being close to total recall. He could dive in and close out everything around him that wasn't on the printed page. It not only educated him but aroused and satisfied the curiosity that seems to be one of his prime qualities."

"That he indulged twenty-four hours a day," she said dryly. "I've been wondering if I was mistaken, Sam. After being isolated for nine years, I thought his passion for books would be a gentle way to open the world for him. Did I just furnish him with another prison?"

"With me as the prison guard?" Sam grinned. "Hell, no. It was sound reasoning. Particularly hiring a brilliant educator like me. You did the best thing you could do under the circumstances."

"Then why is he suddenly—what's going on with him?"

"Only Luke knows for sure, and I'm not sure that he's not pretty confused." He lifted the coffee to his lips. "You want a guess? You gave him a cocoon in which to wrap himself when you brought him here. He stayed there and spun a comfortable web for himself."

"So? He deserved a time of peace and security."

"Absolutely. But have we taken into consideration that what he deserved did not have anything to do with Luke's experience and character? Yes, he suffered, but what was done to him developed a child who was not a child, a boy who was forced to use his wits and his mind just to survive." He looked thoughtfully down into his coffee. "He was used to being totally on his own, not expecting help from anyone because everyone was the enemy."

She flinched. "I know that. Do you realize how much that hurts me?"

"And you want passionately to protect him in any way you can."

"Wouldn't you?"

"I'd probably be worse than you. At least, you're not pushing the boy. I know how hard it is for you to give him his space. You're going slow. I have a tendency to give little shoves to get him to take the next step." He took a sip of coffee. "But that may not be necessary from now on."

"What do you mean?"

"That cocoon may be breaking open. He could be tired of being immersed in his books and the worlds they bring to him. He has a boundless curiosity, and perhaps he's ready to toss the cocoon aside and find out all the answers for himself."

"Don't scare me like that."

"You knew it would come sometime."

"Do you know how often I've worried that Luke will just take off and go somewhere on his own?" she asked unevenly. "I have no hold on him as any other mother

might. As you said, he's been independent all his life, and if I tried to put him in
any kind of prison, he'd leave me. I couldn't
stand that, Sam."

"Yes, you could. But if he left you, you'd
be his shadow until you could persuade
him to come back. Even if it took the rest
of your life."

That was true. She would never stop.
She had lost Luke once, and she would
never let it happen again. "Okay, you think
he's getting bored? What can we do?"

"Not bored. He's too bright to be bored.
He always finds a way to challenge himself. I believe he may be exploring ways to
bridge the gap between the past and present." He added, "Did I tell you he'd asked
me to give him lessons in karate?"

"No, you did not."

"He said that since I'd worked for the
CIA, I should be good enough to teach
him." He chuckled. "I made him pay for
that. But he learned the basic moves very
quickly. He's a natural."

"He knows enough about killing and violence, Sam. He doesn't need you."

"If he wanted to know, he'd find out

everything from one of his books. I just made it easier." He finished his coffee and set the cup on the sink. "Don't dwell on it. It's just an example of the way Luke is thinking. He's pulling memories and skills from his past and elaborating on them. He may not even know whether he has a purpose or not."

"And neither do you."

"I'm just along for the ride. I'll see where it takes me," he said gently. "I like the kid, Catherine. This isn't just a job to me."

"I know it's not." She squeezed his arm affectionately before she turned away. "And I'm grateful, Sam. I never worry when I'm away if you're on the job."

"That's a lie. You're thinking about Luke all the time. But he'll always be safe with me."

"If he doesn't decide to go off on his own tilting at windmills or something."

"I'd be right behind him."

"I know you would. Good night, Sam."

The next moment, she was moving slowly up the stairs. She should shower and go to bed. It had been close to thirty hours since she'd slept, but she wasn't sure she'd be able to do it now. The conversation with Sam had not made her feel less uneasy.

She wanted Luke in that cocoon, dammit.

It was the only way she could be sure of keeping him safe and give her a chance to teach him how much she loved him. But she couldn't bury her head in the sand if there was something happening with Luke. If as Sam was judging, he was becoming— What? She didn't even know what Luke was thinking. There were times when she was almost sure that the bond that they were forging was getting stronger, but he was still a mystery.

A beloved mystery.

Dear God, how she loved him.

All she could do was stay close to him and watch every nuance of change. Find a way to let him know she loved him without making him feel uncomfortable.

And if he wanted out of that damn cocoon, she'd break it herself before he got the chance.

"Water, Venable," Hu Chang called from the bedroom. "And the vial with the orange liquid on the stand next to the black-lacquer cabinet."

"I'm not your nurse, Hu Chang," Venable said testily as he got to his feet. "Is there anything else?"

"Not at the moment. You sent Agent Gregory to the fishmonger to get the oil?"

"Yes, over an hour ago."

"Then he should be back. I told Li San to have it ready. Your man is very inefficient."

Arrogance. "I'll send him in to you to chastise when he gets back."

"You're being sarcastic, but discipline is important. And it's you who must reprimand him for dawdling. It's your duty as his superior."

Venable handed Hu Chang the vial and set the water on the nightstand. "I'll take your suggestion under advisement." He watched him lift the vial to his lips and drain it. "What is that stuff?"

"Herbs, oils, venoms, and a few spices. Very potent." He lifted the glass of water and drained it in three swallows. "But that's almost the last of it. I'll need to make more."

Potent? For the last twenty-four hours, Hu Chang had been gaining in strength at an amazing pace. His cheeks were flushed, his eyes bright and alert, and his movements lithe and apparently accomplished without pain. "It must be good stuff. But doesn't the water dilute it?"

"I hope so," Hu Chang said. "Otherwise, I'll be dead within two minutes. The really good potions are always those that have a fair amount of risk. The efficacy factor depends on the power."

"It's poison?"

He nodded. "Deadly. Sea-snake venom. You can add the deadliest of poisons as long as it is tempered. It's all in the balance." He smiled faintly. "And the balance must have been good this time. I'm still alive."

"And you're healing?"

Hu Chang opened his shirt. "See for yourself. I removed the bandage. It's no longer necessary. There are still surface wounds, but the inner damage has healed itself."

Venable muttered a curse as he stared at the wound. "It's damn near incredible."

"Yes, I am." He buttoned his shirt. "I'm sure that Catherine told you that I was extraordinary."

"I'm beginning to believe her. But why don't you take out a patent on these hotshot potions? You could be a billionaire."

"Incredible does not happen every day. It requires attention and effort. Some fool would be careless and alter my formula, and I would have a dead client. I'm too much of a perfectionist to allow that to take place." He glanced down at his chest. "The potion is beginning its burn. I can feel it working. I may not need that last vial after all."

"If you're feeling so well, this may be the time to have our talk."

"We are talking. And in the very best manner. You are admiring, and I am accepting your admiration. That could be—" He broke off as his phone rang. He glanced at the ID, then punched the access. He said something in Chinese that Venable didn't catch, then listened.

A moment later he hung up the phone. "But I'm afraid our discussion will have to end for the time being. That was one of my neighbors who lives down the block. He told me he saw a package being dropped off at the alley door. I think perhaps you should retrieve it."

"A package?" His gaze narrowed on Hu Chang's face. "What kind of package?"

He didn't answer the question. "I don't believe there is a threat now. I would have been told. But a retrieve is definitely necessary."

Venable turned on his heel and left the bedroom and headed for the alley door. He waited, listening.

No sound.

He pulled out his Glock and stepped to one side before throwing open the door.

The man who had been hunched against the door fell forward into the shop at Venable's feet.

Agent Gregory. Eyes wide, staring into nothingness.

His throat cut from ear to ear.

CHAPTER 3

Louisville, Kentucky

It was after seven, Catherine realized drowsily as she opened her eyes. She would lie here for just a moment and enjoy the sensations of home after the weeks of camping out in the jungle alternating with a crummy hotel room in Lima.

Not like this.

She stretched like a cat.

Crisp cotton sheets and a familiar mattress, the scent of lotus subtly mixed with one of the clean yet haunting fragrances that Hu Chang sent her to tuck inside her pillows. She had told him once that she was sure that the fragrance was some kind of sleeping powder that caused her to fall into a deep sleep. Hu Chang had smiled.

But he had not denied it.

Catherine jumped out of bed and headed for the hall door. It wouldn't take her that long to get down to Eve and Joe's lake house, but if she could get Luke moving, they might have time to breakfast together before it was time to leave. Those breakfasts were to be treasured. She had missed so many of them after Luke had been taken from her. Little things. Breakfasts. School pictures. Birthday parties.

So treasure every moment, every event big or small.

"Breakfast!" She threw open Luke's door. "We'll make it together. Do you want pancakes or—"

Luke was gone.

The bed neatly made, but Luke was not in it.

Panic surged through her.

Luke, only two years old. She had put him to bed and kissed him good night. Three hours later, throwing open the door and finding that bed empty.

Not again. Please God, not again.

"Catherine?"

Luke's voice.

She whirled and saw him coming toward her down the hall. Relief. Blessed relief. She reached out and grasped the doorjamb. Don't let him see that moment of weakness. She was supposed to be the strong one in this relationship. She drew a deep breath. "Hi, I guess I'm a little late. I was going to wake you up, but you're all dressed. Where have you been?"

"Down in the library. I thought I'd take a couple books with me when we went to see Eve and Joe." He nodded to the two books he was carrying. "We were talking about Hu Chang, and I remembered that he gave me this one the day we left."

"You haven't read it yet? That's a surprise. You usually devour a book as soon as you get it."

"I read it." He frowned. "But I don't think I understood it. I thought I'd try again."

She glanced at the top book and started to laugh. "Luke, that book is in Chinese. Of course, you wouldn't understand it."

He shook his head. "I don't think that's it. I think I should have understood it."

She flipped through the book. She did understand the script, and it appeared to be a chemistry book of some sort. "Pretty dry stuff. I'll have to talk to Hu Chang about his choice of reading matter." She smiled as she handed the book back to Luke. "I wouldn't strain my brain trying to puzzle this out. Unless you really want to learn the language. Tell Sam, and he'll help you." She paused. "Or I could. I'm not as good a teacher, but it might be fun."

He shook his head. "You're busy." He tucked the book under his arm. "But I'll try to do it on my own first. I should be able to understand it."

She smothered the disappointment and smiled. "Far be it for me to discourage you. How about helping me to fix breakfast?"

He nodded. "If that's what you want."

There were so many things that she wanted from him. Stop being maudlin. The thing she wanted most was for him to be happy. "That's what I want." She started down the stairs. "I've got to call Eve and tell her we're coming, but there's no real hurry. We can take our time. Maybe Joe will cook barbecue for dinner. I know you like that."

He nodded. "I'd never had barbecue before I visited Joe and Eve."

"It's very good, isn't it?"

"But I think it's more than food. It's sort of like a ceremony, isn't it?"

"Ceremony?"

"People gathering around the fire, talking, singing, watching the food cook. It reminds me of ceremonies I've read about in my books . . . but different."

"We don't do much singing, but that's very perceptive of you. I guess perhaps it is a kind of American ceremony. It's certainly a custom."

"I don't know why, but I . . . like it."

"Then don't take it apart, just enjoy it. Orange juice?" She headed for the refrigerator as he nodded. "Me, too. I don't think I've had one glass since—" Her phone rang, and she glanced at the ID.

Venable, dammit. She was tempted not to answer.

Not now, Venable.

Luke was looking inquiringly at her.

She punched the button. "I don't want to talk now, Venable. You must have heard that everything went well with the job in Peru. We retrieved the dirty bomb and the code, and it's wrapped up. I'll send you a report later. Now I'm hanging up. I'm having breakfast with my son."

"It will have to wait. I need you on a plane here to Hong Kong in the next two hours."

"No way. Get someone else to do the job. I'm taking a break."

"I can't get someone else. You're the only one who has a chance to get it done. He may listen to you." He paused. "If he lives until you get here."

"Why me? I've just gotten home. I haven't seen Luke for the past—"

"It's Hu Chang, Catherine."

She stiffened. "Hu Chang. What the hell are you talking about?" She tried to remember what he'd said. "And what do you mean if he lives until I get there? What's happened to Hu Chang?"

"Do you want me to catalog it for you? He's been severely beaten, he's been shot in the upper torso and should have died except he's been dosing himself with some high-caliber meds, and he's responsible for getting one of my agent's throat cut."

"Shot? Why?"

"Because he wouldn't obey the Special

Forces guys I sent in to save his neck. He said he had something to do before he could be rescued."

"Rescued?" Every word was scaring her more. "None of this is making sense. Whose throat was cut?"

"Agent Gregory. You've never met him. He was a decent enough guy, but he was out of his depth."

"And how did you get involved with Hu Chang, Venable? He doesn't work with the CIA or any other country's security organization. He's a loner."

"Tell me about it. For the last few days, I've been trying to persuade him he'll end up in the bottom of the China Sea if he doesn't let us help him. He's not talking. Not to us, and not to the sons of bitches who nearly made chopped liver of him."

She moistened her lips. "They were beating him to make him talk? About what, Venable? What's he done?"

"I see you're not assuming he's an innocent victim."

"Hu Chang stopped being innocent a long, long time ago. He's capable of doing anything that he chooses. But he doesn't usually choose anything that would get him into this kind of trouble. What's he done?"

"I'm not sure. I think he's concocted some potion or drug that's fairly world-shaking."

"Why would that get him beaten?"

"It might be that it has commercial potential. I saw how fantastically one of the drugs in his shop performed. It blew me out of the water."

But there was a note in his voice that caused her to ask. "But you think it's something else? Of course you do, or you wouldn't have gotten the Company involved."

"I could have wanted to help out a friend of yours."

"You wouldn't have called in the Special Forces. You would have done it yourself. Talk to me. What's Hu Chang up to?"

"I can't be sure." He paused. "But the field agent's informant here in Hong Kong said he'd heard that Hu Chang was involved in some big-time stuff in which Hugh Nardik was very interested."

"Nardik?" Her mind was working quickly, bringing up memories and bits and pieces of information. Smuggling, weapons dealing, rumors of links to occasional high-profile assassinations. He also provided mercenary soldiers to third-world countries to fight their wars, and those were the stories that Catherine remembered most vividly. She had never been sent on a mission concerning him, but she had been told about the atrocities of his forces in Rwanda. "He's very nasty. Can't you reel him in?"

"I would if I could. Right now, between bribery and his bodyguards, he's untouchable. I was hoping that he'd show up when they grabbed Hu Chang, but it didn't happen. He hired some locals here in Hong Kong to take care of the job. He was probably going to take over if they didn't get him what he wanted."

"And what did he want from Hu Chang?"

Silence.

"Tell me."

"My guess? An assassination. Drugs and poisons are Hu Chang's specialty. If you didn't want anyone to be sure that a world leader or dictator had been murdered, wouldn't poison be the best way to take him out?"

"If there was no way to detect it. But that's not possible. There are some poisons that

come close, but with time and sophisticated forensic techniques, there's always
a way to identify it."

"Perhaps I have more faith in Hu Chang
than you do."

No one had more faith than Catherine,
and no one knew how brilliant Hu Chang
was more than she did. He was always
evolving, making advances, turning curi-
osities into miracles.

Oh, Hu Chang, what have you done
now?

"Is that what your informant was saying?"

"He said there were rumors."

"That doesn't mean anything. Hu Chang
wouldn't talk about any of his drugs. Maybe
it was somebody's pipe dream."

"Maybe. You'll have to ask Hu Chang."

"You ask him."

"I leaned on him pretty heavily after my
agent was killed. He won't talk to me." He
paused. "As a matter of fact, I guess I'd
better confess that he's disappeared."

"What?"

"Calm down. I believe it was purely vol-
untary. He probably realized that I wouldn't
keep on trying to get him to talk without

you as a backup. I'm turning Hong Kong upside down trying to locate him."

Which wouldn't do any good, she thought. Hong Kong was Hu Chang's city, and he could slip away without a trace. He had too many friends, too many bolt-holes he'd used through the years. "Okay, let me try calling him."

"Not a good idea if you don't want him to just dig in deeper. The one thing he told me was to not tell Catherine Ling about all this."

"Shit."

"Of course, you could forget about him, let me try to handle it. He's proving very troublesome, and you don't want to leave your son."

"You're damn right I don't." She was silent. "He almost died?"

"If he hadn't had his magic elixir, he'd be a dead man. Next time, he may not be so close to his supply. They didn't mean to kill him until they got what they wanted from him. But accidents happen."

And Hu Chang wouldn't give them what they wanted no matter how much they tortured him. She had seen his stamina and endurance in a dozen different situations.

"I'll come." Her hand tightened on the phone. "You keep searching for Hu Chang. I'll come."

"Good. I'll do my best. There's a Delta flight to L.A. out of Louisville in two hours that will connect to Hong Kong. I'll meet you at the airport."

"No, stay and keep looking for him." She tried to think. "But I want this over as quickly as I can do it. I want help. I don't know anything about Nardik. Get me an agent who has dealt with him before."

"That may not be easy. We haven't been able to get an agent close enough to Nardik to claim to be an expert."

"Find somebody." She closed her eyes. "And you make sure Hu Chang is alive when I get there, or I'll come after you, Venable."

"You don't need to threaten me. When I'm not pissed off at him, I like the guy." He hung up the phone.

That was a concession from Venable. Hu Chang was arrogant, difficult, enigmatic, and completely his own person. He never tried to make anyone care about him.

And she loved him more than anyone in the world except Luke.

"Hu Chang is in trouble?"

She turned to see Luke standing behind her. She forced a smile as she hung up the phone. "Have you been eavesdropping? Didn't Sam tell you that isn't polite?"

"Yes, but I heard you say his name, and I wanted to know what you were talking about."

And politeness went down for the count. Luke was seldom bound by rules he didn't understand. "Hu Chang has been hurt. I have to go to him."

He shook his head. "Something bad happened to him. Someone hurt him?"

"Yes, I don't know who or why yet. I have to go and ask him."

He frowned. "And then you'll kill whoever did it?"

What was she supposed to answer? To hell with being anything but honest with him. "It may come to that. If he tries to attack Hu Chang again. I won't let my friend be hurt."

"I . . . wouldn't like that to happen." He was silent a moment. "I could help you."

She felt a ripple of shock. "To kill someone? No, I don't think so, Luke."

"It wouldn't be that different for me. I

probably killed people when I went on those raids with Rakovac. I aimed, I pulled the trigger, just as he told me to do."

Yes, he probably had killed before. One of the cruelest aspects for her of Luke's captivity had been Rakovac's hideous determination to twist her son's character out of all semblance to the loving boy she had known. Rakovac had been involved in the final remnants of the Georgian-Russian conflict and from early childhood had exposed him to the blood and death of that war. She smothered the fury that memory always brought. "But that's over now."

"Is it?" he asked. "Once he tried to get me to kill one of his men who had betrayed him. He wanted me to press the gun to his head and pull the trigger. I wouldn't do it. It seemed different than the raids. That was sort of like war. But I didn't like the idea of shooting a man who couldn't shoot back."

"Thank God." The idea of forcing a child to commit cold-blooded murder made her want to have Rakovac here before her so that she could kill him again. "It would have been wrong."

"But it's not wrong to kill someone to

save your friend. In all the books I've read, that seems to be okay."

Right and wrong. Do as I say, not as I do. "There are differing opinions. When you get older, then you can make decisions like that. But give yourself time, Luke. It may not be necessary for you to hurt anyone ever again."

He shook his head. "I think I should go help you."

She drew a deep breath. "And I think you should stay with Sam and let me go protect my friend. Will you do that for me?"

"Why?"

"Because I would worry if you came along. It would make me feel bad."

He tilted his head. "You worry a lot, Catherine. I noticed that."

"Right, it goes with the territory when you care about someone as I do you. Then don't make me worry any more than I do right now." She met his eyes. "I don't want to leave you, Luke. I know it seems as if I drop in, then take off in the blink of an eye. But I really have to do this. Will you forgive me?"

"Why?" He was looking at her in bewilderment. "It doesn't matter."

Pain shot through her. She smiled with an effort. "That's right, how foolish of me. I thought you might be disappointed." She started up the stairs. "Now you go make yourself some breakfast while I throw some things into a suitcase and call Sam and tell him that you're going to be free today after I leave for the airport."

"Catherine."

She looked back over her shoulder.

Luke was still standing in the doorway, gazing up at her. "Is it all right if I go to the airport with you?"

It could mean nothing at all. Still, she felt a warm surge of hope. "I'd like that very, very much, Luke."

Catherine gazed at the crazy quilt of fields below her as the plane gained altitude.

Good-bye, Luke.

Sam and Luke were probably still down there at the terminal. She'd been late getting to the airport, and Sam had said that he and Luke would watch her plane take off, and then go to one of the restaurants and have lunch.

I'll be back as soon as I can. Think about me. I'll be thinking of you . . .

But now she should be thinking about Hu Chang, trying to think of a way to persuade him to stop whatever stubborn mischief he was creating.

Providing she could find him.

And providing that Nardik had not found and killed Hu Chang already.

Don't think about that possibility. Hu Chang was incredibly intelligent and had survived wars and archcriminals and governments who wanted to use him or destroy him. He wouldn't have permitted himself to be killed by a sleazebag like Nardik. As he had told her many times, it was his duty to make his death as glorious as his life.

She found her lips curving involuntarily at the memory of those words.

Arrogant. So damn arrogant.

She couldn't believe how arrogant when she'd first met him.

She leaned back in the seat, staring blindly at the clouds outside the window.

But then, she'd been arrogant, too. Fourteen years old going on fifty with a ferocity and confidence born from living on the streets and surviving everything that existence had thrown at her. She'd had that sense of immortality that youth always possessed and the recklessness that went along with it. Hu Chang had always shaken his head and cautioned her against that recklessness.

She had been so different from Hu Chang in many ways and yet so alike in others . . .

Hong Kong
Fifteen Years Earlier

"It's not enough." Choi Meng looked at the coin Catherine was holding up. "Aren't I one of your best informants? I watch and listen all the time for you."

"It's all you're getting," Catherine said flatly. "The last time I followed up on one of your tips, it turned out to be nothing."

"That wasn't my fault."

"Yes or no?"

He nibbled at his lower lip, gazing at the money. "Yes." He snatched the coin and shoved it into his pocket. "The apothecary. Hu Chang, the Master of Medicine, who has a shop on the next block. Bruce Wong and his gang are going to rob him tonight when he closes up his shop."

"And that's all you have?" Catherine frowned. "That's of no use to me. How can I sell that? Give me my money back."

"No." Choi Meng hurriedly backed away from her. "It has worth. You can either offer the information to Hu Chang to save himself. Or to Bruce Wong to prevent you from telling the police."

"And you think that's a threat? You know the police won't come down to this neighborhood unless there's a bribe. And apothecaries don't make enough money to pay me to make it worthwhile for me to risk going against Bruce Wong and his gang."

"Are you frightened?"

"No, I'm cautious." And Choi Meng had known that she'd be crazy to get involved with Bruce Wong when he'd offered her the information. Wong was the head of the neighborhood triad gang and as vicious as a striking cobra. There were over fifty triad gangs in Hong Kong, ranging from neighborhood street gangs to sophisticated syndicates that resembled the powerful Mafia. Wong was small stuff, but he had

ambitions, and she had run into him several times on the docks when he had been
trying to get the whores to accept his triad
to pimp for them. She'd decided the smart-
est thing to do was just stay out of his
way.

"Of course, you're only cautious." Choi
Meng smiled slyly. "I understand. Even
though I hear Hu Chang is soon going to
be a rich man with his fine potions, you
wouldn't want to take the chance. You are
only a woman, really little more than a child.
You're right to be afraid to go up against
Bruce Wong." He grimaced. "Bruce. I knew
him before he took that name. He was Shim
Wong when we were growing up here. But
then he began seeing all those Bruce Lee
movies and thought everyone would think
he was as tough as Bruce Lee when he
joined the triad."

"Then he was even more thickheaded
than I thought," Catherine said dryly. "I
heard the reason Bruce Lee ran away to
America was that he got in trouble with
the triads who controlled the film industry.
None of the big crime triads would be impressed."

He shrugged. "Perhaps he did not hear

that story. You know things many others do not."

"Information is my business."

He smiled. "Because you have loyal people like me trying to help you make your living. You are right to be afraid. His triad would probably rape you, then kill you. I hear Bruce Wong murdered a prostitute last night."

She stiffened. "What? Where?"

"The docks. You didn't know?"

"I wasn't at the docks. I was at Kowloon last night. Who?"

"Lucy Tain. He beat her to death. You know her?"

She felt as if she she'd been punched in the stomach. Oh God, not Lucy.

"You're pale. You did know her."

"Yes." She swallowed to ease the tightness of her throat. "She was only thirteen." Small and delicate and scared of everyone and everything. Except Catherine. When Lucy had first been brought to the docks, she had trailed around behind Catherine like a lost puppy. Catherine could only guess that it was because they were close to the same age. At first, Catherine had been impatient. She'd had no time to spend explaining things and trying to comfort her. It was a hard life, and everyone had to pull their own weight. Catherine had never had a childhood, and she couldn't understand why Lucy was clinging to hers. Then something had happened.

Lucy had . . . touched her. Catherine had grown used to seeing her, indulgently listening to her chatter, trying to rid her of the fear that was always with her.

"She was so scared." Catherine could remember Lucy's eyes wide with panic as she'd huddled close to her, afraid to come out when her father had called her. "Her father was acting as her pimp and wouldn't let her give Wong's triad a percentage. I told her to run away to Macau and try to get work in the fields."

"She would probably have ended up as a whore in Macau, too."

Damn him. Damn all of them.

"Why?" Her eyes were blazing. "She would have had a chance. She didn't have to stay a whore. She could have been anything she wanted to be if she worked at it hard enough. Wong should have left her alone. She was only thirteen."

"And you're what, fourteen? Only a year older."

That was different. She didn't feel fourteen or any particular age. The years passed and were marked only by what she learned and how far she had come from the last year. Lucy Tain had been a scared child, not understanding that she was only a pawn. A child who had been caught between a greedy father and a brutal gang leader. "I don't suppose anyone called the police."

He shrugged.

Of course they hadn't. No one in this neighborhood would risk being a target of a triad gang.

"I can see that you're upset," Choi Meng said. "It's a good thing that I told you about the apothecary. You'll want to run down to his shop and warn him about Bruce Wong."

She drew a deep breath and tried to smother the anger and sadness. This was life and had to be accepted.

And so did the fact that Choi Meng was trying to manipulate the situation to his own advantage.

"Don't try to play me," she said coolly.

"Give me back my money, or I'll break both your arms and remove your testicles."

Choi Meng said quickly, "Everything I've told you is true. All right, stay away from Bruce Wong. Hu Chang gets fine prices for his potions. He can afford—" He broke off. "I need the money, Catherine. I haven't eaten in two days."

"And that's a reason for me to feed you?"

"I've given you good information for the last year."

"Not last time." She hesitated. Choi Meng did look emaciated, and she knew what it was to have hunger gnawing at you. What was she thinking? He was probably back on the opium. If you were soft, you ended up in the gutter like Choi Meng, to be used and manipulated. Everyone had to take care of themselves.

"Hu Chang will pay you a fine fee for saving him from being robbed," he wheedled. "I give you my word."

The man would probably swear his way into heaven for the food that coin would buy. Swear and lie and cheat. It's what people did when they were hungry and cold and without hope. She had lied and stolen fish from the market when she was younger just to keep her belly full.

The memory was suddenly before her: all the fear, the hunger. Catherine at five years slipping closer to the booth and waiting with heart pounding for the crowd to get big enough so that no one would notice one small girl moving near enough to snatch a bit of raw fish, then tear away through the market.

Oh, dammit, what difference did it make whether he was playing her for a fool? She had money to live for the next few weeks, and she could always make more. She was not a weak fool like Choi Meng. "If he doesn't, I'll come after you." She turned away. "And if you've already spent the money, you'll owe me. And you know I always collect."

"I know." His voice was eager. "You won't be sorry. Thank you, Catherine." She heard his footsteps running on the cobblestones, and, when she glanced over his shoulder, he'd disappeared from view.

With her money. She probably would be sorry.

No, she wouldn't. She wouldn't allow herself to regret a decision. It was done.

Perhaps if she hadn't been upset about Lucy's death, she wouldn't have been so soft, but she had to accept her moments of weakness as she did her moments of strength. There was a possibility she could get something out of this. Now she had to explore the situation and see if she'd been cheated only just a little or a great deal. But she'd better get moving, or there would be no chance to bargain with this Hu Chang.

She checked her watch. Choi Meng had said that Bruce Wong and his gang were going to attack Hu Chang when he closed up shop in the next hour, and she'd already wasted time arguing with Choi Meng.

Move.

She ran down the alley, up the street, and turned left. Hu Chang's shop should be the third house on the left . . .

Yes, there it was. A small hole-in-the-wall shop with a bamboo door.

A door that was flung wide with such force it had been torn off one of its hinges.

She skidded to a stop. Dammit, it appeared Choi Meng's information about Wong waiting until the store closed to rob the apothecary was not correct. She could hear the sound of glass breaking and laughter inside the shop.

And the sound of harsh breathing and flesh on flesh.

Bruce Wong was clearly enjoying one of his favorite pastimes. Evidently Hu Chang had not been cooperative about giving up his money.

Should she walk on by?

It was obviously too late for her to bargain with either Hu Chang or Bruce Wong. It would be smart of her to forget about both of them and let fate decide who was going to survive.

Except she didn't believe in fate.

And she hated Bruce Wong.

And all she could think about was Wong beating Lucy Tain as he was now beating Hu Chang.

She glided toward the shop. Wong usually took one or two of his gang with him when he was on a job. There was no one on guard outside, so they must all be inside.

She stopped at the door.

Only two men. Wong, big, muscular,

dressed in the black jacket with the triangle embossed on the leather, was beating up Hu Chang, who was pushed against the cabinet. Another shorter man with a crew cut wearing a similar leather jacket was leaning against the wall to the right of door. She'd seen him down at the docks with Wong. Kwan Lin.

Take out Lin first. He was grinning, completely absorbed in the brutal show Bruce Wong was furnishing him. He didn't even realize she was there. Had he been just as entertained when Wong had killed Lucy Tain?

Fool.

The garrote? No.

The next instant, she was springing forward. He barely had time to turn before she kicked him behind the knee and caught the back of neck with the hard edge of her hand as he started to fall.

He was unconscious by the time he reached the floor.

Bruce Wong whirled away from his victim at the sound. He was breathing hard, his face flushed with pleasure. For an instant, he didn't recognize her. "You!" He shook his head to clear it. His gaze went to the man on the floor at Catherine's feet. He started to curse. "What are you doing, bitch?" He reached into his jacket and pulled out his gun. "I'll blow your head off, you stupid whore. No one interferes when I have—" He screamed as the knife she'd thrown entered his hand.

Then she was across the room and on top of him, grabbing his gun.

He slapped her so hard her ears rang. Dizzy.

He was trying to get the gun . . .

She hit his temple with the barrel as hard as she could.

He collapsed, unconscious.

Kill him? It would be the smart thing to do. If she didn't, he would track her down, and she'd have to do it all over.

"No . . ." It was the shopkeeper, Hu Chang. He'd raised himself on his elbow. "Don't do—" He coughed up blood. "I'll take care of— Go."

"No. I'm in too deep now. If Wong doesn't kill me, one of his gang will do it. They swear all kinds of blood loyalty oaths. I'm not going to—" She broke off as she heard the familiar wail of a siren. "Dammit, it's the police. Someone must have called them.

Why do the police always come when you don't want them? They didn't come when Lucy needed them."

"Lucy?"

"Never mind." She stared at him in frustration. "I'm not going to let the police interfere. And I'm not going to let you ruin everything by dying on me." She moved across the space separating them, put her arm around Hu Chang, and lifted him. "It won't be for nothing," she said fiercely. "I won't have it. I don't give a damn about you, but I won't be beaten. Now help me, and I'll get you out of here before the police or the rest of Wong's gang shows up and cuts you into little pieces."

"That does not sound pleasant. But I'm fully able to care for myself." He was hobbling painfully toward the door. "I do not need you."

"No? You were being beaten to death, you crazy man." She glanced up and down the street. Just a woman and her little girl at the corner market. No one who appeared to be a threat. But the police sirens sounded closer. "I'd have given you maybe another five minutes, and you would have been dead or in a coma."

"You're wrong. I had at least seven minutes. And I was about to make my move to dispense with that scum."

She looked at him in disbelief. He was staring blandly back at her from the torn and bruised ruin of a face.

"And how would you have done that?"

"With deftness and intellect. Not the roughness that you displayed." He flinched as he took a deep breath. "But you may have been of some assistance. I believe I have a broken rib, and that would have made it difficult to function. Where are you taking me?"

"I thought I'd drop you off at the British Hospital. Wong would have a hard time reaching you there."

"No, the British don't like me, and I don't trust them. They tried to use a truth drug on me once."

"What?" Perhaps the beating had addled his brains.

"You will take me home with you." He tilted his head. "I believe I can trust you. Though I'll have to be very careful. You're not much more than a child, are you?"

"Who saved your scrawny neck," she said through her set teeth.

"Yes, you must tell me why you did that. I will give you compensation, of course."

"How? Wong wrecked your entire shop and all those pretty little bottles."

"You like my bottles? You have excellent taste. I engraved and painted them myself. I was very upset to see them broken, but I can do others. And each potion, each work of art I do becomes better with practice."

"I don't care about any of that. How are you going to pay me?" she repeated as she took more of his weight. "I have to earn a living, and I'm going to have to stay out of Wong's way for a while. I should have killed him when I had a chance."

He smiled. "But I could not allow you to kill for me. Perhaps when you're a little older, I would have no objection." His smile ebbed, then vanished. "But you appear to be well versed in the art of violence. Have you killed before?"

She didn't answer.

He was studying her face. "You *have* killed, haven't you?"

"I didn't say that."

"But your silence spoke. I listened."

"It has nothing to do with you."

"And you do not wish to discuss it? I would not betray you, Catherine."

She stiffened. "How do you know my name?"

"I've seen you running around the neighborhood, listening, asking questions. I've asked questions, too. You interested me. They call you the Gatherer."

"Do they?"

"Yes, because you gather information from one place and distribute it to another. But I can see that not having the freedom to run the streets would affect your livelihood. I will have to consider how to make sure you won't suffer for it."

"Yes, you will. You should pay. Unless I decide to take care of it myself."

"I believe I'm getting very tired. I need to rest. Why are you dragging me down to these docks?" He was looking at the small fishing boats and even smaller junks huddled almost on top of each other near the shore. "Are you going to drown me or take me to where you live?"

She scowled. "I haven't decided. You're a bother, old man."

"I'm not old. Children always think that the fully mature are old."

"Then how old are you?"

"Old enough to be extraordinary, young enough to still have my vigor."

"You have gray flecks in your hair."

"A mistake of nature. I'll take care of that someday. I just haven't gotten around to it yet."

"You'll still be old."

"That's where you're wrong. It depends on how I decide to take care of it."

"I'm tired of talking to you," she said, exasperated. "You make no sense." She stopped in front of the tiny junk where she lived. "Get on board and lie down. Maybe you'll go to sleep, and I'll be done with you for a while."

"It's entirely possible. It's very small, isn't it? Barely nine or ten feet." He climbed on board and looked at the cardboard boxes and the single pallet beneath the small, shaded tarp. "Cluttered. And not as clean as I'd like."

"It's clean. Maybe you'd prefer I dump you in the sea instead?"

"I think not. The harbor is even more disgusting." He lay down and closed his eyes. "There is only one pallet. Where will you sleep?"

"I'm not tired." She dropped down and leaned back against the mast. "And I can sleep anywhere. If I decide I want my pallet, I'll get you up and take it."

"Yes, I can see you doing that." He didn't speak for a moment. "This section of the docks is used by the whores. If you get a customer, will I prove an inconvenience?"

"No, I'm not a whore. This boat belonged to my mother. When she died, her friend, Natasha, took it over and let me stay with her here."

"Close quarters. It must have proved educational. How old were you?"

"Almost five."

"A great age."

"Old enough. This was just a place to get out of the weather if I needed to do it. I lived on the streets."

He opened his eyes. "And you didn't decide to follow in your mother's footsteps?"

"Why would I? Men used her. No one will ever use me. Go to sleep and stop asking me questions."

"But I'm curious about you, Catherine." He turned his head and looked out at the sea. "It's a lovely name. Did you take it for your own or were you given it at birth?"

"Why would I try to change what I am? My mother was half-Russian, and I suppose she liked the name."

"And what happened to this Natasha? Why are you in possession of this fine vessel?"

"She died last year of an overdose. Just like my mother. I was making enough money to pay the rent myself by that time."

"I can see how you'd be very self-sufficient. Buy and sell information and remain very independent . . ."

"That's right."

"Interesting . . ." He closed his eyes again. "Little gatherer . . ."

He was asleep.

Catherine drew a deep breath and closed her own eyes. She was glad to be free of his questions. In her world, people kept to themselves and just worked to survive. This potion maker was . . . different. Not totally annoying. And she was beginning to be curious about him, too. Crazy? Perhaps. But he was not boring. Not in speech, not in appearance. He was dressed in a black tunic and pants, was a little taller than middle height, and was slim yet muscular. His hair was thick and black with only a few threads of silver, and his face was angular, with high bones and olive skin. His eyes slanted only a little, and they were large, night-dark, and almost hypnotic in intensity. When he'd stared at her, she'd felt as if she been held, captured, unable to break free. His lips were large and well formed and almost as expressive as those eyes. He was probably a blend of several races, as was common in Hong Kong, she thought idly.

And the cuts on his face were still bleeding.

So what? She was not a nurse. He was nothing to her.

But if the cuts became infected, that would just be another problem with which to deal. She muttered a curse and got up and got a cloth and dipped it in the bucket of water. Then she knelt beside Hu Chang and began to dab at the cuts.

"You have no gentleness," Hu Chang said without opening his eyes.

"Shut up. It has to be done."

"Is the cloth clean?"

"Clean enough."

"I will make sure to cleanse the cut when I wake."

"You said you'd trust me."

"Not with my personal cleanliness. I will have to teach you more about that. That's the way. Gently."

Catherine hadn't realized that her touch had altered. "Enough." She threw the cloth into the bucket. "Go back to sleep."

"You disturbed me." His lids lifted, and she was suddenly looking into those large dark eyes that she'd noticed were almost hypnotic. "Who did you kill, little Catherine?"

"I'm not little." She moved back to her former place across from him. "I think we're safe here for a little while. Wong will be coming after us. But I moved the junk two nights ago to another dock when I saw the triad trying to take over the one where I was before. Go to sleep, so I can get rid of you, old man."

He chuckled. "I'm not sure you'll ever get rid of me. Would that not be an interesting development?"

"A nightmare. When you're better, you leave. I'm not going to take care of you. I have enough trouble taking care of myself."

"But perhaps we could take care of each other . . ."

He was asleep again.

She leaned her head back against the sail and closed her eyes, listening to the sounds of Hong Kong.

The toot of the British dinner boat leaving the dock on the far distant side of the harbor with its formally dressed upper crust.

The fishermen putting to sea to gather their catch for the next day.

Jen Lin in the second junk down the line had an early customer. Catherine could hear the sound of their coming together and the creak of her boat as it moved beneath their bodies.

Different lives, different futures.

Which one would be Catherine's?

Why even wonder? she thought impatiently. It would be the one she chose. But she'd better choose soon. She could see how easily Hong Kong could draw a man or woman into its darkest webs.

As Lucy Tain had been drawn to her death.

But she was not Lucy.

And she would never be a victim.

CHAPTER 4

"What are you reading?"

Hu Chang was awake again and gazing curiously at her. More questions.

She put the paperback down. "It's *Atlas Shrugged.* Some of it I don't understand, but I like it."

"I've never read it." He glanced at the book. "English. Where did you learn English?"

"I can read and write English. Hong Kong is ruled by the British in case you didn't notice."

"Not for much longer. Soon they'll hand it over to the Chinese," he said absently.

He glanced at the box of books tucked under the seat. "Chinese, Russian."

"My mother and Natasha were both half-Russian. I taught myself Chinese from living on the streets. Knowing different languages helped me."

"I can understand that." His gaze went back to her book. "British . . . But you didn't learn to read and write English down here at the docks."

"No."

He waited.

She shrugged. "When I was ten, I was picked up by the police for stealing fruit in the market. There was a British social worker who decided I had to be saved. She sent me to an orphanage that she ran outside the city. I was there until I ran away two years later."

"Why did you run away? It would seem a decent life, an education, a full stomach when you went to sleep at night."

"I didn't mind the books. I just didn't want to be there." She got to her feet. "I'm hungry. I'll go see what I can find in the market. If you want to stay for a while, I'll feed you. But you have to go soon."

"Why did you run away?"

She shook her head. "Stop asking me questions. I don't like it. How would you like it if I pried into your business, old man?"

"I'd applaud you for your interest. I'm definitely worthy of scrutiny. But although I'm sure you're calling me 'old man' to annoy me, I have to point out that it's totally inaccurate." He sat up and flinched. "I believe my diagnosis is correct. I have a cracked rib. Which means I'm not yet ready to confront this Bruce Wong. We'll have to think of something else." He looked around the boat. "For I refuse to spend another night in this place."

"Good." She jumped onto the dock. "I'll be back with something to eat. Get ready to leave."

"No, you didn't understand. I have to take you with me, Catherine. I consider it my duty."

She glanced back over her shoulder. "You're crazy. You're leaving, I'm not. Get ready." She strode down the dock in the direction of the market.

She would fetch the food as she'd said, but she would also go back to Hu Chang's neighborhood and see if Bruce Wong had recovered enough to stir up trouble. As she'd told Hu Chang, she doubted if there were more than a few people in the city who knew where she lived, but it only took one.

Hu Chang's shop had been burned to the ground.

Not only his shop but the laundry next door had caught fire and was blackened, its windows gaping scorched holes.

Catherine stared at the ruins in shock from where she was standing in the alcove of the house across the street. She shouldn't have been this surprised at the viciousness, she told herself. Wong was always ugly, always trying to prove his power. It was clear he had rallied and was demonstrating that no one could go against him without suffering the consequences.

"Get out of here, Catherine." She turned to see Choi Meng coming out of the side street. "I've never seen Bruce like this. He's going to kill you. He's been going from house to house and asking everyone where he can find you." He smiled sourly. "The cheap bastard is even offering money to anyone who will turn you over to him. That should show you how badly he wants you and the apothecary. He'd much rather beat information out of someone."

"And which method did he use with you?"

"I took the money. I told him I'd watch the shop and send someone to get him if you showed up here."

"And have you done it?"

"I'll give you three minutes' head start, then I'll call. I can't afford to do any more than that. Someone else may have caught sight of you, and I want to keep his money." He shrugged. "And my head. There are stories that Bruce likes to chop off the heads of people who go against him. Remember that gang leader who was trying to take over the triad drug deliveries? They found his head under the bridge. He thinks it sends a message."

"Then why are you doing this, Choi Meng?"

"I don't know. You gave me money when you didn't want to do it? I don't like that bastard, Bruce? You're a beautiful little bitch, and I've always wanted to take you to bed." He turned away. "I'd hate to see that pretty head floating in the harbor. Hurry. Move. He'll find you, Catherine. He'll turn loose all his gang on you and Hu Chang.

Someone will talk. Someone will follow you. Lose yourself somewhere until he forgets what you did to him."

"I can't lose myself. I have to be on the streets. I have to earn money to live."

"Then do what your mother did. There's always a way for a woman to make her way. I'd pay to get between your legs." Softly, he added, "I'd kill to get between your legs."

Smother the rage, the urge to strike out at him. That was what all men valued. From the time she had been old enough to be able to be aware of what those men were doing to her mother, it had been drummed into her. Choi Meng was just another one who saw women as only important for the pleasure they gave him.

But for whatever reason, he had given her warning, and it might have saved her life. She owed him for that. "I'll remember what you did. But I'll find another way to pay you." She turned and started up the hill at a run. "Three minutes."

Use every back alley.

Avoid the markets, where someone might recognize her.

Run!

*   *   *

Hu Chang was sitting on the side of the boat, dangling his feet in the water, when she ran down the dock. "It's very difficult getting clean in this vessel. I tried filling that bucket, but it was not—"

"Get on your feet. We have to get out of here." She jumped onto the boat and began to throw clothes into a duffel. "Wong burned down your shop, and he's bribing everyone to try to find us."

"You're afraid?"

"Didn't you hear me? Move. He wants to hurt you. He burned down your shop. That means you have no way to make a living. Can you go to a relative until he stops looking for you?"

He shook his head. "I am alone, like you. But that is not too worrisome."

"Where will you go? Where will you live? You can't stay here. This place isn't safe now."

He was staring at her with that curious glance that had annoyed her before. "You are afraid."

"No, I'm angry, and I want to hit someone." She glared at him. "I want to hit *you*. I should never have interfered with Wong. I can't hide myself away and concoct brews and medicines. I deal in information, and to do that, I have to contact people. I make my living on the streets, and I'm going to have to dodge around and find a way to do it without getting myself killed. I'll have to find a place to live where someone won't run to Wong and tell him where I am."

"Perhaps you should find another way to earn your living . . . at least for a little while."

"What?" She said tersely, "Are you like Choi Meng? You think all a woman is good for is to whore? Go away, Hu Chang. I've had enough of you."

"But I've not had enough of you," Hu Chang said. "I believe you may be trainable." He was putting his shoes on as he spoke. "You didn't get me any food. I'm hungry."

"Too bad. We have to stay away from the markets."

"I believe I may have something to eat at my shop. We will go directly there since you were so neglectful."

She stared at him in amazement. "Are you mad? I told you that your shop was burned to the ground. You're not going to find anything there but ashes."

"Ashes can be valuable. Sometimes potions that have been treated with high temperatures are transformed into something even more valuable than the original. I wish I'd known that you'd gone there."

She said through her teeth, "I am not going to go back and sift though those ruins for your valuable ashes."

"I understand." He got to his feet. "Perhaps I'll send you later."

"Go yourself. You'd deserve what Wong would do to you when he catches you." She drew a long breath. "Look, Hu Chang. I know this has been a shock to you. But you have to realize that your shop is gone. I know how long it probably took you to scrape together enough money to have your own shop. But you'll have to start over."

"That is true. Many of my medicines were destroyed by that ugly man. We will have to work very hard to replace them." He started down the dock. "Now come along. I've not eaten since last night. First, you try to infect my wounds with that unclean water, then you try to starve me."

"I did not infect—" She hurried to catch up with him. "I don't know why I care, but I'm not going to let you go back to that burned-out shop and have Wong cut off your stupid head." She grabbed his arm and whirled around him to face her. "You're coming with me, or I'll give you a karate chop that will drop you where you stand. Then I'll find a place for us until you come back to your senses."

He stared down at her, then a slow smile lit his face. "You do not know why you care? I know, Catherine Ling. It is because you have a great heart." He turned away. "And great hearts should never be either wasted or broken. Now come with me, and I may be persuaded to feed you as well as myself."

She stared at him, stunned. No one had ever spoken to her like that. But she had never met anyone like Hu Chang before.

She called after him. "I meant what I said. You can't go back to that place. I won't let you."

"Did I say I was going to return to that lowly shop at this time? You misunderstood. You do not listen. I have another place a good distance away. Now come along."

She did not listen? She wanted to strangle him.

He slanted a look over his shoulder, and

there was the tiniest impish gleam in his glance. "Trust me, Catherine. Neither of us is good with trust, but perhaps we can learn together."

She hesitated. Why should she trust him? She barely knew him, and he was probably as crazy as she thought he was.

But she wanted to go with him. She didn't know why, but she didn't want anything to happen to him. He shouldn't have mattered to her. Just a crazy, old man . . .

"Wait." She ran to catch up with him. "I'll go with you, but don't expect me to trust you. I'll watch you every minute, old man."

"Do not call me old. Someday, when you're my age, you will look back and think what a foolish child you were. I wish to save you from that embarrassment." He thought about it. "Or perhaps not. I may wish to use it to curb your ego. I can see it exploding until you are unbearable. By all means, make as many mistakes as you wish during this tadpole period."

Tadpole. She opened her lips to fire back at him, then closed them without speaking. It was what he wanted her to do, and she wouldn't give him the satisfaction.

"That's right," he murmured. "We are

already learning each other. Is that not a fine thing? I believe that—" He broke off as he looked over her shoulder. "I think perhaps we'd better hurry. Is that a few of those triad gang men coming down the dock?"

She tensed as she looked over her shoulder. Not Wong, but the men wore black jackets with the triangle insignia. They were going slowly, checking out every junk. "I was hoping we'd have more time." She grabbed his arm and pulled him up the dock toward the long, concrete steps that led to the main town. "Come on. Keep out of sight."

"That is hard to do. I think we need to go somewhere and wait until after dark." He started slowly climbing the stairs. "I know a place. Come with me."

They had reached the top of the steps when she heard shouts from below on the dock.

"Don't look back," Hu Chang said.

Who was he to tell her what to do? She looked back anyway.

Her junk was on fire, the flames licking at the masts!

The two triad gang members were standing laughing on the dock.

"No!" She turned and started back down toward the steps.

Hu Chang grabbed her arm. "It's too late."

She could see that for herself. The boat was completely engulfed.

She had to give herself a minute before she could push her rage aside. She shook off Hu Chang's grip. "Bastards." She turned and started climbing the steps again. "Dirty bastards. That junk was the only home I remember. It felt as if it was *mine.* They had no right."

"It seems we've both lost property this day," he said quietly. "I regret you lost yours because you helped me."

"So am I." But she had to be honest. "It wasn't really because of you. I was angry with Wong anyway."

"And it seems he's very angry with us." He went ahead of her as they reached the street. "Come. We'll find a place that we can hide out of sight for a while."

"It's a temple." Catherine stared up at the Buddhist temple as she stopped at the bottom of the steep stairs just inside the narrow gate. "This is where we're going to wait until dark?"

"Can you think of a safer place?" Hu Chang asked as he climbed the stairs. "I don't know of any triad who would be coming to a temple."

Neither could Catherine, and she hurried after him up the steps. "No, I've seen tourists come in here, but no one from the neighborhood. What temple is this?"

"It's called the Temple of One Hundred Names."

"Do you come here often?"

"Not often. It is a good place to meditate when the need is there." They entered an antechamber, where thirty or forty spirals of burning incense whirled up to the ceiling from the burning tapers. The scent was nearly overpowering.

Catherine started to cough. "Meditate? Are you sure the triad isn't selling them drugs? I'm dizzy just smelling that incense."

He smiled. "No, but I trust the priests. They are very sincere. They believe that smoke is a way to communicate between the world of the living and the world of the dead. They think a temple should be a welcome portal for the ghosts."

"That's foolishness."

"You don't believe in ghosts?" He led her down a hallway. "Come along, we'll go in the back chamber. The incense is less heavy there."

The walls were completely covered, from chest level to the ceiling, with hundreds of tiny tablets, smaller than paperback books. Each one was inscribed with a name in Chinese, a date, and sometimes a picture.

She frowned. "What is this?"

"You know that according to traditional Chinese beliefs, everyone who dies without a family to conduct funeral rituals and tend their grave will become a 'hungry ghost'?"

"Superstition. Foolishness. Dead is dead."

"Not everyone thinks that's true. They believe that ghosts roam restlessly between heaven and Earth, sometimes causing mischief for those still alive."

She pointed to the plaques. "So what are those?"

"After the bubonic plague, the community had a huge problem. They did believe in ghosts and couldn't face having to live with unsettled ghosts wandering around. But they couldn't afford to send the remains of the dead back to their families back in their villages either. So they built this temple. The ashes of all the dead without family are brought here so that the whole community can pray for them and feed them offerings as if they were their own ancestors."

"It's not at all practical."

He slanted her a glance. "And you disapprove."

"I didn't say that. If it was practical, it would be less . . . lonely." She looked away from the wall. "But it's really foolish to build a temple to a bunch of ghosts. How long do we have to stay here?"

"Just a few more hours." He gestured toward a chair against the wall. "Sit down and rest."

"You should be the one resting. Wong didn't beat me up."

"No, you defended yourself very well."

"And you," she added pointedly.

He smiled. "And me, Catherine."

She gazed restlessly about the chamber

at the cluttered altar, the silk-draped statue of Tin Hau, the Goddess of the Sea. "You didn't like my boat because it was messy, but this place is worse. How can you meditate when you have all this stuff around you?" Her glance fell on one of the priests near the altar. "And are you sure he's not on the triad payroll?"

"How cynical. Not everyone can be bribed."

"It's safer if you assume they can."

"That is true. You're very young to have discovered that."

Her gaze shifted back to him. "You don't like me to call you old, but you keep saying how young I am."

"Does it bother you?"

"No, but it's stupid since my age doesn't matter." She studied his face. "And I can't really tell how old you are." His face was unlined, the contour as defined as that of a young man. "But if you are an old man, you should have been smarter about fighting Wong. You could have just given him the money."

"I was considering it, but he didn't give me the opportunity to make up my mind. He's a savage, isn't he?"

"Yes." She looked away from him. "He beat Lucy Tain to death the night before."

"Lucy Tain?"

She lifted one shoulder. "Just a prostitute who worked out of one of the junks down on the docks."

He was studying her. "But you felt affection for her."

"I knew it was a waste of time. She wasn't smart. She was scared all the time. She wouldn't listen to me."

"But you still liked her."

"I wanted her to *live.* I wanted her to *fight* them." She drew a deep shaky breath. "Now she won't have the chance. She's dead. And nobody cares." She looked around the chamber. "Any more than anyone cares about all your ghosts in this temple, Hu Chang. It's all lies. You can't believe it."

"As time passes, you'll realize that truth, as well as lies, is in the eyes of the beholder. And perception changes as the mind changes."

"That's pompous bullshit."

He chuckled. "I do believe that I like you, Catherine."

"And I don't care whether you do or not."

She leaned her head back against the wall and watched the curling smoke of the sandalwood waft up to the ceiling. She was dizzy with the heavy incense and the heavier bitterness and sadness. It must be that same smoke that was making her eyes sting. "It's hard to breathe in here. All this smoke . . ."

"Do you know that it's because of the aroma of incense that the city got its name?" he asked softly. "Chinese fishermen passing by all the temples along the shore would always smell the smoke and sandalwood. They began to call the island *Heung Gong,* fragrant harbor. Some said when you breathed in the smoke, you were really breathing in a spirit that came alive within you."

"More ghosts? Not true . . ."

"Not if you don't want it to be true. Close your eyes," Hu Chang said. "Try to sleep. I'll watch out for priests who might be less than honest and ghosts that might do you mischief."

"But you said that the ghosts were happy here."

"But you don't believe me."

She wanted to believe him. In that moment, she wanted desperately to believe in a second chance for Lucy Tain, who'd had no chance at all. "You're right." Her eyes closed. "I don't believe you."

"Catherine."

She opened her eyes to see Hu Chang's face above her as he bent to wake her. The scent of sandalwood was still thick in the room, but the light was much dimmer except for the glow of the lit tapers on the altar.

"It's time we left," Hu Chang said. "It's dark, and we have a long way to go."

Catherine nodded, trying to shrug off the effect of the incense that still seemed to be filling her lungs and her mind. She got to her feet. "I'm ready."

"Not quite." He handed her a damp cloth. "Wash your face. It will make you feel better. You have to get used to the incense. It's almost like a drug until you become accustomed to it."

"Drugs . . ." She shook her head to clear it. "But you don't get used to them. They just take you away and don't bring you back."

"Like your mother?"

"Yes, and Natasha." The damp cloth felt cool and fresh on her cheeks. "Lucy's father tried to get her to sniff opium, and he was angry with me when I threw it into the harbor. He thought it would make her more willing when they . . ." She shook her head again. "But you weren't talking about drugs, were you? It was about the incense. I was confused . . ." She gave him back the cloth. "Let's go."

He nodded and strode toward the door.

She started after him, then she stopped and looked back at the altar. The burning tapers, the smoke that Hu Chang had said was a bridge, the plaques that showed the world that a soul had passed that way seeking comfort.

Everyone had a right to seek comfort and an end to loneliness, didn't they?

"Catherine."

"I'm coming." She strode to the altar and grabbed a taper from the box. This was stupid. Why was she doing it?

Because she wanted to do it. That was reason enough. She lit the taper and put it on the altar. She watched as smoke began to slowly curl up into the air.

I'll remember you, Lucy. You're not alone.

She whirled and strode away from the altar. She didn't look at Hu Chang as she passed him. "I don't want to hear you say anything," she said fiercely. "I know it made no sense. I still don't believe anything you've told me about this place."

"No, it made no sense at all." He followed her out in the darkness and down the steep flight of stairs. "But since it's done, it should be done correctly. You were too impulsive. I'll call the temple priest once we're settled and have him put up a plaque . . ."

"What is this place?" Catherine stared at the small sod house set back in the shadows of the screen of the bamboo trees. It was over two hours later, and Hu Chang had led her out of the main city to this tiny farm community, ignoring her questions with that silent serenity that annoyed her even more than when he spoke to her. "Who lives here?"

"We do." He was leading her toward the door. "Or rather I do. But I'm willing to share with you for the time being. Provided you learn quickly and don't talk too much. I've noticed that you have a tendency to ask many questions."

"You're the one who has been asking me questions ever since I saved you from Bruce Wong. The only question I have is why you brought me outside my city to this barren countryside."

"It is not barren. You're obviously not accustomed to the bounty that the earth gives us. Tell me, have you ever been outside Hong Kong?"

"No, why should I? Hong Kong has everything anyone could want. What it doesn't have, people bring to it."

"Very logical. So you intend to stay the rest of your life in Hong Kong and become the person to whom everyone comes for information? Your own little kingdom."

"I didn't say that. Nothing stays the same. I have a little time to decide." She watched him throw open the door. "But what is this place? I don't understand why you brought—"

Rows and rows of bottles and vials on finely crafted wooden shelves. The sun coming through the window fell on the crystal and glass and turned it into glittering rainbows of color. "Another shop? Out here in the middle of the country?"

"Not a shop." He strode across the

room. "My laboratory. It's where I create all the magnificent medicines and potions that I sell in the city. I have a garden in the back where I grow my herbs. Here I'm free to work without worrying about the interference of scum like Bruce Wong."

"It's . . . different." His shop in the city had been shabby, with bamboo doors and shelves and only a few bottles on display. Every cabinet, every shelf, every piece of glass in the place looked sparkling clean and beautifully crafted. "But couldn't you have this place closer to your shop in Hong Kong?"

"Too dangerous. I take orders from my clients and make the remedies here, then take them to the shop in Hong Kong. Some of my potions are very expensive, depending on the depth of the pockets of the client. It's best that no one knows how expensive or how valued my services are. People do not notice the poor in the city. There are too many. But prosperity casts out a light all around it that attracts the buzzards."

"And are you prosperous, Hu Chang?"

"Sometimes. When I want to be." He went to the corner and lifted the lid of a large white refrigerator box. "I have dried meat, powdered milk, and tea. You may prepare me something to eat while I rest from the journey."

"And why should I do that?"

"Because I am furnishing you sustenance and will offer you shelter." He moved toward the beaded curtain at the far end of the room. "And because my side is hurting, and I fear I've overextended myself by walking this distance from the ferry. You would not want me to collapse and make it necessary that you take care of me."

"You're hurting?" Suspiciously, she asked, "Are you lying to me?"

"Possibly. You will have to study me and find out how to tell when I'm doing that. Until then, you'll have to rely on your feelings. And since I've discovered that your feelings can be manipulated by one wise enough to do it, you'd better learn me very quickly." He pushed aside the beaded curtain. "Call me when it is time for me to eat."

She stood looking at the rows of amber beads that were still in motion. She had no intention of waiting on Hu Chang. She could leave this place and be back in the city she knew in a few hours. He was clearly safe, far safer than she, and she did not have to be concerned about him.

But she was concerned. He had been moving very slowly when he had left the room, and his lips had been drawn with pain.

She stood there, gazing at the curtains, her fists clenched before she turned on her heel and headed for the white refrigerator box. It would do no harm to let him have his way until she was sure that he had not seriously harmed himself by the long walk from the ferry.

Then she would leave him and go back to her life in the city that had nothing to do with Hu Chang.

"You let me sleep for a long time." Hu Chang lifted his cup to his lips and gazed at her over the rim. "I fear your softness is becoming more evident with every passing hour. You will have to be more careful."

"I took a nap myself." She nibbled on a rice cake. "And then I got hungry, or I would have been on my way. I thought I might as well share." She smiled. "Since it was your food after all. Sustenance. That's a strange word. As strange as you, Hu Chang."

"Words are like bits of crystal, the more faceted, the more beautiful. Speech should not be boring." His gaze shifted to his bottles and vials on the shelves. "Any more than those containers should be boring. What I create is magical, their containers should be equally deserving of admiration."

"You had one or two of those painted bottles in the shop in Hong Kong, but none this fine."

"I save my rejects for Hong Kong. I keep the best for my own pleasure."

"You don't care what your customers think?"

"Do you?"

"No. But nothing about trading information for money is pretty. Your bottles are pretty. I like the one that has the lotus flower on it. How did you get the petals so thin and graceful?"

"Time . . . and talent."

She made a rude noise.

"Now, if we're going to be together, you must not do that disgusting thing again," he said. "Even if I deserve it. It offends me, and we must not offend each other."

"But we are not going to be together. I'm going back to Hong Kong tonight."

He shook his head. "I've decided that I will accept your services for the next week or two. Naturally, you won't be permitted to do anything of real importance. I will teach you how to blend trifling potions like the ones I sell to the prostitutes for birth control. That will repay me for your food and lodging." He paused. "And keep you out of harm's way until it becomes safer for you in the city. You may thank me now."

She put her cup back in the saucer with great precision. "Good-bye, Hu Chang."

He smiled. "Too arrogant? Forgive me. Sometimes I cannot resist. It is my nature. But this time I meant to amuse you."

"I was not amused. I don't need you, Hu Chang."

"Perhaps. Perhaps not. 'Need' is such a cloying word. But though we may not need each other, it might be pleasant to help carry each other's burdens. Just for a little while. Then we go our own ways." He leaned back. "And you can never tell when you might need to know how to concoct a fine potion for one of your friends. I might teach you how to create my cure for migraine."

"That's crazy. I have no friends who have migraine headaches."

"No," he said softly. "You have no friends at all, do you? Perhaps Lucy Tain might have come close. Neither do I. Life is too difficult to maintain friends when you often have to concentrate on keeping alive."

"I don't need friends. I do fine."

"So do I. But perhaps we can pretend to be friends for these few weeks and see what comes of it. A kind of experiment."

"I don't pretend."

"You *are* difficult, Catherine. I offer you safety, the opportunity to better your mind and skills under my tutelage, and the chance to explore a relationship with one of the finest and most creative men of any generation."

"And the most conceited."

"That doesn't matter. It's perfectly natural." He added softly, "It's a long way back to Hong Kong. Stay until morning, and we will talk some more. There's a pallet in the small room next to mine. The room is no larger than that boat you lost today. You can curl up there like a little cat."

She was silent, looking at him.

"You're trying to think of every danger

that I could hold for you." He tilted his head. "Let me address them. I will not rob you. You have no money. Nor make a slave of you in my laboratory. You have no skill. I will not rape you. It is against my code, and, besides, that's not the feelings you stir in me. I'm not sure what those feelings are, but I believe them to be without harmful intent." He got to his feet. "Now I'm going back to bed. You may wash these dishes, then go to your pallet."

"No." She looked him in the eye. "We will do these dishes together. You will not make me a kitchen slave any more than one in your laboratory."

He hesitated, then shrugged. "Very well. It's not worth the battle. We will divide labor at a later time." He began to stack the dishes. "Then we are in agreement?"

She didn't answer for a moment. "I don't mind staying for a week or two. But don't pretend that you won't be lucky to have me. You said yourself that you had to replace all those potions that were in that shop in Hong Kong. I can help. I can't believe it will take too much intelligence to just pour those pretty-colored concoctions together."

"Very well, Catherine." Hu Chang smiled faintly as he picked up the cups and saucers. "You're right, I will not pretend that I am not the most fortunate of men to have found you. That would be indeed sacrilege."

CHAPTER
5

"I'm tired of making these herbal drinks," Catherine said as she carefully corked the glass vial. "It's boring. Give me something else to do."

"You're not ready for anything else."

"I've been doing this for more than two weeks. In that time, you could have taught me to blend up a cure for the common cold."

"Two weeks? I believe that has been a mystery for centuries. Even I could not teach you to bridge that gulf in two weeks." He added a tiny mist of powder to the liquid in the wooden cup before him. "Those herbal drinks are very important. They can keep a child alive and perfectly healthy even if they're deprived of food for many months."

"Really?" She looked at the drink in the vial before her with new respect. During the last weeks, she had learned that Hu Chang might boast, but he never lied about anything connected with his work. "Some kind of vitamin stuff?"

He grimaced. "To put it without even a hint of elegance."

"And who do you sell the drinks to?"

"I don't sell, I donate. There are many parched and starving lands in this world. These will go to some charity organizations in Ethiopia."

"Donate?"

"That means give without compensation. I can understand how you'd not understand the word."

"You're right, I do well to feed myself without worrying about anyone else." She reached for another herb from the bowl he'd given her. "And how do you manage to do it? You have food here but little else."

"I have what I need. Even if I didn't, I

would still donate the herb drinks. I regard giving as necessary to right the balance."

"What balance?"

"You're very curious today."

She was curious about him, and that curiosity had been growing every day. "What balance?"

He didn't look up as he added a minute amount of creamy liquid to the mixture in his cup. "Life and death."

She stiffened, her gaze narrowing on his face. "And how do you right this balance, Hu Chang?" Her eyes dropped to the wooden cup in front of him. "What's in that cup?"

"Many things, all very complex and very, very lethal." His gaze shifted to her face. "There's a great market out there for poisons of all descriptions. In a world that regards the taking of life as the ultimate victory, a man who can supply the quickest, safest way to do that is in high demand." He added gravely, "And I am the grand master. I make the poisoners of the Renaissance appear amateurs." He tapped the side of the bowl. "When this is brewed, it will only take a whiff to make a victim go into cardiac arrest."

She was staring at the mixture in fascination. "Who do you sell it to?"

"Whoever can afford it."

"What about your precious balance?"

"Do you mean does my conscience bother me? No, I supply, I do not judge. Occasionally, I refuse a client. But that is rare." His mouth twisted. "I look upon my poisons as bullets. I do not aim the gun. I merely create the bullet that's fired by the murderer. It is his decision, not mine." His gaze was studying her expression. "But that troubles you."

"It shouldn't."

"Because you've killed?"

"I have no right. It's just that poison is so . . . intimate."

"Yes, it is. But unless specified by the client, it is very quick and almost painless."

"How long have you done this?"

"Since I was a boy in Siberia. My father was Chinese, my mother Turkish and Russian, and they ran the only apothecary shop in over a hundred miles. There were several Masters of Chinese Medicine, but no one had the skill that my father possessed. We were very poor, barely eking out the sparsest living. It was natural that my father decided to branch out into more lucrative sidelines. Suddenly, we were no longer poor. I learned the art of creating poisons from my father. He was very good."

She smiled. "But not as good as you?"

"No, I am not good. I am magnificent."

"And he taught you that it was good to sell these poisons?"

"He taught me that money is good and poverty terrible and let me learn everything else for myself. By the time I had learned enough to realize that my soul was probably doomed by many people's standards, I had already been involved in over a hundred deaths. It was a little late to try to redeem myself. Not that I would have done it anyway."

"Is your father still making his poisons?"

"No, one of his clients in Moscow, Peter Rudov, decided that he had to erase all of his tracks after he gave one of my father's potions to a political rival. Rudov was very important in the government and wanted to make sure there were no leaks. One night, my father and mother were shot by a hired killer, Boris Zartak, as they drove from our home to the shop. I was already at the shop and managed to escape when he came after me. I was shot in the leg, but I pried out the bullet and put on one of my salves to heal it."

"And then left Siberia and came here?"

"Eventually." He took out a plastic bag and began carefully to pour the poison into the container. "But I was only a boy of fifteen and I had no patience or philosophy of life. I decided I had to revenge my parents." He sealed the bag. "So I did."

She waited.

His brows rose. "How? First, I tracked Boris Zartak, waited for an opportunity, then did what I'd been trained to do. He liked a straight shot of vodka before he went to bed every night. It helped him to sleep. So I poured a few drops of one of my favorite remedies into the bottle." He smiled. "He did not sleep well that night. Nor for several nights after that. Have you heard of Ebola? The symptoms were reminiscent of that terrible disease. The poison ate into his organs and caused him excruciating pain. It gradually devoured his liver like a hungry parasite. The doctors couldn't help him. They thought he'd been bitten by some rare African mosquito."

"You can do that?" she whispered.

"Yes, does it frighten you?"

She thought about it. "No, but it makes me wary."

"Everyone should be wary. It's healthy."

"What about Rudov, that man who hired him?"

"I waited a year before I killed him. He developed a strain of pneumonia that was completely incurable. He lived a month fighting for air before he died." He smiled. "And then I decided to travel the world and increase my knowledge and competence. I didn't settle here in Hong Kong until many years later."

"Why Hong Kong?"

"It's a city that has many interesting facets and is the center of wickedness as well as beauty. Balance. It pleased me."

"Until Wong decided to try to beat you to death."

"I would not allow that episode to affect my attitude. Though I admit he did catch me off guard. I was glad to have you step in until I could get my breath."

"What? I believe I did more than give you breathing room. He might have killed you."

"No, as I told you, I was about to make

my move." He held up his right fist. "Is this not a fine ring?" The gold ring on his index finger had a lapis star in the center that glittered in the candlelight. "You notice the prongs holding the lapis?"

"And?"

"Any pressure on the prongs releases a poison that will kill in ten seconds. All I would have had to do was strike Wong once, and it would have been over."

"Then why didn't you do it before? He was breaking you into pieces."

"I had to decide if I wished to take drastic action. It's a responsibility to kill a man. One has to decide whether it's required." He smiled. "But when he cracked my rib, I decided that it was definitely called for."

She was gazing at the ring. Death. Just a slight pressure and death.

Hu Chang followed her gaze. "During the Renaissance, poison rings were very popular, particularly among the Borgia family. But they had containers of poison that had to be emptied into wine. This is much more efficient."

"I can see it would be. If you aren't clumsy and could be sure to control the pressure."

"Oh, I have great control. You don't have to worry that I would strike and kill you by accident."

"Only by intent," she said dryly.

"Exactly." He got to his feet in one fluid motion. "And now it's time to sleep. You might make a mistake and damage my reputation if you grow too tired."

"I think that your reputation would be more damaged if you made a mistake. I'm not dealing in deadly poisons." She had a sudden thought. "Or am I?"

"You doubt me?"

"I don't know anything about these herbs. They may not be what you say they are."

"But you do know more about me now, don't you?" He reached down and lifted her to her feet. "What do you think? Did I tell you the truth?"

It was a challenge.

She reached down and took one of the herbs and put it on her tongue. It tasted faintly bitter. "If it's poison, you'd better have a remedy, Hu Chang."

"Don't swallow it."

She quickly spit it out.

"It wouldn't have killed you." He chuckled. "But it would have given you a stomachache when not balanced by the other herbs."

"Balance, again." She rubbed her tongue on the top of her mouth to get rid of the taste. "You wanted to make me nervous."

"It was an opportunity I couldn't resist. You have such formidable composure for a woman of your young years." He turned toward the beaded curtains that hid his pallet from view. "And it could have given you more than a bellyache if you'd chosen the herb right next to it. That was belladonna. I use it sometimes in my milder poisons."

"But the blend of all those herbs will keep a starving child alive for months?"

"Balance, always the balance." He stopped at the beaded curtains to look back at her. "Go to bed. You've worked hard today."

She shook her head. "I don't want to sleep. I'm going to go and sit outside in the grass for a while."

His gaze searched her face. "You're restless."

"Maybe. I feel as if I can't breathe."

"Did what I told you, disturb you?"

"No." She shrugged. "I've known whores and pimps and thieves all my life. And I've run across men like Bruce Wong, who like to hurt as well as kill. Everyone I know would kill if they had to do it to survive. At least, you told me the truth." She looked at him over her shoulder. "But I don't know why you told me. You're not like anyone I've ever met. Sometimes you make me uneasy."

"You'll learn someday. And I'll learn, too. I'm not sure why I told you, either. All I know is that there must be a reason why we came together. I believe we must explore our relationship to see what that reason could be." He smiled. "We are both alone. Perhaps we were not meant to be alone. Maybe that is the reason. So simple."

"I don't mind being alone. I don't need anyone."

"Don't you?"

"No." She turned and went out the front door. She took a deep, slow breath of the night air before she sank to the ground beside the front door. It was cool out here, but she needed that freshness after the closeness of the laboratory.

Closeness. Yes, that was the word. The air was warm and close, and Hu Chang's words had also woven another kind of closeness between them that she instinctively rejected. He was a solitary man, just as Catherine was solitary. Why think that they could comfortably accept anything else? Yet these weeks had been strangely serene, filled with learning and flashes of dry humor . . .

"May I sit with you?"

She looked up to see Hu Chang standing in the doorway. "You were going to go to sleep."

"I changed my mind." He dropped down beside her and leaned back against the house. "It was more important that we clarify our situation. You were becoming upset."

"No, I wasn't." She looked up at the stars. "You were just talking nonsense. I couldn't understand you."

"And I was coming too near. I had a small bit of trouble at the thought that I was going to have to accept you into my life, but I—"

"You don't have to accept anything," she broke in. "I don't need you. You don't need

me. I shouldn't have come with you. This
is no place—"

"Please don't interrupt. As I said, I have
years of experience and maturity that allow me not to struggle against the inevita-
ble. You do not." He put his fingers on her
lips. "And you will not make that disgusting
sound again. It is true. You may be far more
grown-up than other girls your age, but that
experience has been confined to a narrow
channel here in Hong Kong."

She brushed his hand away. "That's not
true."

"It is, you know. There's so much world
for you to explore. I wish I could be there
with you to open your eyes." He was not
smiling. "That would give me great pleasure. Do you know that whenever I was in
my shop in the city and saw you striding
about the neighborhood, I would stop and
watch you? You were so slim, almost fragile, and yet bold and graceful, and you lit
up the entire street. Sometimes I would
worry about you because it would be natural for anyone to want to stretch out their
hands to touch you." He chuckled. "And
then I saw how you treated one of your informants who did reach out and touch you,

and I didn't worry any longer. Where did you learn karate, Catherine?"

"Lee Kai. He was very respected and had a studio on Kowloon. I was strong, but there were so many men who were stronger. Karate seemed to be the answer. But Lee Kai taught only young boys and men until I asked him to teach me. He didn't want to do it, but I had to have a way of protecting myself. So I found a reason to make him agree." She added impatiently, "I offered him money. I'd saved up a little. He wouldn't take it. He was so sure that I wouldn't be worthy of his teaching. He was like you, Hu Chang. Arrogant."

"I'm certain that he didn't remain that way when you finished with him."

"I was almost as good as he was by the time I stopped going to him. I would have been better if I'd stayed another five weeks, but I'd thought I'd learned enough to survive on the streets."

"From what I observed, I believe you're correct. And how did you get Lee Kai to agree to teach you?"

"I watched him for three weeks to see what he wanted more than money."

"And what was that?"

"He had a young wife, Mai Sung. He had bought her from her father in the old custom when she was fifteen. She was very beautiful. But she was seventeen and hadn't given him any children. He blamed her for it." Her lips twisted. "Though he was in his late sixties, he wouldn't admit there was a possibility the problem might be with him. He was a bull of a man and a great fighter. How could he be to blame? But he became very suspicious and jealous when she began to disappear for hours in the afternoons. He thought she was having sex with one of his students, Han Lo."

"How did you know this?"

She shrugged. "I told you, I watched them."

"And put the pieces together."

"That's what you have to do. Grab a little information here and there, then put it all together. I went to Lee Kai and told him that I'd follow his wife and see if he was right about her being unfaithful with Han Lo. I'd give him a report, and, in return, he'd teach me what I needed to know."

"And he agreed?"

"I knew he would. He was like a slavering dog when he was around her. And she wasn't even a whore. I guess some men feel like that about all women."

His lips quirked. "I guess they do."

"Two weeks later, I handed in my report to him. I told him that Mai Sung wasn't going to bed with Han Lo. That she was going to the Buddhist temple to pray to conceive a child. He began to teach me karate two days later."

"Was it the truth?"

"I don't lie. It was the truth. She wasn't going to bed with Han Lo. It was a young gardener she'd met in the park. And she started going to the Buddhist temple the day I talked to her, so that's the truth. I told her that she had to do it or I'd tell her husband. I also told her that she should stop her lover from using birth preventatives when they met. All she needed to do to be safe was get with child and tell Lee Kai it was his. Otherwise, he'd probably end up killing her."

"Quite probably. A very satisfactory conclusion."

"Are you making fun of me? It was the best thing for everyone. Mai Sung will live to be a young, healthy widow. Lee Kai will have a child. And I got what I needed without telling a lie."

"I'm not making fun of you. I'm lost in admiration."

"No, you're not. You can't be interested in how I— Why don't you go to bed?"

"Truly. You are amazing." He turned and looked her in the eye. "And you're wrong, I'm interested in everything you've ever done or said. I regard it as important. Why else would I have risked my life?"

She frowned, puzzled. "Risked your life?"

"I put my life in your hands when I told you about the murder of my father and mother. I confessed to the killing of Zartak and Rudov. I gave you names and circumstances. You could do me great harm if you went to the police."

She had never considered that he had given her that power. She had listened to him tell of his background as if it were only a fascinating story. That was odd in itself since it was natural for her to weigh every spoken word for value. "Why did you do that? It was stupid of you."

"Sometimes one takes chances if the

stakes are high enough. And for some mysterious reason, I trusted you. You were asking me questions. I answered them."

"I never asked you if you'd killed someone. I wouldn't do that."

"But I regarded it as a return in confidence. You'd already told me that you had killed." He paused. "Why did you kill, Catherine? Who?"

She didn't answer.

"Who?" he repeated softly.

"Why do you want to know?" she asked fiercely. "Do you want to make sure that I don't go to the police about the men you killed? I couldn't do that if you knew everything that—"

"I want you to trust me as I do you."

"Why? I'm nothing to you. Tomorrow or the next day, I'll go back to Hong Kong, and we may never see each other again."

"Listen to me, Catherine." He reached out and cupped her face in his two hands. "We will see each other. We're together now, and we can't escape it. Do you know that some people believe that we go through life after life and meet and interact with the same people?"

"That's crazy."

"No." He gently stroked her hair back from her face. "I knew many people in India who were certain of it. I only thought it an interesting concept. Now I'm beginning to believe it. I think . . . I recognized you, Catherine."

"I'm not listening to you," she said unsteadily. "Bruce Wong must have knocked something loose in your head."

"Quite possibly." He smiled. "Perhaps a lost memory or two. I don't mean to frighten you. I just have to say it. Because it may have meaning. We were together once. I don't know in what manner. But there was affection. You could have been my wife, my sister, my daughter . . ."

"I'm going to bed, Hu Chang."

He nodded, and his hands dropped from her face. "My daughter perhaps. I feel such pride in you." He got to his feet. "Perhaps this time we will only be friends. But I could never hurt or betray you, Catherine." He looked down at her. "Any more than you could betray me. Trust me. I'll help you. We'll help each other."

He turned and went into the house.

She was shaking. Crazy. When he had been speaking, she had almost believed him. She had felt as if they were bound together in some strange way. But he had been wrong, he had not frightened her. There had been something warm and strong and river-deep in those moments.

Perhaps this time we will only be friends.

Trust me. I'll help you. We'll help each other.

What would it be like not to be alone?

No, she would have to yield too much. Believe too much.

She turned and went into the house.

She would forget that strange conversation. She would go to bed, and everything would be different in the morning. Perhaps it was time she went back to Hong Kong.

Yes, she would lie on her pallet and make a decision about leaving Hu Chang before she went to sleep.

Go on, Catherine told herself. This was foolishness. You haven't been able to sleep all night. Why worry about waking him? He was the one to blame for all this.

Catherine stopped before the beaded curtains and braced herself. "Hu Chang?"

"I'm not sleeping. I was waiting for you. You took a long time."

In the dimness, she could see him sitting up, his legs crossed, leaning against the wall. "It was your fault. You had to mutter all that nonsense that I had to sort out. I wasn't used to all that—"

"Sit down and stop chastising me. I knew it would be difficult for you. You are not like me. Everything has to be clear and have a beginning and an end. Only sometimes that doesn't happen, Catherine."

She dropped to the pallet and crossed her legs as he was doing. How many times during the last weeks had they sat like this across from each other at his worktable, preparing his potions? "I'm going to go back to Hong Kong today."

"I thought you might."

"I couldn't stay here forever, playing with your herbs. I have to face Wong and get on with my life. This is your life, not mine."

"And you have worlds to conquer."

"I'm not stupid. All I want to do is make a living and try not to do it by running drugs or whoring or hurting everyone around me."

"That is a laudable ambition. But conquering worlds could be fitted into that picture. You have the capability. I have faith in you."

She could not see his face in the darkness, but his voice was firm and held absolute certainty. He believed what he was saying, and the knowledge was shaking her to her core. How could she be hard and practical and all the things she needed to be when he did this to her? "Because I was your daughter or wife or sister in some other life?" she said sarcastically. "Because you think you know me?"

"I do know you. But we will forget past lives. If it will make you more comfortable, we will deal only with this one. Hu Chang and Catherine."

"That is our life, dammit."

"I should not have rushed you. It was just that I had only recently reached the obvious conclusion, and I wished to share it. I should have realized that we were not at the same stage."

"Since you consider yourself as all-knowing, that was a gigantic mistake."

"You're ranting at me, but your voice is shaking a little. I've noticed that paradox when you are profoundly upset and trying

to disguise it. Why did you come to me tonight? Why not wait until morning?"

"Why shouldn't I be upset? And I'm not
ranting. I'm just—" She stopped. She was
not being honest. She had come to him for
a reason, and she should not be a coward.
"I knew I wouldn't sleep, and it's a long
walk back to the ferry to Hong Kong. It's
not practical not to get a good rest before
starting out."

"And you're always reasonable and
practical."

She drew a deep breath. She was glad
that it was dark because he couldn't see
how vulnerable she felt. "You . . . trusted
me. You said you wanted to be my friend. It
made me— I don't know why I would want
a crazy, old apothecary for a friend, but I—"

"Shh. It will come. You're getting off track.
Start over."

"I'll do it the way I want to do it. As I was
lying on my pallet, I thought maybe it
wouldn't be so bad not to be alone—to
have a friend."

"Even if it's a crazy, old apothecary."

"Perhaps you're not so old. You tell me
you're not."

He chuckled. "And you're willing to concede one point."

"I don't care," she said roughly. "Some people would wonder why you would want to have someone like me for a friend." She added quickly, "Though I'm just as good as anyone I know and better than a lot of them."

"Much better."

"Then it's settled, we're friends," she said brusquely. "It doesn't mean anything, but I'm glad it's out in the open."

"Then is this good night?"

"Not quite." She moistened her lips. "I have to say one more thing. It's sort of . . . an exchange."

"I know where you're leading," he said quietly. "It doesn't have to happen, Catherine."

"You told me what you did to the men who killed your parents. You asked me to trust you. If you're my friend, don't I have to do that? You asked me who I'd killed. You want to know, so I have to tell you." She braced herself. "His name was Donald Carruthers. He was British."

He was silent for a moment. "That must have caused you some difficulty. The British here in Hong Kong take care of their own."

"Yes, they do. And some of them think that anyone who doesn't look like them and talk like them are only good to treat as toys." She added fiercely, "I wasn't a toy. He shouldn't have done it."

"No, you're not a toy." He asked gently, "How long ago was it, Catherine?"

"Two years ago. I was twelve. You remember I told you about the British woman, the social worker, who put me in that orphanage when I was ten?"

"Yes."

"Her name was Emma Carruthers. She was on the board of the orphanage and had a fine house next door. She gave all kinds of society parties for her charities and would bring them to the orphanage to show them how generous she was to us. I didn't like her, but I didn't mind the orphanage. I had food to eat, and I was learning things. But when I was twelve, she sent for me and told me that she was sending me to her husband at his house in town. She said that she was going to make it look as if I'd run away from the orphanage and that I must be good and do whatever he said. If

I didn't, she'd tell the police to take me away and put me in prison. She said her husband liked young girls, and no one would care what happened to a half-breed Chinese slut who everyone knew would end up a whore like her mother. I tried to run away, but there was a man at the door who chloroformed me. When I woke up, I was tied to a bed." She was starting to shake as the memories rushed back to her. "And then he came."

"You don't have to say any more," Hu Chang said quietly. "We'll consider the exchange made."

"No, we won't. You haven't heard it all. He kept me locked in that room for a month. He called me his little China Doll, his beautiful toy, and made me do . . . things. When I'd fight him, he'd beat me. He liked that. It made him feel powerful. He was big and muscular and proud of being so strong. He'd brag about being strong as Hercules. He even had a brass statue of Hercules on the bedside table that he showed me and asked if it didn't look like him."

"You don't have to tell me that you didn't agree with him even though it would have been the wise thing to do."

"Wise? I told him he was fat and ugly and a coward."

"And you paid for it."

"Yes, but it was worth it. He told me that I wasn't the first girl from the orphanage his wife had sent him. He was an important man in the government, and he had to be careful of his reputation. They lived apart, but she liked the position and prestige of being his wife, and they came to a compromise that suited them both. When he was done with the girls, he arranged for them to go to a house in Macau. But that night he said I was special, that he'd keep me for a long, long time." She paused. "And that's when I knew I was going to kill him."

"Enough, Catherine," he said gently.

She barely heard him. She was back in that scented room with Carruthers's sweaty body over her, hurting her. "But I didn't know how to do it. He liked to keep me bound. Ropes. Chains. Handcuffs. He never trusted me because I was always fighting him. But that night I realized what I had to do. He was calling me his little baby whore and saying what else he'd make me do before he turned me over to anyone else, what he'd teach me." Her fists knotted into fists. "But I didn't have to be taught. I'd grown up with whores. I knew what they did to make a man do what they wanted. Carruthers liked to think he was powerful. All I had to do was pretend to be beaten, then do the things I'd seen my mother and Natasha do to their customers. I began to touch him, use my fingers, my tongue. He liked it. No, he *loved* it. It was easy.

"The first night he was surprised, but he still kept me tied. The second night I told him what else I'd do to please him, things I said my mother had taught me. But that I couldn't do any of those things bound up as he had me. He was tempted, I could tell. But it wasn't until the fourth night that he took off both the ropes and the cuffs. As he was doing it, I lay there on the bed and watched him. My heart was beating hard, and I knew that everything I'd planned was going to happen.

"He stood there, looking down at me. 'You're smiling,'" he said. 'I always knew that this was all you were good for, all that would make you happy.' He lay down beside me. 'Now show me, little whore. Give it to me.'"

"So I did.

"I crawled over him and started touching him. He closed his eyes. I reached for the brass statue of Hercules on the nightstand.

"I called his name before I hit him with it. I made him open his eyes. I wanted to make sure he knew it was coming and that I had done it. I hit him, and I hit him again, and kept on hitting him until I was sure he was dead."

"And then you ran away?"

"That's what I started to do, then I stopped. I wasn't going to have the police after me for the rest of my life for killing that scum. I got dressed and ran out of the house. Two hours later I was at Emma Carruthers's house adjoining the orphanage. I woke her up and told her what I'd done. I told her she had to fix it so that no one would know I'd killed him, or I'd tell everyone what he'd done and that she'd sent me to him. Her fine life of prestige and privilege would be over. If she covered up his death, I'd disappear, I'd go back on the streets, and she wouldn't hear from me again."

"She agreed?"

"She was still fuming and cursing me when I left her. But the next day I read in the paper that Carruthers had tragically fallen down the stairs of his fine home on Graham Street and was found dead by his devoted and bereaved wife the next morning."

"And she's caused you no more trouble?"

"No, the police never picked me up. I went back to Wen Chai, where I was before I went to the orphanage."

"Not quite where you were. Experiences alter us."

"I'm not sorry I killed him. I'd do it again," she said fiercely. "He had no right. I'm not a whore. I'm not a toy."

"Shh." He was on his knees before her. His hands were stroking her hair with the gentlest of touches. She felt as if she was enveloped, surrounded, in that cloudlike tenderness. How strange . . . "Shall I tell you what you are? You're a child of the sun. You're all golden and ebony and silk on the outside. On the inside, there is strength and clarity and honesty. I look at you, and I believe that life is good. Remember, I told you I was proud of you? I'm a hundred times more proud now to have you for my friend."

She couldn't speak for a moment. "You talk like a damn poet or one of those stuffy books they had me reading at the orphanage." Her eyes were stinging. "You're right, I am strong. I didn't let that bastard hurt me or change what I am. But I'm not proud of what I did. And you're very strange to value me more because I had to kill him. I don't think more of you because you poisoned those men who killed your parents. Though I can see why you did it."

"We are different. I'm a little beyond your experience. You'll catch up someday. You were terribly hurt, but not enough to take joy in revenge or to do it properly." She couldn't see him smile in the darkness, but she knew he was doing it. "I'll take that joy for you." He took her two hands in his. "I thank you for the gift of your trust. I will treasure it."

Warmth. Comfort. Bonding. The absence of loneliness. It was too much, too intense. She had to back away from it. "This doesn't really mean anything. I'm still going back to Hong Kong in the morning."

"Of course, but the gift has been given. You can't take it back." He dropped her hands. "Go back to your pallet. You will sleep now. When you wake, you will pretend that nothing has happened, and so will I. But when you're in need, you will know that something has changed, that you have someone to fill that need." He stretched out with one graceful motion. "Tomorrow, the day after, next year . . . Who knows how long? We'll have to see, won't we?"

Catherine stood there, hesitating. She didn't want to leave him. She wanted to talk to him, feel that bonding again.

She was being foolish. People came and went in your life, and you couldn't expect any of them to stay. "Friendship" was only a word. She turned to leave. "Sleep well, Hu Chang."

She had reached the beaded door when he answered. "Stop worrying, Catherine. It will come together. We've started to blend a powerful mixture, now we only have to seek the balance."

"Balance? Everything is balance with you." But she was feeling her spirits rise as she said it. "I'd rather throw everything in the mix and see what comes of it. And I'm not worrying. Why should I? I can take care of anything that comes along." She heard him laugh as she went through the beaded door. She liked the sound of his laughter. It was so familiar now. She had grown accustomed to hearing that laugh, the dry humor of his remarks, the way he looked quizzically at her when she was impatient or questioning him.

She would miss him.

The knowledge stunned her. She had known the apothecary for only a few weeks. She couldn't remember missing anyone but her mother for a little while after she had died. But she had been so young then that sadness had faded in the urgency of just staying alive.

But she would miss Hu Chang.

CHAPTER
6

"Here is something to eat on the way back to the city. Fish and a little rice and bread." Hu Chang handed her a foil-wrapped package. "It would be wise of you to avoid going back to the docks even if you have people who might help you there. Wong will be keeping an eye on that area."

"I wasn't going to be that stupid." She tucked the package in her jacket pocket. "Though Wong may have become involved in one of his gang-turf battles and forgotten about me."

"You do not believe that."

"Anything is possible. Isn't that what you tell me, Hu Chang?"

"Where will you live if you're avoiding the dock area?"

"There are empty warehouses near the dock. I can shelter there until it's safe to move somewhere permanent."

"You could shelter here." He held up his hand as she opened her lips to protest. "If you find it necessary. My door is open. Even if I am no longer here."

She stiffened. "Where are you going? Not back to Hong Kong?"

He smiled. "You think it would not be safe for me? But I was only the victim, not the aggressor."

"That doesn't matter. You were there when Wong was humiliated. They burned your shop to the ground."

"Yes, that did annoy me."

"You're not being sensible."

"And you're being amazingly protective. I am touched."

And he was being mocking and faintly patronizing. "Protective? Why should I care what happens to you?" She whirled away and started toward the front door. "I have enough problems just keeping myself alive. It's just not smart to risk going back to the city if you have nothing to gain from it. You can't rebuild that pile of ashes."

"I could if I find it worthwhile. But I have another interest in Hong Kong. I'll look into rebuilding the shop later."

"Not me, Hu Chang. I don't need your help. I won't take it."

"I'm aware of that." He waved his hand. "Now be on your way. You need to get to the city and find shelter before dark."

He was treating her like fathers she'd seen in the city whisking their children off to school. It should have made her feel indignant. It did not. It made her feel . . . warm. She turned away. "Good-bye, Hu Chang."

"Wait. It might prove safer if you stay away from your usual clients and sources in the city. Most of them are in the neighborhoods Wong considers his turf."

"Yes, but how do I earn a living if I stay hidden inside a warehouse and off the streets? That's not possible." She added caustically, "As I told you, it's not as if I can close myself away brewing potions and medicines as you do."

"That's true. Particularly since you have no real talent for anything but the easiest of mixtures." Before she could shoot a reply back at him, he added, "No, I was thinking that you should take your present endeavors to the next level. Do you ever sell information to the police and Chinese military?"

"Sometimes." She shrugged. "But the police don't pay well, and the military has the reputation of getting rid of informants if the information is what they call 'sensitive.'"

"I can see why that would deter you." He paused. "Have you ever dealt with the Americans?"

"I sold the American ambassador information about a Russian general who was having meetings with the Chinese."

"No, that's a onetime transaction, not what I'd call regular work. What about the American CIA?"

She shook her head. "I've heard they're hand in glove with the British in the city. I don't deal with the British if I don't have to do it."

"I can see how you'd have reservations. Do have any prejudice against the Americans?"

She shook her head. "My mother said my father was an American soldier. He left her before I was born, but he never hurt us."

"Neglect is not hurt?"

"He just went away. People go away. Why do you ask?"

"Because I believe you should reconsider the advantages of dealing with the CIA. They have a gigantic thirst for information and might keep you from having to deal with anyone else who might prove dangerous right now."

She shook her head doubtfully.

"Think about it. I believe you may be wrong about the attachment of the CIA to the British. There's a new field agent in town by the name of Venable. I've done business with him, and I'd judge him to be totally committed to his own country's agendas."

"What kind of business?"

He smiled. "No, he didn't purchase a poison from me. Though that would not have surprised me. He needed a truth drug that had certain special properties. He paid promptly and, other than threatening me with a dire fate if I'd cheated him, the transaction was not unpleasant. I would not recommend him as a new source of income to you if I'd had any apprehensions. His office is at the Princess Hotel, far away from Bruce Wong's turf."

"I'll have to face Wong sometime."

"If one of his gang rivals doesn't kill him first. There is always that happy thought." He turned back to his laboratory. "Remember, the CIA agent's name is Venable . . ."

Fourteen Days Later
Hong Kong
1:40 A.M.

Catherine glanced cautiously down Sun Ti Street before she ran across to the door of the deserted warehouse. There had been no sign of Bruce Wong and his triad anywhere near this area since she had come back to Hong Kong, but that didn't mean he might not appear. She had been careful, on the streets only at night and trying to contact only her informants who had some loyalty to her. But as far as she knew, there was still a bounty on her head from the triad, and money sharpened people's eyes.

She ran up the flights of stairs to the third floor, where she had her blanket and thermos. This place seemed as safe as any other, but she should probably find another warehouse next week. Moving around was always a better plan than going to ground in a single hiding place.

A few minutes later, she'd settled on her blanket and pulled another one over her. She should be tired, but she was still wired from the day. She'd done another job for Venable today, and they were always a challenge . . . and usually a little dangerous. When he wanted information, it was something that she had to walk a tightrope to get for him.

That was all right with her. He paid well, and he'd never tried to cheat her during the last two weeks. Hu Chang was right, Venable was proving one of the best customers she'd ever had.

Hu Chang.

She felt a sudden pang of loneliness as she remembered those words. Loneliness? Forget about him. Perhaps the loneliness had always been there, but she had never been so aware of it until those weeks with that crazy apothecary. She had been right to leave, to get back to her own life, to leave him before he left her.

And she was only lonely in moments like this, at the end of the day, when she was a little tired. It would go away entirely after a month or two. She would be—

Sounds from downstairs in the warehouse.

Footsteps.

Catherine listened.

They were trying to be quiet, but their boots creaked on the loose boards. She counted. One. Two. Maybe three. It was hard to tell.

Two or three men. Either way it wasn't good. It was after midnight, and no one should be in the deserted warehouse. Unless she'd been seen when she'd come back from seeing Venable tonight.

And if she'd been seen by someone, then she was now prey.

Bruce Wong?

Logical answer. There were all kinds of scum on the streets, but it was Wong who was targeting her.

Get prepared.

There was no elevator in the warehouse, and he would have to come up the spiraling wooden stairs to where she was on the third floor.

He would probably have weapons. Knives, perhaps even guns. She had no weapons except a knife that was in the holster on her thigh, and the board with nails that she'd put in readiness by the staircase. No, her ability at martial arts was also a weapon, and Wong would be using caution with her in close quarters.

But three against one was not good odds, and she should probably hit them, hurt them, then get away.

No sound. They mustn't realize she was awake.

She glided to the window and quietly raised the sash. No one was on the street below. She threw down the rope she'd already fixed to the wall beside the window.

They were coming up the staircase.

She ran back to the steps and grabbed the board with the embedded nails.

"Watch out!"

It was Wong's voice, but it wasn't Wong who was first on the stairs, she realized with disappointment. It was Kwan Lin, his lieutenant she'd put down at Hu Chang's apothecary shop who exploded up the final few steps.

He had a knife in his hand, and he was cursing. "I'll cut your heart out, bitch."

She swung the board, but he ducked, and the nails only grazed his head.

He screamed with rage and dove at her, knife raised. She hit him again with the board, and the nails sank deep into his skull.

He fell to the floor.

But another man had emerged from the staircase.

Again, not Wong. Son of a bitch. Coward. Attack.

She jumped forward and swung her leg, connecting with her toe to his throat. He gasped, and his stride broke. But he recovered and plunged forward again.

"You fool, get her. She's only a woman." It was Wong on the steps behind him. "Do you want everyone on the street to know that she beat you?"

Catherine was breathing hard as she sidestepped the lunge. "Did you tell them how I took you down, Wong?" She grabbed his lieutenant, put her arm around his throat, and held him in front of her as a shield with her knife to his throat. She told him, "Don't move, or I'll slit your throat." She looked at Wong over his shoulder. "No, you probably didn't tell them. You were too ashamed. All your lieutenants and your whores would have laughed at you. But I see you brought help this time."

"I don't need help." He drew a pistol out of his jacket. "I wasn't expecting any trouble when I went after the apothecary. You caught me off guard."

"Excuses, Wong?" She couldn't get close enough to grab the gun. Better to get out and live to fight another day. She started to back away from Wong toward the window, dragging his lieutenant with her. "What did you just say? 'She's only a woman.' It's too bad you're not a man."

He was cursing, his mouth twisted, ugly. "You'll see if I'm a man, you bitch. I'll stake you out and screw your brains out. I'll keep you alive for the next month and chain you and beat you and make you scream like the whore you are."

Chains.

Stakes.

Whore.

She couldn't breathe, her stomach was clenching with anger . . . and fear.

Don't remember that other time. Carruthers had not won out over her then. The memory must not beat her now. And Wong would not have his chance at her. Not if she did not panic.

She took another two steps back toward the window.

"Would that make you feel like a man? Hitting women? I can see you puffing up like a rooster. You like to see people helpless, don't you? Is that how you felt when you were beating up Hu Chang?"

"Yes, but he wasn't important. He was just in my way."

"Make her let me go, Wong," his lieutenant croaked. "You didn't tell me this would happen."

"Why should I tell you anything? You should have just obeyed orders."

"I'm bleeding. She's cutting me."

Two more steps, and she'd reach the open window. "I'll let him go, Wong, if you put down the gun and give me a head start down those stairs."

He laughed. "Oh, no, you got away from me once before. It's not going to happen again." He lifted his gun. "I've had enough of this."

Dear God, he was going to shoot!

Catherine's arms dropped down and she dove to the side as the bullet tore into the head of Wong's lieutenant.

Another shot, this time, grazing her arm.

She reached the window and rolled over the sill, catching the rope as she fell.

She jerked, the rope burning her palms.

Move quickly.

She had caught Wong by surprise by leaping out the window, but that surprise wouldn't last long.

She let herself half fall, half climb down the rope.

He was right above her, leaning out the window.

A bullet tore past her head, taking out a clump of hair.

She swung to the side to spoil the next shot.

She had to get off the rope.

Ten feet to go.

"Let go. Jump!"

Hu Chang. Somewhere below her in the darkness.

No time to think or wonder.

Trust.

She let go of the rope.

She was falling.

Then she was snatched out of the air and both she and Hu Chang staggered sideways into the wall of the building.

Another shot.

Wood splintered next to her cheek.

"Into the doorway." She dragged Hu Chang to the right and under the protection of the overhanging beam over the doorway.

Wong was cursing above her.

"How many?" Hu Chang asked. "I saw three go in."

"Only Wong left, but he has a gun."

"I noticed," Hu Chang said dryly. "And he's no doubt on his way down those stairs right now."

"What are you doing—" No time to ask questions now. She grabbed his arm. "Come on, we have to get out of here. He'll kill you. He may have more triad members on the way. I won't let him—"

"Hush. We have time. I saw no one else on the streets."

"He has a gun, and I had to drop the knife I had when I grabbed the rope." She heard the thunder of Wong's shoes on the wooden flights of stairs. "Let's go. Stop arguing with me, dammit. He just shot one of his own men because he was in his way."

He was shaking his head. "If we leave, you will have to fight him again. We must grasp the opportunity."

"We? This is my fight. You should have stayed in the country, tending your herbs."

"I told you I had things I had to do in the city." He tilted his head, listening. "He's running through the warehouse toward the door. I believe you must use some of the skills Lee Kai taught you and disarm him."

"If I get that close, I'd better do more than disarm him." Hu Chang was not moving, she realized with exasperation. And Wong couldn't be more than a few yards away.

Time had run out.

Surprise him.

She gave Hu Chang a shove to the side and leaped through the door.

Wong was only feet away, and he stopped short.

But he was lifting the gun in his hand.

She kicked him in the belly, and when he bent double with pain, she jumped closer, and the edge of her hand lifted and came down on the wrist of the hand grasping the gun.

The gun fell to the floor.

Catherine dove toward it, grabbed it.

"Bitch." He was on top of her, his weight heavy on her slight body, his eyes glittering in his contorted face above her. "I won't wait to kill you. I want it too much." He was twisting, trying to take the gun. "You've been nothing but—" He suddenly arched, his head going back. "What is—"

"Hold out just for a few seconds more, Catherine." It was Hu Chang's voice from where he stood behind Wong. "I know it's distasteful having him that close to you, but it will be better soon."

Wong's face was no longer flushed but pale. "What did you—hurts."

"I believe it's called a rabbit punch. I hit you with my fist on the back of your neck. Not very hard." His star-shaped lapis in the center of his gold ring shone as he held up his hand. "It really wasn't necessary."

"Sneaky bastard. I should have—" His voice was hoarse. Catherine could feel his body begin to shake against her own. "I feel—"

"Two more seconds, Catherine," Hu

Chang said. "It would be wise to push him off you now. He will be a deadweight." His lips curved in a faint smile. "I truly would not have used that phrase if I'd thought. Much too James Bond."

Catherine shoved with all her strength and wriggled out from under Wong's weight. She had no trouble. His eyes were glazing, and she doubted if he knew she was still there. She drew a deep breath. She felt dazed, her gaze on the lapis ring, and all she could think to ask was a weak, "What do you know about James Bond?"

"Am I not a cosmopolitan? Who does not know of him?"

Wong was falling, his body stiffening.

"It's over." Hu Chang reached down and took her hand and pulled her to her feet. "And now we should leave this place and disappear for a while. Someone must have heard the shots."

"In this neighborhood, they hear, but they don't respond. Particularly in Wong's territory," Catherine said. "But the Royal Police have been riding the triads pretty hard, and it would be best to not be seen. Let's go hop on the ferry and get out of this neighborhood." She looked warily down at his hand, still holding her own. The star lapis was shimmering in the moonlight. "When you pulled me to my feet, you used the hand that you hit Wong with. I'd appreciate your being very careful. I wasn't sure that I believed you when you told me that you were only waiting for the right moment when he was beating you in your shop."

"You should have believed me." He took her elbow and nudged her out the door. "I will always tell you the truth. And there was no danger to you. The prongs retract the moment they leave the flesh."

She looked back at where Wong was lying crumpled on the floor. "He looked as if he was in pain before he died."

"Only a small amount. I was more annoyed than angry with him. But he should not have shot at you." He touched her temple where the bullet had torn away a small patch of hair. "If he'd truly hurt you, I would have had to delay his punishment to make it more fitting."

"How long have you known I was sleeping in this warehouse?"

"Since the second day you found it. I followed you from Venable's hotel."

"Like some Hitchcock movie? Why were

you so secretive? Why didn't you let me know that you were in Hong Kong?"

"I'm secretive by nature. Haven't you noticed? You needed space from me. I gave it to you. We both had tasks to accomplish." He glanced at her. "And you accomplished yours, didn't you? How do you like Venable?"

"He's honest. He's smart. He believes in what he's doing." She paused. "And he can probably be as ruthless as anyone I've ever met."

"But if you're on his side, he'll protect you."

"But I'm not on his side. I just do jobs for him." She jammed her hands into her pockets and looked out at the glittering harbor as they waited for the ferry. "And I can protect myself, Hu Chang."

"I did not say that you couldn't."

"But you sent me to Venable anyway."

"It does no harm to offer a destination when you see someone trying to choose a path. He will not be easy, but he will give you options. You have very few now." He smiled. "Of course, you could choose to stay with me; but, as you've told me, I am arrogant and set in my ways. You would

grow restless. And I would become accustomed to you and not want to let you go.
Since I am very clever and extremely self-
serving, I might succeed in that." He chuckled. "Or you might end up by using my own
ring on me and laugh while I writhe at your
feet."

"That's an interesting picture."

"I thought you'd enjoy it. Someday, perhaps. But for the present, it's better if we
go our own paths and only intersect every
now and then." His smile faded. "As good
friends do, Catherine."

He was going to leave her. Just as
everyone she had ever known had eventually left her. "I wouldn't know." She took
a step forward as the ferry pulled close to
the dock. "Not that it matters. Go away. I
won't miss you."

"How cruel. But you'll be the one to go
away. I'm comfortable here in Hong Kong.
I can conquer all my worlds from here." He
helped her onto the ferry. "Good-bye, Catherine. Go to the Princess Hotel and tell Venable you're available for any job he wants
to send you on. Stay away from this district.
Someone will replace Wong as head of the
triad, and he may try to target you. Just

fade away until you're forgotten by the police and the triad. That's the first step to conquer your worlds. If you need me, I'll be here."

"I won't need you." She was lying. She already felt empty inside. She hated it. One person shouldn't matter this much. She turned, her hands clutching the rail. "You're not going on the ferry?"

"No, I'll stay here and make sure that there are no repercussions from my removing Wong. I'll contact you if I see any problems on the horizon."

"You shouldn't have even been there tonight. Why were you?"

"I've been outside the warehouse every night since I found out where you were." He added simply, "I wanted to be there if my friend needed me."

What was she to say? All her defiance, all the walls that kept her safe, were melting away. "You picked the wrong friend. We've been in trouble since the day we met. You could have been killed."

"Why should I be afraid? Do you not see that we work well when we are together? Almost as if it had happened many times before."

"Don't be ridiculous. Get that stupid idea out of your head. I wasn't your daughter or your sister or your great-aunt in another life. I met you for—" The ferry horn sounded. Catherine felt a frisson of panic. "I suppose I should know where to find you. When do you go back to the country?"

"I'll stay in the city until there's no more reason for me to be here." He smiled. "Don't worry. We won't lose each other, Catherine."

"I wasn't worried." The ferry was starting to move away from the dock. "Why should I—"

"Something for you to read while you're on the ferry. You'll find it interesting." He reached into his jacket and brought out a folded newspaper and thrust it at her before the ferry pulled out of reach. "Keep well, Catherine."

"Keep well, Hu Chang," she said unevenly.

He lifted his hand in farewell, then turned and disappeared into the crowd on the dock.

What had she expected? Hu Chang to stay on the dock until the ferry was out of sight? He was not a man of sentiment in

spite of his odd ideas about past lives. Neither was Catherine. She would turn away
and find a seat on the bench by the rail.

In a few minutes.

It would do no harm to stand here and
let the cool breeze touch her cheeks as
she watched Hu Chang stride down the
dock.

As if he felt her gaze on him, he turned
and smiled, then proceeded on his way.

He had known she was watching him
leave her. Well, why not? She would do as
she pleased. She would not do anything
according to his rules. They were different
as night from day.

**I wanted to be there if my friend
needed me.**

Perhaps not all that different. She would
stand guard over Hu Chang if she was
needed. It was strange to know that after
years of being alone, she had someone
she actually wanted to watch over. When
she had walked into that apothecary shop,
something had happened that she would
never have dreamed would occur.

He was out of sight now. And he had
not told her how to reach him, dammit.

No matter, if she wanted to see him, she

would find him. She knew this city, and now she knew Hu Chang. She dropped down on the bench and looked down at the folded paper in her hand.

Something for you to read while you're on the ferry. You'll find it interesting.

She started to unfold the paper. It was today's issue of the *Hong Kong Sun Times*. She frowned in puzzlement as she noticed it was just one section of the newspaper.

She stiffened.

The obituary section.

Her gaze flew down the column to the obituary that had been circled.

There was a photograph of the deceased to the right of the text. The woman was heavyset, sleekly coifed, and her smile was less warm than superior.

Catherine knew that smile.

Emma Jane Carruthers. 59. Widow of the late James Carruthers. Mrs. Carruthers was chairwoman of several charities and social organizations, and Ambassador Ralph Douglas issued a statement that she would be sorely missed in the fabric of Hong Kong society.

Mrs. Carruthers fell ill fourteen days

ago of a disease that her physicians describe as possibly a bacterial attack with symptoms similar to Ebola. Results have been sent to London and Atlanta CDC for confirmation.

Ebola.

She remembered sitting and watching Hu Chang's face as he calmly told her about his killing the murderers of his parents.

He did not sleep well that night. The poison ate him from the inside. Have you heard of Ebola? It finally devoured his liver and he died.

Fourteen days.

It was a long time to suffer when you were in intense pain. Emma Carruthers must have suffered horribly during those final days.

Hu Chang had to have given her the poison on that first day, when he had followed Catherine to the warehouse from her meeting with Venable. Then he had waited to be sure that Emma Carruthers was dead, and Catherine was safe.

You'll catch up someday. You were terribly hurt, but not enough to take joy in revenge or to do it properly. I'll take that joy for you.

And this had been her first lesson. How did she feel about it? Her first reaction had been a surge of fierce pleasure. The woman deserved to die. She had served Catherine and other little girls up to her husband as if they were some kind of primitive carnal sacrifices. The only way Catherine had been able to keep herself from acting against her was the knowledge that the woman had the power, and Catherine might hurt only herself.

But that had not stopped Hu Chang. He had made the decision, acted, and not cared about the consequences.

And it had been done for her sake.

Another link in the bond that was growing stronger with every hour, every act, every encounter.

It was a dark act, a cruel act, as Hu Chang could be dark and cruel on occasion. But the cruelty had been toward Catherine's enemy, and to Catherine, there had been only mercy.

And she knew that the principal emotion she was now feeling was passionate gratitude.

Together with the knowledge that if the situation had been reversed, she would

have taken that same step for Hu Chang
as he had for her. It did not even come as
a surprise.

So, is that how it's always going to be
between us, Hu Chang?

She slowly folded the newspaper and
tore it into several pieces and dropped
those pieces into the dark waters of the
harbor. She watched the remnants of that
obituary whisked away by the currents.

Yes, I believe it is . . .

Present Day

"We're going to land in fifteen minutes,
Ms. Ling." The flight attendant smiled as
she bent over Catherine. "It's a shame to
wake you, but I thought you'd want to see
Hong Kong from the air. It's pretty spectacular."

"Yes, it is." Catherine pushed the blanket
aside and sat up straight in her seat. "But I
wasn't sleeping. I was just thinking." Thinking, remembering, letting those times with
Hu Chang flow back to her. "Are we on
time?"

"Yes, even a little early." The flight attendant started down the aisle, checking the passengers' seat belts.

It can't be too early for me, Catherine thought. She needed to get off this plane and into action. The flight from Atlanta had seemed excruciatingly long. She gazed out the window at Hong Kong below her. Yes, it was spectacular, and would be bizarre, wicked, and everything she remembered. It had changed over the years since she had met Hu Chang when she was only fourteen. It had become more crowded, a little more touristy, but some places always retained their character.

Like some people. Like Hu Chang, who was most at home in this city though he traveled all over the world. It suited his complex, dark personality, and he knew every nook and cranny of Hong Kong.

And it was going to be hard as hell to hunt him down if he didn't want to be found. She was not as familiar as Hu Chang with the new Hong Kong, and he knew everyone in the city.

But she would do it, dammit.

If this plane ever got on the ground.

CHAPTER 7

"Agent Ling? I'm Agent Jeff Carmody. Venable sent me."

Catherine turned away from the Customs desk to glance at the tall, good-looking, fair-haired man who was smiling tentatively at her. He didn't look a day over twenty-five. She had been younger when she was recruited, but Carmody lacked the necessary edge. Lord, is this what the Company is hiring to please Washington these days? "Hello, Carmody." She grabbed her suitcase. "I told Venable I didn't need anyone to meet me. Sorry you've wasted your time."

"It's not wasted if I'm doing what Venable

wants me to do." He grimaced. "He's been very testy since I arrived here from Sydney. I'm the replacement for Gregory, and he doesn't like to lose agents. All I know is that he told me to meet you and stay with you. I guess he wants to make sure you're safe."

"No, that's not what he wants." She headed for the exit, and said bluntly, "He wants Hu Chang, and he's afraid that I'll find him and not let him know about it. Isn't that what he told you?"

He was silent as he hurried after and opened the door for her. "Yes, that's what he told me. But I'm sure that he doesn't doubt your loyalty, Agent Ling."

"Catherine. And you don't know any such thing. Right now, you're wondering if I've gone rogue and if Venable is going to have to have me put down. And you're probably worrying if it will be you who will have to do it."

He suddenly chuckled. "Not worried. Just regretful. Though you'd be a gorgeous corpse, Agent—Catherine."

She looked at him in surprise. He was more cool and savvy than he appeared. If she was going to have to put up with him for a while, she might as well clear the decks. "It won't happen. Venable and I go back a long time. If he thought I posed a danger, he'd take me out himself. All he wants from you is to spy and report. He knows that I care more about Hu Chang than any mission and that I'll do what's best for him. If it's also good for the Company, then that's a plus. As long as you don't bother me with questions, I'll let you tag along and assist. Until you get in my way." She met his eyes. "And then you're gone, Carmody. Understand?"

"You're very clear." He had paused beside a gray Mercedes and opened the passenger door for her. "But that sounds very permanent. I hope that's merely a turn of phrase."

"You'd know if I meant permanent. And I wouldn't be so sexist as to claim you'd be a gorgeous corpse."

He made a face. "What can I say? All of those politically correct seminars just never took with me." He got into the driver's seat. "Though no one ever told me talking about gorgeous corpses was sexist. I guess it never came up."

She was beginning to like him. He was dryly rueful and amusing. "If it was a CIA politically correct seminar, I would have thought it might be first on the agenda." She didn't wait for an answer. "Venable was supposed to find me someone who'd had experience with Nardik. Has he done it?"

He shook his head. "He was still working on it when he called me into his office. He said it wasn't easy. Most of the agents who have tried to infiltrate Nardik's operations end up dead."

"I don't care if it's hard or not. If Nardik is after Hu Chang, I need to know everything there is to know about him. I'm not going to let him—" She drew a deep breath and tried to temper her voice. "When you call in your report on me to Venable this evening, you tell him to get going and find me a source."

"May I suggest you call him yourself? I'm very low on the totem pole in the Company. He may not listen to me."

"No, you may not suggest it. He will listen to me, but I'll probably end up by pissing him off. That's not productive."

"Point taken. Now what hotel am I supposed to take you to?"

"No hotel. Hu Chang's apothecary shop. I'll stay in the bedroom quarters in the back."

Carmody didn't speak for a moment. "You do know that he's not there? Do you expect him to come back?"

"No."

"Then why—" He broke off. "No questions. But Venable will want me to stay close to you. It's not safe. He found Gregory's body in the alley in back of the shop."

"You can find your own spot on the block to set up surveillance. There are all kinds of shops on the street. Hu Chang's place is too small."

"You've been there before?"

"Every time I come through Hong Kong. He keeps a small room in the back for me."

"That's convenient."

"Sometimes." She remembered the last time she had been there with Luke just months ago. She'd just freed him from those hideous years of captivity and brought him with her to Hong Kong because she'd promised Hu Chang that she would return immediately after using the weapon he had given her to kill Rakovac. She and Luke had shared that small room, and she had thought that Luke would object since he was accustomed to being alone, and she had been a stranger to him. He had not complained. He'd just curled up on his pallet across the room and gone to sleep. He had surprised her many times during those days in Hong Kong. "We weren't here long. I just stopped by to have some dental work done."

"Hu Chang is a dentist? I knew he was a Master of Chinese Medicine."

"He doesn't practice dentistry, but he wears many hats. It was urgent that I have a tooth redone immediately. He made me promise to come back within a few days of when I popped off the cap."

"And he was the only one who could do it?"

"The only one I'd trust. He'd injected the tooth with mamba venom, and he was afraid that it might get into my system after I replaced the temporary cap."

"Mamba venom," he repeated. "Interesting. I hate to keep breaking your rule about questions, but I'm wondering why you'd inject your tooth with mamba venom. Feel free not to satisfy my curiosity. Is it what I'm guessing?"

"Probably." She had the sudden desire to shake him. She bared her teeth, then snapped them shut. "What does a mamba do but bite? I had a man who had made my son suffer, who I had to kill. I knew I wouldn't be able to use conventional weapons."

"I see. Your Hu Chang must have been a great help to you if he could offer you those services."

"That was an extraordinary occasion. I don't generally ask him to be anything but my friend."

Which is all that she wanted right now. Just to find him and make sure that he'd stay alive. Where are you, Hu Chang?

She checked her watch. "We're about ten minutes to the ferry that will take us to Wen Chai." She took out her phone. "I need to call my son and tell him I've arrived."

He grinned. "I'll be very quiet."

"Thank you." Not that it would make any difference. Her conversation would be brief and more for Catherine's benefit than Luke's. She quickly dialed. It rang only twice before it was picked up by Sam. "Hi, Sam, I'm here. May I speak to Luke?"

"Sure, he's here in the kitchen having a snack. Good flight?"

"Smooth as glass."

"Well, better boring than turbulent."

It hadn't been boring, she wanted to tell

him. Having the time to relive those first days with Hu Chang had been bewildering, exciting, and yet curiously bittersweet. But never boring.

"Here's Luke."

"Hello, Catherine," Luke said the next minute. "I've been reading Hu Chang's book."

"The one in Chinese? That must be a challenge. Have you had to ask Sam for help?"

"For a few things. But the Internet language webs are great." He paused. "And Hu Chang's notes kind of explain themselves."

"I don't see how. They're in Chinese, too."

"But somehow I can understand them. Is he okay?"

"I don't know yet. I've just left the airport. I'm on the way to his shop."

"At Wen Chai. I'd like to go back there now that I'm reading his book. Could we do that?"

"I don't see why not. Just not right now. Give me a week or so."

"You're worried about him."

She wouldn't lie. "Maybe a little. It will be better when I corner him and make him tell me what's going on." She changed the subject. "What are you and Sam doing besides studying?"

"We went to a movie last night." He paused. "And I called Kelly and asked her if she could come to see us this weekend."

"Kelly?" That was strange. Luke seldom initiated contact with anyone. Yet Luke and Kelly Winters were as good friends as an eleven- and fifteen-year-old could be with all the adolescent conflicts that frequently erupted between them. Both were amazingly intelligent and mature for their ages and Catherine considered that little anomaly healthy for both of them. "Why did you do that?"

"I want her to look at Hu Chang's book. You know she's good at seeing patterns in stuff."

Not good. Brilliant. Genius. Kelly had a talent that was off the charts in that area. That was why she spent a good portion of the year in a science think tank at that college in Virginia. "Wouldn't it just be better to have the book translated? Why are you fighting having it done, Luke?"

"I don't know." He paused. "Because I don't think it's the language. I think there's something there I'm not seeing. Maybe Kelly can see it."

"Can she come?"

"Yeah, she said she'd make it. She tried to make me think she was doing me a favor, but I know she's just curious."

"And doing you a favor."

"I guess." A pause. "You okay, Catherine?"

"I'm doing fine."

Another silence. "I've been wondering why Hu Chang gave me that book."

"Because he liked you."

"He likes you, and he didn't give you anything."

"You're wrong, he gives me things all the time. Sometimes when I least expect it."

"Maybe he gave it to me because I'm your son."

"I don't believe Hu Chang would do that. He judges and responds to everyone as an individual. Believe me, if Hu Chang had not liked you, it wouldn't matter if you were my son."

"When I was in the lab, he watched me all the time. I told you that, didn't I?"

"Yes, that should show he was interested in you. When he let me mix some of his potions, he watched me like a hawk. He's very careful."

Another silence. "When you go to the shop, will you look for something for me?"

"Of course, did you leave something when you were there?"

"No, it was a bottle that's in the book. I guess it's a bottle, or vial or something because it was with a bunch of other vials. Anyway, I think I remember seeing one like it at Hu Chang's shop."

"Most of Hu Chang's bottles are unique. He makes them himself."

"Yeah, he told me. But would you look when you get there and see if I'm right?"

"No problem. What does it look like?"

"It's about eight inches tall with an ivory background with branches or vines or trees painted on it."

"Sounds pretty fancy. But I suppose it's possible. I've seen a few things that Hu Chang has done that look like works of art." They had drawn up to the Star Ferry. "I have to go now, Luke. We're at the ferry. May I call you back?"

"No, that's okay. You'll probably be busy."

"Not too busy." Don't push him. "Call me if you want to talk. Tell Kelly that we miss

her, and it's about time she came to visit.
And that she just doesn't have to be on
call at your command."

"I told you, she's curious. Good-bye,
Catherine."

"Good-bye, Luke." She hung up and
tucked her phone back into her handbag.
That business with Luke's obsession with
Hu Chang's book was bizarre. But perhaps she was making too much of it. Luke
had known that she was going to Hu
Chang. Wasn't it normal that he'd be interested in anything associated with him?

"Everything all right?" Carmody asked.
"It sucks being away from family."

"Yes, it does." She nodded jerkily. "He's
fine. I miss him more than he does me. Do
you have kids?"

"I have a little girl, Dany. She's four. My
wife and I are divorced, and she has custody. But I get to see her for weekends
when I'm in Sydney." He shrugged. "She's
better off with my wife. I'm not much of a
father. I'm gone a lot, and I miss birthdays
and stuff." He smiled. "But I do love that kid.
They make a big difference in your life."

They were driving onto the ferry now.
"Yes, they do." Love made all the difference

in the world, and it had been Hu Chang who had first made Catherine take those first steps toward trust and love. He had opened her eyes and pushed her gently forward. Dammit, she would *not* have anything happen to him.

And she was suddenly feeling a wrenching ache that Luke, the child who was center of all that love, was not with her. Carmody didn't even realize how lucky he was to have a relationship that could be so easily healed with just a little effort. She was suddenly furious at his blindness. She jumped out of the car onto the ferry and whirled to face Carmody. "So don't give me that bullshit about not being a great father for your daughter. You can be anything you want to be. I don't care if you're cheating yourself, but don't cheat her by giving her anything but your best."

He blinked. "Yes, ma'am. Of course, it's none of your business."

"She's a child. A child is everyone's business." And he didn't even realize his good fortune in having a daughter who was safe and had known only love. She wanted to deck him. "What the hell. You're probably right. You don't deserve her." She strode over to the rail and looked down at water. "And I'm seriously overreacting. Don't come near me until we get to Wen Chai."

He smiled faintly. "Or you'll bite me with your mamba teeth?"

"Tooth, singular." Her lips twisted ruefully. "And I save that for special people. You've got to prove yourself to me."

"I believe I'll decline the honor." He moved down the rail. "I'll see you at Wen Chai."

"You have a key?" Carmody watched her unlock the door of the apothecary shop. "Hu Chang must trust you. Venable said some of the medicines he has in there are very valuable."

"He gave me a key on the day they finished rebuilding his shop. It had been burned to the ground, and Hu Chang didn't get around to building a new one for two years afterward." She threw open the door. "Okay, you've seen me to his shop. You've done your duty. Now go find somewhere to stay down the street, someplace you'll be as unobtrusive as possible."

He looked around the shop, then strolled back to the rooms in the back. "No one lurking."

"Hoping for Hu Chang?"

"Or anyone else I could catch and receive a commendation." He smiled as he handed her a card. "If you need me, call. Though Venable told me that you'd resent my saying that."

"I do. If we knew each other, I'd resent it more. I can take care of myself, Carmody." She wearily nodded at the door. "Go on. I know you're only doing your job."

"Look, if we know you and Hu Chang are so close, don't you think Nardik would be privy to that info? If he can't get his hands on Hu Chang, wouldn't he go after a hostage?"

"Very reasonable. Now, will you leave?"

He tilted his head, studying her. Then he gave a low whistle. "That's why you're here. You're setting yourself up as bait. And you don't want anyone around who would make the bait less tempting for the rats to snatch."

"Right. And that's why Venable has set you to watch me. He not only doesn't trust me to go the Company way if I find Hu Chang, but there's a chance of a bonanza. Now get out of here and don't come back unless I call you."

He nodded as he headed for the door.

"You're going to be a very difficult assignment, Catherine."

"Then go back to Sydney and work on being a father to your kid." She closed the door and leaned back against it. She should probably not have been so hard on Carmody, but she was tired, and her emotions were both splintered and raw. Venable had deliberately put Carmody into her path as an obstacle to overcome. It was going to be difficult enough to locate Hu Chang and try to find out what kind of mess he'd gotten himself into without having to dodge Carmody.

She shot the lock on the door and gazed around the interior of the shop. It looked the same as it usually did, as she'd last seen it. The mahogany cabinets gleaming pristine clean, the bottles and vials with their colorful contents backlit by the strong lights. In most Asian apothecary shops, she was always aware of the scents of incense, but not in Hu Chang's shop. He demanded that there be no smells at all and for good reason. She could remember him sitting at his low table and looking at her scornfully after she'd asked the question.

"Nothing must interfere with the scent

of the medicines. You should realize how distracting those smells can be after our hours in that temple. Other than those herbs I have you working on, I do not deal in potions for children, Catherine. I can't afford to make mistakes. A potion may look the same as another, but it never smells the same. Not if you've educated yourself to the nuances." He thrust a vial beneath her nose. "What do you smell?"

She sniffed. "Only rosemary."

He looked at her in disgust. "There are at least forty other scents in that potion. You're a total failure. It's a wonder I'm so patient with you."

"It's a wonder I let you abuse me and still work at making these silly health potions for you."

"Because you realize what a master I am and are grateful that I spread my knowledge." He smiled slyly. "And that I satisfy your curiosity when you ask absurd questions."

She found herself smiling as she remembered the exasperation mixed with the humor she had felt during those moments with Hu Chang. Every moment had been different, every path new to her. So many paths that had changed her, opened her mind, opened her emotions.

The vials.

She'd promised Luke to look for the bottle that he'd thought he'd seen here. She crossed the room and studied the rows of bottles on the shelves. Mostly crystal. A few plain vials, one small hand-painted bottle that was indeed a work of art.

But no bottle like the one Luke had described.

She'd try one more place, the small lab downstairs. It was where Hu Chang did his special preparations and might have kept a few valuable containers.

She opened the door beside the sleeping quarters, turned on the light, and went down the flight of stairs. The ceiling was so low that there was barely headroom and only a single worktable and cabinet.

And one stool where she remembered Hu Chang had deposited Luke when he had taken him down here while he worked.

She crossed to the cabinet and looked up at the vials on the shelf. Two empties,

one containing a liquid that was almost co-
balt blue. Definitely no bottle that met Luke's
description. He must have been mistaken.

But Luke had a phenomenal memory.
She had half expected to find the bottle.
Well, it wasn't here, and it didn't really matter if it was or not. She had other things to
worry about right now.

She went back upstairs and flipped off
the light. Not that there was anything precious down there unless it was that dark
blue liquid. But you could never tell with
Hu Chang what was treasure, what was
trash. She had learned to respect everything connected with his work as if it were
a jewel beyond price.

But right now she didn't want to think of
Hu Chang or the beautiful bottle that had
intrigued Luke. She wanted to take a shower
and change clothes and perhaps grab
some sleep.

After she slipped outside and reconnoi-
tered the neighborhood to see if there was
anything or anyone suspicious of which
she should be aware. She knew most of
Hu Chang's neighbors and should be able
to spot anything unusual with no problem.
If she was going to act as bait, it was go-

ing to be with full information about ways to exit if it became necessary to save her neck.

Are you out there, Nardik?

Vancouver, Canada

Jack Tan was the name on the caller ID.

Hugh Nardik pressed the button on the first ring. "Have you found him, dammit?"

"Not yet. I've searched every—"

Nardik cursed. "Then why are you calling me, asshole? I told you I didn't want to hear from you until you found Hu Chang. You should never have lost him in the first place. I expected a professional when I hired you. All you had to do was get the information, then kill the son of a bitch. Instead, you not only let him escape, you let the CIA find out my connection with him."

"I told you, we wounded him. And there's still a chance. I don't think he's playing ball with Venable. He made him take him back to his shop on Wen Chai to recover."

"And then you killed a CIA agent on his doorstep."

"He had that package. I thought that it

might be some of the stuff you wanted. Was it?"

"No, it was sea-snake venom. And you scared Hu Chang off for a bunch of nothing. You could have grabbed him again. Now Venable has seen that he's gone undercover."

"Not Venable. He's scurrying all around trying to find him. If Hu Chang's hiding, he's on his own." He paused. "But Venable has called in someone he thinks can find Hu Chang. Catherine Ling arrived in Hong Kong today."

Nardik stiffened. "You're sure?" He went to his desk and opened the dossier on Hu Chang. It was spotty in places, but the recent section since Hu Chang arrived in Hong Kong a number of years ago was fairly complete. He looked at the picture of Catherine Ling. Beautiful woman and as deadly as she was gorgeous. He had a dossier on her, too, in case he needed to use her in some way to get at Hu Chang. It hadn't seemed necessary since she appeared to be out of his life at present. But there was no doubt that at some periods during Hu Chang's past, she'd figured prominently. How, it was hard to determine.

Had they been lovers, friends, partners? I don't have time to probe the depths of the relationship, he thought impatiently. All that was important was that she meant something to that bastard, and that might mean she could be the key he needed to unlock the treasure chest. "Where is she?"

"She's staying at Hu Chang's place. I was wondering if she expected him to meet her there. That's why I called you. What do you want me to do?"

Nardik thought about it. "It's probably a trap. If she was going to meet him, it wouldn't be at that shop. That would be stupid."

"So you want me to hold off."

"No, I want you to figure out a way that wouldn't be stupid." He added softly, "And there had better not be any mistakes. You'll take her, you'll find out if she knows anything, then you'll use her to get Hu Chang. And if you don't, you'll not get another chance. If I have to take over and deal directly with this mess, I'm not going to be pleased. Do you understand?"

Tan didn't speak for moment, and Nardik could sense the anger that he was trying to smother. Too bad. Tan might be a heavyweight in his own little corner of the world, but he had to learn that Nardik could manipulate that world whenever he lifted one finger. There were varying degrees of power in the hierarchy that Nardik ruled, and Jack Tan was very low on that ladder.

"I'll work it out," Tan said curtly.

"Report back as soon as you have something besides excuses to give me." Nardik hung up.

He glanced back down at the photo of Catherine Ling. Would Tan be able to handle her? She had an impressive résumé and was probably far cleverer than Tan. She would be a challenge for a man on any level.

And the level that was luring him now was horizontal and purely sexual.

He was experiencing a surge of pure lust that had come out of nowhere. Ling was so strong, so sleek, so silken, and yet he knew she would fight until she broke. What would it be like to handle her body, to break her, to make her kneel, before he plunged inside her? He had never found a woman who gave him the heady sensation of total sexual domination that would come only from a battle so intense it would probably end in death. That could be the true meaning of power.

And he was getting hard just thinking about it. He suddenly wanted to call Tan and tell him he was coming to Hong Kong to take over the search for Hu Chang.

"You want her." Ken Fowler, his assistant, had been watching him from across the room. "You want that bitch."

And Fowler was so jealous that it was eating him alive, Nardik thought. He had taken Fowler as a lover when he'd first come to work for his organization as a means of cementing his loyalty. It was important someone in his close confidence be completely dominated on every level. Sex was the great enslaver, and Fowler had been easy. The fool thought he loved Nardik. He meekly accepted his affairs with other men as well as women. These days, Nardik did not even have to pretend that Fowler was more than an occasional diversion for him to keep him in line.

"Yes, it's a pity she wouldn't appeal to you, or we might share her."

Fowler flinched. "You don't need her. Kill her."

"I'll do as I please, Fowler. Anything I please. You know that. Don't try to tell me what to do."

Fowler flushed. "I didn't mean—" He whirled and strode out of the office.

Fowler must be upset to risk his anger and step out of the place that Nardik had carved out for him. Nardik must have been more obvious than usual in his lust for Catherine Ling. That might be a sign that she was proving a distraction. He would have to consider any disruption in his concentration on the main objective.

And Catherine Ling was only a woman, and imagination was often more tantalizing than the reality. There was a greater prize on the horizon than any sexual triumph. He would let Jack Tan have her to interrogate and concentrate on victories of which Tan could only dream.

He flipped the folder shut and strolled over to the window to gaze out at the majesty of the mountains towering over the skyscrapers of the city. Vancouver was a city where a man could effortlessly dominate his surroundings if he had money and influence. He moved from place to place because the authorities were constantly

trying to find him, but he was most comfortable here. He liked the idea of pulling
the strings in the underbelly of this slick,
cosmopolitan city and making everyone
dance.

And how they did dance, he thought with
fierce pleasure. He could do anything, take
anything. Drugs, jewels, money, whores.
Hell, he could rule the world. Dictators and
presidents and Mafia czars came to him,
and he decided whether to give them what
they wanted.

And it was going to get better still as
soon as Tan found Hu Chang.

Ultimate power.

Dammit, how could Tan have let that
Asian son of a bitch slip through his fingers? All he'd had to do was obey Nardik's
orders and he'd be— Smother the anger.
It was going to go well from now on. Either
with Jack Tan or without him, Hu Chang
would be in Nardik's hands.

And, perhaps, so would Catherine Ling.

CHAPTER
8

Hong Kong

Catherine woke, totally alert.

She had heard something in the main shop. Not a footstep, just a . . . change, an addition of sound. Then she realized what it was. The front door had opened, and she was hearing distant street sounds.

But she had locked that front door.

She got to her feet in one lithe motion. She drew her knife from the holster on her thigh.

Then she was at the door between the shop and the sleeping area.

She tensed.

Now she *did* hear a footstep.

"I don't hear you, but I know you're there," Carmody said from the other side of the door. "Don't get bent out of shape. It's only me."

Her breath expelled with exasperation as she threw open the door. "What the hell are you doing here, Carmody? And did you pick the lock on that front door?"

"I'm guarding you. And yes I did. It's one of my many talents. Venable told me that you're not so bad at it yourself."

"I'm very, very good. And, if it had been me, I'd have closed the door instantly behind me so that there wouldn't have been any street noises for a target to hear."

"I'll remember that next time. But you're not my target. I'm guarding you." He looked down at the knife in her hand. "That was for me? I'm glad I spoke up."

"Why are you here?" She tucked the knife back in her holster. "And why didn't you call me instead of burgling the place?"

"I was in a hurry. I've been posted a few houses down the block, and I saw a black Mazda at the top of the street. It drove by, then turned around and disappeared out of sight. I hadn't seen a car on the street all evening and I always look for something unusual that sticks out."

So did Catherine. It was standard CIA procedure when you were doing surveillance. "So?"

"I ran up to the top of the street and looked down the block. The Mazda was backing up and parking next to the entry of the alley that runs by the rear of this house." He nodded as he saw her stiffen. "That caught your attention." He was moving toward the rear door. "Let's be on hand to welcome them."

"How many were they?"

"Two." He grinned. "They must have thought that would be enough to handle a helpless little lady like you. They probably haven't heard about your affinity to mamba venom. Do we go out or let them come to us?"

"We let them come to us." She glided toward the door. "And I want at least one left alive to question. So press against that wall and—"

The alley door burst open as the jamb was splintered by a kick.

Guns, Catherine realized. The tall man facing them had a Glock.

The other stockier man behind him had an AK-47 and lifted it the moment he saw them. "Don't kill the woman."

"Shit!" Carmody dove to the floor, reaching for his .38 as the shop was sprayed with bullets from the AK-47.

No time for the knife. She dove forward and knocked the tall man with the Glock to the floor. She gave him a karate chop to the throat before she rolled him over to use him as a shield against that damn AK-47.

She could only hope Carmody would take him down with his .38.

But the room was being peppered with shots, and she heard the sound of breaking glass and bullets splintering wood.

She grabbed the Glock that had fallen to the floor and rolled behind the cabinet.

Another spray of bullets tearing, chewing at the cabinet.

Stop it. Put a bullet in the hand that was holding the automatic.

Aim. She got off a shot. She heard a gasp, then cursing, as the AK-47 fell to the floor.

Another bullet in the right kneecap.

She aimed again.

A shrill scream.

Then he was whirling, cursing, as he limped toward the door.

Go after him. Don't let the bastard get away. She *needed* him.

By the time she reached the door he was halfway down the alley. He was crippled. Good. She'd be able to catch up with him before he reached the Mazda at the end of the alley.

"Catherine . . ." It was Carmody.

She shot a quick glance behind her.

Oh, shit.

Carmody was lying crumpled on the floor. Blood. So much blood. And his tattered jacket had more holes than she could count. One of those sprays of bullets from the AK-47 must have been aimed at him.

"It's okay." She was beside him in seconds, falling to her knees. "Don't try to talk. I'll try to stop this blood."

"Little late . . . ," he whispered. "I don't think . . . I have any left. Didn't think it would end like this. I guess . . . you never do. Thought I had—all the time in the world . . ."

"Don't give up, dammit." A wound on his

chest. How close was it to his heart? "We can get through this." Put pressure. But there were so many wounds. "You're young. That's on your side. I'm not going to let you go. Do you hear me, Carmody?"

"You act as if you're going to shake the man, Catherine," Hu Chang said from the alley doorway. "As usual, you lack gentleness in these matters. If you want him to live, I suppose I'd better take a look at him."

She wasn't even surprised to see him. He always came and went as stealthily as a shadow. "I do want him to live." She sat back on her heels and glared at him. "Do something. You're always telling me what a wonderful master of everything in the whole damn universe you are. It's your fault that he's full of holes. Now make it right."

He moved forward and looked down at Carmody before saying to him, "She has a tendency to be excitable in certain circumstances. It's true, I'm extraordinary. But it's not as if I have superhuman powers. But I will try to help you." He glanced at Catherine. "Continue that pressure. That's the most dangerous wound. You were doing the correct thing. I will see if I can find him a potion that will help him until you can get him to a hospital." He grimaced as he turned to the cabinet. "Look at this catastrophe. I don't believe there's a bottle left unbroken. Was it necessary to bring this havoc down upon my splendid shop?"

"Yes. Find something for him." It was true, she couldn't see any container that was still intact. "What about that blue stuff down in the lab?"

"Quite deadly." He knelt and opened one of the cabinet doors. "But I have something that might work if there is any left. I used it on myself recently and didn't have time to restock it."

She looked down at Carmody. "Hold on. He can help you. I promise." She took out her phone. "I'm calling Venable and getting help out here."

"By all means."

She got through to Venable in two rings. "Carmody's down. It's bad. Get medical help out here to Hu Chang's shop right away."

He muttered an oath. "Are you okay?"

"Yes. Stop asking questions and get an ambulance out here." She hung up.

Hu Chang had a vial of orange-colored liquid in his hand as he knelt beside Carmody. "This tastes terrible," he told him. "If you'd rather die, I can understand. But I have to offer it to you since Catherine is so upset." He lifted Carmody's head and put the vial to his lips. "It will burn going down, but that's a good thing."

"No use . . ."

"I never do anything that is without use. It would waste my time, and my time is more valuable than you can imagine." A smile suddenly lit his face. "You are close to death, it is true. But close is not there. So drink this medicine so that Catherine will not heap me with any more blame."

Carmody hesitated, his gaze on Hu Chang's face. Then he opened his lips and drank the potion in the vial in three swallows.

He gagged and wheezed.

"I told you it was terrible." Hu Chang laid him down again. "But it will give you your chance."

Carmody's eyes were bulging as he gasped for air. The next moment, he was unconscious.

Hu Chang got to his feet. "Keep the pressure on him until you can get him a transfusion, Catherine. I can heal what's inside, but I can't do anything about the bleeding." He moved toward the door leading to the alley. "Perhaps someday . . ."

"And where do you think you're going?"

"You no longer need me. I've done what I came to do. More. Since you made me take care of your friend. One of Venable's men?"

"Yes."

"He can't be very good if he got himself shot up in that fashion. Venable should have assigned you someone else."

"He's young. He'll get better. Stop criticizing and tell me how you knew to barge in at this particular moment."

"You know I have friends in the neighborhood who are always eager to do me favors. I'm a very valuable man to call friend. When I realized that you'd probably come here after Venable phoned you, I called in the favors."

"You must have been very close. This all went down within ten minutes. Were you staking me out?"

He paused at the door. "Of course. Just as you were setting me up. Very reckless, Catherine. See who you drew instead?"

"No, I don't know who they are." She met his gaze. "Why don't you tell me?"

"That man lying over there by the cabinet is Kim Soo. Dead?"

"Yes."

"Very efficient. And the man who ran down the alley is Jack Tan."

"Are they the men who shot you?"

"Possibly, or more likely it was one of their underlings. They had a good many more men with them at the time when Venable plucked me away from them. But Jack Tan gave me many unpleasant hours trying to convince me to tell him what he wanted to know. I became very angry with him." He glanced at Carmody. "Perhaps I should not condemn him too much for being so unprofessional as to get himself shot up like this instead of helping you. I must have looked a great deal like him when Venable threw me into the helicopter." Quickly, he added, "But I had reason and extenuating circumstances."

"Don't you always?"

He smiled. "Always." His smile faded. "Go home, Catherine. I don't want you here."

"Go to hell. What's happening, Hu Chang?"

"I merely encountered Lucifer, and he thinks I can bring him out of hell and give him back paradise. I don't wish you to have to deal with him."

"And is Lucifer's name Nardik?"

"Yes."

"I've heard of the bastard. How did you get mixed up with him, Hu Chang?"

"Through mutual acquaintances. But 'mixed up with him' is not the proper phrase. I avoid Lucifer if I can. I understand his ambition and recognize it in myself. It's just another name for power, and it can be a heady brew."

"Venable says you've got something Nardik wants. A drug?"

"Go home, Catherine."

"Don't tell me that." He was smiling at her, and she wanted to shake him. "You're the most exasperating man on the face of the Earth. It's no wonder you got shot. It's only surprising it didn't happen before."

"I find it strange also. But I never had to deal with Lucifer before." He turned to leave. "It may prove a challenge."

"Wait. Don't you dare leave, Hu Chang."

His lips quirked. "But it's the perfect opportunity. You can't follow me because you're forced to keep that pressure on your friend to keep him alive." He looked back at Carmody. "He'll probably curse me when he wakes. I didn't tell him that the burning lasts for six hours or so."

"Will he live?"

"Probably. I did."

Her gaze raked his face. He appeared a little thinner than when she'd last seen him, but he moved with the same springy litheness. "And how are you now? Venable said you almost died."

"And you're concerned even though you're sure I deserved it? How many times must I tell you that you must be harder?" He shook his head. "You'll never learn, Catherine."

"Not from you. You were the one who was lurking around the neighborhood like a cat burglar."

He chuckled. "True." His glance shifted back to her. "Go home to your son. That's where you belong. How is Luke?"

"Fine," she said curtly. "He's reading that book you gave him."

His brows rose. "Is he? Interesting."

"Don't change the subject. Let me help you, Hu Chang. Don't try to handle Nardik by yourself."

He turned away from her.

"You're my friend, dammit."

"Yes, I am. Good-bye, Catherine."

The next moment, he was gone.

Her nails bit into the palms of her hand as she stared at the empty doorway.

Dammit. Dammit. Dammit.

She wanted to jump up and run after him.

But she couldn't do it. Hu Chang was right, she couldn't leave Carmody until help came.

Clever Hu Chang, who knew her better than anyone in the world. Just by keeping Carmody alive, he'd made sure that she was held hostage here. As he said, he might have done it just because she'd asked him to save him. But she could never be sure what motivated Hu Chang at any given time. He was always a puzzle.

"I'm . . . going . . . to kill him," Carmody whispered.

Her gaze flew to his face. His face was a little flushed, his lips no longer ashen. "Don't talk. Venable will be here soon."

"Hurts. Kill the bastard— Tortured me. You . . . let him do it."

"Yes, I did."

"Burning . . . me alive. Throat. Chest."

"Six hours. He said it would be only six hours."

"Kill . . . him."

"Shut up. You're alive, aren't you? I would have bet you wouldn't last this long. You should thank him instead of whining." Perhaps that was a little rough. She shouldn't take it out on Carmody because she was angry and worried about Hu Chang and impatient that Carmody didn't realize how lucky he was that Hu Chang had been willing to help him. Hu Chang had a very high pain tolerance. If he said that potion was very painful, then it was probably excruciating. "Maybe it would be better if you try to go back to sleep. It will be over sooner."

His eyes closed. "Burning . . ."

"Six hours," she repeated. Come on, Venable. Maybe if Carmody got a sedative, he wouldn't feel the effects of Hu Chang's potion. Hurry.

But Venable and a team of local hospital EMTs didn't arrive for another ten minutes.

"Good." She sat back on her heels and

got out of the way of the EMTs as they swarmed around Carmody. "I know he needs blood and something for pain. He was complaining of a burning sensation in his throat and chest cavity."

"Burning?" Venable's gaze narrowed as he turned to look at her. "What happened here, Catherine?"

"Enough to almost kill Carmody. You shouldn't have assigned him to me, Venable." She ran her hand through her hair. "The man over there is Kim Soo. There was another man, but he got away down the alley. His name was Jack Tan."

"How do you know? I'm sure they didn't introduce themselves."

"No time for introductions." She stood aside as the EMTs carefully put Carmody on a stretcher. "But you have an ID, and you should be able to find out more about them." She glanced at Venable. "They were the ones who grabbed Hu Chang and ended up shooting him."

"Really? And did you find that out before you encountered these hoods or after the fact?"

"After." She met his gaze. "I think you know Hu Chang was here. You were with him after he was shot, and he told me he took the same medicine as he gave Carmody."

"Well, it was bonanza night for you, wasn't it? You got Hu Chang and these slimeballs. You must be pleased with yourself." His lips tightened. "Why the hell didn't you keep him here?"

"I was busy." She stood aside as the EMTs took Carmody through the door. "In case you didn't notice."

"Okay. Okay. Do you know where he is now?"

"No, he told me to go home. Idiotic bastard. Who does he think he is? Who does he think I am?" She drew a deep breath. "Carmody. He has a divorced wife and a little girl in Sydney. Maybe you should let them know and bring them here if he has to be in the hospital for long. If he manages to get through the next couple days."

"What did Hu Chang give him? Orange liquid in a clear vial?"

She nodded. "I told him to give him something, anything. Carmody was dying, Venable. He still may be dying."

"Maybe." He shrugged. "But I think I'll see if I can arrange to bring his wife and kid right away. That stuff Hu Chang brews up is pretty heavy. I was impressed. Do you know what it is?"

She shook her head. "And he may not ever repeat that exact recipe. He's never satisfied. He gets bored and tries to do something different, something better."

"I'd be satisfied with that one. And I'd bet that Carmody is going to be satisfied, too."

"Not for the next six hours." She turned and started toward the back sleeping areas. "There's no use my staying here now. I'll go get my bag, and you can drop me off at a hotel."

"Which one?"

"The Princess." Her lips twisted. "It will bring back memories. You were staying there when I first met you."

"Sentiment, Catherine?"

"No, but I remember that in order to impress you with my value so that you would take me on, I did a complete security check of the hotel. I even told you how an assassin could get at you."

"And you were right. You were only a fourteen-year-old kid, but you brought up holes none of my men had thought of."

"If I can find Hu Chang again, I'll take

him there, and he'll be as safe as I can make him. If the stubborn bastard will let me." She turned before she opened the door. "Hu Chang said Nardik is Lucifer. He never exaggerates, so that must be a good description. I may not be able to get Hu Chang to cooperate, so I may have to go directly after Nardik. Did you get me my agent who has experience with him?"

"I have a possibility." He held up his hand as she started to speak. "Leave me alone. I'm getting there, Catherine. I'm close."

It was the best that she could hope. "I can't wait much longer. Hu Chang isn't going to stay in hiding. I'd bet he's already got a plan, and it doesn't include me. So I'll have to go after Nardik on my own if you can't get me help."

"What about me?" he said dryly. "I'm not entirely unskilled."

"But you go by the rules when you can, and Hu Chang doesn't understand rules except in nature."

"I might bend the rules in this case," he said soberly. "The circumstances might warrant it."

Her gaze narrowed. "You've heard something else."

"Just rumors."

"That you're not going to tell me?"

"They might just be rumors. But it's from a source I respect, and it scared the hell out of me. And if they're not rumors, I may have to do something that I wouldn't like, that you wouldn't like."

She stiffened. "You're talking about a sanction on Hu Chang, aren't you? No way, Venable."

"If I don't think I can keep Nardik from getting that potion from Hu Chang any other way, I'll remove the possibility of their connecting." He added grimly, "So find Hu Chang, Catherine. Find him and make sure I don't have to do something I don't want to do." He turned. "I'll wait outside in the car for you to pack. After I drop you off at the hotel, I'll go to the hospital and stay with Carmody until I'm sure he's out of danger."

"If he's out of danger, it's because Hu Chang helped him. But that doesn't make a difference, does it? Hell, you'd probably send Carmody after him."

"I wouldn't be that lacking in intelligence. Carmody wouldn't be a good choice. You have some time, Catherine. Not very much, but it may be enough." As he went out the door, he added grimly, "You let Hu Chang get away tonight. Don't do it again. I don't promise it wouldn't be a fatal mistake."

Vancouver, Canada

"Fool."

Nardik pushed viciously at the disconnect button on his phone and turned to Fowler. "Jack Tan blew it. I'm going to castrate the son of a bitch. He not only didn't get Catherine Ling, but he lost a man and got himself shot up." Through clenched teeth, he added, "And we still don't have Hu Chang."

"That's not good." Fowler frowned. "You've made promises. Or at least I've made them for you. There's a time frame, and they want a test case first."

Nardik whirled on him. "I never promised anyone a test case. I thought it was a done deal."

"They said there's too much in the balance. They won't take our word."

"Screw them." Political assholes, out to cover themselves and leave him out to dry.

Someday, he'd control all of them, make them toe the line. But first he had to have Hu Chang. "What time frame?"

"Fourth of July."

"That's less than a week away. I'll need at least another month."

"It has to be that weekend. They say if we can't deliver, they'll find someone else to do the job."

"They're bluffing."

"Do you want to risk it?"

No, he didn't want to risk it. He could use Hu Chang's drug in another situation, but this was the ideal showcase for other similar jobs. He'd been looking at the Mideast, which was in constant turmoil. Hell, give him another few years, and he'd rule the whole damn area. "No, we'll give them their son of a bitchin' time frame. But they can't have their test case. I may have to use the dose of the drug I have on hand for the actual kill if I can't get my hands on Hu Chang in time." He turned away and opened the folder on the desk. Catherine Ling's face seemed to jump out of the photo, and he once more felt that intense surge of lust. It seemed he was going to be able to toy with her after all.

Okay, you've been playing with amateurs, whore. I hope you enjoyed yourself with Jack Tan. He's nothing, less than nothing. Wait until you see how a real man operates.

"You should tell them to go to hell," Fowler said. "You're too important for them to try to set the rules. Arrogant bastards."

"No." He would be diplomatic although it gagged him for them to think he was only another one of their underlings. Perhaps it was going to be good that he'd have Catherine Ling on whom to expend all his rage and pent-up sexual energy. He could hardly wait to get his hands on her. "Tell them we'll give them what they want except for the test case. They won't argue. They want it too much."

"Whatever you say." Fowler shrugged. "But I suppose I'll have to stall. They can't know you're not absolutely sure that the drug will work on their target until we get hold of Hu Chang."

"Of course you'll have to stall."

"Shall I call Jack Tan back and give him any orders?"

"No, tell him that I'll be there myself to take over the search." He strode toward the door. "And order my yacht in Macau moved to Hong Kong harbor. We'll be flying there tonight."

Hong Kong

Dawn was rising over the harbor when Catherine finished her shower and shampoo and walked out onto the small balcony at the Princess Hotel. It had been a long, frustrating night, and the morning breeze felt good as it stroked her cheeks. She'd always liked this hotel for reasons other than the one she'd told Venable. It was an older skyscraper than the other hotels along this stretch of harbor. Not nearly as grand as the behemoth Ritz-Carlton down the street, yet it had a flavor she identified as quintessential Hong Kong. Her hands clenched on the rail as she gazed down at the junks, barges, and ferries on the bay far below.

Where the hell are you, Hu Chang?

Don't think about him. Go to bed. Get the sleep you need to function efficiently and start out a new day.

Her phone rang, and she took it out of the pocket of her terry robe.

Venable.

"I just thought you'd like to know that Carmody is going to pull through," he said when she picked up. "They're still running tests, but they got out all the bullets and there doesn't seem to be major damage except for the wound in his chest."

"That's good. Send him home to Sydney and let him work out what he wants from his life before he loses it. He came close this time."

"I agree." He paused. "I meant what I said about Hu Chang, but I wouldn't want to do it, Catherine."

"I know. You make hard choices, and at least you gave me warning, so that I can stop you in your tracks. I won't let you kill him no matter how necessary you think it would be for the whole damn world." She didn't give him a chance to answer. "I'm hanging up now. If you can offer me help instead of threatening Hu Chang, call me." She hung up and shoved the phone back in her pocket.

The sad thing was that in spite of his

ruthlessness, Venable was one of the good guys. There were so few good guys in her world, and it was one of the things that had made her become a CIA agent. There was a chance to make a difference in a world that was getting dirtier by the day.

But she wouldn't allow Venable or anyone else to kill Hu Chang in the name of making civilization a better place. Who was anyone to judge him who did not know him? *She* knew him and was aware that Hu Chang was far from pure in thought or action. Money would not tempt him, but a challenge might lead him into all kinds of trouble. But if Hu Chang was being tempted by his Lucifer counterpart, then she would step between them. She would not allow anyone else to get near him.

She was getting upset again just thinking about it. Calm down and give yourself time to plan, she told herself.

Call Luke before she went to bed? No, she refused to lie to him, and what she could tell him? That Hu Chang was looking completely well, but that there might be a sanction placed on him at any moment? No, she'd give herself time to work this out before she talked to Luke.

She turned and went back into the bedroom and drew the blackout curtains over
the French doors. That was another thing
she liked about the hotel. It was tastefully
luxurious but not ostentatious, and it catered
to businessmen who did not necessarily
operate nine to five. Casino employees,
restaurateurs and—she smiled sardonically as she ended the mental list. And CIA
agents like Venable and Catherine Ling.

She climbed into bed, pulled up the covers, and stared into the darkness.

Are you still watching me, Hu Chang? I
bet you have friends in this hotel, too. You
have friends everywhere. Well, maybe not
friends, people who owe you, people who
fear you, people who want something from
you. You're very selective about your friends.
Well, so am I. And I won't let you go.

So go ahead and have anyone you wish
watch me and report back to you.

I'm not going home.

She woke seven hours later, and was instantly awake.

Spice with the faintest hint of lemon.

The scent was teasingly faint yet so
familiar that she would have identified it if

she'd smelled it in the middle of a crowd the size of the Super Bowl.

Not here in this room. Not on the balcony.

That elusive scent was coming from the sitting room.

Her heart was pounding as slipped out of bed and put on her robe. The next moment she was throwing open the door to the sitting room.

The man who was sitting in the chair near the door, with his legs stretched before him, smiled at her. "Hello, Catherine. I tried not to wake you."

John Gallo.

CHAPTER 9

She felt the breath leave her body as she stared at him. He was just the same, tall, dark eyes, a faint indentation in his chin, a thread of white in his dark hair . . . and the powerful magnetism that made his stunning good looks pale in comparison. It was because she hadn't expected Gallo that she was feeling this shock, she told herself. It wasn't because of the sexual tension that always seemed to be present whenever they were together. She had that under control and never allowed it to interfere. But it was interfering now, she realized. She hadn't seen him in weeks, and she hadn't been sure that she'd ever see him again. Their relationship had been full of distrust, at one time she had even thought him a murderer. Yet that fear of betrayal hadn't been able to smother the fact that she was physically drawn to him. "How did you get in here, Gallo?"

He nodded at the door. "The usual portal but not necessarily the usual manner. It took me a little while. You had it booby-trapped."

"You could have called me. Or would that have been too easy?"

He smiled. "It would have spoiled the challenge. And I regarded it as kind of an audition."

"Audition? What the hell do you mean?"

"Venable says you have a job for me but that you'd have to approve my application. He said that if I could get beyond your security measures, you'd be inclined to look on me with favor." He added softly, "And are you looking at me with favor, Catherine?"

"No, I'm pissed at myself that you got in without my knowing."

"I was only in here for a minute or two. You must have heard something."

"Maybe." She was not about to tell him that it was the scent of him that had woke her. That was too intimate, and she was trying to keep intimacy at bay with Gallo. It was ridiculous that she should feel so sensually intimate with a man with whom she had never slept. They had walked around the volcano and felt the heat but had been too wary to make that leap. At least, she had been wary. Gallo was more reckless, and Catherine wasn't sure when or if he would make a move that threw both of them into that inferno.

"You're not asking me questions." He tilted his head. "That's not like you, Catherine. You're always firing away until you know the complete layout of the land."

He was right. She was not behaving normally. He had caught her off guard, and the last thing that she wanted Gallo to know was that he had managed to shake her. Stop thinking about Gallo, the man, and think about what he had said. "I'll try to remedy that. Venable? Audition? What job?"

He chuckled. "That about covers it." He got to his feet. "Suppose I call room service and get a pot of coffee, then we'll talk?"

"No, later."

He shook his head. "Actually, I was trying to be tactful. I was going to give you the chance to throw on some clothes while I made the call." He added bluntly, "You're naked under that robe, and you're disturbing me. Unless you want to postpone the conversation indefinitely?"

She could feel the blood rise to the surface of her skin beneath the terry robe. Her breasts were tautening, and her pulse was beginning to pound. She forced herself to shrug as she turned toward the bedroom. "Why didn't you say something? It's not like you to not be frank." She moved across the room. "Okay, just give me broad strokes, and we'll fill it in later."

He made a face. "Even that sounds sexy as hell to me at the moment." He held up his hand. "I'm getting to it. You need someone who's familiar with Nardik's operation. Venable sent for me." He turned toward the phone on the table beside him. "Now go get dressed."

"What do you—" But he'd picked up the phone and wasn't looking at her. And she didn't want to look at him right now either, she realized. He was wearing dark jeans that made his stomach and buttocks appear tighter and his thighs more powerful. She was suddenly as vividly aware of her nakedness beneath the robe as he appeared to be. She felt ready . . . and available. She needed to get away from Gallo to clear her head. "Ten minutes."

She closed the door behind her and drew a deep breath. That had not gone well. She had not had her usual calm composure, and Gallo would have had to be blind not to have noticed. Gallo was definitely not blind. He had been aware of the explosive tension between them from the very beginning and had not even tried to fight it. It was Catherine who had struggled and managed to keep things on an even keel. Besides the fact that she had never felt this intensity with any other man, he had a history that was disturbing, and she did not want to experience an all-consuming relationship with any man. She had Luke, and she had no right to concentrate on anyone but him right now.

"I can feel you there, Catherine," Gallo said softly from the other side of the door. "Remember when you were hunting me up in the woods in Wisconsin? During those weeks, we got to know everything about each other without a word or a touch. It was as if we were inside each other and could feel every muscle, know every thought. It's still with me, Catherine. Is it still with you?"

She didn't answer. Of course, it was with her. It was during those weeks of hunting, of playing cat and mouse, that she had learned how dangerous he could be.

"Let me in, Catherine. We'll talk later."

Let him into the room, into her body . . .

Talk? That wouldn't happen.

She drew a deep breath and pushed away from the door. The next moment, she was slamming the door of the bathroom behind her to make sure he would hear it. Not that it was necessary; he would be able to sense that she was no longer there.

A shower and in ten minutes she'd be calm and able to function efficiently again. She stripped off the terry robe, and the air was cool on her flushed and still-taut breasts.

Well, maybe fifteen.

She turned on the shower and stepped under the spray. Yes, that was better. She was beginning to think with her head and not with her body. She felt a surge of resentment that he could disturb her so easily. She had never understood why Gallo should have such a powerful physical effect on her. She was only grateful that it was physical and not emotional.

Perhaps she couldn't entirely rule out emotion considering their history and who John Gallo was to the people she cared about. He had come into her life because he had been her friend's, Eve Duncan's, lover many years ago, when Eve was a teenager, and had been the father of Eve's daughter, Bonnie. He had been an Army Ranger and a prisoner of war in North Korea and never learned about the birth of his daughter until years later. Nor that Bonnie had been kidnapped and presumed murdered by a serial killer when she was only seven. When Gallo had become a suspect in her murder in later years, Catherine had gone on the hunt for him as a service to her friend, Eve. It had been a dangerous and turbulent time even after she had discovered that Gallo had not killed his daughter.

And now that he was here, life was

beginning to be just as turbulent again, dammit. Why had Venable chosen to throw him back into her path?

Because Venable had no idea that she would have this response when confronted by Gallo. He had only been on the periphery of their relationship before and had merely sought to give her what she needed. He had assumed she would be totally professional.

And that's exactly what she would be from that moment forward. This wasn't about her or Gallo or anything that had happened in the past or might happen in the present.

This was about keeping Hu Chang alive in any way she could.

"I thought I heard you come out of the bathroom." Gallo was pouring coffee into a white china cup from the carafe on the table. "Black, right?"

"You know it is." She crossed the room and took the cup and saucer from him. "And you didn't 'think' you heard me. You have hearing like a forest animal. I found that out when I was hunting you in those woods in Wisconsin. I'm very good at tracking prey, but you got away from me dozens of times just when I thought I had you."

"You are very good." He was pouring himself a cup. "I learned about hunting and keeping alive in those woods as a boy, but you grew up here on the streets of Hong Kong. Very urban. How did you get that good, Catherine?"

"After I became an agent, I taught myself. I knew it was a skill I needed, so I developed it." She sat down on the chair by the window. "It was the professional thing to do." She stared him in the eye. "And I am a professional, Gallo. I do my job and don't let myself be distracted."

He nodded. "I thought you'd go on the attack when you had time to think. You've always been very defensive." He sat down across from her. "Actually, I didn't mean to try to seduce you the minute I walked into this suite. I just saw you and . . ." He shrugged. "I've always lived for the minute, and it's hard to break the habit." He smiled. "And I've been wanting you for too long. I've never hidden that from you."

No, and that awareness of his desire had only intensified her own.

"I don't care that you want to screw me,"

she said bluntly. "That would only get in the way. And that's not why you came here. You told me that Venable sent you because you knew about Nardik's operations. How?"

"I was sent to kill him several years ago when I was still working for Army Intelligence."

She stiffened. "A sanction?"

"Whatever you want to call it. I thought about it more as stepping on a tarantula and grinding his guts out. Particularly after I did my research on him." His lips tightened. "Ugly. Very ugly."

"You did research on him? How much?"

"Plenty. Enough to get me close to him. About that time, I was being sent on suicide missions by that bastard, Colonel Queen. As you know, after those years in that North Korean prison, I wasn't exactly sane, but I knew that much. I just didn't care. But I wasn't going to make it easy for anyone to take me down."

Easy? She had been told he had the skill and mad ferocity of one of those Viking berserkers. "Why were you sent to kill Nardik?"

"What was the story they gave me about my so-called mission? Nardik was supposed to be involved in a drug deal with the Pakistan government that was going to enable them to bribe key military bigwigs in India to back off when they invaded one of the disputed northern provinces." He lifted his shoulders in a shrug. "And possession is everything."

"Why didn't you go through with the killing? Evidently, Nardik is still hale and hearty."

"They yanked me out just before I was to go in and do the job. Queen told me that India had got wind of the plan, and Pakistan had backed out of the deal with Nardik as part of the resulting chain reaction."

"And you believed him?"

"Not particularly. But it didn't matter. There was always another job to do." He lifted his cup to his lips. "Though I had a few regrets after going over Nardik's involvement in a couple atrocities in the Congo. I was anticipating with extreme pleasure removing him from the scene."

"You could find and get to him now if it becomes necessary?"

"I'd have to tap a few contacts to get updates. As I said, it was several years ago."

"But you could do it?" she persisted.

He nodded. "I wouldn't be here if I couldn't give you what you want." He smiled. "And I don't mean in the carnal sense. Though I'd be happy to discuss that at any time."

"No, we won't," she said curtly.

"Whatever you say. Are there any other questions you'd like to ask me?"

"Probably a hundred or so once we get into locating Nardik." She met his gaze. "But I have a couple I want answered right now. Why are you here? Why did you come when Venable asked you to do this job? You have plenty of money these days, and you haven't had to work for Army Intelligence or any other security department for a long time."

"You're asking me if I'm willing to risk my neck for the chance to get you in bed?" He smiled. "Oh yes, it would definitely be worth it." His smile faded. "But that's not why I'm here. I owe you, Catherine."

"Bullshit."

"Typical response. But it's still true. You helped me find my daughter's body and the one responsible for her death."

"You know I didn't do it for you. Eve is my friend, and she deserved to be at peace after all those years of searching for her daughter, your daughter. I wanted her to have some kind of resolution. You weren't important."

He made a face. "Cruel but honest. But in spite of my lack of importance, you still gave me resolution, too. It might have been just a by-product, but the result was the same." He looked down into the remaining coffee in his cup. "And there were times when you had more faith than anyone else that I hadn't killed Bonnie. That meant a great deal to me."

"Why? It wasn't because I thought you were such a great guy. I knew who and what you were. It was just that everyone around you wasn't thinking clearly. Too much emotion. Someone had to put two and two together and come up with something besides six."

"I'm glad you set me straight," he said solemnly. "Heaven forbid that you thought I was worthy of the battle. Will you at least accept that I feel differently and want to pay off a debt? You believe in the payment of debts yourself, or you wouldn't be here, would you? You think you owe a debt to Hu Chang."

She shook her head. "This isn't about debts. Hu Chang and I have gone way past that point. I just can't imagine my world without him, and I won't tolerate anyone's trying to take him out of it."

"Really?" He was studying her expression. "That's an extraordinary commitment. Hu Chang is a lucky man."

"Hu Chang makes his own luck." She added curtly, "And can also be a complete asshole."

He chuckled. "I take it that's his present status?"

"If I could corner him and get him to talk to me, I might be able to tell you. Did Venable tell you he had to pull in a Special Ops team and an F-16 to get him away from Nardik?"

"Extreme measures. He must think Hu Chang is worth it if he went to the trouble."

"He thinks that Hu Chang is going to cause some kind of major catastrophe if he can't stop him." She put her cup down. "And he'll stop him any way he can. Did he make you an offer to turn Hu Chang over to him after we find him?"

"Yes, quite a nice one. You're right, he

wants Hu Chang badly." His brows rose. "Are you going to ask me if I accepted?"

"No. If you'd taken the offer, you'd lie. But I tend to think that you wouldn't betray me. You don't need the money, and you wouldn't let Venable tell you what to do."

"That sounds promising. Are you telling me that you're going to let me help you nail Nardik?"

"If I find I have to do it. I don't give a damn about Nardik. All I want to do is get Hu Chang out of this bonfire he's gotten himself into. If you think that you owe me, I'll take it. I'll take anything anyone can give me to wrap this up."

He nodded. "Then we find Hu Chang and put Nardik on the back burner. It's settled. In the meantime, I'll make a few phone calls and see if I can update my info on Nardik." He stood up. "Because we both know that if Nardik wants Hu Chang that much, then he's going to be very troublesome in short order." He inclined his head. "Or you wouldn't have had Venable request my services. Now what else would you like me to do? I'm at your disposal."

"As if you'd pay attention to my orders any more than you would Venable."

"You're wrong, this is your territory. I can obey orders if they make sense." He smiled. "Or if I think that there will be pleasurable consequences." He saw her frown, and said, "No, everything I told you about my motives was the truth. This is a payback as far as I'm concerned. Will I try to get you into bed? Hell, yes, that goes without saying. It won't interfere with anything. And we've been heading in that direction since the first time we saw each other."

"I don't give a damn what happened in the past between us. As far as I'm concerned, this is a clean page. I don't want to think about it. I don't want to talk about it."

"A fresh start? That might be appealing. I'll try to comply. But I have certain memories that keep intruding." He added, "So give me orders if you like, Catherine. I may not obey them in the conventional way, but the result will be the same."

And that would frustrate her no end. "I'd rather keep you under my eye than tell you what to do. It's safer. Just get me that info on Nardik."

"Right." He turned and headed for the door. "I checked into the room next door. I'll give you a key in case you need me. I'll go and make my calls, then come back, and we'll go out to dinner and talk again. You can show me Hong Kong."

"I'm no tour guide. You've never been here?"

"A couple times, but I haven't seen *your* city. That should be interesting . . ."

The door shut behind him.

She should have told him he didn't want to see her Hong Kong. It had been seamy and full of ugliness.

But he would probably have found that ugliness as interesting as the more beautiful sights of the city. He had boundless curiosity. He would study it and see how it had shaped the person she had become.

No.

She instantly rejected the thought. She was too vulnerable to Gallo now, and she did not want to get any closer to him.

Unless that closeness was in bed. Admit it, that was the one place where she knew there would be pleasure, and the only vulnerability would be physical. She could handle that far better than any psychological probing.

What was she thinking? She could handle either one, but it was better if she kept Gallo at a distance on all fronts. She got to her feet and headed for the bedroom. She would call Luke and tell him what she could without disturbing him. He would probably realize that she was being deceptive, but she wanted to hear his voice and was ready to run the risk. Anyway, she was probably as overprotective as Sam claimed. It would do no harm.

And it would do no harm to go out to dinner with Gallo. They had to eat, didn't they? It would be different sitting down at a dinner table with him in a situation where they had no agenda. They might have grown intimate sitting over campfires and trekking through acres of woods, but they didn't know the simple, civilized things about each other.

Civilized? That might be the wrong word. There were elements of savagery about both of them, and they instinctively reacted as warriors when the situation called for it.

What the hell? They could pretend to be civilized.

As Gallo had said, it might be interesting . . .

*   *   *

Gallo knocked on her door forty-five minutes later. He had slipped on a black sports
coat over his black jeans and a white shirt
that was open at the throat. He looked
very tough, totally masculine, and riveting.
"Ready?" he asked tersely.

"Yes." Her eyes narrowed on his face.
"What's wrong?"

"We may not have to go hunting for
Nardik. I got my update, and he arrived in
Hong Kong today. He evidently wasn't
pleased with the way you decimated his
hired help and decided to take over operations himself. He had his yacht, *Dragon
King,* brought to the harbor from Macau,
and he should have boarded it already."

"He's here?" She shouldn't have been
surprised. If Hu Chang was important, Nardik would be determined to have everything
go well. "Where's he anchored?"

"I couldn't find out everything. I should
get a call in about thirty minutes." He gestured for her to precede him. "But I refuse
to have him delay dinner. I have an idea
he's going to get in our way too much as
it is. I figured we'd go downstairs and sit
on the veranda facing the harbor. Who

knows? We may see him streaming past us."

"Not likely." She stopped at the elevator and pushed the button. "That's not all, is it? What else did you find out that was upsetting you?"

"Other than Nardik's landing in our lap before we were expecting him? Not a thing." He got on the elevator and punched the button. "Except he's been exhibiting a good deal of interest in Catherine Ling. He has a dossier on you and has been asking questions."

"What's unusual about that? It's no secret that I'm close to Hu Chang. It would be stupid of him not to check me out. We'd do it."

"It's not unusual. It just pisses me off." He looked at her. "And don't ask me to be reasonable about it. I don't feel like being reasonable. Absurd as it might seem, I'm feeling protective."

It was totally absurd, but it still gave her an equally unreasonable rush of warmth. "That's your problem. Get over it."

"I'm working on it. No one knows better than I do how capable you are." He reached into his pocket and drew out his phone and handed it to her. "Access the photos. You probably already know what Nardik looks like, but he has an assistant slash lover who travels with him. Ken Fowler. Watch out for him."

She gazed at the photo. Blond, wavy hair, boyish good looks, and a South Beach tan. "Lethal?"

"Cunning more than lethal. He likes to inflict pain, and Nardik uses him for that purpose. He's totally devoted to Nardik." He changed the subject. "How is your son doing?"

"Very well. I phoned him while I was waiting for you. Our friend, Kelly Winters, was on her way from the airport. She's staying with Sam and Luke this weekend. She'll keep them both on their toes." She smiled reminiscently. "I'm sorry I'm not there to watch her do it."

"I can see that." He was studying her face. "You're definitely wistful. If it wasn't for Hu Chang, you'd have told Venable to go to hell."

"You bet I would. I've got a chance of having a home and family now. I don't even know how that would feel." She added wryly, "A very dysfunctional family, but I'm working on it. I've seen signs of promise with Luke. It always helps when Kelly is there."

"You regard her as part of your family?"

"Why not? She has a mother who thinks she's some kind of freak because she's a genius. She just wants her to be normal or go away. That's why Kelly spends so much time at school." The elevator stopped, and she stepped out of it. "I met Kelly when I had to go in to rescue her and her father in South America. He was a coffee executive, and they'd been taken hostage by the head of a drug cartel. I was able to get her out, but her father was killed. It was hideous for her. She was fourteen, but she had more guts and endurance than a woman twice her age." Her lips twisted. "And instead of wanting to bring Kelly home and comfort her, her mother wanted to send her to a rehabilitation home for therapy. It was less trouble for her."

"So you felt sorry for Kelly?"

"Hell, no. I wouldn't insult her like that. She was strong enough to fight her own battles."

He nodded slowly, studying her. "But you might have identified with her. Oh, I know your backgrounds were different, but you were both alone and forced to fight for survival at a young age. It would be natural for you to become close."

It was perceptive of him to connect the dots and come out with that conclusion. "Very natural. Just as it's natural for Luke and Kelly to strike sparks off each other."

"Fighting for maternal attention?"

She burst out laughing. "That's the last thing either one of them wants from me. I'm having to work all the time to keep from intruding on their space. Neither of them looks on me as a mother figure. No, they strike sparks because they're too intelligent, too independent, too sure they're right. The last is typically teenage, and I welcome it." She slanted a glance at him. "Why are you asking all these questions?"

"Is it odd that I want to know about you? You're a unique personality, and I'm intrigued."

"It's not as if we're strangers."

"But now I can delve into the details. In the past, we were too caught up in the events to have any time for anything but the basics. Though those were fascinating enough."

Basics. Sexual attraction. Fear. Suspicion. All the basic elements of the hunt . . . and even when the latter two were erased, the sexual attraction remained dizzyingly strong. Looking at him now she could feel the pull of that strength. "The details of my family life are hardly that interesting." She stopped as they came to the entrance of the restaurant. "You already knew about my son."

"Yes, I'd like to meet him."

"Maybe someday."

"Soon."

She met his gaze. "Why are you being persistent?"

"I don't know. Why don't we find out together?" He turned to the maitre d' who was approaching them. "I told them a table on the harbor. We should be able to see a fantastic sunset."

"It's a wonderful sunset," Fowler said softly as he came to stand beside Nardik at the rail. "It reminds me of the one we saw that evening in Tahiti a few months after I came to work for you. Do you remember?"

Fowler was always trying to jog his memory about the period when they'd been lovers, Nardik thought with annoyance. Usually, he let it go, but he was on edge tonight and wanted to strike out. "No, I'm afraid that I don't. It must not have been that important to me."

Fowler stiffened. "It was important to me," he said hoarsely. "And you know it."

"But I have more important matters to think about." He had turned the knife enough and had received the required response. "What did you find out about Catherine Ling? Where is she?"

Fowler didn't speak for a moment. "The Princess Hotel. You'd think that she'd be nervous after that encounter with Jack Tan and go into hiding. She must be very stupid."

"Or very confident. There's something very sensual about a confident woman. It makes one wonder how long it will take to rob her of that confidence. She's being watched?"

"Yes, she's not had contact with Hu Chang. And she's having dinner on the veranda overlooking the harbor with a man registered at the hotel. John Gallo."

He didn't recognize the name from the report he had on her. "Find out more about him." He was beginning to feel a rush of excitement as he stared out at the harbor. Ling was going to prove a challenge. He could feel it. These days, he relished a challenge that would break the boredom. He was glad he was here and able to ready himself for the battle that was looming ahead. He could scarcely wait until she knew that he was here. He had a sudden thought. Why not? he thought recklessly.

He turned to Fowler. "Tell the captain that I want to move the yacht to a position near the Princess Hotel."

"Now?" he asked, startled.

"Now. He doesn't have to dock. But I want to be close enough for her to see us."

"She won't know the *Dragon King.* It would be senseless."

"It would be senseless if it were you," he said sarcastically. "But she's very sharp. She'll know about the yacht by now. It will have meaning for her."

Threat. Intimidation. Warning of what was to come.

Yes, she would recognize the message and know that the game was about to start.

*   *   *

"Have you had dinner here before?" Gallo asked. "Venable seemed to think you knew the hotel inside out."

"I do, from necessity." She lifted her wine to her lips. "But I seldom stay here. Most of the time I'm with Hu Chang. And no, I've never dined here. It's beautiful."

She was beautiful, Gallo thought as he gazed at her across the table. She was dressed in a simple black dress with a boat neck and no sleeves. Her long black hair shone in the light of the setting sun, which also made her olive skin more golden. He had thought she was beautiful the first time he had seen her and had wanted to reach out and touch her. But even then, he'd realized how dangerous she could be, and that had been part of the appeal. He'd learned other things about her since, the honesty, the loyalty to her friends, the love she held for her son. All fine qualities, and they should have impressed him more.

"What are you thinking about?" she asked.

Tell the truth? Sure, why not? She was always brutally honest with him.

"I was thinking that I was a shallow son of a bitch because I couldn't appreciate your sterling qualities." He lifted his glass to her. "And that it was your fault because I look at you and all I want to do is take your clothes off and to hell with anything else." He added softly, "You shimmer in this light. There's a balcony upstairs in the suite. You'd look wonderful stretched out with the light on you . . . and me over you."

"That's a matter of opinion." Her tone was cool, but he could see the pulse pound in her throat. He was always aware of her responses, and those responses drove him crazy.

"Yes, but I can't get the thought out of my head." Back off. He was talking too much. And, dammit, he was getting hard just looking at her. "I think that you're having a few problems with that, too. Just what is your opinion, Catherine?"

She looked out at the harbor. "That we shouldn't be talking about anything that doesn't pertain to finding Hu Chang."

But she wanted it, she wanted him. He could feel it, sense it in every move she made. Lord, and he wanted her. It had been like this between them for too long. They needed it, dammit.

But not now. She might be lured to bed,

but she'd resent it later. Cool down. It would come in time.

"Whatever you say." He drew a deep breath. "But you'll have to be the main contributor to the conversation. I'm having trouble concentrating. Hu Chang. Do you have any idea where he could be in the city?"

"Of course not. If I did, I'd be there." She frowned, thinking. "He's a will-o'-the-wisp when he wants to be. We won't be able to find him. He'll have to come to us."

"And how will you draw him?"

"He worries about me. That's why he came back to the shop when he heard I was staying there. He was watching me then. I'd bet he's watching me now."

"So all we have to do is wait until he thinks you're in danger?"

"We may not have to wait long. You said that Nardik is here in Hong Kong now." She shook her head. "But I don't like that idea. If we draw Hu Chang to me, then we're setting him up for Nardik. That's probably why they'd be tailing me anyway, hoping we'll lead them to Hu Chang. No, we have to go at it another way." She took another sip of her wine. "I was thinking about what

Venable told me about the night they rescued Hu Chang off that island. He slipped away from the Special Ops guys before he went to the helicopter. He told Venable he had something to do. What could be so important that he risked his neck to do it? That delay could have been suicide. Hu Chang isn't reckless."

Gallo was thinking, too. "He was either searching for something." He paused. "Or he was hiding something."

She nodded. "He wasn't sure that he'd get away, and he didn't want Jack Tan to find whatever he was looking for when he was torturing him." She was taking it step by step. "And he didn't have it on him when he got to the helicopter. He was wounded, and Venable had to do first aid and would have known."

"Then it's on the island. If Hu Chang hasn't already gone back to retrieve it. He would have had time since he left the shop after Agent Gregory's murder."

She nodded. "But if he thought it was safe, then he might not have wanted to risk being followed back to the island. Or Jack Tan could use that cottage on a frequent basis and still have men stationed there."

"We're saying 'it.' What are we looking for, and how can we find it?"

She shrugged. "A drug, a formula, the name and address of the place that either could be found. Or something else entirely. I have no idea. But we do know that Hu Chang didn't have much time to get elaborate when he was hiding it."

"You told me that he was a genius. It might not take much time if he had made contingency plans."

"We can guess until we're blue in the face. This is all supposition."

"And you intend to go to the island anyway. In spite of what Hu Chang might have decided was best to keep Nardik off the trail."

"Hu Chang won't work with us, so we have to work around him." Her lips tightened. "We're going to that island, Gallo."

"It's going to be dangerous as hell. We have to get in and get out without being followed."

"Then we have to make sure that we have a sure exit strategy." She lifted her glass to him. "You said that you'd obey orders, Gallo. Let's see you do it."

"In other words, you're going to shove

all of us under the bus and expect me to put on the brakes."

"Can't you do it?" Her dark eyes were gleaming, teasing him. "And I thought I could trust you. We played this game before when I was on the hunt for you. Have you gotten soft, Gallo?"

He chuckled. "That's not a word you can ever use in our relationship." He was feeling the familiar surge of tension and excitement that was always present when Catherine was issuing a challenge. "Oh, I can do it. But it may mean blowing up the bus. Will that be all right with you? I don't believe I can arrange for an F-16 to zoom to the rescue as Venable did."

"Really? I'll be disappointed, of course. Hu Chang will rub it in that he was important enough to rate a jet, and I couldn't—" She stopped, her smile vanishing. Her head lifted as she sat up straighter in her chair. "Someone is watching me."

"Every man in the room who isn't blind or gay." But his gaze was darting about the restaurant. Catherine had wonderful instincts, and she would know the difference between casual lust and something more threatening. "You said that Hu Chang would probably be watching you. Can you spot him?"

She shook her head impatiently. "He wouldn't be that obvious." She paused. "And it's not Hu Chang. I'd know it if it were."

"Then maybe it would be a good idea if we went back to your suite and had our dinner sent up." He added grimly, "You're a target out here on the veranda."

"The hell we will." She rubbed the nape of her neck before turning to look out at the bay. "It's somewhere out—" She stopped, her gaze on a yacht that was some distance offshore. "What was the name of Nardik's yacht?" She answered herself. "*Dragon King.*"

Gallo muttered a curse as his gaze followed hers to the white yacht. The damn ship was close enough to read the name emblazoned on the side. "Son of a bitch."

"Don't be rude to a guest when he's come calling. He obviously wants to call attention to himself. I don't doubt that he has his binoculars trained on me this minute." She pushed back her chair and stood up. "Stay here. Let's give him a better look."

"Catherine."

She wasn't paying attention. She strolled

slowly over to the ornate wrought-iron railing that overlooked the bay. She turned and looked directly at the *Dragon King.*

Shit. Was she close enough to be picked off by a rifle? Gallo calculated. No, but he wouldn't have been able to stop her anyway without knocking her unconscious.

God, she was magnificent. Her slim body was warrior-straight, her chin lifted with defiance, her dark hair tossed back. She was smiling and she lifted her glass in a mocking toast to the man on the *Dragon King.* She held the glass high for a full half minute, took a sip of wine, then hurled the glass to splinter on the rocks below.

Without another glance, she turned on her heel and sauntered back to the table.

"Satisfied?" he asked, through set teeth. "Now that you've pissed him off and made yourself number one on his kill list, may we leave?"

"No." She sat back down. "We'll finish dinner and have dessert, then an after-dinner coffee, I think. Why make him think he's of any importance?"

"And you want to rub his nose in the fact that you certainly don't think he is. One thing I found out when I was researching him was that he has a gigantic ego."

"That doesn't surprise me. Hu Chang called him Lucifer." She watched the waiter set down a fresh glass in front of her and poured the wine. "Lucifer had a very good opinion of himself, too." She looked at him across the table. "You're annoyed with me."

"You could say that." He was also on edge and scared shitless. She had caught him off guard and had set off a chain of imagined scenarios that had shocked him. He should have been cool and admiring, even amused. He could even see himself making that same taunting gesture under other circumstances.

But this wasn't him, this was Catherine. And that protectiveness he felt toward her that they had both found so strange was now raising its head again.

Crush it down. Lust was fine. And he could handle gratitude. But this overwhelming desire to take care of Catherine could tear him apart. She would not accept it, and he could probably not keep himself from doing it.

"Screw you," Catherine said gently. "I

did what I wanted to do." She lifted her wine to her lips. "And it felt *good*."

"Did it? Then that's all that's important." He lifted his wine. "I'm making a list of the things that make you feel good. I'm hoping it will come in handy." He looked out at the *Dragon King,* sleek on the blue waters of the bay. "That's an interesting name he chose. Do you suppose he thinks of himself as a fire-eating dragon?"

"It's possible."

"Would it make you feel good if I lay the head of the dragon at your feet? I might enjoy that, too . . ."

"I can kill my own dragons. That's not why I wanted Venable to send me help."

"Then will you kill a couple for me? You do know that Nardik will draw a bull's-eye around anyone with you? He may only be glancing casually at me through those binoculars, but he's taking note."

"Of course, I know." She didn't speak for a moment. "After I make contact with Hu Chang, I'll try to get you out of this."

"Everything for Hu Chang."

She nodded jerkily. "It has to be that way. As I said, I'll try to—"

"Be still, Catherine," he said quietly. "I'll

stay or go as I please. This has always been my choice." He gazed out at the ship. "And how can I resist meeting Nardik? He's old unfinished business. I'm looking forward to him almost as much as I am to getting to know Hu Chang . . ."

CHAPTER

10

Bitch.

Nardik's hands tightened on the binoculars. Catherine Ling was leaning back in her chair on the veranda and leisurely drinking her coffee. She hadn't cast one look at the *Dragon King* after the defiant gesture that had made him want to strangle her. No, that would have been the final thing he wanted to do to her. He was going to take his time and make the pain excruciating.

"She had no right to try to make a fool of you," Fowler said. "You should send Jack Tan to teach her respect."

And that would avoid any possibility that Nardik might change his mind if he came in contact with her. Did Fowler think he couldn't see through him? "There's no way she could make a fool of me," he said harshly. "And I reserve sole right to prove that to her."

"Then let me help," Fowler said eagerly. "Remember Carl Falek? You said that I did a good job with him. I made it last a long time."

He lowered the binoculars as Ling rose to leave the restaurant. "I'll consider it." It wasn't a bad idea. Fowler was a vicious bastard when he was jealous, as he had been of Carl. He was sure he would prove even more inventive with Catherine Ling. It might be more entertaining watching him work on her than doing it himself. He turned and smiled at Fowler. "You want to please me, don't you?" He reached out and stroked his cheek. He could see the pulse leap in Fowler's throat. "Yes, I can see you do. Then start thinking of Catherine Ling, every minute, every second." He whispered, "It has to be very special."

"When?"

So eager. Well, he was eager, too. He

had been thinking of Ling as a bonus when he succeeded in getting the potion from Hu Chang. Now he was thinking that she might prove the pièce de résistance. "I've told Jack Tan that she has to be taken in the next two days either with Hu Chang or without. If he doesn't do it . . . well, you may have another way to please me."

His hand dropped away from Fowler's cheek, and he turned away and started down the deck toward the dining salon. "I believe anticipation has made me a little hungry. Or maybe it was watching that bitch at the restaurant. She's given me an appetite in more ways than one. Tell the cook that I'm ready for dinner."

"Where have you been?" Catherine threw open her door and glared at Gallo. "You disappear for a full day and don't answer your phone. Even Venable didn't know where you were."

"I was busy." He came into the room and shut the door. "You put me in charge of exit strategy from the island, and I thought I might as well take care of our arrival as well."

"And you couldn't have told me?"

"Did you tell me when you decided to taunt Nardik into a fury at the restaurant? Neither one of us is good at communicating . . . unless it's life-or-death." He went out on the balcony and looked down at the waters of the harbor. "His yacht is still down there, like a cat waiting at a mouse hole."

"Cat and mouse. That's what he wants me to think. It's supposed to be a war of nerves." She joined him on the balcony. "He's been there ever since last night." She smiled and waved. "Screw you, Nardik."

He shook his head. "I'm surprised he hasn't made a move yet."

"Cat and mouse," she reminded him. She turned and went back inside. "And I've seen to it that he knows where I am if he wants to see me. How do we get to the island?"

"A seaplane will drop us off tonight on the north end of the island, and the pilot will wait for us until we come back."

"Tonight? *Yes.*"

"I'm glad you're enthusiastic."

"Waiting has been driving me crazy. I wanted to murder you when I couldn't get in touch."

"I'm sure that isn't the first time. I did a flyover of the island today, and the cottage seems to be occupied. Tan must use it as a permanent base. It's not going to be a walk in the park. I arranged for a speedboat to pick us up several blocks from the hotel and take us to the docking area for the seaplane. It should be dark in another hour, and by the time we get to the island, we should be able to slip in and slip out with no trouble." He made a face. "But that never happens, does it?"

"Not in my experience," she said dryly.

"I left getting us out of the hotel up to you. Venable told me that you know this hotel like the back of your hand."

She nodded. "We'll go down to the gift shop on the mezzanine and slip out their emergency door and down the stairs to the delivery area in the alley." She headed for the bedroom. "I'll get a duffel and my jacket and be right with you."

He nodded. "I'll be here."

"You weren't for the last twenty-four hours," she said sarcastically.

"Because I was off doing your bidding." He paused. "And I thought I'd better stay away from you for a while."

She looked back at him over her shoulder, then wished she hadn't. Intensity. Readiness. Lust.

"Yes," he said softly. "It doesn't go away. I'm trying to work with it, but I'm going to have to pace myself." He turned back toward the balcony. "I think I'll go out and let Nardik see me again. We can't let him concentrate too heavily on you. I believe in sharing."

She shut the bedroom door behind her and stood there for a moment. How the hell could he shake her with only a look, a few quiet words? Ignore it. Use Gallo for the task at hand and nothing else.

Use him? Gallo wouldn't be used for anything that didn't please him. She should be grateful that it pleased him to help her because of a sense of gratitude. But she couldn't even be sure that was the real reason. The sexual tension between them was so strong that it blurred everything else.

Clear your head. Stop thinking about him. Tonight we have a job to do.

She crossed the room and grabbed her duffel and black leather jacket. The only thing she should be concentrating on was the fact that they were good together on the hunt. We'll need to be, she thought ruefully. Since she had no earthly idea for what they were searching.

The seaplane glided in silently some distance from the shore, and the pilot, Ned Talbot, called cheerfully back to them, "There you are. Couldn't be any quieter. But you'll have to row at least a quarter of a mile to get to shore."

"No problem." Gallo was throwing the raft into the water. "Just be ready to go when I call you." He met Ned's eyes. "You have your orders."

Ned nodded. "Right."

Gallo turned to Catherine. "You're sure you want to do this? It's not very practical. You admit you don't know what he hid in those woods. The odds are against our stumbling over whatever it is." He added grimly, "And the odds are better that Jack Tan's men will find out we're on the island and come after us."

"I want to do it." She jumped into the raft

and grabbed an oar. She had been telling herself the same thing since Gallo had arrived at the hotel, but for the past hour she had become more and more certain that she was doing the right thing.

Every instinct was beginning to whisper to her.

And she usually listened to those instincts.

She stared at the island's shadowy outline, and that same feeling was surging through her.

Okay, Hu Chang, we're here. Now let's see just how stubborn you are.

"When we hit the shore, we go through the trees, skirt the cottage, then go into the woods. Right?"

He nodded as he sat down opposite her in the raft and started rowing. "And hope there's no sentry on the shore or in those woods."

"I'm turning on the flashlight. There's no way we can see anything without light," he said when they reached the woods. "I think the brush is heavy enough to keep anyone in the cottage from seeing the light. I figure we'll examine the trees and any crevices for anything that looks out of place."

"That's a good idea," she said absently. She stood there, her gaze wandering around the wood. "You go ahead."

"Me?" He shot a glance at her. "What about you?"

She nodded. "In a minute."

He gazed at her, his eyes narrowed. "What's going on? You know trying to find anything in these woods is going to be a disaster."

Her gaze was searching the trees. "Maybe not."

Come on. I know you're there.

"Catherine," Gallo said. "Talk to me."

Silence all around her.

Dammit. Dammit. Dammit.

"You're right, we can't find anything here. It's not working." She pulled her Glock out of her jacket pocket. "We go to plan B."

She pointed the gun in the air and let off four shots in rapid succession.

"What the hell!" Gallo grabbed her wrist. "Are you nuts? You're going to bring Jack Tan's goons running."

"They should already be on their way."

She didn't look at him. "Get out of here, Gallo. Get back to that seaplane."

"You are crazy. I'm not going anywhere without you."

"No. You go on. I'm staying here." She raised her voice so that it rang out loud and clear. "I'm not going without you, Hu Chang. So you come out of there or watch Jack Tan's men take me down. Do you hear me?"

"How could I help it?" Hu Chang came out of the trees. "You're being exceptionally noisy." He stopped before her and shook his head. "Only you, Catherine."

"Shut up. This is all your fault. All you would have had to do was come out of hiding and we wouldn't have had to come here and go to all this trouble." Her hands clenched into fists. "You knew we were coming here. Did you follow us?"

"No, I knew you'd come. I've been waiting a few hours." He tilted his head. "And I believe I hear the uproar you meant to cause."

She was also hearing shouts from the cottage. "Then we'd better get the hell out of here. Do you have what you came to get?"

"Oh yes, it only took a moment."

"I don't suppose you're going to tell me what it is."

"Eventually." He turned to Gallo. "I believe we have not been introduced. I am Hu Chang. I understand you are John Gallo?"

"Not the time for polite introductions," Catherine said as she turned. "We have to get back to the plane."

"Not that way," Gallo said. "The cliff side of the island." He turned to Hu Chang. "The same way you went when you were heading for the helicopter. Only this time, you take the path down the cliff toward the sea."

She looked at him in bewilderment. "Why? The seaplane is on the far side of the—"

"Don't ask questions," Gallo said roughly as he started to run up the incline. "I'm pissed off enough at you for making me listen like some outsider while you and Hu Chang played your games. I was supposed to be a part of this operation. Or did you forget?"

He wasn't waiting for an answer, and Hu Chang was right behind him. "He seems to know where he's going, Catherine. It would be wise to follow him."

She was already following him. Gallo always knew what he was doing. Though she had no idea what was happening or where he was going. She just had to trust him.

They had reached the cliff top and were going down the twisting path leading to the rocky shore. She was aware of the salt wind in her face and the sound of the surf crashing on the rocks below.

The surf was so loud that she couldn't hear the pursuers behind them. But at least there were no shots.

Gallo was almost at the bottom of the path and was lifting his phone and talking into it.

No boat. No plane. Just surf skimming the rocky shore. And the sea was so rough here that a boat couldn't possibly get close. What the hell were they supposed to do?

She looked over her shoulder. Still no pursuit. That was weird as hell. Jack Tan's men should have reached the top of the cliff by now.

Hu Chang was starting to chuckle. "Oh, very good, Mr. Gallo."

She swung back around and her gaze followed Hu Chang's out to sea.

A small submersible pod had emerged from the water a quarter of a mile out to sea.

"Swim out to board her," Gallo said curtly as he waded out into the surf. "The pilot can't come any closer."

Catherine covered the last yards to the shore. "Tan's men will be able to pick us off in the water as soon as they reach the top of the cliff."

"They won't reach the top of the cliff . . . I hope." He started swimming. "Ned is staging a distraction with the seaplane on the other side of the island. I told him to give us ten minutes if he could before he took off."

"How did—" Questions later. They had to concentrate on getting out of here. She struck out for the submersible. "Hu Chang?"

But he was already ahead of her in the water and was overtaking Gallo.

She could hear the sound of shots. But not directed at them, distant . . .

They'd taken the bait.

The hatch of the submersible was opening up ahead, and she saw Gallo enter the sub.

"Come, come, Catherine." Hu Chang turned and looked at her. "You're keeping me waiting."

"Bastard. Get inside and out of my way."

He chuckled and climbed aboard the sub.

Gallo was reaching a hand down in the water to pull her into the pod. He turned to the pilot. "Get going, Bill."

He scowled. "Then sit down and let me get under way. This pod isn't supposed to accommodate four. Three is a tight squeeze."

"You don't have to rely on oxygen for more than ten minutes," Gallo said as he sat down in the other pilot seat. "Just enough to get us to the next island."

"And I assure you that it wasn't my choice to inconvenience you." Hu Chang huddled on the floor in the back of the pod. "Though this is an interesting mode of transportation. When Venable called in the F-16, he didn't actually let me ride in it. This is much better."

Catherine dropped down beside him

and leaned back as the pod started to move. "I'm so glad you approve."

"I approve of the technology," he said quietly. "I do not approve of being hijacked. Though it's not entirely unexpected."

"You didn't leave me any choice." To Gallo, she said, "Why?"

"Every exit strategy should have a backup." He added grimly, "Though I didn't think you'd trigger the need to use it."

"Trigger," Hu Chang repeated with a smile. "What a fitting verb to use."

"It was purely unintentional."

"Too bad. But I'm sure you're clever anyway. How else would you get permission to use this submersible?"

"It's a research sub. I offered a sizeable contribution to their current project."

"Well, bribery isn't clever, but it's efficient." He was studying Gallo's expression. "I believe I'll not discuss this until we're back on dry land. You're a trifle on edge."

More than a trifle, Catherine thought, as she glanced at Gallo. "What island are we heading for?"

"I don't think it has a name. It's not much more than a sandbar in the middle of the ocean. But I told the pilot of the seaplane,

Talbot, to pick us up there if he heard shots on the island." He gave Catherine a cool glance. "Plan B. It appears we both had one. But mine was aimed at saving our necks, not sacrificing them to bring Hu Chang into the fold."

"It was a last-minute decision. I knew he was out there in the woods. I had to take the chance."

"But he's quite right," Hu Chang said. "And he has reason to be angry."

"Shut up, Hu Chang," she said through her teeth. "It was a big chance, it was a risk. But I'd do it again."

"I know." He leaned his head back and closed his eyes. "As I said, only you, Catherine. But this is very close quarters for such volatility. I can feel the thunder crashing, and it's upsetting to such a peaceable man as myself. We'll go into it later."

"Oh, yes," Gallo said softly. "You can bet we will."

"You look like drowned rats," Ned Talbot said as they climbed from the dock into the seaplane. "Though I can see how you'd choose a dunk in the sea over those guys who were shooting at me. They were pretty determined. Two of them tried to get a boat out to board the plane. That's when I decided it was time to take off. I'm glad I gave you enough time."

"You did the right thing. I wanted you to stall, not get yourself killed or your plane blown up." Gallo grabbed the towel Ned was handing him and started drying his hair and neck, then dabbing at his damp clothes. "I'm going to go up in the cockpit with you. Catherine and Hu Chang can keep each other company. I'm sure they have a lot to talk about." He headed for the cockpit.

"He's very annoyed with you." Hu Chang handed her a towel, then began to dry his hair. "And me, too, perhaps. It's difficult to tell."

"He likes to run things. I threw him a curve, and he doesn't appreciate it." She threw the towel aside. "This isn't doing any good. I need to wash the salt off and start over." She made a face. "Ned's right, drowned rats."

"You could never look like a rat," Hu Chang said. "This Ned was mistaken. I hope he's better at flying than with words. Perhaps you resemble a water sprite."

"And you're crazy." She sat down in the seat and buckled up as the plane took off. "Water sprite, I'm not. But Gallo was right, we do have to talk. What did you pick up on that island?"

"I always enjoy conversation with you." He paused. "As long as it's the topic of my choice."

"Bullshit."

"Let me elaborate. You have caused me to realize that it may be more dangerous keeping you at a distance than to let you help me. I will consider changing my mind about involving you, but that decision is not yet made." His voice was silken but iron firm. "Until that time, we will not speak about it."

She gazed at him with frustration. "You're not being fair. What would you do if it was me who—"

"The same as you. But I don't have to be fair. I only have to be right." His gaze went to the cockpit. "John Gallo is interesting. Of course, I knew he would be when I did my research on him."

"Research?"

"Naturally, when he showed up at your hotel room, I had to know what kind of man he was. So I made phone calls and delved deep." He smiled faintly. "I had to go very, very deep. His background is exceptionally obscure. But very interesting, and I can see that there are close ties between you. I'm sure it has some connection to your feeling for your friend, Eve Duncan, but I don't sense that same kind of bond. I'll have to examine him and see if I approve."

"And when did your approval ever make a difference to me?"

"Whenever you make the admission that it does."

It was the truth of course. "He's only here because he thinks he owes me a debt."

"Gratitude is an admirable quality. And the other reason?"

"He doesn't like Nardik. He thinks the world would be a better place without him."

"I'm beginning to appreciate his judgment. And I already thought his innovative flair was commendable. He's starting to grow on me. Though I've always thought that expression brought to mind leeches or parasites." His expression was thoughtful. "But I don't believe Gallo could ever be a parasite. What else he could be is questionable. I was told at one time he was thought to be mad."

"After seven years of torture and imprisonment, anyone would be a little unbalanced. He survived and got over it."

"Is that what he says?"

She was silent a moment. "No, he says he still has moments of uncontrollable rage. Who wouldn't, dammit?"

"I'm not attacking him." His lips curled in the slightest smile. "You're defending him."

"He was honest with me. And I've never seen him in a situation where he couldn't control himself."

"But that time might come. I'd be curious to see what your reaction would be."

"It would depend on the situation." She smiled recklessly. "We both know that I'm not always entirely balanced in my own attitudes if my emotions are involved."

"No, you can't be cool if you care about someone."

"I don't care about Gallo," she said quickly.

"I was speaking of my humble self." His hand touched his chest. "Since I regard our relationship as the only one of importance to me. The rest is just curiosity and amusement."

"I don't believe you feel either curiosity or amusement about Nardik. If you did, you'd have no objection to telling me what's happening with him."

His smile vanished. "It started out as curiosity. Supreme wickedness has always intrigued me. A man has to cross so many barriers to reach that level. But then, when I discovered he was Lucifer, I realized that I had to step back before he touched me."

She frowned. "What do you mean?"

"Sin. We're all so close to the edge. One touch, the right touch, would send us over. And as I studied Nardik, I realized that he takes everyone with him on the journey. He reaches out and touches and the mark can never be erased and the evil spreads and spreads. Particularly in a man like me."

She felt a chill, then immediately shrugged it off. She shook her head emphatically. "You're wrong. He's a man like any other. No, he's more egotistical, and that's a fault that can be used against him. So stop talking nonsense."

He threw back his head and laughed. "Whatever you decree. I didn't think I was talking nonsense. I thought I was being deep and philosophical. Why can I never impress you, Catherine?"

"You do impress me. You impress me with your stubbornness and your sheer contrariness." She paused. "And with your inability to realize that we've been together for too long to sit on the sidelines when one of us is in trouble. You've never closed me out before. Why now?"

"Because I may have made a mistake, and I can't have you or your son hurt because of it," he said quietly. "That's why I told Venable not to bring you into this."

"What mistake?"

He didn't answer.

"I am in this," she said fiercely. "It's too late. Gallo said his informants told him that I was already targeted."

"And you made certain by that display in the restaurant. If you hadn't put on such a splendid show, I would have been really furious with you."

"You were there?" She frowned. She had been able to sense Hu Chang in the woods on the island. Why hadn't she known he was in that restaurant? "I didn't realize that."

"I was careful." He inclined his head.

"And you were distracted. Both when you were talking to Gallo and when you decided to fling the gauntlet down to Nardik."

"It was a wineglass."

"Don't quibble."

"Anyway, you shouldn't have been anywhere around me. Nardik would have been on the watch for you. That's why Jack Tan went on the attack at the shop."

"And you shouldn't have gone to the shop or the island or come to Hong Kong at all." He waved his hand. "We will not argue. I am always correct, and I would not have you feel less than you are. I will meditate and come to my decision." He leaned back and closed his eyes before saying softly, "You were truly splendid in the restaurant when you were confronting Nardik. Bold and blazing with defiance. I was proud of you."

And the fact that he admitted to that pride filled her with warmth. The words completely disarmed her. He'd probably known they would.

"Yes," he answered her unspoken thought. "But just because affection and admiration is spoken, it doesn't mean that it's not true. I've been proud of you since the moment we came together and became one in friendship. It's like being proud of myself."

She wanted to reach out and touch his hand, but that would be a weakness she couldn't allow herself. "But you certainly have no lack of pride in that direction."

"I deserve it. First comes intellect, then comes labor, then comes pride. Now hush while I go over possible consequences of your intervention."

She thought about it, then decided that she had made her argument and stated her intentions. It would be best to give him the time he requested, then go after him again if the result of that meditation didn't meet with her approval.

She gazed out the window at the sea below her. "We'll be arriving at Hong Kong in less than twenty minutes, Hu Chang."

He didn't answer, and she knew that he was already involved in the process of weighing results and consequences as he had said he would do. She had seen him in this state of complete absorption many times before.

She just hoped that total absorption would bring the result she so desperately wanted.

"Is he sleeping?" Gallo had come out of the cockpit. "Wake him up. We're going to land."

"I'm awake." Hu Chang opened his eyes. "I assume you did not allow the pilot to fly to the same area where he usually lands?"

"No, he's landing near the docks at Kowloon," Gallo said curtly. "I'd be pretty stupid not to figure that Nardik might be able to find out from whom we'd rented the seaplane and send some of his men there to meet us."

"And you're not at all stupid, are you? I'm becoming more and more aware that your presence could be an advantage to Catherine. Have you arranged a place for her to stay that would be safe?"

"It's Catherine's decision, and she thinks the hotel would be safe." He was silent a moment. "But if she changes her mind, I found a flat above a tattoo shop on Kowloon that might do for tonight."

Hu Chang laughed. "You see, Catherine, I like a man who comes to the table prepared."

Gallo met his eyes. "And I come prepared to stop you if you try to split after we land. I'm not having Catherine put her head on the chopping block again just to find you. We both know she'd do it."

"I fear that's true." He paused, then nodded. "And so the threat is greater if I don't allow her to go after Nardik than if I do. Therefore, the decision is made." He turned to Catherine. "And I have to live with my mistake. You're sure that this is the way you want it?"

"What mistake?" Gallo asked.

"You'll both know in time." His gaze was holding Catherine's. "It will be very ugly, and you will not like it. You're sure?"

"You know I am."

He nodded soberly. "You always were sure once you made up your mind. I believe the question was to make me feel better about opening this door." He turned back to Gallo. "You have a plan to go after Nardik?"

"I'm working on it. It will take a little while to pull it together."

"From the reports I've had, you're

singularly effective whether you have a plan or just act spontaneously. This cannot be spontaneous. There is too much at stake." He turned to Catherine. "And the first thing you must do is call your Sam O'Neill and tell him he must get additional protection for your son. Nardik will go after you any way he can."

"I know that," she said shortly. "I called home again after I went back to my room after the restaurant incident. Before that, I was just a way to get his hands on you. I made it personal. Sam is calling on some of his CIA buddies to stake out the house and keep Luke safe. He's going to try to keep Luke and Kelly in the dark about what's going on."

"Very good. No need to disturb the children." He nodded. "Though Luke is a child only in years. Still, every vestige of childhood is precious. I was thinking that when he was helping me in my lab when he was here. He was cheated of his childhood and deserves to have it back."

"Too late," Catherine said. "It doesn't matter what he deserves; all I can do is help give him the best life I can."

"And you will," he said gently. "But we

must make sure that his life is preserved so that you can do it."

Just talking about Luke's being in danger was causing her to start to panic. "Why are you telling me this? Do you think I don't know? Let's just go after Nardik. We take him out, and he can't give any orders to even touch Luke."

"It may not be easy to take him out even though you have such fine help in Gallo. But I may be able to point the way in his direction."

"How?" Gallo asked.

"We'll discuss it later." The plane was skipping over the surface of the water now. "I believe we've landed. I trust you've seen fit to protect our pilot?"

"I told him Thailand was beautiful this time of year and gave him a bonus to keep him happy there for a while."

"Excellent. You're spending a good deal of money on my behalf. Of course, I'm worth it, but I still appreciate your generosity."

"How are you going to help me get Nardik?" he asked again.

"Catherine, tell Gallo that I'm not to be coerced."

"I'm asking, not coercing." Gallo went to the door and flung it open. "You'd know the difference." He gestured to Catherine to precede him. "The hotel or the tattoo shop, Catherine?"

"The hotel is no longer secure," Hu Chang answered for her. "And the tattoo shop is a fair idea, but Catherine would attract attention on the streets. People remember her face. I will take you to a place that is more secluded. It's a palace belonging to a friend who owes me a service. You will find it charming."

Gallo ignored him. "Catherine?"

Catherine hesitated. Then she shrugged. "I've never stayed at a palace before. Why not? And I don't care about charming as long as it's secure."

"It's as secure as Gallo will make it," Hu Chang said as he got to his feet. "And I'm certain he will take extraordinary measures to make it safe since he has little trust in anyone but himself."

Hu Chang was slyly baiting Gallo, Catherine thought with frustration. And Gallo had been difficult and combative since the moment Hu Chang had appeared out of those woods on the island. She supposed she couldn't expect anything else since it had been her action that had stirred the conflict.

"Right," Gallo said as he jumped on the dock and reached up to swing Catherine down beside him. "Sometimes extraordinary measures are the only thing that works. I don't like palaces any more than I do hotels. I prefer small spaces that can be controlled." He gave Hu Chang a cool glance. "Okay, where the hell is this palace?"

CHAPTER
11

"It looks more like a temple than a palace," Catherine said, as Hu Chang drove the sleek blue speedboat closer to the large red-roofed structure on the bank. "It even has the high walls and the bell hung at the gate."

"It was a Buddhist temple at one time. But when it was abandoned after it fell into disrepair, it was sold by the Chinese government to the highest bidder." He cut the engines and threw the rope to the young Chinese boy on the dock. "Then it was only a question of repair and restoration. It took Chen Lu nine years, but she managed to fulfill its potential."

"Nine years and a fortune I'd imagine," Gallo said as he stepped out of the boat and helped Catherine to the dock.

"Oh, yes. They call this place the Golden Palace. That bell in the belfry is gold. It's ten karat because it has to be durable, but she couldn't resist. And there are golden vases and doorknobs all over the place. Chen Lu isn't afraid of being ostentatious."

"And who is Chen Lu?" Gallo asked.

"No one threatening. You don't have to go into battle mode." He rang the bell at the gates. "You'll meet her in a few moments. I called her while we were approaching to make sure we'd be welcome."

"That's short notice."

"It was a mere courtesy. She will not object. We have an understanding."

"An understanding?" Catherine's eyes brightened with sudden curiosity. "Is she your mistress, Hu Chang?"

His brows rose. "Why would you think that?"

"I don't think anything. You've just never introduced me to a woman with whom you have an 'understanding.' You're always very secretive with me about your relationships."

"And shall continue to be. Chen Lu deserves my discretion. You must decide for yourself if—"

"Hu Chang!" The door was thrown open by a white-haired woman in a gold caftan. "I should have you tossed into the harbor. You've not come to see me in over three months." She turned to Catherine. "You must be Catherine Ling. I'm Chen Lu Moriarty. Welcome to my home."

"Thank you." She was as startled by the small, slim woman's exuberance as she was by her appearance. She had been expecting someone of Chinese descent, but she had been wrong. Not only were those words of greetings spoken with an Irish accent, but Chen Lu's irregular but fascinating features were definitely Caucasian. Her hair, worn in a high chignon, was snow-white but she couldn't have been more than in her late forties or early fifties. Her skin was firm and without lines, and her blue eyes were sparkling with enthusiasm in a face whose turned-up nose and slightly winged brows gave her a roguish charm. But the vitality and vigor that she carried with her was like a strong breeze that swept all other impressions aside. "This is John Gallo, Madame Moriarty."

"Come in. Come in." She stepped aside. "Call me Chen Lu. Everyone does. My husband loved everything Chinese, and started calling me that when we first moved here. After he died, it was easier to keep the status quo." She turned to Hu Chang. "You said trouble. How much?"

"A good deal. I am wanted by an exceptionally bad man who wishes to pluck me bare, then kill me." He nodded at Catherine. "And she brings you additional problems. She has seen fit to antagonize him."

She frowned. "Who is he?"

"Hugh Nardik."

"Never heard of him."

"That is to your great benefit and the fact that you spend so much time within these handsome walls." He shut the door behind him. "Where is Rory? Gallo will wish him to show him all over the palace. He is very protective of Catherine."

"But not of you?" Her gaze was studying

each of them shrewdly, weighing words and expressions. "Doesn't he realize your value?"

"Catherine has been trying to convince him I'm worth all this bother."

"Oh, you're worth it," she said softly.

"You'll forgive me, but he has to prove it to me," Gallo said coolly. "Who is this Rory?"

"Rory Benedict, my nephew. He's sort of my majordomo," she said. "I love the Chinese, but I need someone around me who has the same roots. Rory is in the garden teaching a history class for the servants' children. They go to school in the city, but I prefer they don't get the twisted version that's served up there." She glanced at the man coming down the hall. "Here he is. Rory, this is Catherine Ling, a friend of Hu Chang. And this is John Gallo."

"Delighted to meet you." Benedict gave them a beaming smile. He appeared to be a man in his late thirties or early forties, with curly red hair and the same blue eyes as his aunt. "It will be good to have company. Chen Lu loves to show off the palace."

"And so do you." Chen Lu gave him an affectionate smile. "Don't pretend you don't love every stick of it. But Mr. Gallo is concerned about the security of the palace."

"Really?" Rory Benedict's bushy brows rose in surprise. "Nothing to be concerned about. Chen Lu takes better care of her place here than they do of the crown jewels in the Tower of London."

"Stop bragging and show the man how safe we are here. Give him the grand tour of all those boring exits and tunnels and introduce him to your team. Then take him to his room."

"I'm not bragging, merely expressing pride in our achievements," Benedict said. "And it will be my pleasure." He gestured down the hall. "Mr. Gallo."

Gallo nodded but turned to Catherine. "We need to talk. I'll call you when I'm finished."

She had been expecting that from him. "I'll be waiting." She watched him walk down the hall with Rory Benedict before she turned to Chen Lu. "I'm sorry to intrude. Hu Chang said that you wouldn't mind."

Chen Lu's laugh rang out. "No, I don't mind as long as I come out of it alive. Hu Chang has always made sure so far that I have. I like life too much to risk it without the proper precautions. Come along with me, Catherine. I'll show you to your room." She smiled at Hu Chang. "You have the same quarters as usual. I'll come and see you after I get your friend settled. We have to discuss a few things. I'm getting impatient."

"You were born impatient," Hu Chang said. "You will get along well with Catherine. You suffer from the same malady."

"I've been very patient . . . for me," Catherine said. "But I have to know what this is all about. I'm going to have a shower and change out of these clothes. And then I'm going to come looking for you."

"You'll probably find me in the garden with the children. I, too, must change, but I like being with the young. They have clean minds that one can write upon."

"Like Luke?"

"It is very difficult to make an impression on Luke's mind, but I think I succeeded. In the end, we got along very well." He turned and went down the opposite hall from the one where Gallo had disappeared. "I look forward to seeing him again . . ."

"Then heaven help him," Chen Lu called after Hu Chang before turning to Catherine and leading her down the hall. "Hu Chang told me about you and your son. I told him I wanted to meet you, but he wouldn't commit. He seems to want to keep you to himself."

"I was thinking the same thing about you. I'd never heard him mention your name. I was wondering if . . ." She stopped and quickly changed the subject. "This place is wonderful." Her gaze went from the polished cherry floors to the paintings on the walls they were passing. They were a mixture of traditional Chinese and old masters. A decorator would probably have been horrified, but Catherine liked the combination. The colors were bright and the paintings zinging with life. The furniture she had passed had the same combination of color and rich comfort. Contemporary but clean lines, and the colors were the delicate lemon, beige, and cream popular in Hong Kong. "The interior certainly doesn't look like a temple."

"There are thousands of temples. I didn't want to imitate any of them. This place was a disaster, so rotten it was almost falling into the bay. No one wanted it but me. Hong Kong is crowded and growing more crowded every day. I wanted the peace and the space, and buying the temple was my way of getting my way." She grinned. "You should have seen the Chinese cultural minister trying to get me to listen to him on the duty of restoring this to its former Chinese glory. He was horrified at what I was doing here. They would have taken it away from me if I hadn't tied the purchase up with a mountain of clauses, then bribed the politicians in Beijing to make them irreversible." Her face was suddenly alight with enthusiasm as she grabbed Catherine's hand. "Come, I have to show you why I'd never give up my Golden Palace." She pulled her over to the full-length panel of glass on the landing. "Look at my garden. Have you ever seen anything more wonderful?"

"Never." Catherine stared, stunned at the acres of beautiful flowers and trees of every description. Roses, day lilies, cherry trees, too many plantings to identify . . . The planting beds were lush and varied and breathtaking and several white fountains with sparkling sprays reached for the sky. Catherine didn't know where to look next. "It's positively . . . amazing."

"Yes." Chen Lu smiled with satisfaction. "I put the first plantings in myself after I bought the property. The rest I imported from all over the world. Tonight, we'll have dinner on the veranda that overlooks my gardens. You'll love the scents." She started up the stairs again and shot a glance at Catherine over her shoulder. "Now that the distraction of my lovely palace has been put to rest, what were you wondering?" Her eyes were twinkling. "Let me guess. Did you think that Hu Chang was my lover? No, though I'm sure that he would be an excellent one. Our relationship is much more complicated. And I'm guessing that yours is equally complex."

"You could say that," she said dryly. "I'm sorry that I misunderstood. He told me you had an understanding and implied that you'd be willing to go to a great deal of trouble for him."

"I would do anything," she said simply. "He did a great service for my late husband, Donal, and an even greater one for me. You need not worry that we won't keep you safe here."

"I . . . see."

Chen Lu threw back her head and

laughed. "No, you don't, and you're fighting against throwing discretion to the winds and asking me to tell you what the hell I mean."

"Yes." Catherine grinned back at her. "And Hu Chang will tell you that I'm not known for my discretion, so I'm really suffering."

"There is no reason why I shouldn't satisfy your curiosity. It's a fine tale, and I'm proud of every minute of it." Chen Lu shrugged. "My husband, Donal, and I knew and loved each other from childhood. I married him in Dublin when I was seventeen. We had no children, but the love was so strong that we needed no one but each other. We traveled, we climbed mountains, we sailed the seas, we loved, we laughed. I helped him start his business, and it prospered. Oh, my, how it prospered. We found China, and we grew to love it. Donal even gave me a Chinese name that he said suited me much better than the one I was given at birth. He said Margaret had no magic, and I should have magic all around me. I did have magic. I led a truly magical life with my Donal." She paused. "But sometimes the magic stops, and you can't get it back. He fell ill with a blood disease, and they told me he was dying. He was in terrible pain. It had to stop. I told all the doctors to make it stop. They just looked at me and said . . ." She drew a deep breath. "You know what doctors say when they don't know what to do. They said we'll put him to sleep. Morphine is so good, Chen Lu. He may live another year, but he'll be asleep. No pain. My Donal, who loved every minute of our life together, and they wanted to put him to sleep for the last year of it. That year was precious. Then I heard about Hu Chang from one of my maids, and I went to see him. I won't tell you how hard I had to plead with him to find a way for Donal. All I'll say is that he agreed to try and he came to see him. When he left, he said that it was too late to save him, but he would do what he could. Three days later he sent me a small vial with instructions. The next day Donal's pain was gone, but even better he was my Donal again. He lived another eighteen months, and he lived it with joy and free of pain. Hu Chang came to see us frequently during that time, and he and Donal formed an attachment. And when my Donal died, Hu Chang was there for me." She smiled. "So there's my story. It's a good story, Catherine, a good life. But like all good stories, to make it meaningful, there must be a wee bit of sadness. But can't you see? It's full of joy, too."

"I can see it was," Catherine said with a smile. "I'm afraid I wouldn't be so philosophic. I'd fight and yell and howl. But I can see you have a very Gaelic attitude."

"How can I help it? I'm only a poor Irish lass, and I'm older than you. The years teach you to accept what you can't change." She stopped before a beautifully carved door. "This is your suite." She opened the door. "You have no maid. I sent most of the servants away when Hu Chang called. I kept only the ones I can trust implicitly. But I imagine you can take care of yourself."

"No problem."

Chen Lu nodded. "I had no servants at all until years after I married Donal. But you'd be surprised how quickly I became used to them. You'll find a caftan in the armoire in the sitting room to change into for dinner. I've always found caftans fit everyone, and they make us look like empresses. Isn't that wonderful? Dinner will be on the veranda in two hours. That should allow you time to refresh yourself and still have time to try to dig information from our mutual friend, Hu Chang." She smiled. "I'm lost in admiration that you think you can succeed. Your relationship must be much closer than even I can claim with him." She didn't wait for an answer, but was gone in a flash of gold-embroidered silk and a lingering trail of boundless energy.

I *will* succeed, Catherine thought as she gazed after Chen Lu. This woman and the Golden Palace she ruled were both dazzling and distracting. She genuinely liked Chen Lu, and her story had touched her. But it didn't change the scenario or the reason Hu Chang had brought them here.

She entered the luxurious suite and shut the door behind her. The situation was getting more and more dangerous. Hell, she'd even had to safeguard Luke. She couldn't allow it to go on.

She tore off her clothes, which were now dry but caked with salt from that swim in the sea, and headed for a door that must lead to the bathroom. She would shower and change, then go down and find Hu Chang.

And before she left him, she would know everything.

*   *   *

"Jack Tan is here," Fowler said as he came into the yacht's lounge. "Shall I show him in here?"

"No, tell him to go away and not come back until he finishes the job." He couldn't believe the incompetence the asshole had exhibited. The numbskull had actually had Catherine Ling and John Gallo on that island, and his men had failed to catch them. She had made fools of them.

As she had mocked him on the veranda.

That sting was like an open wound.

Why had she gone to the island? Because she was working on Hu Chang's orders to retrieve something he had left there?

Of course, that was why she'd taken the risk to go to the island. And he knew exactly what she'd been after when she got there. Jack Tan's fault. Another reason to be angry with the bastard.

"I thought that might be how you felt," Fowler said. "So I thought you might want me to ask him a few questions. He said to tell you there was a third set of footprints in the woods. A man's prints, a medium-size foot," he said. "Hu Chang?"

"It wouldn't surprise me," he said through his teeth. "That would make this disaster complete."

"He's trying to trace the seaplane. He's got the pilot's name, Ned Talbot, and the woman who lives with him, Sue Kim. He works out of Hong Kong, but the plane hasn't been seen there since he dropped off passengers and took off again. The woman is still at his place in Kowloon." He paused. "He dropped off three passengers in Hong Kong."

"Three. Hu Chang. They *are* together."

"Tan said he's got men all over Hong Kong asking questions and trying to find where they went after they left the seaplane. He has a report that they may have rented a blue speedboat on the docks and taken off south. Tan has sent men out in the bay to scan the coastline, trying to locate the boat. Those rental boats all have numbers."

A break? It was about time that Tan came up with something promising. "Tell him to confirm it. Find them."

"Anything else?"

"The pilot, Talbot, may know something. Tan's got to locate him. See if his woman will give him up to you. If she doesn't talk, kill her. If he feels anything for her, that may bring him back so that Tan can grab him."

Fowler nodded. "Very clever." He started to leave the lounge. "You've always found it efficient to go through people close to the target."

"You're damn right it's efficient. That was why I was trying to get Ling. But it's time to start going down the chain." He reached for his phone. "According to her dossier, Ling has a child. Even a bitch like Ling may have maternal feelings." He smiled. "I'm going to enjoy seeing how she likes seeing you work on the kid."

Hu Chang was dressed in a black tuxedo and sitting on a low chair, gazing out at the sun going down over the harbor, when Catherine reached the veranda. "It is beautiful, isn't it? Why do you think God made the end of the day so much more beautiful than the beginning? Do you suppose it is supposed to have some correlation with death and birth?"

"I have no idea." She dropped down in the chair opposite him. "And I have no desire to think about it . . . or discuss it."

"Not at the moment anyway." He smiled. "Did Chen Lu make you comfortable?"

"Of course, it's a fantastic place. Everything is meant to please the senses. How could I help but be comfortable?"

"Yes, comfortable but a little on edge." His gaze traveled from her shining dark hair loose to her shoulders, down her body garbed in the scarlet silk caftan, to the red silk slippers on her feet. "I see she furnished you with dinner regalia, too. Chen Lu loves to dress up." He touched the lapel of his tuxedo. "She always keeps one of these here for me. I wonder if she managed to find one on such short notice for Gallo. You look magnificent in that scarlet caftan. You're like a sunset yourself."

"I don't want to talk about sunsets. And I don't want to talk about Chen Lu, either. Though she's definitely interesting."

"You have no idea."

She brought the subject back to where she wanted it to go. "How did you get into this mess, Hu Chang? What the hell is this drug that Nardik wants so damn much?"

"I call it Pondera. It's Latin for balance. I was going to call it Octatok, which is the Russian word, but Pondera flowed better."

"Pondera, balance. From the first day we met, you've always been hung up on balance."

"It seemed fitting in this case."

"Why? I don't care about the name. Tell me what it does and why it has caused all this trouble."

"What did Venable tell you?"

"That it had something to do with a fool-proof poison that could be used for assassination with no possibility of detection. I found that hard to believe. Forensics is so sophisticated these days that there would be some test that would give it away."

"You're quite right, and someday in the far-distant future, they will possibly develop a test to detect traces of my Pondera in the body." He smiled. "But not yet, Catherine. And not for a long, long time."

She stared at him, stunned. "The perfect murder, Hu Chang?"

"Convulsive heart failure. Perfectly natural in every symptom."

"Why?" Her hands clenched into fists. "Why did you do it? You don't need any more money. You've told me yourself what people pay for your medical potions and drugs. You could be a bloody billionaire just from those medicines if you chose to go that route."

"Money is always desirable." He lifted one shoulder in a half shrug. "But in this case I wasn't commissioned to produce this particular drug. It came as a by-product of another potion I was creating. That happens often, but I wasn't expecting such a powerful side effect. I was quite amazed."

"Not too amazed to exploit it. How many times have you used it?"

"Only once. Lab experiments were inadequate, and I had to look farther afield to make certain that my findings were correct."

"How far afield? In what direction?"

"You would have approved. He was quite atrocious, a dictator who had been torturing his subjects for some twenty years. His prime minister had recently been won over to democratic principles and wanted to take over the country. But there were too many equally ambitious men in the cabinet who merely wanted to take over the dictator's slot and continue the oppression. The prime minister knew everyone would be accusing each other of the assassination, but they'd have to prove that it was murder.

If he could stir the population while all the uproar and the forensic tests were going on, he had a chance of seizing power."

"Who was it?" She was thinking hard, discarding possibilities. "Mideast?"

He nodded. "I thought since there was chaos there anyway, I'd give the people their chance. It worked out very well."

"It was Ben Salan, wasn't it?" The tiny Mideastern country he'd ruled was the only one who'd had a revolution after the death of its dictator. "You killed Ben Salan."

"Actually, his prime minister, Ali Gazaran, did it. I only provided the means." He frowned. "But Gazaran didn't deserve my help. He had become a little too Westernized. He broke his promise of silence and told his pretty wife about my drug. She was very shallow and loved to party when she was out of the country. After Gazaran became president, at one of those parties, she made a few indiscreet remarks that attracted the attention of Nardik. So one night when she was vacationing in Switzerland with friends, she disappeared for a matter of a few hours. It was only a short time, but Nardik's men are very capable.

Her sports car was found smashed against a tree at the bottom of a ravine just after midnight. Her terrible wounds were thought to be as a result of the accident."

"She told Nardik everything."

"Yes, without doubt. And now I'm suffering the consequences of not handling the matter myself and depending on Gazaran. I truly thought that he would keep his word. But one can never tell what a man will do when he's infatuated with a woman. It tends to blur honor and judgment." He poured a cup of tea and handed it to her. "I meant well, Catherine."

"And you couldn't leave it alone and walk away. You had to *know*." Her hand tightened on the delicate cup. "I've seen you create incredible formulas, then just abandon them and go on to something else because you were bored. Why not this one?"

"I wasn't bored," he said simply. "And I couldn't walk away from this one. I had to know every single aspect of it."

"Well, now you do. And it's causing chaos all around you."

"To disperse the chaos, we have only to remove Nardik. I guarantee that he's not disclosed the details he found out from Gazaran's wife. He's not a fool, and he's very ambitious."

"And it will be your secret again?" she asked bitterly.

"Until I choose to share it."

"Not again, Hu Chang," she said flatly.

A smile lit his face. "You are concerned. I do not wish you to worry. We will compromise. Suppose I promise that I will let you choose the cases when I wish to share. Yes, that will please both of us."

"Why don't you just—"

"A compromise," he said gently but firmly.

And he was not going to budge. At least, she had won this much from him. And he had given her a surprising amount of power in the decision. All she had to do was say no. She nodded. "Though I wish you'd abandon this entire project, Hu Chang."

He leaned back in his chair, and his gaze shifted once more to the sunset. "I know what you wish. You've never hidden your feelings from me." He chuckled. "Nor from anyone else. I notice that Gallo is having to accept that same stinging honesty. You clearly know each other well for such a short acquaintance."

"We've been through a good deal together in that short time." She looked out
at the sunset as she sipped the tea. "He's
very good. Maybe the best agent I've ever
worked with. We think alike on a lot of
things. I know he's been antagonistic toward you, but he won't let it interfere."

"You don't have to explain him to me,
Catherine. I can read him very well. I know
who he is and what's driving him. And the
antagonism is partly due to the fact that
he realizes that he senses that I know.
Has he contacted you yet?"

"He called me before I came down.
Rory's tour is taking longer than he thought.
I'll meet him in the garden just before
dinner."

"Good. Then we have time to sit here
together in peace. It's been a long time
since we were together."

"Not so long. Luke and I came to Hong
Kong several weeks ago."

"But I was too busy studying and preparing the ground with your son to enjoy
that reunion."

"Why would you want to 'study' him?"
she asked curiously.

"Because he belongs to you, and I must

make him part of my life. If I had made that effort right after you gave birth to him, you might not have suffered so terribly those nine years after he was kidnapped. It would never have happened. I feel a certain guilt that I allowed myself to step back from you at that time."

She stared at him, stunned. He had never spoken of Luke or that time before this. "Don't be ridiculous. You had no reason to have any guilt feelings. I'm the only one responsible for my son."

"I might have stopped it. I allowed my feelings to interfere and left you alone."

"I had my husband, Terry. I was not alone."

"If I was not there, you were alone. When you left the CIA and settled in Boston to have your child, I felt . . . displaced."

"What?"

"I realize it was irrational. I was mortified that I could be subject to such emotions. I wanted you to have a full life, but I wanted to be part of that life."

She stared at him in bewilderment. "We kept in touch. I'd never let you go."

"It . . . was not enough. Our bond was

strong. But I had to come to terms with it, so I stayed away and did not try to draw you back to me. It was a grave mistake." He shook his head. "The child was taken."

"Hu Chang, your not being there had nothing to do with it."

He shook his head. "I must make sure that I am part of your son's life so that I can keep him safe. I will not make that mistake again."

"Listen, my husband was shot by that butcher who took my son. If he couldn't stop him from taking Luke, why would you think you could?"

"Why, because I am extraordinary." He waved his hand. "But we will not discuss this any longer. I answered you with truth because it is right that there be no secrets between us. And now you know that your son will remain under my protection, and that will bring you infinite solace."

"And will show that you have the biggest ego in the universe." Yet in spite of her words, she couldn't deny she did feel a sense of intense relief. Hu Chang was a formidable force, and she embraced the idea of Luke's being surrounded by all the power and protection she could gather about him. "It's not as if I can't care for Luke myself."

"Catherine."

He knew her so well, and she owed him the honesty that was such a strong part of their relationship. "I thank you for your concern for my son," she said jerkily. "It means a great deal to me."

He chuckled. "That was very difficult for you. I think you should lean back and rest after the ordeal."

"Not so difficult." But it was good to lean back and relax as he suggested. "I'm not the fourteen-year-old girl you met all those years ago."

"Yes, you are. I still see flashes of her in the mature woman you've become. I cherish those flashes."

And she cherished the closeness, the total acceptance, the lack of loneliness that he always brought her. No one else had ever given those unique gifts. He was the most difficult man she had ever met, but those offerings made solving the constantly shifting puzzle of Hu Chang worthwhile.

And for the moment, there was no conflict, no tightrope walking, no striving to keep even or ahead of him.

They could sit here and be together and forget what might happen in the hours to come.

"You look relaxed," Gallo said, as she walked down the garden path toward him. "Good God, even serene. I've never seen you like this. Are you sick?"

"I'm fine." And he looked absolutely stunning in the tuxedo that Chen Lu had evidently found for him, she thought. He was always high-impact, but the stark black and white contrasting against the delicate blossoms of the garden made him look all the more masculine. "I just took time to sit down with Hu Chang and watch the sun go down. I can be relaxed on occasion. It's just with you the occasion never occurred." She sat down on the stone bench by the fountain. "You'll want to know what I found out from Hu Chang about the formula for his drug, Pondera. He discovered it as a side effect from another formula he was creating. It's a poison that could not be detected by any means of forensic testing."

"No way. That's hard to believe."

"Believe it. He decided that it had to be tested outside the lab and chose Ben Salan."

"Shit." She could see he was thinking, going over what he remembered of the news stories. "No proof of foul play after all those hundreds of tests. He actually did it."

"He wouldn't say he did it unless it was true. But there was a leak, and Nardik found out and decided it could be the premier weapon in his dirty arsenal. Now he wants it very badly."

"I think we have proof of that," he said dryly. "Anything else?"

She shook her head. "Nothing that would concern you."

"Personal stuff? Heaven forbid I interfere with that."

She ignored both the words and the faint edginess in his voice. "Well, are you satisfied that you know every hole and cranny of this place?"

"Yes, there are at least five ways of exiting if it became necessary." He paused. "And at least two that were capable of being a danger if anyone tried to get in. I had Rory assign extra guards to those areas."

"Good. I'm sure Chen Lu will be grateful for your expertise, too. She doesn't impress me as someone who would care to be vulnerable in any situation."

"Rory seems very capable, and it's clear he cares about her. That's one of the prime requisites in a security chief."

"She called him her majordomo."

"Then he wears more than one hat. He was in the Army in Ireland with special duty fighting the IRA before he took this job. Beneath that sunny smile and broad Irish accent, I bet he's very competent in caring for Chen Lu." He paused. "He thinks very highly of Hu Chang."

"What did he say?"

"Not much. But the respect was there."

"Are you surprised? Everyone has respect for Hu Chang. I told you, he's remarkable."

"Yeah, you told me."

She looked up at him and could feel his tension. "And you should believe me." She was suddenly impatient. "If you can't see him for what he is, then you're a blind man."

"I'm not insulting your friend, Hu Chang." His lips twisted. "I wouldn't dare. He seems to hold everyone in a trance around here.

He's like a—" He broke off and drew a deep breath. "Forget that. I'm reacting to an overdose of the power of the mighty Hu Chang. I instinctively fight back."

She nodded. "You're antagonistic."

"And defensive. He's like fighting a ghost."

"Why fight him at all? He's agreed to work with us now."

He was silent.

"Why?"

"He has too much influence with you. Do you want to know the truth? I think I'm jealous."

"I don't believe it," she said flatly. "You're too confident to be jealous of anyone. And you have no reason to have feelings like that concerning me anyway."

"Absolutely. On both counts. It doesn't make a damn bit of difference. I never thought I'd feel anything like this, and I don't like it."

"Neither do I. Hu Chang is my friend, and I've known him for years. I've only known you for several weeks. Naturally, he can influence me. But he accepts it when I refuse to listen."

"Which I haven't noticed occurring very

frequently." He added with frustration, "It's as if he hypnotizes everyone around him. Hell, even I was tempted to believe that every word he said was wise as Solomon's."

"You resisted that temptation very well," she said dryly. "You couldn't have been more skeptical."

"I was fighting a losing battle. I hadn't figured out what I was going to do or what was happening. I reacted instinctively." He gazed down into her eyes. "So when we were flying into Hong Kong, I had time to think, and I tried to put the pieces together."

She stiffened. "What pieces?"

"First, I had to accept that Hu Chang has more influence on you than I would ever have thought. From casual things you mentioned, I thought he was just a good friend to you."

"For God's sake, that's what he is."

"No, he's more than that. You have a fixation about him." His lips tightened. "He's like your alter ego. You love the bastard."

"Of course, I do," she said fiercely. "He's worth loving. And I'd be proud to be his alter ego. You have no idea how much we've gone through together." Her eyes widened.

"You think there's something sexual, don't you? You're crazy. There's nothing like that between us. Hell, Hu Chang says that maybe I was his daughter in another life. That's almost as crazy as what you're thinking, but it gives you an idea of how wrong you are."

"I didn't say that I thought anything like that. You were the one who jumped the gun," he said roughly. "I'm saying that you met him during a time when you were still impressionable, and you've put him on some kind of pedestal."

"That's ridiculous."

"Is it? What about—" He stopped, hesitating. "I'm probably going to regret this."

"Don't you dare stop," she said through set teeth.

"Oh, I wasn't." He smiled recklessly. "When have I ever stopped on the edge of a cliff? I'm like you in that, Catherine. I was just remembering some of those pieces I put together, things you've told me about your past. I was thinking about your husband, Terry. He was in his sixties when you married him, and you were still in your teens."

"So? That doesn't mean anything. Venable turned me over to Terry to mentor me when I joined the CIA. He was a great agent and a wonderful man. We wanted the same things, a home, a child . . ."

"Sex?"

"Of course there was sex."

"But you mentioned only the practical things . . . the mature things." He repeated. "Maturity, yes, that was the impression I received."

"The worthwhile goals," she said. "It's your own interpretation of my words. Now what the hell are you driving at?"

"Maturity. Why would you choose a man who was decades older than you to marry? You'd had a hard life, but you weren't looking for a cozy little cave and an ordinary family environment."

"You're wrong. After I had Luke, I wanted him to have everything that was normal and good."

"But not before you had your son. Shall I tell you why you married your Terry?"

"I'm sure you're going to do it anyway."

"Because the only man with whom you'd had a rich and rewarding relationship was Hu Chang, who was older than you. You instinctively were drawn to a more mature man because you were hoping to repeat the experience."

"Bull. I never thought of Hu Chang's age after the first day I met him. I don't even know how old he is. I know Terry was older. At least, I think he was. Hu Chang's always seemed . . . ageless to me."

"And how could a younger man compete with ageless when you were looking for a relationship? It brings to mind priceless treasures and weighty volumes that last through eternity."

"I did care about Terry."

"I don't doubt it. And you care about Hu Chang." His eyes were glittering in his taut face, and that recklessness was back in his expression. "And I've decided I don't care about what you felt for either one." His voice was thick, intense. "Because I *can* compete. I'm not ageless or some philosophic guru. I'm flesh and blood and young enough to make your head spin and your body want what I have to give you. And you *will* want me, Catherine."

She wanted him right now. She couldn't look away from him. She should be angry. She had been angry only a moment before. She couldn't believe what he had said to her. It wasn't true. Or was it?

But either way, it didn't change the fact that her body was readying, her breasts swelling. Or that she wanted to stand up and step closer and rub against him. She wanted to inhale the spice-lemon scent of him. She was acutely aware of the hardness of his body, the muscles and tendons. She was suddenly aware of her own softness in contrast to that hardness.

"You see?" His gaze was on her face, reading her thoughts. "I can compete, and I will. We've wanted this since the first time we came together. You can have your intimate little philosophic discussions with Hu Chang. I don't give a damn. Because you'll know when I'm looking at you, I'm thinking of everything I want to do with that gorgeous body. Every move that's going to bring you pleasure, make you arch, and move against me. And when you come to my bed, I guarantee you're not going to think of anyone but me."

She couldn't breathe. She was burning hot. The muscles of her stomach were clenching helplessly. He had said that he could make her dizzy, and he was doing it. He wasn't even touching her, and she felt as if she was opening, accepting.

She had to get away from here. "I'll think what I please." She jumped to her feet. "Who the hell do you think you are, Gallo?"

"Your lover." He met her eyes. "You just haven't recognized me yet. I just realized it myself. I probably would have taken more time if I hadn't gotten so pissed at Hu Chang. I've never been jealous before."

"So you said all those stupid things about Terry and your weird theory about why I married him. You're wrong, Gallo."

"Maybe." He reached out and touched the skin in the hollow of her throat. "Think about it. Be honest with yourself as you've always been with me."

Her skin was hot, burning beneath that light touch. She could feel the pulse leap beneath his fingers.

He could feel it, too. She felt his body tense in response. "Do you know what that does to me?" He put his two thumbs in the hollow and gently rubbed back and forth. "There's a rhythm to that beat. I want to make a rhythm, too . . ."

If she didn't step back, she'd move forward, go into his arms. If she went into his arms, they'd end up screwing like two frantic animals in the grasses of this beautiful garden.

And Lord, how she wanted to do that.

But you didn't always do what you wanted. You didn't act on impulse with a man who had this searing effect on you. She had never felt this intensely about anyone, and it was shaking her to her core. He had said she should think, but she wasn't going to do it if he kept touching her.

She stepped back, and said breathlessly, "I'm going to the veranda. I'm . . . sure it's time for dinner." She turned and started down the path. "Are you coming?"

"Not at the moment. I'll join you after I cool down a little." Ruefully, he added, "It may take a while. Tell them to start dinner without me."

She glanced back at him then wished she hadn't. "Whatever you say." She jerked her eyes back to the arched door of the house. "I'm sure that Chen Lu will—"

"Catherine." He was shaking his head. "You don't have to run away. It's not going to be an attack. It will be a seduction. I just had to let you know that it had officially begun. I owed that to you."

"You don't owe me anything. And we shouldn't think of anything but Hu Chang and making sure he's safe from Nardik."

He smiled. "Now that I've established my course of action, I'll spare some thought to Hu Chang. I'll even be civil to him. Run along to dinner, Catherine."

He was speaking to her as if she were a child, and only the moment before, the words he had been saying had been almost inflammatory. She welcomed the surge of irritation that was dissipating some of the heat he'd stirred. "I'll walk, not run, and if you speak to me again like that, I'll castrate you, Gallo."

He laughed. "I'll watch my tongue. Neither one of us would like the results of that particular move."

She gave him a frustrated glance and hurried down the path away from him. Away from his words and the feelings they'd stirred within her. The evening had been a confusing and disturbing one on several levels. Revelations from Hu Chang, the accusations from Gallo regarding the reason she had married Terry. The latter had to be a complete fallacy. It was just some psychological bullshit that had no basis in fact.

Or did it? She had never been one to examine her own motives. She knew who she was and usually responded instinctively.

As she had responded sexually to Gallo in those minutes before she had managed to break away. But in that case, the response had nothing to do with her basic personality. It had been mindless and almost animalistic. And she was not an animal. Her mother had been a prostitute, and Catherine had grown up with whores. She had seen that animal response all her childhood. She had even known it herself a few times since her husband's death. But it had only been for a single episode, then she was able to control it and walk away.

This time she had walked away from it before it even happened.

Because with Gallo, she wasn't certain that the control would be there to walk away afterward.

CHAPTER
12

Louisville, Kentucky

"What are you looking at, Kelly?" Luke asked impatiently from the desk across the bedroom from where she was standing at the window. "You promised you'd go over this translation with me."

"And I will. I'm thinking about it." She continued to stand there gazing down at the street. "Luke, I like your tutor, Sam. He's cool. And he must be really capable if Catherine picked him out for you. She trusts him?"

"Yeah, sure." His head was bent over Hu Chang's book.

"And you trust him?"

WHAT DOESN'T KILL YOU   337

Luke raised his head and his eyes were suddenly wary. "Yes, why do you ask?"

"No reason. You don't trust many people. I was just curious."

"You don't trust people either, Kelly."

"More than you." She suddenly grinned. "But I do guess we're two of a kind, and that's why you wanted me to work on your precious book with you."

"No, I did it because you're smart," he said with a straight face, but there was the faintest hint of a twinkle in his eye. "Or maybe you've just got a lot of those professors fooled. I hear it's easy to send those ivory-tower teachers down the wrong path."

"And where did you hear that?"

"I've been studying about politics and all those advisors in the White House. They seem to be pretty confused and causing big messes."

"And what would be your solution?"

"Blow it all up and start over." He looked down again at his book. "I like a clean slate."

That was typical Luke, she thought. His experiences had made him ignore everything but the main objective and the quickest way to get to it. "So do I. But I think there would be a few problems with that particular action. Maybe we can work out something less violent and still effective." She headed for the door. "I'll be right back. I left that translation I pulled off the Internet downstairs in the library."

He lifted his head and gave her a level glance. "I'll be waiting."

She didn't know if he believed her. It was difficult to tell with Luke. At any rate, she'd better get back to him as soon as possible to allay any suspicions. She closed the door behind her and ran down the steps.

Sam O'Neill was coming in the front door and looked up with a smile as she reached the landing. "I thought you and Luke would be tied up all day on that book of his. He told me that there would be no lessons today and that I wasn't needed."

"That was rude of him. It's just Luke's way."

"I know that. Luke and I understand each other."

"Yes, he said he trusts you." She gazed searchingly at him. "Should he trust you, Sam?"

His smile vanished. "Yes, why do you ask?"

"Because something is going on. Last night when I came here, I went out on the porch for some air. I saw you down the street. You were talking to a man near that oak tree on the corner. This morning I saw you talking to someone in a car on the other side of the street."

"My, how suspicious. Maybe I'm just a friendly neighbor."

"One time wasn't suspicious. A second time I had to think about it and decided to check. I took a course in body language at school. I thought it might help in my studies in working out patterns and projections. Do you know what I'd guess from watching you?"

He tilted his head. "I'd be fascinated to hear."

"You were superior, in charge, the other men were accepting orders. You're former CIA and very capable. Why would you have to give orders to someone outside watching the house? Catherine wouldn't put you in charge of Luke if she didn't have absolute trust in you. So I thought there was a good chance that you'd explain if I talked to you."

"And not lie?"

"I hope not."

"What would you do if you thought I wasn't telling the truth?" he asked curiously.

"I'd have to take Luke away if I couldn't trust you." She held his gaze. "I love Catherine. I couldn't let her lose Luke or even risk having him hurt. The scenario I'm hoping for is that you're only protecting Luke, but even so you're trying to deceive us. That's not fair, and neither Luke nor I will let you do that. What's happening, Sam?"

His smile was rueful. "I'm staring at you and what's coming out of your mouth doesn't compute. You look like a young angel, big, innocent, blue eyes, fair hair in that ponytail. And you're how old? Fifteen?"

"That doesn't make any difference. You're dodging. What's happening?"

He shrugged. "No ugly plot. At least on my part. Catherine is dealing with a man who might be interested in taking his hatred out on her son. He's vicious, has means at his disposal to hire scumbags to carry out his orders, and she thought the possibility was strong enough to alert me to take on extra men to protect him. I did as she ordered and pulled in four guys I worked with when I was with the CIA."

"And she told you not to tell Luke?"

"She's a mother. She wants to protect his sensitive feelings."

Kelly snorted. "Luke is tough. She should know that."

"She does. She just doesn't want to admit it. Because it hurts her to remember what made him that way."

Kelly nodded soberly. "Yeah, she hurts all the time. I want it to go away."

"She's working on it." He gazed at her quizzically. "So have I passed the test? Do you believe me, Kelly?"

"Yes. Catherine told me you were a good guy, but I had to be sure." She turned and started back up the stairs. "There wasn't any use in telling Luke until I knew what I was talking about."

"You're going to tell him? Catherine won't be pleased."

"Catherine's not here. And Luke can handle it." She thought about it. "He might enjoy it. I think he's a little bored."

"Are you insulting my teaching regime?"

"I'm saying he's stuffed so much into his

head since we got him out of Russia that he might need something in the real world to clear it."

He chuckled. "I understand you cram a lot of stuff in your head at that think tank at your college, too." He was going down the hall toward the library. "Maybe you're just being sympathetic."

"Maybe I am." She rounded the landing and stopped short.

Luke was sitting on the top step, looking at her. It took a minute for her to get over her surprise. "Hi, Luke. Were you, by any chance, eavesdropping?"

"Not by any chance. Deliberately. You were acting . . . weird. So I decided to follow you down to the library. But Sam came in, and I decided to just sit here and listen."

"That's not considered polite."

He shrugged. "I've done it all my life. I had to know what was going on. It was a way to protect myself."

"Sorry, I can see that." She climbed the rest of the stairs and sat down beside him. "And I'm sorry I was weird. I just had a hunch, and I didn't want to bring you into it in case I was wrong."

"You said that you had to protect me because of Catherine." He frowned. "I don't need any help, Kelly."

"Okay, I hear you. But it doesn't change that I'd have to do it. Catherine saved my life, and I have to do whatever I can for her." She wrinkled her nose at him. "And since you were rude enough to listen, you know I was coming up to tell you what Sam said."

"Would you really have told me?"

"Yes, because I would have wanted to know myself. I wouldn't have wanted anyone to treat me like I was some kind of delicate namby-pamby kid who couldn't take care of herself."

"Namby-pamby?" He lifted his hand. "Never mind. That explains itself, but it's very peculiar." He continued, "Yes, I would have been angry. I don't mind Sam's trying to do his job. That's why Catherine hired him. But I should know, I should be able to protect myself if Sam can't do it."

"Sam's very smart," she said gently. "He'll be able to make sure security is tight. Trust him."

He shook his head. "I can only trust myself. That way no one is to blame but me if anything happens. That's the way it should be. In the end, we're all alone."

And that independence and poignant solitariness must be terribly hard for Catherine to handle, Kelly thought with a pang. "Maybe you're right, but it's nice to have people you love come and visit with you." She added deliberately, "Like Catherine."

He was silent.

"Luke?"

"What do you want me to say?" he said roughly. "I know I should love Catherine. You're always telling me that. But I can't seem— Sometimes I think I remember her from the time before Rakovac took me. And it's strange and warm and . . . kind of happy. I think I loved her then. Maybe I love her now . . ." He shook his head. "I like it when she's with me. I . . . think I miss her when she's gone. And every now and then, when I think about her, I get confused . . . It's like listening to a shell where you hear the ocean but can't see it."

Kelly made a rude sound. "Boy, are you screwed up. I don't know why Catherine bothers with you. You don't deserve her."

He didn't answer for an instant. "I think it would hurt if anything happened to Catherine. I've been . . . worried about her lately. I've been wanting to help her."

"Wow, that's a breakthrough. It's almost a normal reaction. I may get through this weekend without wanting to strangle you after all." She paused. "Maybe even a few days longer. We need to work on that translation."

His brows rose as he looked at her. "You said you had to get back to class." He stiffened. "You're staying because of what you said about watching out for me because Catherine would want you to do it."

Tell him the truth. He would know if she tried to deceive him. "And what's wrong with that?" she said brusquely. "You may think you're alone, but as long as Catherine thinks you're worth loving, then I'm going to be right here with you. I know you know more about taking care of yourself than I do, but two is always better." She searched his expression but didn't see any softening. "And you know something else? I'm also staying because, weird as you are, I like you. I've taken you on as my friend whether you like it or not. And I don't leave my friends alone when they're in trouble. If you have a problem with it, that's too bad, Luke. Adjust."

His expression didn't alter for another

moment. Then a faint smile touched his lips. "Who are you calling weird? You're the one who's staying here when you could be safe and cozy with those ivory-tower professors. That means you're more weird than I am."

She drew a relieved breath. "They're not cozy, but they're safe and, consequently, very boring. We can find something more interesting to do here." She got to her feet and started down the stairs. "Let's grab a sandwich, then get back to work."

"Go on to the kitchen." He was following her down the stairs. "I need to talk to Sam first."

"Why? You're not going to give him a hard time about this, Luke? As you said, he's just doing his job."

"No, I need to know how to recognize the men he's hired to stand guard. And I want to know their names, too."

"Why?"

He shrugged. "It helps. How do you know the bad guys from the good guys? I always knew who the sentries were who guarded the house where Rakovac kept me."

"But they were all bad guys there."

"But then if I knew them, I knew what

kind of mistakes they'd make. Stop asking questions, Kelly. I know what I'm doing."

She imagined he did. He'd had to learn to survive those nine years alone, with only ugliness surrounding him. "Oh, very well." She'd reached the bottom of the stairs and headed for the kitchen. "Sam was headed toward the library. It shouldn't take you long. I'll start making your sandwich."

Golden Palace
Hong Kong

The dinner was served on exquisite china, and the food was excellent. Chen Lu was dressed in another silk caftan, this one a bright violet, and she was so vivacious she lit up the head of the table.

Hu Chang leaned forward to murmur to Catherine as a servant was pouring wine into their goblets. "You're very quiet."

"I didn't have much chance to talk, did I? You and Chen Lu were catching up on old times."

"We were rude?"

"No, you tried to include us."

His gaze went to Gallo, who had just

been pulled from his chair by Chen Lu and dragged to the stone balustrade overlooking the garden so that she could point out a rare orchid to him. "And neither you nor Gallo was in a mood to be very gregarious. Actually, I felt I had to distract Chen Lu from you. She's very curious and has a bold tongue."

She stiffened. "I don't know what you mean."

"Don't you? She calls a spade a spade no matter how graphic. She's not tactful as I am." He picked up his goblet. "But she's very tolerant. She would just tell you to go to bed with him and get it over with. That way she would keep her fine palace from going up in flames from sheer combustibility."

She felt the heat in her cheeks. "And that's supposed to be tactful?"

"As tactful as I can be considering the situation." His long, graceful fingers were moving on the delicate crystal of the wineglass. "I realized you were heading in that direction, but I didn't know it would turn explosive this soon. It came as a shock when I was forced to endure the physical vibrations that appear to be rocking your world."

"I don't want to talk about this, Hu Chang."

"Nor do I. I find it disturbs me. I'm more selfish than I thought." He gazed at Gallo, smiling down at Chen Lu at the balustrade. "Your Terry didn't bother me. I thought that would be the test . . . It seems it was not."

"Terry. Everyone is talking about Terry tonight." Her hand clutched her glass. "Do you know what Gallo thinks? He says it was because of you that I married Terry. He said that you were the only man for whom I'd had any affection, and it was natural that I tried to find someone older, more mature when I was looking for a relationship. Isn't that ridiculous?"

"Is it?" He smiled. "I should not be so vain, but Gallo's opinion pleases me. Perhaps I like him more than I thought." He tilted his head. "Or perhaps not. I will have to consider it."

"I married Terry because he was a good man, and I knew we would have a happy, stable life together."

"Stability. Yes, I can see how that appealed to you. You would not have to

deal with the primitive lust that your prostitute mother brought into your life from
infancy."

She stared at him, stunned. Only earlier
that evening, she had admitted that fact to
herself. "I've come to terms with my background, Hu Chang."

He shook his head. "Not yet. You're the
strongest woman I know, but everyone
hides from something." His gaze shifted to
the cream-colored candles and watched
the flames flicker. "Do not hide from this,
Catherine. I'm selfish, and you're part of
my life. I would like to tell you to send Gallo
away. I do not want to share you. But he's
like a storm that you must survive to become stronger."

"That's bull. All you're talking about is a
jump in bed, not some great psychological
revelation."

"Whatever you say." He smiled. "I felt it
my duty to tell you my thoughts. I will be
happy if you ignore them. But I'm not sure
you will be as happy." He nodded at Chen
Lu as she turned away from the railing and
smiled at him. "They seem to have finished
their horticulture discussion. Now we will
be very civilized and have her special Irish

coffee with our hostess. It is amusing how she surrounds herself with silks and pearls and pictures of dragons and still loves her Irish coffee. We will meet in your suite afterward, and Gallo can tell us how we can get to Nardik and end this."

He had changed the subject, and she should be relieved. The entire conversation had been bizarre and upsetting. It was as if he had given her his blessing to go to bed with Gallo.

As if she needed anyone's blessing to do anything she wanted.

Gallo was walking toward them across the veranda.

The light from the three tiers of candles on the dozen outdoor chandeliers was playing over his dark hair and throwing his cheekbones in shadow. His lips were open slightly, and his teeth were white against his olive skin. He looked totally male, totally sensual.

She felt a sudden tightness in her chest just looking at him.

Stop it, dammit.

But he was looking at her too. She knew what he was thinking. He had told her how it would be.

"Be careful," Hu Chang murmured. "I would not have Chen Lu embarrass you."

She tore her eyes away from Gallo. Control. This was not about her past or whatever hang-ups she might still have from that past. And it was not about her own damn emotions. It was about Hu Chang and his formula that could possibly wreak chaos.

She forced herself to smile at Chen Lu. "You were a long time. Did you have to start at square one, telling Gallo all about your plantings? You must have thousands."

She nodded. "Yes, but Gallo has an amazing memory. He tells me he made a fortune at card counting in the casinos. Then he parlayed that base into even higher stakes in the stock market."

Catherine knew about that. What Chen Lu had probably not been told was that he had trained that memory in the depths of a Korean prison just to retain his sanity. "I'm sure he didn't try to memorize all your wonderful plants."

Gallo smiled. "Only a dozen or so that I'd never seen before. I'm rebuilding my place in Utah that burned to the ground and a lot of these plants wouldn't survive the winters." He seated Chen Lu at the head of the table, then sat down beside Catherine. "But most of the time I prefer the hardy plants anyway. There's a special beauty to a flower or tree that doesn't bend, doesn't break, and can survive to bloom again." He looked at Catherine. "They offer both a challenge and intense excitement."

Bastard. She refused to look at him. "Chen Lu, you must find the same problem with your place in Ireland."

Chen Lu nodded. "But I'm here most of the year. I only go back when I need a good jolt of reality. You can't live forever in paradise." She looked at Hu Chang. "Though I do try, don't I?"

"That's because you're an eternal optimist." He lifted his glass to her. "And there are too few of you in the world today. I will always help and applaud that optimism."

"You'd better." She sipped her wine. "We need all the help we can get." She turned to Catherine. "You're very lucky to have Hu Chang for a friend, you know. Treat him right, and he'll give you the world."

"Chen Lu," Hu Chang said.

She grimaced. "Oh, all right, I'll be quiet. But it's true, dammit. I'll talk about something else." Her eyes were suddenly twinkling. "How is this? The real reason I took so long with our friend John Gallo was that I'm considering becoming one of those cougars I saw on television. I'm at least as attractive and clever as those women. Gallo seemed a good candidate for experimentation." She shot him a mischievous glance. "How about it, Gallo?"

He chuckled. "Anytime."

Catherine was not laughing. Any other time, she would have been amused at Chen Lu's bold, outrageousness. Instead, she was feeling an entirely irrational surge of anger.

Get over it.

"Good. I'll start thinking seriously about it," Chen Lu said.

"Well, now that we've settled that world-shaking question, I believe I'll say good night, Chen Lu." Catherine smiled as she put her napkin on the table. To hell with civilized customs and Irish coffee. "Wonderful dinner. Fantastic hospitality. Thank you."

"I think we've got a few other important matters to discuss before we let you retire for the night." Hu Chang rose to his feet. "Good night, Chen Lu."

"I'm being abandoned?" She turned to Gallo. "You, too?"

He stood up and inclined his head. "With the greatest reluctance."

"Oh, I do like you, Gallo. You lie so beautifully I can't even tell if you're doing it." She waved her hand. "Go away. I'll call Rory, and we'll go to the garden and drink ourselves into a sublime state of oblivion." She looked up at the stars. "Isn't it a lovely night? The stars seem so close you can hear them sing to you."

"You must be already in that sublime state," Hu Chang said. "Stars don't sing, do they?"

"They do if you listen. That's what life's all about. You only have to listen." She reached for her phone. "Rory, meet me at the fountain near the veranda and bring a bottle of champagne." She jumped to her feet. "Go do your thing, you boring people." She gave them a final exuberant grin over her shoulder as she headed for the steps to the garden. "Maybe, if you're lucky, you won't even know what you're missing."

"Tan has located the speedboat," Fowler said as he hung up the phone. "It was parked at the dock of a restaurant near the ferry access to Lantau Island." He held up his hand. "No, they weren't in the restaurant, but Tan found out that the boat had been taken to the restaurant by a Chinese servant who paid very well to rent the space."

"Whose servant?"

"The woman who owns a huge place nearby, a former temple." Fowler unrolled a map on the coffee table. "Chen Lu Moriarty. She seems to be well-known in the area." He pointed to a place on the map. "There it is. They call it the Golden Palace."

"And she has a connection to Hu Chang?"

Fowler shrugged. "Tan doesn't know if she does or not. No one seems to know anything about who Hu Chang's friends are."

"Except Catherine Ling." Nardik stared down at the map. He almost had them in his hands. If he handled this right, he could have the bitch. "What kind of security?"

"Tan is checking it out. He thinks it may be heavy-duty. You don't own a palace in Hong Kong without the means to protect it from predators. And Chen Lu Moriarty has contacts with the Chinese government in the city. She can call on them if she needs to do it."

Not good. He didn't need to cause an uproar that might call attention to him right now. The deal was too finely balanced and the client too nervous.

Shit. But he knew where they were. He couldn't let the opportunity pass. Even if the chances weren't as good as he liked, he had to try. He could still see Ling's mocking expression as she'd lifted that glass. He felt the blood pound in his temples as he remembered how he'd felt in that moment.

Do you feel safe in that Golden Palace, bitch? You're not safe, you'll never be safe from me. There's always a way, and I'll find it.

"What do I tell him?" Fowler asked.

"We go after them." He got to his feet. "But we don't screw it up. I can't have any publicity. It has to be done with a scalpel, not a machete. Tell Tan to come and pick me up in thirty minutes."

"You're going?" Fowler asked, startled.

"Didn't you hear me? I told you, I can't risk a bungle."

Fowler moistened his lips. "Do you wish me to go along?"

And Fowler was praying that he wouldn't say yes, Nardik thought. He was tempted to tell him that he was to come just to see him wet himself from sheer panic. "Why? You're not any good at this. Save your strength for something you can do right." He could see the relief on Fowler's face. "But when I bring you Catherine Ling, you'd better entertain me."

CHAPTER 13

Catherine headed for the bathroom as soon as they reached the suite. "I'll be right with you as soon as I change out of this caftan. I don't feel as comfortable in all this silken splendor as Chen Lu. I think there's a bottle of wine in that cabinet over there if you'd like a glass." The door closed behind her, and she drew a deep breath. It had been a strange, volatile night, and she wanted to get back to the familiar. She tore off the silk caftan and kicked off the matching slippers. The next moment, she had pulled on her black jeans and black sweater. Her boots were in the other room by the bed, she remembered. She ran her fingers through her hair and went barefoot back into the room.

Gallo and Hu Chang were standing together on the balcony. Not speaking. Well, even if they hadn't been definitely cool toward each other, she hadn't given them more than a few moments alone. They could hardly have started much of a conversation, she thought as she joined them on the balcony.

"I feel better now." She gazed down at the garden below. She could see Chen Lu sitting by the fountain some distance away with Rory. The next moment she heard Chen Lu's robust laugh ring out. "She's certainly enjoying herself. I've never seen anyone quite like her."

"No, she's quite rare," Hu Chang said. "I had to take that into consideration in our association. One can't always compare her reactions to what others might feel."

"Is that supposed to make sense?" Gallo asked. "If it is then, I'm missing something."

"It makes sense to me." Hu Chang smiled. "I'll try to make my thought process more simple for you to understand."

The jabs had been gentle, but definitely pointed, and Catherine wasn't having any more. "We're not here to discuss Chen Lu." She turned and went back into the suite. "I want to know how we can get Nardik before he gets us." She dropped down in a chair and tucked one leg beneath her. "Where is he vulnerable, Gallo?"

"Nowhere. He has four bodyguards around him at all times when he's out of an area he regards as secure. He has no problem with delegating mayhem and hiding behind his goons. We'll have to pick a time and place where he chooses to come out of the dark."

"But he came here to Hong Kong."

"Hu Chang was the impetus." His lips tightened. "And you added fuel to the fire. He has an ugly temper. I'd judge Hu Chang was a business decision. You're a different matter entirely."

"You always manage to make yourself an exception," Hu Chang said. "In this case most regrettable."

"Not necessarily," Catherine said. "If I piss him off enough, he might be persuaded to take a wrong step and blunder into the trap. It might be the quickest way."

"No," Gallo said sharply. "That's not the way we're going."

"I agree." Hu Chang leaned against the wall and crossed his arms across his chest. "Don't be in such a hurry, Catherine. We have a little time. We don't need to stake you out as bait for the tiger."

"What do you mean 'a little time'?" Gallo's gaze was fastened on Hu Chang's face. "What aren't you telling us? You dribbled a little information out to Catherine tonight, but it's not nearly enough."

"Indeed? Then I'm sure that Catherine would have asked me to elaborate without your assistance. She's never shy about pinning me down."

"Neither am I," Gallo said. "And I have the advantage of not trusting you any farther than I can throw you. While she regards you as a friend who seems to have the ability to mesmerize her on occasion."

"Mesmerize?" He chuckled. "I regard that as a compliment but a major fallacy. Not with Catherine, Gallo."

"Stop this," Catherine said. "Ask your questions, Gallo."

"Oh, I'm asking. I've been thinking long and hard about what I've learned about you, Hu Chang, and how it fits into what's been happening. The story is that Jack Tan captured you and took you to that island to torture you into giving over the formula. Now you're very clever according to Catherine and Venable. Off the charts. Unless they caught you off guard, I'm surprised they'd be able to get you so easily."

"Easily? I fought like a lion."

"I don't think so. I think you wanted to be taken by Tan."

Hu Chang's eyes were suddenly bright with interest. "Now why would I have wanted to do that?"

"Why? Because you wanted something that Jack Tan had in his possession. My bet is that it had to do with your precious Pondera. Maybe the drug itself? You hid something of value in the woods that night, and we all took it for granted it was something that Jack Tan was trying to squeeze out of you, something that you'd managed to hide from him. Venable assumed it was maybe a formula you'd hidden in a body orifice or something and were desperate to keep from Tan or anyone else."

"Very logical of Venable," Hu Chang said.

"Unless you turn it around and go on

the premise that Tan had something you wanted, and you were willing to risk being taken by him to get your chance at stealing it. Maybe that dose of Pondera you were so desperate to get back?"

"*Very* good. I'm truly impressed. But you're phrasing is wrong. You can't steal your own property, Gallo. And you're not totally correct but very close."

Catherine was staring at him in disbelief. "Hu Chang?"

He shrugged. "I would have told you, Catherine. I was just trying to decide how best to do it. It was a little complicated."

"Since you set Venable up," Gallo said. "You leaked info through one of his informants that not only put you in the position of victim but gave just enough information about the importance and deadliness of your formula. He had two reasons to come and save your ass."

"After all, I had to have an exit plan." Hu Chang nodded. "I knew that it was going to be a bit risky."

"Risky?" Catherine's voice was shaking with anger. "You almost died. You willingly walked into their hands? I could strangle you. *Why,* dammit?"

"I didn't walk. I told you, I fought like a lion. It wouldn't have seemed authentic if I hadn't." He grimaced. "I'd known for several days that I was being stalked by someone, but I was able to elude them. Then Jack Tan grew impatient and contacted me and told me that his employer, Nardik, had the remainder of the drug that I'd given to Ali Gazaran, the prime minister who had rid the world of Ben Salan. But Nardik needed to know how to administer it so that there would be no question of any suspicion falling on his client. The prime minister's wife had told them under torture that I'd said Pondera was very volatile, that I'd made her husband give me every detail of Ben Salan's physical condition before I could guarantee that there would be no interference in the way that the drug worked. It was quite true. It was necessary that I know every detail of the health of the potential victim so that there would be no chance of its failing. The height, health, race, age, and any possible weaknesses due to past illness or accidents. Everything. I had to make sure nothing would keep it from being a valid experiment."

"Experiment," Catherine repeated.

"A trifle cold-blooded for you? But it was an experiment for me. Would you prefer to think of it as the glorious victory of democracy over oppression? It was that also. By all means, choose whichever pleases you."

"It pleases me to know how you managed to manipulate Jack Tan."

"And it pleases me to know why the hell you let a dose of that stuff float around for anyone to pick up," Gallo said harshly.

"Don't be absurd. I hadn't been able to judge the exact amount since this was the first time it had been used outside my lab, so I gave Gazaran an extra dose in case it was needed. But I told him that any excess was to be destroyed immediately after Ben Salan died. He lied to me and told me he had done it."

"You should have known better," Gallo said. "It was too tempting to have that extra insurance in case he ran into another political 'impediment.'"

"I realized I was taking a chance. But I truly believed in Gazaran's integrity. I respected the way he'd turned his country from a dictatorship to a democracy with just a little help from me." He added sadly,

"But in this world, honor toward one's country doesn't necessarily translate to every endeavor. At any rate, I knew I had to get the drug back before it was used in a manner of which I did not approve."

Catherine shook her head. "So you decided to try to trick Jack Tan."

"He seemed to be the logical path. Not too bright. Nardik had told him that Pondera might prove ineffectual depending on the physical condition of the intended victim. Only I could determine whether it would work or not." He paused. "And also that I was the only one who could furnish the additional amount of the drug if I judged the dose would prove too weak. It was clear they realized at least that was the truth. Nardik had probably already tried to have the drug duplicated." He smiled. "No one duplicates a drug that I create. I learned long ago how to prevent that from happening. They were finding it very frustrating that they had to come to me. I had all the answers. I could give them the formula. Or I could possibly give them a safe way to use the drug they already had in their possession."

"So what did they do?"

"First, Tan tried to bribe me for the formula. While I was stringing along negotiations, I was able to pull enough information from him to realize that Nardik already had a target in mind. I had to find a way to identify that target. So I backed away from the deal, and Tan started to use threats."

"So what happened when Tan took you to the island?" Catherine asked. "Other than that they gave you a beating that you probably deserved for being so crazy."

"It was not crazy. It was necessary. I had a chance to either get back that extra dose of Pondera Nardik had stolen or discover the name of the potential victim." He shrugged. "But it went as you guessed. Very painful. Tan started with trying to get the formula. And then, when my endurance proved exceptionally stubborn, decided to postpone that tactic and went on to try to determine if the dose Nardik had in his possession would prove adequate for the current job. That was the direction where I was trying to lead them after I realized I wasn't going to get that dose of Pondera back. There had been the slimmest chance Tan might have the actual dose himself, but I soon found I was out of luck on that score. But Tan had indicated he'd been given a basic profile of Nardik's target while he was trying to bribe me before I let myself be taken. I had to get my hands on that profile. When Tan was questioning me on the island, he took out a dirty leather book in a waterproof sleeve and was firing questions at me. Medical questions concerning a victim's age, possible effect on the victim of past injuries, and so forth." He made a face. "Some profile. It was just Tan's dog-eared leather notebook in which he'd obviously scrawled some notes he'd gotten over the phone from Nardik. Another disappointment.

"I was getting very irate about the punishment I'd taken for so little when the Special Ops team broke in and did what they do best. I managed to grab the book with the victim's supposed profile, then allowed myself to be extracted from the jaws of death by those valiant warriors." He thought about it. "Or at least serious harmful consequences."

"Then why hide it in the woods? Venable wouldn't—"

"Venable is a clever and patriotic man,

but I couldn't have him involved with Pondera. I didn't know what might be in that notebook. Venable would do what was best for the CIA and his government. That would mean that I'd lose control of the drug." He added gently but firmly, "That cannot happen."

"Yes, you've done such a great job of keeping it out of the hands of the bad guys," Gallo said sarcastically.

"That will be rectified." He met Gallo's gaze. "It is my creation. Therefore, it is mine to do with as I choose. I will not have governments or bureaucracies trying to get in my way. Would you not feel as I do?"

Gallo stared at him for a long moment, a dozen emotions flitting over his face. "It's possible. I haven't had the best experiences with government interventions in my life. There are too many ways Big Brother can be manipulated. That doesn't mean I wouldn't try to stop you if you decided to make a deal with Nardik."

"He wouldn't do that, Gallo," Catherine said.

"But you can see as far as Gallo knows, everything is still on the table as far as I'm concerned," Hu Chang said. "He didn't like it that I was not immediately up-front about my dealings with Jack Tan." He said to Gallo, "I truly would have confessed all soon. I was searching for a possible way to remove Catherine from the entanglement." He beamed. "Which would involve substituting risking your life to any danger to her. That would have made me very happy."

Gallo's lips were sudden quirking. "I can see how it would. Too bad you blew it."

For God's sake, Catherine thought, from suspicion and enmity they were beginning to bond in some twisted way. "You did blow it, Hu Chang. I thought we were on the same page."

"Always, Catherine. But you can hardly blame me for wanting to preserve that page." He reached into his inner jacket pocket and drew out a small, gray, leather notebook. "But speaking of pages, would you like to see the profile Jack Tan was so eager to have me approve for execution?" He moved across the room and handed her the tattered and stained book. "In spite of the waterproof sleeve, the binding is a little stained from being in the dampness of the woods. I hid it in the trunk of a tree. But the ink is still clear except for a little

running on page three." He added distaste-
fully, "Though Tan's less-than-clean finger-
prints and scrawl are uglier than any other
damage. As you can see, Gallo, I was prepared to share it with you."

Gallo was ignoring him as he strode
across the room to sit on the arm of Catherine's chair. "Is there a name?"

"No name," Hu Chang said. "That would
have been too much to hope for. I told you,
I was very disappointed in the scantiness
of the information in this profile. However, I
should have realized Nardik wouldn't trust
Jack Tan to any great extent. He'd give
him what he needed to delve for the information he needed, and that would be all. I
had a chance to go through the book earlier in the evening, and there were a few
items of interest. You'll notice at the top of
page one there's a date scribbled."

"July 3," Catherine said. "No year."

"If you were planning an operation on a
certain day, you wouldn't need a year,"
Gallo said. "Unless it was a year other than
this one."

She was going down the page. "'Height
6 foot 3, weight 185 pounds, eyes blue,

hair brown, age 46. Race Caucasian.' This reads like a driver's license."

Gallo nodded. "Date of birth April 3, 1965. But no name, dammit." He flipped to the page Tan's scrawl had labeled Medical Records. "Johns Hopkins, Baltimore, Maryland, Hermann Hospital, Houston, Texas. St. Luke's Hospital, St. Louis, Missouri." He flipped the page again. "Just the names of the hospitals, no records."

"Tan was probably going to be given authority to access those records if I proved cooperative and agreed to go over them with him," Hu Chang said. "But it would have been a death sentence if Nardik had given Jack Tan those records. Then Tan would know who the target was, and I doubt if he would have lasted more than a few days. Nardik wouldn't have trusted him. So it was fortuitous for Tan that he didn't have to tap those records." He added, "Though I'm sure that he's still in serious trouble that he lost this notebook. It may still yield a good deal of what we need if we work at it."

"July 3 doesn't have to be a target date," Catherine said.

"But it might be," Hu Chang said. "We'll

see how it ties into the picture once we put it all together. But first we have to find out to whom these medical records belong. I told Tan I had to have complete records from birth to the present for any assessment of the efficacy of the drug. I believe our best bet is to go for the birth record and start from there."

"So you mean we find out in which hospital he was born?" Catherine asked. "Do we each take a hospital and try to trace him by this date of birth? Then double-check the other hospitals for additional medical procedures performed on patients with the same name through the years?"

"That sounds like the best plan," Gallo said. "I'll take Hermann Hospital, Houston."

"Johns Hopkins," Hu Chang said. "That leaves you with St. Luke's in St. Louis, Catherine." He added, "But this is going to take a long time to access and call hospital administrations, then find out the names of all the baby boys born on that date.

"We do know he was Caucasian. That will help to narrow it down. May I suggest that we go to our rooms and get some sleep, then meet tomorrow at breakfast to discuss results?"

Catherine nodded. "Whatever. But it's afternoon now in St. Louis. I may try to do some checking now anyway."

"That doesn't surprise me." Hu Chan was heading for the door. "It's your choice, of course." He glanced at Gallo as he reached the door. "As I said, I was impressed with you. I should have known Catherine would not have been drawn to anyone who was less than adequate. You may do very well after all."

"I was thinking the same thing about you," Gallo said coolly. "However, with considerable more skepticism. But only time will tell."

Hu Chang smiled and inclined his head. "That is true." The door closed behind him.

She was alone with Gallo. She was suddenly aware of how close he was to her, sitting on the arm of her chair, the warmth his body was emitting, the sensuous feel of the velvet upholstery against her bare foot that was tucked beneath her. The faintest scent of spice and lemon . . .

"You go, too, Gallo," Catherine said. "I'll see you in the morning."

He rose from the arm of her chair. "We could work on these hospitals together."

His brows rose. "Or am I in disgrace for treating your Hu Chang with disrespect?"

"Why? Hu Chang was playing his own games, and they needed to be exposed. He's always difficult, but he had no right to keep anything from us when we're trying to help him." She stared him in the eye. "But toward the end, the two of you were playing a different game and leaving me out. I didn't like that."

"The game was all about you, Catherine," he said quietly.

"A game to keep me safe and out of the action." She didn't bother to try to keep the anger from her voice. "No one does that to me, Gallo. I've earned my respect and independence. Don't try to rob me."

He stared at her a moment, then slowly nodded. "No disrespect. You're right, I got a little carried away when I was confronting Hu Chang."

"You bet you did."

A sudden smile lit his face. "But I shouldn't have to face this alone. Why don't I go get Hu Chang and let you go after him, too?"

That smile was brilliant and full of warmth, and she could feel that familiar melting. No, she did not want to be drawn by that charisma. Hold on to the annoyance that had kept it at bay. "Hu Chang always knows when I'm annoyed with him. He doesn't need words. I'll see you at breakfast, Gallo."

He gazed at her for a moment, then turned and headed for the door. "I won't push it, Catherine. It's tempting, but it's not the time." He smiled again as he opened the door. "I'm in your bad books. I have to prove that I have the utmost respect for your freedom of choice."

She stared at the door after it had closed behind him. Damn him, he had known exactly how she had felt in that moment. She could still feel the flush of readiness that had begun to ripple through her. It was evident she couldn't be in the same room with him without that response.

Well, he isn't here now. Forget him. Get some air, then get to work.

She got to her feet and went out on the balcony. She drew a deep breath of the intoxicating scents drifting from the flowers in the planting beds below. She looked up at the night sky, at the glitter blanket of stars. So much had happened tonight, so many words spoken, so many memories of the past, so many facts about that past that she'd taken for granted that had been questioned. By Hu Chang. By Gallo.

By herself.

Laughter . . .

She looked down at the fountain a short distance away.

Chen Lu again, joyous and full of life.

For an instant she felt a twinge of envy of the woman who seemed to live each day as if it were her last. Catherine had always tried to do that, but Chen Lu seemed to have perfected the skill.

Foolish. Catherine was not Chen Lu, and if she lived in this beautiful place, she would be bored within a week. She had to go her own path.

And now her own path was waiting for her inside and away from bright stars, gorgeous flowers, and sparkling fountains.

She went back into the suite to start making her phone calls.

Smoke . . .

Catherine lifted her head from her pillow as she came wide-awake and alert.

Yes, smoke.

She swung her legs to the floor and jumped out of bed. She could see the sky was now a gray haze outside the balcony doors she'd closed when she went to bed a few hours ago.

Her phone rang.

"Fire," Gallo said. "I don't think it's in the palace yet. Stay where you are. I'm coming to get you."

"No, go get Hu Chang and see if he's all right. He's in the south wing. He'll be the target. This can't be an accident. I'll see you downstairs in the foyer." She hung up and started throwing on her clothes.

The smoke was getting heavier, and she ran to get a wet washcloth to cover her mouth and nose in case she had problems on the way down that grand staircase.

Explosion!

Somewhere in the garden.

God, Chen Lu and Rory had been in that garden.

She started for the French doors, then stopped. It was a risk to go out on the balcony. She could be a target. But it was more of a risk to go down to the garden and verify if she could see them than do it from up here. Dammit, there wasn't any question that she wouldn't do that.

Take the risk.

She threw open the balcony door.

No shots. The smoke poured into the suite. She darted to the left and pressed against the wall.

Dear God.

Chen Lu's magnificent floral beds were on fire. Acres and acres of blossoms being devoured by flames. Through the heavy fog of smoke she could see several men in black leather jackets torching the garden.

The fountain. Chen Lu and Rory Benedict had been beside the fountain.

Her gaze strained through the stinging smoke to see if they were still there.

A swath of violet silk crumpled on the ground beside the fountain. Chen Lu? The man lying beside her must be Rory.

A powerfully built man stood over them. Black leather jacket, thick gray hair. He had a knife in his hand.

"For God's sake, get off that balcony." Gallo was running into the room behind her. "All hell's breaking loose. On my way up here I took down a man who had blown the door from the veranda to the foyer. I couldn't raise either of the two guards at the dock entrance."

She barely heard him. She was staring

down at the man standing over Chen Lu and Rory. He must have heard Gallo for he had raised his head and was looking up at her on the balcony.

Nardik. He was smiling.

Then he was reaching down and jerking one of the figures at his feet upright by the hair of the head. Chen Lu?

No, the hair was red and curly. It was Rory.

Catherine knew what he going to do.

"No! Oh, my God. *Shoot* him, Gallo."

Gallo was already aiming his gun.

Too late.

Nardik looked up at her and his smile deepened as his knife sliced viciously across Rory's throat.

Blood spurted.

Gallo's bullet splintered the marble of the fountain next to him as Nardik disappeared into the smoke.

Gallo was muttering a curse as he jerked her back into the suite. "We've got to get out of here. I called the shore police, but they may not get here in time."

"Not in time for Rory." She felt sick as she remembered Nardik's knife tearing through Rory's throat. "Maybe not for Chen

Lu." She was stuffing the book with the victim profile into her duffel. Clear your head, she told herself. She couldn't help Rory now, and Nardik had abandoned Chen Lu and disappeared into the smoke. She might still be alive. "That was Nardik, wasn't it?" she asked jerkily. "I've only seen photos, but I recognized him." She grabbed her duffel and headed for the door. "And he recognized me. He wanted to punish me. I smashed a wineglass, and he cut a throat. Son of a bitch."

"It's not your fault. Do you believe he wouldn't have done it anyway? You know damn well he would have." Gallo carefully opened the door, glanced outside, then motioned her to come. "He just had the opportunity to make it count for more, and he took it."

"Where's Hu Chang? I told you to go get Hu Chang."

"And I decided to do exactly what I'd intended to do. I called Hu Chang and made sure he knew what was happening. He was already with Chen Lu's security guards and trying to determine what was happening. I told him we'd meet him at the boats and get you out of here."

"You're crazy if you think I'd leave without knowing if—"

A bullet exploded in the wall next to her.

"Shit." She pulled Gallo down behind the
column at the top of the staircase. "They're
in the house. We may have to use the bal-
conies."

Another bullet.

One gunman near the chest beside the
veranda door. She didn't think there was
more than that.

"By the door." She took out her gun. "I'll
take my shot, then run to the next column.
If he shows, take him out."

"The hell you will," Gallo muttered.

She was already aiming. She might be
lucky . . .

No luck. She rose to her feet and, keeping low, streaked toward the nearest column.

Two shots, almost simultaneous.

The second hit the column before she
dove behind it.

The first?

"Come on, I got him," Gallo said roughly.
"Unless you want to dodge a few more
bullets."

"Stop complaining. It was the fastest

way." Catherine glanced at the veranda door as she ran down the stairs. The man in the black leather jacket was lying against it, his head half blown off his body. "What's the best route out of this place?"

"Rory showed me a tunnel passage below the palace that leads to the next house about a mile along the shore."

Rory.

A vision of him came back to her, being held upright by Nardik while the bastard cut his throat.

"We'll get him." Gallo's gaze was on her face as he pulled her toward the silk wall hanging across the foyer. "I liked Rory. We'll get Nardik, Catherine. It's only a—" He broke off and his head tilted as he listened. "I believe the cavalry has arrived. We may not have to use that passage."

She, too, was hearing the wailing of the sirens of the shore patrol as they sped over the water. They were very close. "Then if we've got them on the run, let's go after Nardik." She headed for the veranda door. "I want that bastard." She stopped. "Wait. Chen Lu. We have to make sure that she's okay."

She opened the door and smoke poured into the foyer.

The gardens were still blazing, and it was hard to see through the dense haze. If there were any of Nardik's men in the garden she couldn't see them. They were probably in the palace or had fled when they heard the sirens.

But that smoke was now as dangerous as Nardik's scumbags.

"The fountain . . ."

But Gallo was already running across the veranda and down the steps to the garden.

She was right behind him.

She started coughing and covered her mouth with the wet washcloth she had grabbed from her bathroom in the suite.

The white fountain loomed out of the haze.

Violet silk . . . and blood.

"I think she's alive." Gallo was kneeling beside Chen Lu, his fingers on the pulse in her throat. "Dammit, I can't feel a pulse . . ."

"Let me see her. That may not mean anything." Hu Chang had suddenly appeared out of the fog of smoke. He fell to his knees. "She's very strong. She has a chance. The pulse can be elusive. There are ninety-seven pulse points . . ." He took her wrist and his fingers probed delicately. "I feel one. Let's get her out of this smoke."

"Rory . . ." Chen Lu's eyes were open and fixed on Hu Chang's face. "Help Rory . . . Hu Chang. Can you . . . save him?"

Hu Chang shook his head as he glanced at Rory's body a few yards away. "Too late."

"No, you can do it. Save . . . him."

"I can't save him. There's no way, Chen Lu," he said gently. "It's too late."

"I'll take her." Gallo gathered Chen Lu up in his arms. "I don't think it's only the smoke. There's blood . . ."

Catherine could see the blood soaking the side of the violet silk of the caftan as she hurried after Gallo into the palace. "It's a knife wound," she said to Hu Chang, who was beside her. "Nardik had a knife. He and his men must have caught Rory and Chen Lu by surprise. They were both lying on the ground when I first caught sight of them from the balcony." Her lips tightened. "But Nardik wanted me to know that he'd completed the job on Rory. He cut his throat." The sirens were still wailing and the burning garden appeared deserted. "They were all dressed in those black leather jackets. What's happening, Hu Chang?"

"Chen Lu carries a lot of influence in the city. Nardik didn't want to stir up the authorities, so he decided to misdirect. Those jackets have the triad symbol of the Mao Sen syndicate. That's the only one that would be powerful enough to risk a raid on the Golden Palace."

Triads. It was logical to choose the crime family on which to hang the blame. Very smart. Her life seemed to be eternally plagued by those bastards.

They were in the palace now, and Gallo was laying Chen Lu carefully down on the yellow brocade couch. Catherine hurried forward to put a throw beneath her to keep the blood from staining it.

"That is . . . good." Chen Lu opened her eyes. "My beautiful couch . . . Men don't . . . understand." Her eyes filled with tears. "Rory understood. He helped me pick out . . . this fabric. He said it was fitting that it be the color of the sun."

"It doesn't matter. It was a stupid thing to do. I just acted instinctively. Furniture can be replaced." Catherine turned to Hu Chang. "What do you need? How can I help?"

Hu Chang was bending over Chen Lu and tearing away the bloodstained material away from the wound. "The small packet in my bag over there. Then leave me alone with her."

"The police should be here any minute," Gallo said. "Shall I tell them to get a doctor?"

"He's a doctor of Chinese medicine," Catherine said impatiently. "I know some people equate that with some kind of primitive voodoo but it works. No one can help her more." She crossed the room, retrieved the packet from Hu Chang's bag, and brought it to him. She watched Hu Chang for a moment as he examined the wound. "Go away, Gallo. He doesn't want interference."

"You, too, Catherine," Hu Chang said.

She looked at him in surprise.

He smiled slightly. "The wound is not serious. I do not need help. Chen Lu and I are better off alone in this. She would prefer it."

"You're sure?"

He nodded. "You and Gallo go meet the

police and file the report for her. Then round up the servants and security and make sure no one is hurt other than the three men who were killed during the first attack. I will take care of Chen Lu." He glanced at Gallo. "And if I decide my primitive skills are not enough, I will send her to your civilized hospital in the city. Agreed?"

He shrugged. "Catherine seems to think you can do the job. I've seen some fairly impressive medical skills among tribes in Africa. I suppose you can't do any worse."

He flinched. "I'm a cut above those tribes I believe. Get him out of here before I decide to operate on him, Catherine."

Catherine gave a last glance at Chen Lu before she turned to the door. "Call me if you need me. Come on, Gallo. You must have been introduced to those security men who worked under Rory. You'd have more authority with them in trying to reorganize a cohesive force."

"Not much. Rory had a lieutenant. I didn't pay much attention to him because I thought I'd be working with Rory." He frowned, trying to remember. "I think his name was Jock Munroe. We may be able to work through him. You go find the police captain and deal with him while I go look for Munroe."

She nodded. "I'll try to bring Nardik into this, but I don't think it will do any good. Even Chen Lu's people will testify that the people who attacked the palace were triad."

They were on the veranda again and being assaulted by the sharp odor of smoke. The beds were still blazing, but high arcs of water were being driven from the fireboats on the bay, and the flames were gradually being put out. The north corner of the curled roof of the palace had caught fire and was now wet and charred. "I guess Chen Lu was lucky that no more of the palace was burned. But those beautiful gardens . . ." She straightened her shoulders and she started toward the group of vinyl-coated policemen streaming toward the palace from the boats at the dock. "But you can replace plants just as you can furniture. I'll see you later, Gallo."

CHAPTER

14

"We almost made it. We came close." Jack Tan took a step closer to Nardik, where he was standing at the front of the speedboat that was tearing across the water away from the Golden Palace. "We'd have done it if we'd had a little more time."

" 'If,' " Nardik said through his teeth. " 'Almost.' 'Close.' I don't use those words. Those are the words of a failure."

"It was your plan. It's not my fault." Tan's tone was surly. "Not this time." Then he added quickly, as he saw Nardik's expression, "It was no one's fault. Gallo was too good. I sent my best man upstairs to get the woman for you. And I went after Hu Chang myself just as you ordered. The police came too damn soon."

Nardik couldn't give him an argument. He hadn't expected a response that quick, either. He looked back at the burning gardens and felt a rush of pleasure. He might not have accomplished his purpose, but the damage he had done was very satisfactory. He had made his mark on the place where Hu Chang had thought he was safe. Nardik had shown him that nowhere was safe as long as he was the enemy.

And he had shown the bitch how a real man avenged a slight like the one she'd given him. He looked down at his right hand and saw a bit of dried blood on the knuckles. If he'd had the time, he would have sliced the throat of the white-haired woman, too. It wasn't often that he permitted himself the personal satisfaction of indulging in bloodlust.

"Are we going back another night?" Tan's gaze was following Nardik's to the burning gardens. "It will be harder now that there's no surprise, but we—"

"Of course we're not going back. That

would be lunacy. This raid was worth a shot, but you don't keep hammering. You attack from a different angle. Or you wait until they attack and scoop them up."

Tan frowned. "Wait?"

"You let Hu Chang steal your notebook with the information I gave you to use as reference for your questioning. Do you think they're not going to try to figure out the target?"

"I had no name in those notes."

"Because I knew I'd be a fool to trust you."

Tan was silent. "So what happens now?"

"They try to stop me." His lips tightened. "And I step in and get what I want, then crush them. As you should have done for me." They were approaching the *Dragon King,* and he could see Fowler waiting on the deck, his expression eager. He was going to be disappointed. Fowler had been looking forward to Nardik's bringing back Catherine Ling for him to toy with.

But why disappoint him, he thought suddenly. Why not furnish him with a substitute? The scenario was going to change and move out of Hong Kong since he had to deal with that damn Fourth of July deadline. This was June 29, and his time was running out. He had to position himself to strike at the target. That meant Nardik no longer needed Jack Tan and all his bumbling, which had so infuriated him.

He turned to Tan as the speedboat came alongside the *Dragon King.* "Come on board, and we'll discuss how we're going to proceed with the next step. You and Fowler get along, don't you? He's transmitted enough of my orders to you." He smiled. "I'm certain the three of us will come up with something very interesting tonight."

"You look like a chimney sweep," Hu Chang said, as Catherine came back into the study three hours later.

And she felt as charred and dirty as she looked, she thought tiredly. Even her hair was spiked with soot. "You evidently had time to wash your face and hands. I did not."

"I'm a physician. Cleanliness is necessary."

"Where's Chen Lu?"

"I had her servants carry her up to her suite after I finished treating her. She's doing well." He paused. "She kept asking me to let her go to Rory. They were very close."

"The police forensic team took his body back to their medical department with the rest of the dead. I made a halfhearted attempt at trying to lead them in Nardik's direction. I even told them we'd witnessed Nardik killing Rory. They were very polite, said they'd certainly look into a possible connection, but that with all that fire and smoke, mistakes could be made. They were obviously focused on the triad and brushed me off. They have big-time trouble with the triads and wanted to have their chance at them." She added, "Gallo was impressed at how quickly the police and fire department responded. He said they couldn't have been more cooperative."

"Chen Lu makes sure that she's on the right side of all local enforcement. She and Rory had a list of birthdays and anniversaries of all the police officers and sent out very nice gifts throughout the year. Appropriate but not extravagant. No hint of bribery."

"I'll tell Gallo," she said ruefully. "Actually,

he did virtually the same thing with the sheriff's department at his place in Wisconsin, so he should be able to relate." She was silent a moment. "If the police hadn't gotten here so quickly, Nardik would have been able to do a hell of a lot more damage. He might have been able to take us down if he hadn't had to cut and run. I'm sure he was royally pissed."

"He did damage enough."

"I'm not saying that he didn't. Besides the deaths and injuries, the gardens look like a wasteland. I'm just saying it could have be worse." She added, "Gallo did a terrific job organizing Chen Lu's security in this short time. They were all pretty upset about Rory."

"Where is he now?"

She shrugged. "He was trying to make sure that everything is safe and the place is on its way to recovery for Chen Lu. He said we can't stay here any longer." She made a face. "Even though chances they'd attack here again would be slim to none since we'd be on the alert. Still, it would be like the mouse having to hole up and wait for the cat outside to find a way to pounce."

"And we have a good deal to do that

doesn't include hiding in the mouse hole," he said. "Had you finished going over those medical birth records at St. Luke's before this uproar?"

She nodded. "Four males were born on that date at St. Luke's. Charles Keller, Montgomery Dexter, Douglas Warnold, and Juan Martinez. Keller and Warnold are Caucasian, Dexter is black, Martinez is Hispanic. So Keller and Warnold are our only candidates from St. Luke's. You had Johns Hopkins Hospital in Baltimore, didn't you?"

"Yes, only three male, Caucasians. James Kilpatrick, Nathan Wolf, and Simon Cassidy." He smiled. "So now we wait for Gallo's input, then we start combing the hospitals for other procedures performed on one of these boys so that we can narrow down the list."

She nodded. "I'll go upstairs and shower and go check on Chen Lu." She turned toward the door. "And I'll call Gallo and tell him that we'll be ready to go when he's ready to get us out of here. He mentioned a tunnel . . ."

"Ah, yes, I remember Rory's telling me about that tunnel." Hu Chang got to his feet. "I believe I'll go do a little exploring there so that we won't get an unpleasant surprise."

Catherine watched him go down the hall as she started up the stairs. She could seldom read Hu Chang's expressions when he didn't want her to do it, but she thought that she caught a hint of sadness. And why not? He and Chen Lu were undoubtedly close, and he had brought this chaos down upon her. No, the guilt had not been his alone. She and Gallo had accepted the security the Golden Palace offered. She had a sudden memory of Chen Lu last night at the dinner table, aglow with life and joy. She had been a little envious of that ability to pull every drop of pleasure from each moment. Had they managed to destroy that wonderful *joie de vivre*?

She was not looking forward to facing Chen Lu again.

Chen Lu was not in her suite when Catherine knocked on her door two hours later. There was only a very upset and tearful Chinese maid, who told her that Chen Lu had gone downstairs to see the Master Hu

Chang and refused to let her accompany her.

Fever? Disorientation?

"You should have called someone," she said curtly as she turned, ran down the hall, and took the stairs two at a time.

"Slow. Do not break any bones," Hu Chang called from the drawing room, as Catherine reached the bottom of the stairs. "Chen Lu was foolish, but did not pay for it. Nor should you."

Chen Lu was sitting on the chaise, and she was dressed in a sleek black dress instead of the caftan in which Catherine had become accustomed to seeing her. She appeared pale, smaller than usual, but very elegant.

"Shouldn't you be in bed?" Catherine asked.

"Probably." Chen Lu smiled with an effort. "But I have things to do, and I can't be bothered with that kind of thing. I had to come down and see my friend, Hu Chang."

"Is there anything that we can do for you?" She added, "I can't tell you how sorry I am about Rory, and your beautiful gardens and . . ." She made a helpless movement with her hand. "And everything, Chen Lu. If I'd known . . ."

"But we never know for certain, do we?" she asked unevenly. "I loved my Rory. He was an old and good friend. But he knew that life has its risks and embraced it. We were alike in that." She moistened her lips. "It was a beautiful night, and we were both so happy. It's not so bad to have life end on a note that sweet." She shook her head. "I won't weep for him. God will be glad to take in a bold, funny lad like Rory." She turned to Hu Chang. "But I have to go to the police and make arrangements to take Rory home to Dublin. He must be with his own folk, not among foreigners in a strange land. No matter how beautiful that land is."

"It can wait, Chen Lu," he said gently.

"No, it can't. I cannot bear to think of him in that . . . cold place with people who don't care about him. I will go and do it now." She drew a deep breath. "But I'm not . . . strong. You must give me something to make sure that I can do this, Hu Chang."

"Chen Lu, you've been wounded," Catherine said. "You'd probably collapse before you—"

"I won't collapse." Her gaze never left Hu Chang's. "I'll be strong enough, won't I? You'll make sure I am."

He held her gaze for a long moment. "You'll be strong enough," he said quietly. He went to the bar across the room and poured her a glass of wine. Then he took a tiny vial from his jacket pocket and poured it into the wine. "I'm diluting it. It will last you for five days, no more. Then you must take to your bed and heal."

"Hu Chang," Catherine said uncertainly.

"Don't interfere, Catherine. Chen Lu and I both know what we're doing." He gave the wineglass to Chen Lu. "And if you do not take to your bed at that time, our association is over. There must always be honor between us."

She nodded. "I'm not a fool. I know how valuable our 'association' is to me." She lifted the glass and drained it. She made a face. "Foul, Hu Chang. Why must everything you create taste this terrible?"

"Not everything. Some have no taste at all. But I have to make an effort to do that. I prefer to make sure that you have a solid impact to remind you what you're taking. Or perhaps it's just my sadistic personality."

He took her glass and returned it to the bar. "I'll make your reservations and arrangements for transporting your Rory while you do the paperwork at the police station. You'll take your maid with you into the city, and she'll accompany you to Ireland. You'll treat her with kindness and not overrule her when she tries to make you rest. Is that clear, Chen Lu?"

"What good is it to be strong if I have to listen to other people?" She waved a hand. "Oh, very well. I'll do what you wish." She frowned. "But I don't feel very different. Are you sure it worked?"

"Diluted," he repeated with a faint smile. "And would you feel up to arguing with me if you weren't stronger?"

She thought about it. "No, I suppose not. But I expected something . . . more."

"You always do. That's why you're the unique individual we all know and love." He turned to Catherine. "Come with me. We'll leave her alone to rest for a few moments. If you'll run up to her suite and tell her maid to pack a bag for her mistress and herself, I'll make those arrangements that I mentioned."

"I don't want to be alone," Chen Lu said. "I *hate* being alone."

"You're feeling Rory's loss," Hu Chang said. "I warned you."

"Shut up. I don't want to hear I-told-you-so." She closed her eyes and rested her head on the back of her chair. "I'll be fine. My heart will hurt, but I'll be fine. Go do what you have to do."

"We will." He whisked Catherine from the room. "In spite of what she said, she's best alone now. You have to become accustomed to loss before you accept it."

"You seem to know a lot about her," she said slowly.

He took his phone from his pocket. "But you knew that before. You've been studying us since we set foot in her lovely palace. But now you want to ask questions."

"A few. What was in that vial that you put in her wine?"

"What do you think?"

"It wasn't orange like the medicine you gave Carmody at your shop when he was wounded. It was almost clear. Does it do the same thing?"

"Approximately. But you know I'm constantly changing formulas and making adjustments."

"It was to give her a temporary rush of strength, not heal her."

"Observant as usual. It would heal her if given the opportunity, but she wanted to take another option."

"It's dangerous?"

"Yes, it's always dangerous to push the boundaries. But sometimes it's worth the risk. Rory was her friend, and she wouldn't be able to bear lying in bed and recovering at this time." He added gravely, "She'll be fine, Catherine. As long as she obeys me, there won't be a problem."

She shook her head. "Hu Chang, sometimes those drugs and potions of yours give me a major headache."

His lips quirked. "A purely unexpected side effect on my part, I assure you."

"Nothing is totally unexpected where you're concerned." She started up the staircase. "I'll get Chen Lu's maid on the move. Though I think Chen Lu intimidates her. It's a good thing you warned Chen Lu to let herself be taken care of."

"Call Gallo and tell him as soon as we get Chen Lu off to the city, we'll be leaving."

"That's what he suggested anyway." She looked down at him and ruefully. "Perhaps we should have chosen the tattoo parlor. This Golden Palace doesn't seem to have worked out well for any of us. Where do we go now?"

He was dialing his phone, and said absently, "Wherever those medical records take us . . ."

"She looks pretty good." Gallo had come up behind Catherine as she stood on the dock watching Chen Lu get into the speedboat with her maid. "I thought she'd be in bed for a couple weeks even if she came out of it okay."

"She and Hu Chang made a deal."

"Is that anything like a deal with the devil?"

"You'll have to ask Chen Lu. I don't believe she would think so." She went to the speedboat, and said gravely to Chen Lu, "I hope everything goes well with you. If there's anything I can do, call me."

"The only thing you can do is take care

of Hu Chang," she said. "Nothing must happen to him."

Catherine nodded. "We've been taking care of each other for a long time. I can't see that changing."

"Good-bye, Chen Lu." Gallo was standing beside the speedboat. "I think I've set everything up so that the palace will look almost the same the next time you see it. The gardens will take longer."

She smiled faintly. "It will give me the opportunity to start again with them. New starts are important." She added, "And I haven't forgotten about my ambition to be the most exciting cougar in all of Hong Kong. I rely on you for inspiration."

He nodded and stepped back. "You don't need inspiration. You just need an audience."

She suddenly chuckled. "That may be true."

The next moment, the speedboat tore away from the dock in a bright spray of water.

"What kind of deal?" Gallo asked thoughtfully, his gaze on the receding speedboat. "Venable told me about the medicine that

Hu Chang used on himself when he was wounded. He said it saved his life."

"She wasn't that bad. She just needed a little something to strengthen her." She changed the subject. "Hu Chang has made reservations to go back to the U.S. He said that since all three of those hospitals were in the U.S., the target is probably also in the U.S."

He nodded, his gaze still on Chen Lu's speedboat. "That would be my guess. Where is he?"

"He's meeting us at the tunnel you mentioned as our best exit. Did you get a chance to check out the birth records at Hermann Hospital in Houston?"

He nodded again. "Five male births on that date. But two were black, one Hispanic, and only two Caucasian. Harry Delwin and William Andrews."

"Good. Now that we have all the possibilities, we can check out all the hospitals and see if any of the children born that day also had procedures at the two other hospitals in the succeeding years. We have to zero in on a name." She turned and headed for the dock. "We can do that on the plane to the U.S. as long as we make sure the plane has satellite phones on board. I know Qantas does and maybe Cathay Pacific. I usually don't carry one unless I think it's necessary. And you usually aren't permitted personal satellite phones on commercial flights. Do you have one?"

He shook his head. "But I'm sure that Hu Chang does, and he could probably finagle any airline into letting him use it," he said mockingly. "Doesn't he supply all your needs?"

"Not in the technical world. He'd just give me some philosophical jargon about why it's not necessary." She glanced at him. "That remark of yours sounded a little sarcastic. I was hoping you were getting beyond that."

He was silent a moment. "I'm not beyond it, but I'm beginning to accept that he can be trusted in certain circumstances. But I'm not certain what the hell those circumstances are yet. And I don't think you know exactly what's going on with him, either. With you, it has to be sheer blind trust."

Close. It was true that she didn't understand everything about Hu Chang. She might never know. But over the years, she had learned some things to which she could cling, and the rest she'd rather accept than do without him. "We've been together for quite a few years and he's never hurt me and everything he's done has always been for my good." She grimaced. "He can annoy me, frustrate me, and completely bewilder me, but I've never once wished he'd never come into my life."

He didn't speak until they reached the tunnel and saw Hu Chang standing waiting for them some distance away. "That's a high recommendation for any man. It's no wonder I'm suffering a tinge of envy. I'm wondering if someday you might say that about me."

"Why should I?" She smiled at Hu Chang as they approached. "You've made it clear that's not what you want from me."

"I did, didn't I?" His eyes were glittering with sudden recklessness. "I've always been greedy. I want it all. But there are priorities and urgencies. I'll take what I can get and worry about the rest later." He added softly, "You're tensing. Yes, we're right back where we were. What did you expect? No philosophic jargon from me. What you see is what you get. What *we* get. And it has to be soon. It would have been nice for us to come together in a beautiful garden with glowing candles and the pretty sound of a fountain, wouldn't it? But that's not going to happen. All that's left of that picture is a bunch of charred cinders. We've lost that chance. It's my fault. I should have pushed harder. But I won't make that mistake again."

"Push?" She could feel the flush heat her body, but she wasn't sure if it was resentment or arousal. "Try pushing me, Gallo."

"Oh, I intend to do that. In every possible way and position. Fast. Slow. Shallow. Deep. Push. Push. Push. And I'll let you decide which you like best."

It was arousal, damn him.

And she could see Hu Chang's gaze narrowed on her face. She was usually transparent as glass to him. He was still too far away to hear Gallo's words, but he probably knew exactly what Gallo was doing to her.

And would continue to do unless she stopped him. She increased her pace and was beside Hu Chang in seconds. "Chen Lu got off several minutes ago. We're ready."

He glanced at Gallo, then looked back at Catherine. "Oh, yes." He smiled as he turned and started down the tunnel. "I believe you're more than ready."

Their Cathay Pacific flight took off out of Hong Kong three hours later en route to San Francisco.

The first-class section was almost deserted, and they had the first five rows to themselves. Catherine made certain her seat was next to Hu Chang's, and Gallo's was across the aisle. She pulled out the leather notebook as soon as the flight was airborne. "Charles Keller, Douglas Warnold from St. Luke's in St. Louis. Harry Delwin and William Andrews from Hermann Hospital in Houston. Nathan Wolf, Simon Cassidy, James Kilpatrick born in Johns Hopkins in Baltimore. The rest is going to be a lot more difficult to zero in on one name out of these possibles. We'll have to persuade the clerks at the hospitals to scan decades of medical records to try to tie them to one of those babies born in 1965."

"Venable?" Gallo said. "We could turn his agents loose on those hospitals and see what they come up with."

"We might resort to using him, but we've got twenty or more hours on this flight. We can see what we can do. It would drive me crazy just sitting here and doing nothing. I'd rather get to work and have a chance of making a breakthrough." She took the St. Luke's Hospital information she'd retrieved as well as the other names. "The first one who strikes pay dirt with a medical procedure on one of these boys at one of those other hospitals in the succeeding years can alert the others. Then we can all narrow down the search to that one name and rule out the other two. But we've got to check thoroughly to eliminate coincidence."

"Very efficient, Catherine." Hu Chang got out his own notebook. "But it may take more than any eighteen hours to plow through those records. First, you've got to have cooperation, then the clerk who's doing the work has to have the time to process it. It's going to be very difficult to accomplish that on the phone. We'd have a much better chance face-to-face."

"Be persuasive," Catherine said. "Lord knows you shouldn't have a problem, Hu Chang. I've heard people swear you're hypnotic. You can almost charm birds off the trees."

"You've got that right," Gallo said dryly.

"I don't recall either charming or hypnotizing you, Gallo," Hu Chang murmured. "Of course, I never made the attempt. But either method generally requires face-to-face contact."

"Then wire bribes into their bank accounts," Catherine said.

"Well, that's certainly persuasive," Gallo said as he started to dial the phone. "I like the way you think, Catherine."

She barely heard him as she gazed down at the names on the list. Which one are you?

Harry Delwin. William Andrews. Charles Keller. Douglas Warnold. Nathan Wolf. Simon Cassidy. James Kilpatrick.

What's going to happen to you on July 3?

And why are you a target?

"William Andrews!"

Eight hours later, Catherine sat upright in her chair as she hung up the phone. "You get the prize, Gallo. It's the boy born at Hermann Hospital in Houston. Twenty-one years later, William Andrews had a football injury to his spinal cord at the University of Missouri and was taken to St. Luke's in St. Louis for an operation and therapy."

"Are you sure that it's the same Andrews that was born in Houston?" Gallo asked.

"No, that's what we've got to find out. It's a pretty common name." But her excitement was growing with every passing second. "But St. Luke's accessed his medical records from Hermann Hospital in Houston before they performed the surgery. They also requested records from his private physician, Dr. Gloria Stovez who has a practice in Sugarland, Texas. I'm trying to get background info now on this Andrews from Venable. I couldn't get through to him before and had to leave a message. Did either of you find anything on any of the other names on our list?"

"Zero," Gallo said. "I'll change course and try to find records of Andrews at Johns Hopkins."

Hu Chang nodded. "That appears to be the reasonable course to follow."

Two hours later, Gallo hung up from Johns Hopkins Hospital. "William Andrews suffered a broken ankle on a hiking trip through the Blue Ridge Mountains four years ago. And he recently had a case of food poisoning that required emergency treatment."

"Food poisoning," Hu Chang repeated. "Interesting."

"Poisoning always interests you," Catherine said. "It could have been accidental."

"Or it could have been a clumsy attempt that convinced someone that professionalism was required." Hu Chang looked down at his notes. "So if William Andrews is the target then he was born in Houston, Texas, moved to Columbia, Missouri, to go to college. But he appears to have spent his last years near Washington. I believe it's time we have Venable tell us who and what Andrews is and why someone is willing to spend a fortune to get rid of him."

"I told you, I left him a message to have him work on it," Catherine said. "Check the personal and credit information patients have to fill out, Gallo. That should tell us something."

"And up the ante in the bribe department," he said wryly. "That's very sensitive info in this world of stolen IDs. It's probably at least a misdemeanor." He waved his hand as she opened her lips. "I know, we need it. I'll get it."

And Gallo did get it after another two hours of probing. "William Andrews is a self-made businessman. Computers. Excellent credit rating. No criminal record. Billionaire. He has no children and recently lost his wife after a long illness. That's all I could find out from the hospital records. It's over to you now, Catherine."

Bits and pieces. But they were building a picture of the man.

Picture.

"We need a photo. See if you can have one sent to us."

"Talk to Venable," Gallo said. "It will be easier for him."

She shouldn't be so impatient. Venable would be getting back to her soon on William Andrews. They had done all they could under the circumstances. "I'll get another e-mail off to him."

After she finished, she leaned back and closed her eyes. William Andrews. Billionaire. What else? Why does someone want to kill you and bury the crime so deep no one will ever find out why or how? "Why, Hu Chang? You've dealt with people who kill most of your life. This is so cold-blooded," she whispered, not opening her eyes. "Because he's rich? Inheritance?"

"Perhaps. Or maybe power. Money often translates to power. We'll have to see." His fingers gently touched her hand, then were gone. "Let it go for now. It will be with you soon enough."

Let it go . . .

Venable phoned her when the plane was an hour outside San Francisco.

"I just got your message," he said curtly. "For God's sake, William Andrews?"

She put the phone on speaker so that Hu Chang and Gallo could hear him. "You sound as if you know him."

"Of course I know him. Or about him. I was wondering why the hell you don't. It is William Scott Andrews you're talking about?"

"William Andrews. Some kind of computer mogul. I don't know anything about—" Then it hit home to her. "You think it's *that* Andrews?"

"Holy shit," Gallo said. "I've heard about him. Though I've been too busy to pay much attention, and I've never heard him referred to as anything but William Scott Andrews. He's some kind of politician."

"He added his stepfather's name of Scott to honor him after he died five years ago. He requested the media use that name as well when referring to him," Venable said. "And you're right, some people call him a politician. Any way you look at him, he's big stuff. What do you want to know about him?"

Catherine was trying to remember what she did know about William Scott Andrews. She usually ignored politicians, but even she had been vaguely aware of the ground swell forming around Andrews. "Everything."

"Let me get this straight. You believe he's Nardik's target?"

"I think there's a good chance."

Venable cursed low and vehemently. "And you said there wouldn't be any way of detecting the means if he was murdered?"

"That's what Hu Chang tells me." Venable had lost his cool, and that didn't happen often. "Tell me about this William Scott Andrews. Is he crooked?"

"No," he said shortly. "What have you found out?"

"Not much. He's a billionaire, a self-made businessman who is into computers. He was born in Houston, Texas, went to college in Missouri, where he played football and suffered a spinal injury. Has no children and lost his wife a few years ago after a long illness. That's it. What can you add to it?"

"He has a good chance of being the next president of the United States."

"What?"

"No, let me correct myself. He's a shoo-in if he keeps on the present track. He's running against Howard Wallace, and Wallace's numbers tanked as soon as William Scott Andrews announced he was running."

"Wait a minute. So he's a political phenomenon?"

"No, he's a patriot. He's already stated that he wants only one term, then he'll step down. He said he'll need that much time to put the country back on the right course."

"Patriot?" Gallo asked cynically. "Maybe until he gets to Washington."

"Well, he's managed to convince the Republicans, independents, and a respectable number of the Democrats. The country is scared. Too many wars, too much oil blackmail, too many bureaucracies sucking the life from the economy. According to the polls, the majority of Americans see us losing our grip and becoming another Greece or Portugal. They want a Superman to save them."

"And this Andrews is a Superman? I may have been out of the country for a long time, but surely I would have heard something more about him if he was a superhero."

"He's only stepped up to the plate in the last six months. And since when have you been interested in politics?"

He was right; she served the U.S. in the CIA, but the only time the government had any influence on her was when she became angry when Congress was meddling in what the Company was trying to do.

Gallo was looking at her and nodding. "If the man only stepped onto the political scene in the last six months, he must have launched himself like a comet."

"A supernova," Venable said. "He went

back to traditional values and the Constitution, refused to discuss social issues. Told the public that he'd answer any question about foreign affairs, the economy, and reinstating the U.S. as the country of power and values it's been since 1776. If that wasn't good enough, he told them not to vote him into office. Because once he was there, he was going to kick ass until he got the job done. And since there wasn't going to be a second term, he didn't give a damn about trying to please a base. The future of the American people was his base."

"My God," Catherine murmured. "Is he crazy? Or a saint?"

"Neither one." Venable paused. "I don't know anyone to whom I could compare him. Maybe Abe Lincoln. But Lincoln was a politician, and Andrews is . . . I don't know. He stands alone. I . . . like him, Catherine."

"You believe he's telling the truth?"

"You should hear him speak. Yeah, you can't help but believe him. He's a spellbinder, and he's smart enough to do the job if anyone can do it. He's brilliant, built a multibillion-dollar business from scratch, served honorably in the Marine Corps during the First Gulf War. He's honest, blunt, and, as I said, he's a patriot. The system is broken. Yes, I'd give him his chance to fix it. I might even volunteer to help."

"From you, that's quite a commitment, Venable. What about Wallace? Could he be Nardik's client?"

"It's possible, Wallace is very ambitious. He's a former ambassador to the U.N., and he's been pushing the U.S. toward a global government." He paused. "He's also very pro-China. It's not enough that we owe China too much right now; he wants us to accept them as Big Brother and let them 'advise' us. Oh, he doesn't say it like that, but he's been subtly maneuvering for the last three years. Under Wallace, we'd end up with a country we wouldn't be able to recognize."

Gallo gave a low whistle. "And that opens a whole new can of worms. China, big business who want their piece of the action, Wallace's handlers, and the lobbyist behind him. It goes on and on . . ."

"And what would happen if Andrews was taken out of the picture?" Catherine asked. "Could Wallace take the election?"

"If it was handled right. If there was no

proof that it was anything but a natural death. It would cause an uproar, but Andrews is a shooting star. Shooting stars are forgotten once they disappear into the darkness. Wallace is a corrupt bastard, but he's strong. Strength and answers will carry the day. When you lose Superman, you reach out for the next best option. Wallace would be sorrowful, sympathetic, might even say he'll adopt some of Andrews's philosophies. Yes, Wallace could be elected."

"July 3. What's Andrews doing on July 3?"

"I have no idea."

"Find out. And send me a picture of William Scott Andrews. Okay?"

"I'll get it to you in five minutes." He paused. "You're sure Andrews is the target? Dammit, no one knows better than I do how dirty it can be out there, but I wanted just once for something to go right."

"Then we'll have to see that it does," Catherine said.

"Tell Hu Chang that he'd better be sure that it does," Venable said roughly. "He can't play games like this without suffering the consequences." He hung up.

"You heard him, Hu Chang," Catherine

said as she pressed the disconnect. "It takes a lot to stir up Venable like that. It's clear Andrews managed to pierce that tough hide of Venable's. I'm curious if he has that effect on everyone."

"Check the Web and pull up any stories," Gallo said as he got out his computer. "That's a peculiar platform he's running on. I'm more interested in that."

Hu Chang was staring at the cloud banks out the window. "A shooting star . . . That's an interesting comparison. When I'm creating one of my drugs, some of them are shooting stars that disappear into the darkness. Others are like suns that are born to stay, burn, and transform themselves. I wonder which Andrews will turn out to be."

"Well, whatever happens, I think Venable is going to heap the blame on you." Her telephone pinged, and she accessed the photo Venable had sent her. "Let's see what a present-day Abe Lincoln looks like . . ."

Not like Lincoln at all, she thought. The photo showed William Scott Andrews standing beside a Jeep Cherokee dressed in casual shirt and jeans. Was he handsome? It was difficult to tell. There was so much power and character in his slightly irregular features that they were the only things you noticed. His dark hair was clipped close to his head, he was tanned, and his blue eyes were narrowed, staring searchingly out of the photo.

"Presence," she said. "Enormous presence. I can see how he'd hold an audience spellbound." She handed the photo to Gallo. "We have to talk to him and tell him what's happening."

Gallo nodded, his gaze on the monitor of the laptop. "His home base is in Houston, Texas. But he has an apartment in Georgetown, D.C. We'll have to find out where to locate him right now."

"And convince him there's such a thing as Hu Chang's Pondera and a plot to go with it," she said dryly. "Which may not be easy to accept."

"Not for a shooting star," Hu Chang said quietly. "Or certainly not for a new sun struggling to be born." He was silent a moment. "And, if I am to accept the consequences as Venable suggests, we must make sure that those consequences do not weigh too heavily upon my soul." His gaze shifted from the clouds to Catherine's face, and he smiled. "So I must rely on my friend to make sure that they do not. I'm afraid we will have to save this Superman of Venable's."

"What do you think we've been working toward? I never intended anything else." She added warily, "Did you?"

"I was reserving judgment. You would accept it as your duty as an agent. I have no duty except to Pondera and what I wish for it to be."

"And what I wish is that you destroy that damned drug and the formula as soon as we get this nightmare over with."

His glance returned to the clouds outside his window.

"Hu Chang."

"I will consider your wishes. We will discuss it after we save Superman and all of the free world." He smiled faintly. "I believe the rhetoric in the comic books goes something like that. Is that not true?"

CHAPTER

15

"Andrews is at his place in Georgetown," Catherine said as she hung up from talking to Venable after they'd landed at San Francisco International. "Venable is trying to get through the staff surrounding him to tell him what's happening. He said that we should hop a plane and head for Washington."

"Excellent. I'll make our reservations." Hu Chang headed for the desk across the terminal. "I'll return shortly."

Gallo watched him disappear into the crowd before he turned to Catherine. "You know the chances of Andrews believing

Venable aren't very good? No proof. A drug that no one knows anything about. We don't even have the name of Nardik's client. Venable will be lucky even to get to talk to Andrews."

"Venable's CIA. That will carry some weight. If Andrews is smart, then he'll listen."

"And if he's not, then we're in trouble. And all this effort to save him may come to nothing." He shrugged. "Sorry. I don't mean to be negative. We'll find a way to stop it from happening." He smiled crookedly. "If only to save Hu Chang from Venable's wrath. Though I can't believe that would bother him much. I can't see him letting anything through that enigmatic shell he wraps around himself. Except you. You appear to be the exception, heaven help you."

"Poor me? Is that what you're implying? Knock it off, Gallo. I thank heaven that I'm the exception."

"I know you do. Though I can't see any signs that he's helped us much since he came back into your life. He seems to have spread chaos wherever he's gone." He reached out and tucked a long strand of hair behind her ear. "You're tired. You didn't sleep at all on that plane. You were too busy trying to pull the rabbit out of the magician's hat."

"So were you." But she didn't step back away from his touch. It was gentle, a comfort, not sexual, and she needed comfort. The world she had left in Hong Kong had been aflame with death and malice. The world she was facing now was full of plots and evil, and again, death was looming around every corner. It had to be faced, but this moment of gentleness was oddly welcome. "So was Hu Chang. We all had to work to make it come together. Stop being protective, Gallo." She made a face. "How many times do I have to tell you that it's one of your worst faults?"

"I'll try to work on it." He smiled down at her. "I know you'll remind me."

Intimacy. Charisma. Electricity . . .

And it was time to step back.

She drew a deep breath and did just that. "You can be sure I will."

He chuckled. "Start now. You need to nap on the way to Washington. Give me your phone, and I'll take any calls from Venable."

She frowned. "As if I would do—" He

had to be joking. She was overreacting. "Bastard. And I'm going to be using my phone. While we're waiting for Hu Chang, I'm going to call Sam and tell him I'm back in the U.S. and check and see if everything is okay."

"By all means." He dropped down in a chair by the windows. "Though I imagine if he's as good as you've told me, that you'd know if it wasn't. Give him my best."

She was already dialing the number. "You don't even know Sam."

"I still wish him the best. He's taking care of your son, isn't he? I don't mind extending the protectiveness to which you object so strenuously toward your son as well. I trust you have no objection to that?"

"No. That's different." Sam was picking up, and she turned away from Gallo and spoke into the phone. "Sam, I'm in San Francisco. Is everything all right?"

"No problem. No sign of trouble. Are you sure I'm going to need that crew I hired?"

"No, I hope you don't. I just had to have a little insurance. No, a lot of insurance. How is Luke?"

"Suspecting that all is not right in Emerald City."

"What?"

"I have two very bright kids here. They were bound to find out that the place was being watched. Don't worry. It's cool. I just explained and they asked questions and then they went back to working on that translation. That's what they're doing right now."

"Maybe I should talk to Luke."

"And maybe you should think about it first. The only one who is worried about this is you, Catherine. If you talk to Luke, he's going to know how you're feeling, then you'll both be uneasy. But you'll be worried about each other and not the problem."

"Stop being so damn logical."

"It's up to you. I'll go find him and give him the phone. Say the word."

She thought about it. "He's not upset about this?"

"Only about my possible lack of ability for protecting him and Kelly. He's sure he can do it better. What can I say? He's your son." He chuckled. "No, he's cool as a cucumber."

"You'll tell him I phoned?"

"And I'll also tell him that you'll be eager

to talk to him if he wants to give you a return call."

Her hand tightened on the phone. "I should be able to wrap this up soon. I'm heading for Washington, and I was tempted to stop by to see him. But I can't do that. I wouldn't risk the possibility of my being under surveillance and drawing attention to Luke. You'll keep him safe for me, Sam?"

"I'm keeping everyone on their toes. I'm even thinking of pulling in another couple operatives. It might be overkill. They'd probably be tripping over each other."

"I don't mind them tripping over each other. By all means do overkill."

"You've got it. I'll keep you updated, Catherine." He hung up.

She pressed the disconnect and turned back to Gallo.

"Luke's okay?" Gallo's gaze was on her face. "You're upset. Not frantic, just . . . troubled maybe."

"He's okay." She grimaced. "Sam says he's better than I am. He and Kelly know about the surveillance. I was trying to keep him from worrying, but it didn't work out. It will probably never work out with Luke.

He's too sharp, and now he's got Kelly, who is just as sharp, to ride shotgun."

"But Sam said he was safe?"

She nodded. "And will have more body-guards than the president." She looked across the terminal. "And speaking about presidents, Hu Chang should be back with our tickets to Washington, shouldn't he?"

"It hasn't been that long. It's only seemed that way to you." He got to his feet. "But I'll go look for—"

Her phone rang and she glanced at the ID.

"It's Venable." She punched the access and the volume. "Did you reach Andrews?"

"No, I didn't have time. I was busy with another call."

"Look, we need you to—"

"I have a message for you. You're not going to like it."

She stiffened. Her first thought had been of Luke, but Sam had just told her that Luke safe. "What are you talking about?"

"Ten minutes ago I got a call from Hu Chang. He told me to call you and tell you to pick up your tickets at the Delta counter."

"What?" Then she understood. "Oh,

shit." She drew a long breath. "And what else did he tell you?"

"He said that he would see you in good time. That he knew you and Gallo could deal with Andrews, but that he had something else he had to do."

"And what the hell is that?"

"I don't know. He said to tell you to let him go. And then something cryptic about it being necessary to safeguard his own shooting star. I thought you might understand."

"Maybe. You were comparing Andrews to a shooting star, and Hu Chang said something about his drugs and medicines were sometimes like shooting stars. He may be trying to find a way of getting his precious Pondera away from Nardik. Dammit, he's going to walk right into Nardik's hands again."

"And you'll follow him."

"How can I? He's slipped away again." She was trying to think. "I can't follow him until he tips his hand. Nardik is going after Andrews, and he'll have the drug. Hu Chang will have to be on his trail to have an opportunity to grab the Pondera before he can use it."

Gallo nodded. "So we'll be playing the same game if not for the same stakes."

"Yes, we're trying to save Andrews, and Hu Chang is trying to save his drug." She added, "And if we're lucky, we might be able to help Hu Chang get out of this alive."

"I'm not overenthusiastic about accomplishing the latter," Gallo said dryly.

"Tough. I'm pissed off, too. But I'm not going to let Hu Chang die. And I'm not going to let him go. He knew I wouldn't." She said to Venable, "We're on our way to Washington. Try to get us an appointment with Andrews. If you can't, we'll find a way to see him anyway."

"And cause an incident that will cause the Company big-time trouble."

"You can handle it. The CIA is golden since we delivered Osama bin Laden."

"You're dreaming. Our part in that was forgotten in a month. We're always the bad guy until proven innocent with politicians."

"But you said Andrews wasn't a politician. He's a patriot, remember?"

"Okay, you got me. But let's see if we can accomplish the objective without the ruckus. But besides the problem of getting in to see Andrews, you know that either

Wallace or Nardik will be having him watched? Nardik will know that you've found out that Andrews is the target."

"I wish I thought that would stop Nardik. But his ego would demand that he go through with it anyway just to prove how brilliant and indomitable he is."

"And whet his appetite to take you down, Catherine. Call me when you get to Washington." He hung up.

"Let's go." She slipped her phone in her jacket and picked up her duffel. "We have a flight to catch."

Gallo fell into step with her. "No running around the airport trying to find our elusive friend?"

"You heard me on the phone. We go where we can find Nardik, and we'll find Hu Chang."

"It will be okay, Catherine," he said quietly. "I know you're upset, but he's not going to let Nardik kill him. Hu Chang's slippery as an eel."

"I know that," she said jerkily. "I'm not worried, I'm mad as hell."

He looked at her.

"Maybe a little worried. But he doesn't deserve it. Why couldn't he work with us?

Why did he have to just take off? We've been together for so long. He should have known that I'd do—" Why was she asking those questions? Hu Chang was a law unto himself. She should have accepted that fact by now. "Forget it. Let's just get the job done."

"It will be easier for me to forget than you. In fact, I'd prefer that Hu Chang be forgotten." He added, "It's difficult to compete with him for your attention. Look at you, you're mad and upset, yet he still has you riveted."

But Gallo had that same riveting effect on her. The nuances were different, but the intensity was the same. Perhaps more riveting because she'd deliberately been keeping Hu Chang between them as a buffer.

But now that buffer was gone.

And she was feeling vulnerable, she realized.

She had temporarily lost Hu Chang to his creative passion for his lethal shooting star, and the loneliness was back. But she wasn't going to reach out for Gallo because of that loneliness. Sex might soothe that hollowness for a few hours, but the aftereffects could be addictive. She would be fine once she got over the shock of Hu Chang's taking off.

She was already fine. She was her own person. She didn't need Gallo. And Hu Chang had made his choice, and it hadn't been her. His loss, dammit.

So deal with it.

"Andrews won't see you," Venable said flatly when Catherine called him from Reagan National Airport. "His assistant, Pat Gower, is running interference, and she says she can arrange a phone call with him for you day after tomorrow at three. If you can catch his interest, you might be able to have an interview. I told her that wouldn't be satisfactory."

"We don't have the time. You told her he could be a dead man if we can't prevent it?"

"That's the only reason that she agreed to the phone call. She's smart, and she doesn't want to take a chance that she could make a mistake. But Andrews has had a zillion death threats since he started his campaign. You don't have a radical agenda like his and not bring out a horde of venomous opponents. She asked if we had proof and what could I tell her that was concrete. Nothing concrete. Suspicion of intent. Even Andrews as the prospective victim was questionable."

"No way to budge her?"

"Loyal and determined. It's a tough combination."

"Then we go around her and straight to Andrews. Give me his address."

Venable rattled off an address. "He'll have security. You're risking getting shot, you know."

And having others get shot as well. This wasn't the best way to handle the situation. She thought about it. "You're right; give me Pat Gower's address."

"Tell me you're not going to kidnap her."

"Okay, I'll tell you. But you'd be nuts to believe me. We need a way to get to him. Her security will be a hell of a lot weaker than his."

"Just remember she's a U.S. citizen just doing her job. You don't treat her as if she were running a drug cartel." He gave her Pat Gower's address. "She has an apartment a few blocks away from where Andrews lives."

"Send me her photo. I'll call you when we have anything." She hung up and turned to Gallo. "Andrews's security system has to be disabled, but we need Pat Gower to get past any guards. That means we have to go after her, too. Which one do you want to deal with? Andrews or Pat Gower?"

"I have a choice? How kind of you. I'll choose Andrews. There's always the question of a woman wondering if rape is a motive and getting hurt fighting off an assailant."

She nodded. "Then get to Andrews's place and disable the security alarms. I'll meet you there with Pat Gower as soon as I can." Her phone was pinging. She glanced at the photo of Pat Gower. Thirtyish. Shoulder-length brown hair, brown eyes, thin, pointed face that appeared a little elfish. Attractive. She was looking out of the photo with directness and intelligence. Catherine glanced at her watch. "It's almost ten. Let's aim for midnight."

"If they're home and not out politicking the night away." He turned and headed for the exit. "Remember, this is Washington."

The security alarms for Pat Gower's apartment had been a little more difficult than

Catherine had thought, but they were not state of the art. She managed to disarm them in a short time.

Next question. Was Gower in the apartment?

She carefully disabled the lock on the front door and swung the door open.

Darkness.

There was another door several yards to the left.

Probably the bedroom.

Quiet. The last thing Catherine wanted was to wake the woman before she was in a position to subdue her quickly. Then she'd be able to have her chance to defuse any resentment while she explained why she was doing this.

A very slim chance, she thought wryly. It was very difficult finding a valid explanation for kidnapping.

She glided forward and silently opened the door.

A bed was against the wall across the room.

Something was wrong.

The covers were tossed to one side, which meant—

Shit!

She ducked to one side as a baseball bat came out of nowhere and down toward her head. The bat missed her head but connected with her shoulder.

Pain.

The bat had not come out of nowhere. It had come from behind the bedroom door.

Catherine crashed the door back against the wall, pinning the wielder of the bat behind it.

Cursing. It had to be Pat Gower. It was a woman's voice muttering expletives even as she pushed against the door to free herself.

Catherine felt like cursing, too. Her shoulder hurt like hell, and this wasn't turning out as she'd planned. She slammed the door again, harder. Then jerked it open and ducked again as the bat came at her again.

"Don't *do* that!" She jerked the bat out of the woman's hands and threw it to one side. "I'm not going to hurt you."

"You bet you're not." Pat Gower dove forward and butted her head against Catherine's chest. "But I'm going to hurt you."

The woman's head striking Catherine's

sensitive breasts was already hurting her. And it was clear she wasn't going to stop.

To hell with trying to do the job with the least mayhem possible.

"I take it back. I *will* hurt you." She stepped forward and gave her a karate chop to the neck. "Nothing lethal. But I don't mind causing you a little discomfort." Then she followed the blow with a right uppercut to Gower's chin that dropped her to the floor. "I don't like baseball bats."

She crossed the room and turned on the bedside lamp to see how much damage she'd done.

Not much. Pat Gower was evidently fairly tough. She was sitting up and shaking her head to clear it.

"I'm not trying to hurt you," she said. "I'm only trying to get your cooperation. My name is Catherine Ling. Venable may have told you about me."

"Oh, for God's sake." Pat Gower stared at her in disgust. "CIA? It's no wonder the CIA is always in trouble with the authorities. You can't go around breaking laws and giving law-abiding citizens karate chops. Now get out of here before I call the police and have you arrested. I might do it anyway."

She was totally fearless, Catherine realized. She had a Brooklyn accent, and it made her tone sound even more belligerent. She was sitting there on the floor, brown hair mussed, bruised, wearing ridiculous pink-poodle pajamas, and ready to take Catherine on again. Ordinarily, Catherine would have admired that courage, but she could use a little intimidation right now. "Let's get this clear. We're in this position because you made a stupid decision, and I'm having to go out of my way to make sure it doesn't hurt William Andrews." She paused. "And if he ever does become president, you'd better get down on your knees and pray that the CIA is still around to make sure that no one blows up the world on his watch. Now get up and get out of those stupid pajamas and into your clothes. We're going to wake up your boss."

"The hell we are," she said fiercely. "You're not getting near him."

"I'm talking to him within the next two hours. John Gallo, my partner, is already at his apartment waiting for us. I could tell Gallo to go on without us, but it might mean gunfire from Andrews's security team, and Andrews might get hurt. We're trying to avoid that happening."

"Or this Gallo might get hurt."

Catherine shook her head. "That's highly unlikely. The best way to avoid having William Andrews damaged in any way is for you to go with us through the security guards outside the apartment. Once we're inside, you can go with us to see him or not." She stared her directly in the eye. "But we *will* talk to him. And if he throws us out, then that's his decision."

Her gaze narrowed on Catherine's face. "And then you'll give up?"

"No, this isn't only about him. I have to keep him alive. I'll just do it without his help . . . or your help." She shrugged. "I can understand your not wanting to stick your neck out. Why should you care? You only work for him."

"Yes, I only work for him." She moistened her lips. "It's a wild story Venable told me. I can understand some crackpot taking a shot at William, but that's different from calculated . . . murder."

"Very different."

Silence. "And I have to keep all the

craziness away from William. He has enough ugliness without having to deal with nonsense like— But what if it's not nonsense? I try so hard to protect him. What if I'm protecting him from the wrong thing?"

Good God, she cared deeply for Andrews. Perhaps she even loved him. "That's the question you'll have to answer. Or do you want me to answer it for you?"

"No, why should I trust you? You come in here and try to kidnap me and—" She was silent again. Then sat up straighter on the floor, and said brusquely, "I want to see your credentials. How can I be sure who you are anyway? Though who else but the CIA would be this arrogant and lacking in—" She stopped again. "I'll get you in to see William, but if you make me look foolish to him, or if this is just some crazy, idiotic scheme, I'll find a way to make you pay, Catherine Ling."

"I'm sure you will," she said gently. "And you won't look foolish to him. I promise you." She showed her credentials, then picked up the baseball bat and looked at it ruefully. "I wasn't expecting this. It hurt, dammit."

"My father gave it to me when I left home

and got my first apartment." She examined the credentials closely and handed them back to Catherine. "He was a Yankee fan, and it was autographed by most of the team. He treasured that bat. But he said that he wanted me to have it and to use it if anyone gave me any trouble." She got to her feet. "You gave me trouble. I'll get dressed now." She scowled. "And these aren't stupid pajamas. My niece gave them to me."

"Well, that makes a difference. Of course they're not stupid. I'm sure the pink poodles are brimming with intellect."

"My niece is twelve years old and saved up her allowance to buy them for me. These are great pajamas." She opened her closet and took out a tailored blouse and skirt. "So shut up about them."

And Catherine would have felt the same if Luke had given her those pink monstrosities. In fact, she would have wanted to treasure them, not wear them. "Sorry. You're right, they're fantastic." She took out her phone. "And while you're busy shedding those fantastic pajamas, I'll call Gallo and tell him that you're going to cooperate and make it easier for us."

"He'll be relieved?"

"Maybe. Probably not. Gallo doesn't like easy. He prefers balancing on the edge. But he'll just have to live with it."

"Gallo, this is Pat Gower." Catherine glanced around the quietly luxurious lobby. With Pat Gower running interference, Catherine and Gallo breezed through the security team outside William Andrews's apartment, and here in the lobby, she saw only one man. "Any trouble?"

"A shakedown, but when Ms. Gower called, they backed off." He inclined his head to Pat Gower. "Many thanks. I don't think I could have tolerated the direction in which they were traveling. I was getting a little uptight. Literally."

"At least, you didn't get hit with a baseball bat." Catherine stepped on the elevator. "Pat called Andrews and told him we were coming. Surprisingly, he wasn't upset about our nocturnal visit."

"He trusts me." Pat pushed the button. "And he'd better keep on trusting me."

"She took out insurance," Catherine said. "She called Venable and double-checked with him. She even sent him a photo of me."

"It was either that or bring my baseball bat," Pat said straight-faced. "You could have stolen and altered credentials." She studied Gallo. "I guess I don't have to check on you. You look pretty much as Catherine described you."

"And so I'm totally innocuous?"

"No." The elevator doors opened. "But I think Catherine can take care of any problem you bring us." She was leading them down the hall. "And if she can't, there's always my bat."

She stopped at a door, rang the bell, and her voice was suddenly intense. "And I'd use it. William is a great man and a great person. No one is going to hurt him. Do you understand?"

"You've made that very clear," Catherine said. "We're all on the same page as far as that's concerned. We'll do everything that we—" She broke off as the door swung open.

"What the hell is going on, Pat?" William Scott Andrews stood there, glaring at Gallo. "And who are you?"

"He doesn't matter. Though I know he looks a little intimidating." Pat Gower stepped forward. "Just listen to Catherine."

"Cut to the quick," Gallo murmured. He stepped aside and gestured for Catherine to enter the apartment ahead of him. "At least I'm good enough to watch your back."

"And who is supposed to watch my back?" Andrews asked as he turned and strode back into his apartment. He was fully dressed in black slacks and an open-throated white shirt, and William Scott Andrews was just as arresting as Catherine had thought he'd be. Force, power, vitality, and spellbinding presence. "It appears I'm the one at risk." He suddenly turned back to Pat. "Are you okay, Pat? You're bruised. Did these bastards hurt you?"

"I'm fine." She smiled. "Catherine and I had a misunderstanding. But I came out on top."

"Your dad's baseball bat?" He smiled. "Good for you." He turned to Catherine, and his smile faded. "I don't like this. If you want to go after me, do it. But Pat only works for me, and I won't have her harassed."

Catherine could see why Venable liked Andrews. He was very genuine. "I'm not harassing—well, maybe a little. But she wouldn't have brought us here if she hadn't

WHAT DOESN'T KILL YOU 451

thought it was necessary. As to who is watching your back, you're looking at them."

"Listen to them, William," Pat said quietly. "It sounds really crazy, but I think there's a chance that it could happen. It scared me."

"Nah, not you." His smile was suddenly even warmer. "You could take on the whole damn world." He turned to Catherine and Gallo, and said crisply, "Assassination plot? Talk to me. Details. Proof. Solutions."

"Over to you, Catherine," Gallo said. "Hu Chang is a little difficult to describe, and you'll be better at it than me. The discourse would definitely be less obscene."

"That's not helpful, Gallo." Catherine gazed directly at Andrews, and said, "Though he's right that it has to start with Hu Chang. But I want to make it clear that Hu Chang is not one of those criminals. I'm sure he'll try to stop Nardik from—"

"Stop defending him and tell the man what Hu Chang has been up to," Gallo said. "He can make the judgment for himself. Of course, if he's going to become president, it may mean he'll have to send Hu Chang to Guantanamo."

"Hu Chang is not—" She drew a deep breath. "Hu Chang is not like anyone else. Let me tell you about him . . ."

And she did tell him, in detail and as completely as she could do it for the next twenty minutes. He listened, silent, his gaze narrowed on her face. When she stopped, she searched his expression for any hint of what he was thinking. Futile attempt. Dammit, he is as enigmatic in his way as Hu Chang. "It's the truth," and she added bluntly, "Do you think we would have wasted our time coming here if we hadn't thought you'd be dead in a few days if we didn't? Now help us, dammit."

"Subtle and diplomatic she's not," Gallo said. "But honest, Andrews. You can always count on honest."

"And full of passion. I respect anyone who cares passionately for anything. Passion burns away everything mediocre in its path," Andrews said. "And what about you, Gallo? Do I detect a hint of conflict between the two of you? Is this Hu Chang all she's saying?"

Gallo was silent. "He's probably more."

"But you don't trust him?"

"I'm not a good judge. I'm a bit emotional

about him, and I can't see beyond the surface. Should you believe his drug can do what he claims? Yes. Will he try to save you if he can do it without endangering his creation? Yes. That's all I can promise you."

"I don't want promises. I want solutions."

"You said that before," Catherine said.

"Solutions are the only thing worthwhile in this world," he said wearily. "You're in Washington, D.C., where we're surrounded by promises. Promises aren't any good." The weariness was suddenly gone, and his entire demeanor was vibrating with the force of his will. "I have to have solutions. I *will* have solutions."

Catherine couldn't take her eyes from him. Total conviction. Total determination. Oh, yes, here was a man who could move mountains. No wonder he was considered a threat to any opponent. "I imagine you will." She moved her shoulders, trying to shake off the effect of that personality. Her job wasn't to help him move mountains. It was to keep him alive. "So let's find a solution to make sure Nardik doesn't get in your way. This is July 1. What are you doing on July 3? Where will you be?"

"He was going to debate Howard Wallace at his ranch in Sugarland, outside of Houston," Pat Gower said. "And on Independence Day, he was going to give a speech at the Astrodome. Those two days should have clinched his bid for the presidency. We're expecting a tidal wave of support after those two events." Her lips tightened. "I'll cancel the arrangements."

"No," Catherine said.

"What do you mean no?" Pat asked fiercely. "You've just told us that Nardik is going to try to kill him. We can stop it by just canceling the Fourth of July plans."

"Until the next time," Catherine said. "Do you really think they'll stop? We have to get rid of Nardik and scare off the people who are paying him. That's the only way to make sure Andrews is safe."

"And you believe Wallace may be paying him?" Andrews asked thoughtfully. "It's possible. Wallace is ambitious, and I stand in his way."

"I don't know if it's Wallace himself or his handlers," Gallo said. "They're desperate to avoid appearing to be involved. That's why they're willing to pay Nardik so highly for the use of Hu Chang's formula. Once we get our hands on Nardik or the man he sends to actually give you the drug, then we might find out more."

"Then get rid of the bastard," Pat said. "Just don't involve William."

"We'll try," Gallo said. "But it may come down to the night of that debate. It's the only time we can be sure that there will be evidence of the—"

"No," Pat said harshly. "Screw your evidence. I won't allow him to go meekly to—"

"When have you ever known me to be meek, Pat?" Andrews asked gently. "And they're right, the best way to get rid of the threat is to make sure that the trap is sprung." He grimaced. "Providing I'm not in it."

"Be quiet, William." Her eyes were glittering with moisture. "I won't let you do this. You're too valuable. I've only known two men in my life who were worthwhile, who made a difference. My father died on 9/11, and now you want to take a stupid chance when everyone needs you. *I* need you."

"Shh." He was suddenly beside her, taking her in his arms. "If I didn't take stupid chances, you wouldn't have come to work for me. Everyone said I was some kind of crazy idealist, and you still stuck around and made them eat their words. This is just one more risk we have to take, Pat. Don't fight me, help me."

He didn't even realize how cruel that request was, Catherine thought. He meant only kindness, and he did care about Pat. Perhaps not enough. But what did Catherine know? She was an outsider and could only guess.

Pat buried her head for a moment in his chest, her arms tightening around him. "I'll help you." She cleared her throat then stepped back. "And I won't let them kill you . . . even if you are being stupid." She turned to Catherine. "You're not to leave me out of this. I'll give you a complete copy of his itinerary, and we'll keep the security force as it is. Anything else would be suspicious." Her lips twisted bitterly. "Someone might think we actually believe someone is trying to kill William. That wouldn't do, would it?" She turned toward the door. "Now we'll let you go back to bed and get some sleep, William. You have three TV shows tomorrow morning."

"Pat." Andrews stopped her as she

reached the door. "Thank you. I couldn't do without you."

"No, you couldn't." She forced a smile. "And you'd better not try."

"Not a chance," he said softly.

"We'll be in touch, Mr. Andrews," Catherine said, as they followed Pat out the door. "Thank you for cooperating."

His brows rose. "In saving my life? I'd think that was a given. I'll take any risk you need me to take. Just give me a solution."

"Solution," Gallo repeated, as they walked down the corridor. "That appears to be Andrews's main theme, or maybe it's his battle cry."

"And not a bad one for a world that's grown so complicated and corrupt that it's starving for answers," Catherine said. "I hope to God he can find us a few."

CHAPTER

16

July 2
Brownsville, Texas

"It will do." Nardik gazed out at the flat land that surrounded the ranch house centered in the middle of the Double Diamond spread. The late-afternoon sunlight made the acreage appear stark and barren. But that was exactly what Nardik had ordered. "You're sure that there won't be any interference from nosy neighbors?"

"No one is going to come around here," Fowler said. "The owners took off after they started being harassed by members of a drug cartel who wanted to use this place as a distribution point. It scared not only them but the neighbors."

"I don't want to be bothered by the cartels while I'm here."

"I've sent out word that you're going to be at the ranch for only a few days and will pay well to have them get us across the border into Mexico when we leave." He smiled. "And I've set up your bodyguards strategically around the place in case the cartels get greedy. There are so many hotheads shooting up the Mexican countryside that the drug families think they can get away with anything."

"Then maybe we should have hired some of them to take Andrews out at that debate," Nardik said sourly. "Since we haven't been able to get our hands on Hu Chang."

Fowler quickly shook his head. "No traces. Wallace is already nervous. It can't look like murder. Andrews can't be a martyr."

"I know. I know." He went out on the porch and gazed moodily at the horizon. "And it will be as perfect as the bastard wants it to be. Wallace will be able to pick the crown out of the gutter like Napoleon did. I still have a day, and I'll make it work for me. Ling is the key. She'll be able to deliver Hu Chang. I wasted my time raiding that palace, but I can't afford to waste any more. Who did we send to Louisville?"

"Mark Townberg. I told him to grab her son and bring him to us. We've used him before here in the U.S. He works alone, but he has contacts, and he's never disappointed you."

"He's not to hurt him." He smiled. "I reserve that job for you. You did very well with Jack Tan."

Fowler flushed with pleasure. "Because I'd do anything to make you happy. You know that."

"Yes, I know that." And that evening of torment for Tan had given Nardik a rush of power that he'd needed to erase the frustration of the raid. "But the child may not be as interesting. Children are weak."

"But you said I could have the woman afterward. You promised me."

"Did I?" He vaguely remembered giving that promise in the heat and thrill of those last moments with Tan. But now he was feeling annoyance that Fowler had tried to manipulate him. Fowler was an expert, but Nardik wanted his encounter with Ling to be more personal.

"You can't back out now," Fowler said harshly.

Nardik could do anything that he wanted to do. Yes, he was definitely annoyed with Fowler. Perhaps it was time to break in a new assistant.

"Did I say that I wanted to break my word?" He glanced away. "When you've been everything that I could wish, Fowler. That would be truly wicked of me. Do you think I'm wicked?"

Fowler didn't answer directly. "I've plans for her. You told me to think about ways . . . A woman's breasts are very sensitive. A woman is different. I could make her—"

"Yes, different." And she would not be in the least desirable when Fowler got through with her. He was not sure he didn't want that result later rather than sooner. "I'm sure you would be wonderfully innovative." He changed the subject. "I've set up a final plan to administer the drug on the night of the debate. We'll go forward with it even if we can't be sure that it's completely fool-proof."

"You're going to double-cross Wallace?" Fowler asked, startled.

"I leave that to chance." He smiled recklessly. "If we get Hu Chang in a position where he'll validate that those medical records assure that the dose I have will do the job, I'll come out smelling like a rose. The perfect undetectable poison. That's the most desirable outcome. Or if I can force him to give me a second dose of the drug to serve as insurance. That would work, too. But if I'm pushed, I'll still have half the money, Andrews dead and Wallace a suspect. Do you think I care about that sleazy bastard Wallace? It's all about me. I disappear for a while, then I go after Hu Chang and the drug again, and we restart the game."

Fowler nodded, relieved. "I didn't think you'd give up so easily. Now about Catherine Ling, I could—"

"No." He was definitely going to have to do something about Fowler. "I've decided I need you to do something more important. I want you to be the one to go to the debate tomorrow night. I need someone to complete that job that I can trust."

"Me?" Fowler's eyes widened. "I don't

think— That's not my—" He added weakly, "I'd be glad to do anything you wish, but I think that someone else would be better."

"But it's not what you think, Fowler. Ledcone will be there to get you away from the ranch, but I want you to be the one to actually administer the drug. When Andrews collapses, you can slip away in the crowd."

Fowler moistened his lips. "I don't want to do this."

Because Fowler is basically a coward, Nardik thought contemptuously. "But you want to please me, and this will please me, Fowler. It will show me how devoted you are to my best interests. You'll be given foolproof credentials and go and do the job. You'll be perfect."

"If that's what I have to do." He looks like a deer caught in the headlights, Nardik thought. "But you're planning on leaving for Mexico right after the killing. How will I get back to you?"

"You and Cambrey will meet me in Acapulco." He smiled. "Perhaps we'll spend a few days there so that I can express my gratitude to you."

"I'd like that." He was still wary. "But

won't you need me to persuade the woman? You said that I could—"

"After I get what I need from Ling, we may take her with us for amusement value." But only Cambrey would be meeting Nardik in Mexico. He'd give orders that Fowler was to be disposed of immediately after they left Andrews's ranch. He had not only committed the crime of boring and annoying him, but it was always smart to remove the man who actually committed the assassination. "But first I have to get her kid, so that I'll have the tool I need. When is Townberg supposed to get his hands on him?"

"You said right away. I told him tonight. Is that all right?"

Tonight. Nardik felt a tiny jolt of excitement at the thought of Luke Ling feeling safe and happy in that house in Louisville. And Catherine Ling feeling equally secure while she tried to ruin Nardik's chances at scoring this bonanza. Soon, neither one them would feel any vestige of safety.

"Yes, it's very much all right, Fowler." He sat down in the rocking chair and started to move gently back and forth while he savored the thought. "I can't tell you how anxious I'll be to hear from Townberg."

Louisville, Kentucky

"It's raining hard." Luke stared from his bedroom window down at the street in front of the house. "Jordack, the agent Sam stationed under the tree on the corner must be nearly drowned."

"You remember his name?" Kelly asked absently, her gaze on the book in front of her.

"I remember everything about him. His name, what he looks like. He's taller than Sam, but he doesn't look it huddling close to the trunk of the tree."

"But it's the same man?" Her tone was no longer abstracted. "You're certain?"

Luke was silent, his gaze on the street. "Yes, I'm certain about who he is." He turned back to face her. "I wish I could be as sure that you're going to be able to tell me about that book. You're supposed to be so smart. Why can't you—"

"Knock it off, Luke. I don't know what

you expect of me. I don't understand any of this." Kelly frowned as she looked up from the book Hu Chang had given him. She impatiently pushed the translations she'd gotten off the Internet to one side. "And what I don't understand the most is why you got me here to help you with it. As far as I can tell, it's just an ordinary chemistry book with special emphasis on Chinese herbs. Sam could have helped you with this translation."

"If that was what I wanted, I could have done it myself. I've learned a lot about computers and how to find out stuff."

"Then why did you think I could help?"

"I don't know." It was the truth, and it made him angry. He didn't like this frustrating feeling that there was something just out of reach that he couldn't quite grasp. That elusive feeling had been with him since he'd started going through the book. "Maybe because you see things that aren't there."

"For heaven's sake, you make me sound like a ghost hunter."

"No, but you see . . . paths, patterns. That's why Catherine thinks you're so smart. You can take a person or fact and see exactly where it's going, where it's going to take them. That's right, isn't it?"

She nodded. "Sometimes it's exact, sometimes I get a little lost."

"But not often."

"No, not often." She looked down at the chemistry book. "This is just a textbook with some handwritten notes. Where do you think it's going?"

"I don't know. It . . . bothers me." He crossed the room and flipped through the book. He jabbed his finger at the photo. "This one bothers me."

"That's the one that you showed me before." She looked down at the photo of the beautifully painted container. "The description says that it's a herbal medicine to cure kidney infections. Pretty container for a nasty illness."

"That's not what it is."

She lifted her gaze to his face. "How do you know?"

"I don't know. I don't know anything." The frustration was searing through him. "But it's for something else, and I should know what it is. I should *know*." She was staring thoughtfully at him, and he said through his teeth, "Stop looking at me."

"I didn't know I was. I'm thinking."

"That I'm weird. You've said that before."

She grinned. "And I'll say it again. But that's not what I'm thinking right now. When you're looking for a pattern, and you can't see it in any obvious place, you look at the weird or unusual. Assume that you're right and examine the surrounding circumstances and explore every possibility."

He was silent. "And that's okay?"

"Sometimes it's necessary." Her gaze narrowed on his face. "You look relieved. I wonder . . . Is that what you've been doing while I've been slaving away trying to find a reasonable explanation? Have you been strolling on the dark side and getting a step ahead of me?"

"No." He suddenly grinned. "Maybe a half step. I'm not like you. I have to depend on finding out things for myself because I can't be sure that I'm not mixed up about things. It's kind of hard for me to put together what I've read and what people have told me. Lots of people don't agree with each other even about what's weird and what's not. But when I couldn't come up with an answer, I had to start looking deeper. You know, like in that *Star Trek* movie where they say 'Where no man has gone before'? But I had to make sure that I wasn't being too weird. You know stuff like that." He made a face. "And you'd tell me?"

"Oh, yes. You can depend on that. And what half step are you taking, Luke?"

"I'll let you know when I figure it out." He was aware of an eagerness and curiosity that was replacing his confusion and frustration. "But it has something to do with taking what I know, then trying to put it together with all the blanks." His smile faded. "And finding out why there should be blanks. Why should I feel as if I should know— That's the weird part." He got to his feet. "But I ran across a book downstairs in the library that might help. It's weird, too. But it could be close to—" He was heading for the door. "Thanks, Kelly."

"Yeah, just use me and toss me away. You're leaving me here to gnaw my fingernails with curiosity? That's not fair, Luke." She stood up and followed him to the hall. "What book?"

"I'll show you later. When I'm sure you're

not going to laugh at me. You do that a lot."

"And you don't do it to me?" She watched him start down the stairs. "When, Luke?"

"Maybe after supper." He glanced out the narrow window beside the front door. "That won't be too long. It's getting dark now."

"That's because it's raining. It's only a little after six. Why don't I go down with you and—"

"Nag me," he finished as he turned and headed for the library. "And then take over and make me mad. Go help Sam fix supper, Kelly."

"Okay," she said resignedly. "Maybe we'll make some stew to share with Sam's security team. Particularly the one who you said looks like a drowned rat. He'd probably appreciate it."

"He might." Luke didn't look at her as he opened the library door. "But check with Sam. He's pretty heavy in the discipline department." He shut the door behind him. He waited a minute to see if Kelly would follow him. She was usually careful of not intruding, but she was curious and might yield to temptation.

Not this time. He heard her go down the hall toward the kitchen.

He moved across the library and climbed the ladder to the third shelf, where he'd placed the red leather-bound book earlier yesterday. Then he climbed down and went over to the cushioned window seat across the room.

The rain was pounding against the glass, and it was beginning to thunder. He stood there, and he could see only a blur of the oak tree on the corner and the man who had stood beneath it.

The man who was not beneath it now.

The door opened behind him, and he knew it wasn't Kelly.

He didn't turn around but continued to look out the window.

"Hello," he said quietly. "I've been waiting for you."

"Go tell Luke supper is ready." Sam turned away from the stove. "While I fill a couple vacuum canisters to take out to the guys."

"Luke wasn't sure you'd want to do it." Kelly smiled as she headed for the door. "He said that you believed in discipline."

"And I do. But my first name is Sam, if you noticed."

"What diff—" She groaned as she made the connection. "Good Samaritan? That's terrible, Sam."

"Not that bad." He finished pouring the stew into the canisters and started putting on the lids. "While I take these outside, you drag Luke out of the library. I don't want his supper to get cold because he's studying some book." He glanced at her. "Particularly that book. He's pretty obsessed with it."

"He's not working on Hu Chang's book. I have it upstairs. He wanted to check something else out in a book he found in the library." She held up her hand as he started to speak. "I don't know. He may honor me with his confidence later." She added grimly, "He'd better. Or I'll strangle him." She glanced at the window. "It's still raining. You're sure you don't want me to hold an umbrella over you when you're playing Samaritan?"

"I'll manage. Go get Luke."

"Whatever you say." She moved down the hall toward the library. It was dim now, and she flicked on the hall light. She banged on the library door. "Luke, supper's ready." She opened the door. "And I've got to tell you about the terrible Samaritan—"

The room was empty.

She stood there in the doorway. The library was as dim as the hall, but she knew that Luke was not here. Why was she standing here assaulted by this sudden chill? Luke could have gone upstairs. Just because he wasn't where she expected him didn't mean there was something wrong.

It didn't mean it, but it could be true.

"Luke!" She turned and ran upstairs. She threw open the door to his bedroom.

No Luke.

She had known he wouldn't be here.

The library. That had been the last place she had seen him. If he wasn't there, he might have left some trace that would lead her to him.

Her heart was pounding so hard it hurt as she ran back downstairs and into the library.

This time she flipped on the light.

And saw the red leather-bound book on the window seat. The book that Luke must have come here to find.

She slowly crossed the room and picked up the book from the window seat.

She held the book up to the light to read the title.

She inhaled sharply. "Oh, my God."

Brownsville, Texas
July 2

"Townberg *has* him." Fowler's eyes were glittering with excitement as he came out on the porch. "He said it went slick as glass."

"At last you seem to have hired someone who can get things done," Nardik said. "When will he be here with the boy?"

"He can't risk trying to get him out of Louisville tonight. He said the place was crawling with CIA, and Sam O'Neill has made sure he has contacts all over the city. He'll try to drive the kid to Nashville and fly out of there."

"Try? That sounds a little weak, Fowler. Rather like Jack Tan."

"It won't be like that. It's just that it has to be a private plane, and arrangements are more difficult to—"

"I know all that." And he was too pleased to give Fowler more of a hard time. Everything was going right for a change. He had that bitch's kid. The boy was the key to getting everything he wanted. He wouldn't have to compromise.

He could have it all.

"Tell Townberg that I want him here at least by tomorrow. And not to drug the kid. I may want him to be able to be coherent if I decide to have him talk to his loving mother."

"It would be better if I could have him here right away," Fowler said. "Then he'd have something to tell his mother."

"I agree. But we're running out of time, Fowler."

Close. It was going to be very close.

Tomorrow night was July 3.

But it was going to be okay.

He was going to have it all.

July 2
Sugarland, Texas

Pat Gower met Gallo and Catherine at the private airport near Sugarland and drove them to Andrews's ranch west of the city. They arrived at dusk, but the large two-story ranch house was blazing with lights, and electricians, gardeners, and laborers were swarming all over the grounds, setting up lights and tables and chairs. The huge covered stage that had been set up some distance from the house was receiving particular attention with at least four electricians and two sound techs bustling about the area.

"It looks like they're staging a rock concert," Gallo said dryly. "It's a madhouse. If it's this bad tonight, I wonder what it will be like tomorrow night before the big show."

"I hope it will be calm and organized," Pat said. "That's the purpose of the madhouse tonight." She smiled. "And it's funny you mentioned a rock concert." She pointed to the foothills to the north. "We're opening the property tomorrow morning, and allowing William's supporters to come and bring their families to the debate. They'll bring blankets and their own suppers and be able to see the debate on giant TV screens we're mounting on the stage. I'm estimating a crowd as big as Woodstock."

Gallo gave a low whistle. "An event."

Pat nodded. "I want the history books to tell about the night of July 3 and how it put William Andrews over the top."

"History books. No one could say you have low expectations," Catherine said.

"No, I expect the world for William, and I'm going to get it." She added, "We'll probably not be ready until just before the actual barbecue begins tomorrow. I wanted this barbecue and debate to remind people of what it used to be like decades ago when an election could be Stars and Stripes and pure Americana. It's got to be just right." Determinedly, she added, "And I'll see that it is."

"You're already halfway there," Gallo said as he got out of the car. "I think I'll drift around and talk to people and see if I can get a feeling for what everyone is doing and their general schedule. Catherine?"

She thought about it. "Maybe later. I want to call Sam and check on Luke."

Gallo turned away. "Then I'll come and give you a report when I'm finished."

"Fine." She turned to Pat. "Will you show me where I'm to sleep?"

"Sure." Over her shoulder, she said to Gallo, "There's only one guest room available in the big house. You'll have to sleep down in the bunkhouse. Tell Charlie I sent you."

But Gallo was already striding away, his gaze fixed on the stage where the debate was to take place.

"It's a nice place." Catherine turned to Pat as they climbed the stairs to the second floor. "I wasn't expecting it to be so homey. After all, Andrews is a billionaire. No grandeur here."

"It's his family's home," Pat said. "They were ranchers for generations until they found oil on the property. I think William would still like to be a rancher. He likes the simple life."

"What about his wife? Did she like the same things?"

"I don't know. Deborah died before I came to work for William. I imagine that she did. I know he loved her and that when she died, he had to search desperately to fill the place she'd occupied in his life."

"So he chose the entire country to do that?" She added carefully, "Most widowers would have just looked for another wife."

"But they aren't William," Pat said. "He's one of a kind."

"And that's all right with you?"

Pat turned to face her. "Stop pussyfooting around," she said bluntly. "I'm pretty transparent. You know how I feel about William. But I can't see that it's any of your business."

"It wouldn't be, except that you're close to Andrews. Ordinarily, that would mean that you wish him well. But if you're frustrated and bitter, that could be a reason for you to look the other way when Nardik tries to take him out. It may come down to split-second timing and pure instinct. I have to know how you're going to react. Positive or negative."

"How am I going to react?" Pat said baldly, "I'd die for him. Is that a positive enough response, Catherine?"

She meant it. The answer was full of both pain and truth. Catherine nodded. "That's all I needed to know. I'm sorry I invaded your privacy."

"That's okay. Anything that keeps William safe is worth a little baring of the soul." Pat's lips twisted. "I didn't want to love him, you know. I wanted to have a marriage like my mom and dad's. Solid, full of humor, love, kids, and all the ordinary things that make life worth living. Then I went to a town-hall meeting with a girl from my office, and I saw William Andrews. For a while I thought that I just loved his ideas and what he was trying to do for the country. I quit my job and went to work for him. It's not often a woman finds a cause that's worth fighting for and a man who reminds her of one of the patriots who started this country. I met him and I heard 'America the Beautiful' playing. The idea dazzled me." She paused. "And it didn't take long until William began to dazzle me, too." She opened the door and gestured for Catherine to enter. "But I don't fool myself that it's mutual. William cares about me, but I don't dazzle him and never will. But life's like that sometimes. You take what you can get. And what I get is pretty damn special." She glanced around the bedroom. "Everything seems to be in order. We keep this room for last-minute guests, but Carmela and the other help are so busy with all the people streaming in here for this debate that I was afraid that it would be in shambles. I should have known better. Carmela would never let anything happen that would make William unhappy."

"She's dazzled, too?"

"Sure, in her way. Carmela Diaz has been housekeeper here since before William was born, two of her kids run the ranch, and another one is in charge of the publicity for the campaign. She practically raised William after he lost his parents when he was in college." She turned away. "If you need anything, call me. But don't bother me unless it's important. I have a lot to do. The barbecue starts at seven tomorrow night, and William will be here by six. There will be good food, bands playing, and flag-waving and I'll be in the middle of it. The debate is at ten."

"And I'll be in the middle of that," Catherine said. "I don't want Andrews to eat or drink anything that you don't see prepared from start to finish."

"You think it will be in the food?"

"I don't know if it can be eaten or injected or inhaled. Dammit, I don't know enough about it." Her lips tightened. "And Hu Chang's not here to tell me. So we'll just have to protect Andrews against everything we conceive as a threat. And hope Hu Chang shows up soon to help us."

"Providing he sees a way to save his

drug *and* William," Pat said harshly. "I've no faith in your friend Hu Chang. As far as I'm concerned, he's a prime candidate for my baseball bat."

"I can see how you'd feel like that. You have a right to be angry."

"You bet I do." Pat turned and strode away from her down the hall.

Catherine entered the bedroom and closed the door. She couldn't blame Pat for her anger with Hu Chang. In her eyes, he was as much a threat to Andrews as Nardik. Catherine had been as persuasive as she could when explaining his position, but who could really explain Hu Chang?

And where the hell are you, Hu Chang?

Okay, forget him. Wondering and worrying about him would do no good now. She had to concentrate on what she had to do. She had gotten the reassurance she needed from Pat Gower. She had been almost certain the woman would be a valuable asset, but almost wasn't good enough in a job like this. She'd had to be absolutely positive that she could count on her.

Now she could go down and check out the surroundings as Gallo was doing.

After she talked to Sam.

Nardik had been too quiet since the attack on the Golden Palace, and she was uneasy. She and Gallo had been moving fast, but she couldn't expect that Nardik had been standing still. She knew Sam would have called her if there had been any trouble, but she would still feel better if—

Her phone rang.

Her heart jumped as she saw the ID.

Sam. It was only coincidence that she had just been thinking about him. It didn't mean anything. Nothing was wrong.

She pressed the access. "Tell me everything is okay, Sam."

"I'm sorry. God, I'm sorry."

Stark fear. "Don't tell me that. You tell me my Luke is safe, Sam. You tell me he's alive and well."

"I can't tell you that, Catherine. I don't know whether he's alive or not. But the chances are that he may be if Nardik wants that drug you told me about."

"Why don't you know, Sam?"

"He disappeared tonight. Kelly said he was looking up something in a book in the library, but when we called him for supper, he was gone."

"That doesn't mean someone took him. How could anyone just walk in the house and take my Luke? You were there, Sam. And you had guards. You said you had guards. You said he was safe."

"I found Jordack, one of my guards, with his neck broken and dragged over behind the bushes. I still don't know how anyone got in the house. I kept that front door locked day and night, and Luke disappeared in the space of a couple hours. I've got everyone searching the neighborhood and asking questions, but we're not getting answers."

She closed her eyes. Oh God, it was happening again, she thought in panic. No, she couldn't lose him again. "I should be there. I'd find him."

"Trust me. I'm doing everything I can."

"You let him be taken. *I* let him be taken. I swore I'd keep him safe, and I broke my word."

"Catherine, I was responsible. I'm the one to blame."

She couldn't talk to him any longer. "You go try to find him, Sam. Call me as soon as you know something."

Silence. "I think you'll know something

before I do. Let me know as soon as you do. Please, Catherine. You know I care about Luke."

"I know." She hung up and dropped down in the chair beside her. Hold on. Don't get sick. Keep control.

Luke.

You'll know something before I do.

Of course she would hear. Nardik wouldn't make her wait too long before he inserted the knife.

Insert that knife in me, bastard. Don't hurt my son.

"Catherine?" The door was opening, and Gallo was frowning at her. "Okay? I knocked, but you didn't— Shit." He was across the room in a heartbeat and falling to his knees before her chair. "Not okay." His hands tightly grasped her own. "What the hell is wrong? You're shaking as if you have malaria."

She hadn't realized that she was trembling. But she shouldn't be surprised when her whole world was trembling. "Luke." She managed to get the word out. "It's Luke."

Gallo muttered a curse and pulled her into his arms. "How bad? Is he alive?"

"Sam . . . thinks he is. A guard was killed.

Luke disappeared. Sam and his security team haven't been able to find him." Her hands slid around Gallo's shoulders, and she held on tightly. He was strong and warm, and she was neither right now. She had to take some of that strength until she could conquer the weakness. "It has to be Nardik."

"That's our best guess. But that means we've got a hope of getting him back if we work it right."

"What do you mean?" she asked fiercely. "We will get him back. Nothing is going to happen to Luke."

"Shh." He was rocking her gently. "Of course we will. We just have to see what Nardik has up his sleeve, then find a way to get Luke away from him. How long has he been gone?"

"I don't know. A few hours."

"If it's Nardik, you should hear from him soon. Do you want me to talk to him?"

"Are you crazy? This is my son," she said jerkily. "I'm the one who is responsible for him." She pushed away from Gallo and immediately regretted it. She was shaking worse than she had before, and she hated to reveal that weakness. Oh, what difference did it make? She had no pride where Luke was concerned. "I should have been there to keep him safe, Gallo. I was given a second chance when I got him back, and I blew it. But I won't let him suffer again. I won't let that happen. I'll do anything to keep Nardik from—" She drew a deep breath and struggled for composure. "But I can't let Nardik call all the shots, or I'll never get Luke back. I have to bargain. I have to be cool. Nardik will take advantage of any softness."

"He's going to want Hu Chang."

"I can't give him Hu Chang." She pressed her fingers to her throbbing temple. "But I can give him someone to trade for Hu Chang."

He stiffened. "I don't like the sound of that."

"Too bad. Nardik has a dossier on the relationship that Hu Chang and I have. It's doubtful that he'd believe Hu Chang would sacrifice himself for me because Nardik would never sacrifice himself for anyone. He wouldn't understand the concept. But if Nardik has me, then maybe he could be convinced that Hu Chang might be persuaded to give him the formula for

Pondera. Or maybe just the information he needs for the assassination. He might take what he could get." She nodded. "Yes, that would probably work."

"I imagine it would," he said grimly. "And do you think that he'd let you live no matter what kind of bargain he made with Hu Chang?"

"Of course not. But it would give me a chance to free Luke, and I can work out a way to save myself if I don't have to worry about him."

"Not I. We. You keep leaving me out."

"Intentional." She looked up to meet his gaze. "I'll use you to help me free Luke, but after that you step back. You take care of my son and let me handle dealing with Nardik."

"Bullshit."

"I told you once that I wouldn't drag you any deeper than I had to. Any debt you owe me is paid."

"That's my decision. I took my job from Venable, not you. I don't usually opt out in the middle of a mission."

She shook her head, but she didn't argue. There was time for that later, and she was too upset now to think of anything but Luke.

Call me, you bastard. Tell me he's alive. Let me talk to him.

"Just lean back and relax. I'll see if there's a coffeepot in this suite." He rose to his feet. "You need something hot to drink. You're ice-cold."

She felt cold, she realized, and dammit, she couldn't stop that shaking. She had to get hold of herself. "Coffee would be good. I think I saw a coffeepot on the—"

Her phone rang, and she jumped on it. "Hello."

"Have you heard from your Sam O'Neill yet?" The voice was deep and mocking. "It wouldn't surprise me if he decided not to call since he failed you so miserably."

"Nardik?"

Gallo stiffened, then leaned forward and pressed the speaker.

"Yes. It's wonderful talking to you at last. Your voice is as alluring as your appearance, Catherine. You have real star quality. I don't believe I'll ever forget you standing by that rail and lifting your glass to me." His tone became edged. "No, I'm sure I won't. Before that, my fantasies about you were purely sexual, but they changed and became very sadistic. But that can be just as exciting. I'll show you when we're together."

"My son."

"I thought that would occupy your thoughts. After trying all those years to rescue your son only to lose him again. What a pity. It must be a mother's nightmare."

"Where is my son? Is he alive?"

"I'm tempted to keep you in suspense, but that would be cruel. I never destroy a bargaining chip before it's been used. That would be foolish. Though my friend, Ken Fowler, is eager to test the boy's endurance. I told him that a child is really no challenge. They break so easily."

Not her Luke. Luke had endured those nightmare years of captivity and never broken. "Then don't hurt him. That would be of no help to you. *He's* no help to you, Nardik. Hu Chang scarcely knows my son. He wouldn't care what happened to him."

"I'm inclined to agree with you. After all, Hu Chang is a very tough customer. How many deaths has he engineered in his lifetime, Catherine?"

"I have no idea."

"But according to reports, he has a soft spot for you. Isn't that peculiar?"

"Most people find it rather strange. But it puts me in a position where I'm a much better bargaining chip than my son. Even you can see that."

"Yes, that's true. Is Hu Chang with you now?"

"No, you must have been told that. You have contacts in D.C., don't you?"

"Oh, yes, I have contacts everywhere. Including a few in that ranch from where you're speaking right now. I was hoping that I'd have some news to greet you when you showed up for the Great Debate. It was very clever of you to figure out the connection to Andrews. Not that it will do you any good." He paused. "I suppose Hu Chang checked on those medical records and found out that Andrews is a prime candidate for the drug?"

As if she'd tell him if he had. "I don't know what he's found out."

"That's right, I was informed that Hu Chang wasn't with you in Washington. Can you contact him?"

"I can phone him. He won't talk to me.

But I can leave a message." She paused. "If I have something worthwhile to say."

"Oh, you'll have something to say."

"Shall we cut to the chase? I'm valuable to you. Luke is not. I'll trade myself for Luke's freedom. Then I'll call Hu Chang, and we'll see how much he cares whether I live or die."

"That sounds reasonable. As you say, the boy is no good to anyone but you." He was silent. "But I might be persuaded to allow a substitution to take place. I'm a bit concerned about making sure that drug will work. I don't like the fact that it might depend on Andrews's physical condition. I want to rule it out. My client is uneasy, and that makes me uneasy. My reputation is at stake."

"What are you asking?"

"I want another dose of Pondera of at least equal strength as insurance that it will work."

"No way. Hu Chang loves that damn drug. He told me he'd learned his lesson, and he's not going to let it out of his hands again."

"That doesn't surprise me. Then I suppose I'll just have to make do with you and see if that will coax him to come out of hiding to save your neck. He might be more amenable after he sees the initial damage on that beautiful body. Now I'll give you my orders for the exchange."

"I want to talk to my son."

"He's not available at the moment."

She inhaled sharply. "Why not?"

"I had a few transportation problems."

"You're lying." She tried to keep the panic from her voice. "He's not alive."

"Think what you like. I'm not stupid enough to kill the goose that lays the golden egg. And you're very golden indeed, Catherine."

The fear began to ebb. "No deal until he talks to me. I have to be sure."

"We're running very close on time, Catherine. I've already decided that Andrews will be given the drug whether there's a risk or not. But I'd like reassurance that the drug will work properly. I also want Hu Chang's formula, and I will have it. But if not through you, I'll find another way. Your son may not be worth anything to me if you keep stalling."

"I'm not stalling. He's my son, but I value my life. I won't let you get your hands on me until I'm sure I'm getting what I want in return. Now when can I talk to Luke?"

He was silent. "Perhaps a few hours. It wasn't easy to arrange to snatch your kid, and I'm going to be very careful not to lose him now that I have him. Your O'Neill had guards all over the neighborhood, and I'm having to move carefully. I'll try to arrange it as soon as possible."

"And when can I see him?"

"Don't be greedy. That will be on the timetable that I decide. I'll call you when it suits me." He hung up.

"Was he lying? Could you tell?" she asked Gallo as she hung up. "Is Luke alive?"

"I'm no psychic," Gallo said. "But it would make sense that grabbing Luke would be a big undertaking."

"But Luke would fight them," she said unsteadily. "He's had to fight all his life. I know he'd fight them. And they could hurt him even if they'd had orders not to do it."

"I don't believe Nardik was stalling. I think that you'll get that call. Perhaps after he lets you sweat a little. His tone was definitely vicious when you came on the line."

"I'd made him angry. Hell, I wanted him

angry and stinging from anything that I could do to him. At the time, I was so angry myself that I didn't even think about anything but telling him how little he mattered to me." She swallowed. "I didn't think about Luke until later."

"I'm sure Luke was already a secondary target when he decided that he might go after you. It's the way he operates. Stop blaming yourself. You did everything possible to protect Luke. If anyone is responsible for the chain of events besides Nardik, it's Hu Chang." He pulled to her feet. "There's no way on Earth that you're going to let Nardik hurt anyone who belongs to you. I know that, Catherine. So find me that coffeepot, and we'll settle down to wait for Nardik's call. Then we'll brainstorm until we find a logical way to free Luke and screw that bastard."

He was trying to get her moving forward and into battle mode, she thought. Gallo and she were so different in a multitude of ways, but they were both warriors in instinct and experience. Tonight, he had given her strength and truth, not lies or pity. Now he realized that this fear and guilt could be paralyzing and was trying to temper it. It could not be erased, but she could deal with it if she kept her mind busy and focused and her imagination at bay. She was suddenly passionately grateful that she had Gallo here to remind her of who she was and that this was only one more battle that she had to win.

And she *would* win it.

"You're right." She reached out and quickly squeezed Gallo's arm before turning away. "We'll screw the bastard."

CHAPTER
17

"It's been over two hours." Catherine's grasp tightened on the coffee cup that contained her fourth or fifth cup of coffee. She couldn't remember how many she'd tossed down. "He should have called by now."

"Easy," Gallo said. "It's not been that long in the scheme of things. It just seems like forever to you." He reached over and took the cup from her and set it on the coffee table. "But the caffeine is probably—"

Her phone rang, and she tensed. "That has to be—" But the ID was Kelly Winters. She answered quickly. "Kelly, I'll talk to you later. I'm expecting a call."

"I know," Kelly said. "Sam told me when I came back with the security guys from searching the neighborhood for Luke. I tried not to call you, but it was driving me crazy, and I had to do it."

"Look, I know how you feel. I know you're sorry about Luke. You don't have to say anything."

"Yes, I do. I have to tell you—it may not mean anything. But it could mean that things aren't quite as they— Anyway, you have to know everything in case you can figure out something that I can't."

"So tell me. Quick."

"Right before Luke went downstairs to the library, we were talking about that blasted book and how Luke was obsessed with it. He was actually relieved that I couldn't find a reasonable explanation about why he felt as if he knew more than indicated by the translation. He said that he'd wanted me to come and help because he'd been thinking about weird stuff, and I'd know if it was okay to go in that direction."

"Weird stuff?"

"Yeah, and who can be more weird than I? Anyway, he went downstairs to the library right after that." She paused. "But he was looking out the window while he was talking to me and mentioned Jordack standing under the tree."

"Jordack is the security guard who was killed?"

"Yes, Luke said that he didn't look as tall huddled against the trunk to get out of the rain."

"You think that the guard had already been taken out?"

"I don't know. I didn't see him. All I know is that Luke saw him and thought he looked different. And then he left his room and went downstairs. I followed him and saw him at the window beside the front door looking out at the rain. Then he went to the library, and that was the last I saw of him."

"But that doesn't tell me anything that will help—" She stopped. If Kelly thought there was a thread to be pursued, then it probably existed. "What are you saying?"

"That there may be a pattern we don't know about. Maybe one that Luke was following. Oh, I don't know, Catherine. But there was something . . . not usual. I had to tell you about it in case you could put the pieces together."

"I'll think about it. Is that all, Kelly?"

"No, one more piece. The book he was reading in the library. I found it on the window seat. I've e-mailed a photo of it to you. I'll get off the phone now. I hope this all helps. God, I hope it does." She hung up.

"Well?" Gallo asked Catherine. "Pretty flimsy. And it doesn't appear to be leading us any closer to Nardik. Is it going to be useful?"

"Kelly is never flimsy." Catherine rubbed her temple. "She instinctively coordinates and builds patterns even if she can't see them. If she thinks there may be an alternate pattern to examine, then we should do it. But my brain is spinning, and this info she heaped on me is making it worse." She was trying to assimilate everything Kelly had told her and find logic.

The Chinese chemistry book that had obsessed Luke since he'd started to read it.

The fact that Luke had recently been worried if thinking in a weird direction was okay.

Luke had possibly seen the killer and his potential kidnapper while he was looking out the window.

If he had suspected that security had been breached, why had he not told Sam?

"The book that Kelly found on the window seat," Gallo nudged gently.

"Yes." She accessed the e-mail on her phone. "It's right here. I'll see what—"

She inhaled sharply as the gold script title jumped out at her. *The Art and Practical Usage of Hypnosis.* "Oh, yes, this is weird stuff all right. Why was Luke—" Then it was all coming together, bombarding her, coming clearer with every passing second.

"Oh, my God."

"Catherine?"

"Another pattern, Kelly said." Her voice was shaking. "Another path."

"And?"

"I've found the pattern. Damn him, I've found the pattern." Her hand was trembling as she started to dial. "Why would he do—" She stopped as she got the answering machine that she had expected. "You answer me, Hu Chang. Pick up. Do you hear me? I'm going through hell, and I won't tolerate this. I just talked to Nardik, and he scared me to death. I think he was either lying, or he genuinely thought he had my boy. But he doesn't, does he?"

No answer.

She drew a long, deep, shaky breath. "If you care anything about me, you'll forget about that stupid Pondera and let me talk to my son."

Hu Chang came on the line. "Catherine, I never create anything that could be termed as stupid. You should realize that by now. I know you're emotionally disturbed by what must be happening at the moment, but I—"

"Let me talk to my son. You have him, don't you? Let me talk to Luke."

"Yes, Luke is with me."

Relief made her so weak her head was swimming. Thank God her guess had been right. Oh, thank God. "Let me talk to him."

"In a few moments. Since I bear responsibility for most of this disturbance you're experiencing, I don't wish to expose him to it until you're calmer. It might upset him." He suddenly chuckled. "Luke is frowning at me. I believe he regards those words as an insult."

"I'm not going to be calmer. Not until I

know he's safe. I still don't know that. Did you make some kind of deal with Nardik to kidnap him?"

"Of course I didn't. I told you Nardik was Lucifer. Would I let him near your son?"

"I don't know what you'd do. How did you get hold of Luke?"

"Actually, he invited me to step into the scene. I was quite shocked . . . and very approving. Of course, I paved the way a little ahead of time, but that only aroused Luke's curiosity."

"What the hell are you talking about, Hu Chang?"

"I had to take care of the boy," he said simply. "I know Nardik. You do not. He always hits at the weakest link. I knew he would go after Luke. I realize you had guards all around Luke, but I couldn't risk one of Nardik's men slipping through the cordon Sam had linked around him."

"Why didn't you talk to me? Do you think I wouldn't have gone to Luke if you'd said one word about the possibility of his not being safe?"

"No, but I had other plans that you might not have agreed to put into place."

"What plans?" She leaped for the most

logical answer. "You have some kind of convoluted scheme to use Luke to get your drug."

"Pondera is important. What's wrong with saving the drug, your fine patriot, Andrews, and Luke? It's a multifaceted plot that serves many purposes. Luke doesn't object. He realizes that it could be beneficial to everyone concerned. He didn't care for the idea that Nardik was going after you with such venom."

"Of course Luke didn't object," she said bitterly. "Why would he? But he has to know what you did to him. Kelly sent me a photo of that book he was reading tonight before you took him. *The Art and Practical Usage of Hypnosis.* Luke realized that one explanation for his obsession with that chemistry book you gave him was that you'd implanted a posthypnotic suggestion concerning it."

"Yes, wasn't that clever of him? Considering that he had to work everything out for himself, and he'd had only scant contact with the subject of hypnosis, it was amazing. I was very proud."

"That you'd subverted his will?"

"Would I do that? It was just necessary that I make sure that the book was safe and useful to him."

"You hypnotized him while he was with you downstairs in the lab in Hong Kong. I didn't even know you practiced hypnosis."

"But you suspected it. You've even joked about it."

"You never confirmed it."

"But if we knew everything about each other, our relationship might grow stale."

"You promise me that you didn't use hypnosis to control Luke in any other way?"

Silence. "Well, I did inspire him to respect and admire me above anyone but you. But I made sure that could be diminished by personal contact if it proved to be false. But I felt I deserved a head start since I'm not with the boy that often."

"Nothing else?"

"Nothing but the contents of the book. You see, it is not so terrible."

"It *is* terrible." She closed her eyes. "But I'm trying to remember that you may have saved my son." Now that Hu Chang had admitted that he had Luke with him, and she knew that Luke was unhurt, the relief was enormous. Hu Chang's silence and manipulation were maddening, even frightening, but he had Luke with him, and her son was safe from Nardik. "But Nardik believes one of his men has Luke. Why?"

"Because his man, Mark Townberg, got close enough to Sam's security man to take him out. I'd been watching down the street and decided I had to step in. So I persuaded Townberg that he was sleepy and needed a nap in my car."

"Hypnosis?"

"No, hypnosis takes time. Drugs are good, drugs are fine. I went back to the oak tree and stood there for a few moments, thinking about my next move. I looked up and saw Luke standing at a window on the second floor."

"And then just decided to walk into the house?"

"I thought he might be ready for me. I was right, he'd unlocked the front door."

She could see why Luke had been ready, Catherine thought. He had been curious and eager to know what was happening to him. And he had welcomed the only man who could tell him. "What happened to Nardik's man, Townberg?"

"I decided he might be useful and that I should keep him alive and functioning. So when Luke and I left the neighborhood, we took Townberg with us."

"Luke was riding around in your car with that murderer?"

"You're speaking like a mother. It was no shock that could damage him. It's not as if Luke hadn't spent most of his years with men like Townberg."

"No, but that doesn't mean I want him to spend one more minute with them." She dropped the subject. "What did you do to Townberg?"

"I persuaded him to make a phone call to Fowler, Nardik's assistant, and tell him he had Luke."

"Persuaded?"

"I have a very good drug that accomplishes amazing feats of persuasion. I also had him stall Fowler and say it would take a little time to get the boy to Nardik. You said that Nardik called you?"

"Yes. And I'm angry as hell that you let him put me through that hell."

"It will fade once you consider the alternatives if I hadn't taken the boy. But I will not ask you to be grateful to me. I realize that would be difficult when you—"

"Grateful? You closed me out. You just got on a plane and ignored everything but what you wanted."

"I wanted Luke alive, Catherine," he said quietly.

"And your damn drug safe and sound." But that first sentence had disarmed her. He had kept Luke alive, and, in the end, that was the most important thing to remember. "I'm supposed to be waiting for another call from Nardik who promised to put Luke on the phone. We're going to arrange to trade me for Luke." She added dryly, "Nardik believes I'm a valuable bargaining chip either to lure you or get you to furnish him information. He doesn't realize that you don't give a damn for anything but your Pondera."

"That was a cruel blow. Nardik is actually correct. He couldn't choose a more desirable lure." He was silent. "I was hoping to find a way to keep you out of it. It doesn't seem to be happening. Oh well, I will force Townberg to call Nardik one last time and tell him that he will be able to deliver Luke sometime tomorrow. Nardik will tell Townberg to call you and put the boy on the phone."

"One last time? You're not to kill Townberg in front of Luke, Hu Chang."

"Am I a savage? I will restrain myself." He was silent again. "I do not like that you're involved in these negotiations. I was planning that Luke and I would handle the matter ourselves."

"Keep my son out of this."

"I will make every effort not to endanger him."

"No, you're dodging. Keep him out of it entirely."

He didn't answer.

Her hand tightened on the phone. "Hu Chang."

"I must get the Pondera back. Luke understands that's a priority."

"How could he? Luke is eleven years old."

"He understands."

She didn't like the sound of that. "Don't you dare hypnotize him again."

"No, that's all over." He added quickly, "I will make do with changing my plans and having you involved, but you must do exactly as I say."

"The hell I will. What do you—"

"I'll call you back," Hu Chang interrupted her. "Townberg's phone is ringing. It's probably Nardik calling him trying to arrange for you to talk to Luke. I'll have to monitor what he says to him." He hung up.

"Dammit," Catherine said in frustration as she pressed the disconnect. "I didn't get a chance to talk to Luke. And I had to tell him how—" She reached up to rub the back of her neck. "It's all crazy, Gallo. Only Hu Chang would be able to pull off something this bizarre." Her lips tightened. "And without consulting me. He left me out in the cold."

"I wish that meant you were going to break with him," Gallo said. "But the anger only goes so far, doesn't it?"

"What should I feel? He saved Luke, dammit."

Gallo's lips twisted. "And who can trump that?"

"No one." She got to her feet and went to the window and looked out into the darkness. "I thought I'd lost Luke again. It was killing me, Gallo."

"I know. I could feel it." He was silent. "So what happens now? Hu Chang seems to be in the driver's seat, but I can't see you letting him stay there."

"Hell, no. He was going to find a way to use Luke to get his damn drug back. Who knows what he'd be having him do?" She shook her head to try to clear it. "But it's hard to think right now."

"What's your objective?" Gallo asked. "I suppose you could take your son and hide out until all this is over. But that's not going to happen, is it? You're already thinking and fuming, now that you know he's safe."

He was right: the terror had turned into pure rage at Nardik. "That bastard, Nardik, tried to take my son. He told me he was going to torture and kill him. If Hu Chang hadn't moved first, he might have done it. And if he slips away, he'll try again."

"That's true. So you have an objective. Now all we have to do is get a plan together."

She turned to look at him. "What are you doing, Gallo? I'm sensing manipulation."

"Perhaps a little." He met her gaze. "Because I have an objective, too. You're upset, bewildered, and vulnerable, and I don't want Hu Chang to take advantage of that condition to stay in the driver's seat. When he calls you back, I want you to have the reins firmly in your hands."

She smiled faintly. "Not yours?"

"Not this time." He shrugged. "Though I admit it's beginning to chafe me." He prompted softly, "Now tell me what you're going to do about Nardik."

"I'm going to take him down. He's not going to touch Luke. He's not going to kill Andrews. And Hu Chang is not going to run the show." She added, "Did you really expect anything else, Gallo?"

He smiled with satisfaction. "Not a damn thing. I just wanted to make sure that you were your usual self, and Hu Chang hadn't thrown you off base by his shenanigans. When Luke is involved I—" He stopped as her phone rang and gestured mockingly. "Pick up. That's probably your Houdini dangling magic and your Luke to lure you back into his fold."

CHAPTER

18

The phone call proved to be from Hu Chang, just as Gallo thought.

"Townberg behaved magnificently," he said as soon as she answered. "With my equally magnificent coaching. Nardik gave him orders to have Luke call you."

"Did you find out anything else? Do we know where he is?"

"I found out previously from Townberg that Nardik is staying at some ranch in Texas with a number of bodyguards and probably a way to exit efficiently after Andrews is killed. He didn't know exactly where the ranch is located. But if you find it, I'm sure that you'll be able to prevent his departure and gather him into the net."

"Really? How?"

"That's your problem. I can't do everything, Catherine."

"I don't want you to do anything," she said through set teeth. "No, that's not true. But you could have stopped after you saved Luke."

"That wasn't an option. I still have important tasks to perform." He paused. "And so do you. Now that you're no longer frightened for Luke, I think I'm sensing a . . . change."

"Of course, there's a change. I'm as angry with Nardik as I am with you, and I'm going to do something about it." She added crisply, "There should be some way we can use the fact that Nardik doesn't know that you have Luke. It could be an ace in the hole. He'll think I'm vulnerable, which means he'll feel safer." She was reaching for a way to do it. "Nardik asked me about Andrews's medical records. You've had time to go over them. Will the drug work on him, or will he need an additional dose?"

"No, it's sufficient."

"And Nardik would walk away with a fortune and more power than even he could hope for and looking for his next score. We don't even know how or when Nardik has arranged to administer the drug. But I'd bet that some plan is in place no matter what happens. Dammit, Andrews is a good man. I don't like the idea of a good man dying. Too many dreams are dying these days." She was frowning with frustration. "Everything is too loose and uncertain. We have to find a way of luring Nardik away from the safety of that cozy little ranch. It could prove to be a fortress for him and make everything too difficult. And we have to get some idea of how they're going to use that dose of Pondera."

"Ah, a double challenge. How are you going to meet it?"

"The extra dose." Gallo spoke for the first time. "Use the extra dose."

"What do you—" She stopped as she made the connection. "Your precious Pondera, Hu Chang. That's what Nardik is principally concerned with at this particular moment. I'm only a bonus. He even asked if you'd told me if the drug would work on Andrews. He said he was uneasy and wanted an extra dose for insurance. What if I tell him that I'd contacted you, and you'd told me that it wouldn't work without that additional dose?"

"And?"

"I'll say that you wouldn't exchange yourself for either me or Luke, but you offered me the extra dose instead. I think that would make sense to Nardik." She paused, searching for the next move. "But I'll tell him that you can't prepare the Pondera and get it to me before tomorrow evening. He'll have to meet me somewhere near enough to the Andrews ranch so that I can give it to him in time for him to get it to the man at the debate who is going to administer it."

"Even if you can set him up, he's not going to let you choose the place, Catherine," Gallo said.

"We'll work with what we can get. Let him choose the place. I'll only demand it be out in the open, so that I can be sure that I won't be ambushed. He'll probably insist on a least one of his men being present. I show up, they search me, he makes the call to release Luke, I hand him the drug." She grimaced. "And after I hand him the Pondera, the trap snaps shut."

"The hell it does," Gallo said. "No way, Catherine."

"That's the way I feel." She met his gaze. "So you find a way to keep the trap from shutting and give me enough time to take Nardik down."

He muttered a curse. "You don't ask much."

Hu Chang chuckled. "But we have confidence in you, Gallo. Look how clever you were at extricating us from that island."

"Can you get me a vial of liquid that appears identical to the Pondera that Nardik will be using, Hu Chang?" she asked.

"Of course." He paused. "But I'd better try to create a small dose of the real drug instead. Nardik wouldn't have been able to duplicate Pondera, but he probably had his lab find a quick way to test the drug for authenticity."

"Can you do that on this short notice?"

"Yes, with some difficulty, but it can be done. May I get you anything else that you might find useful?"

"Mamba venom?" Gallo asked mockingly. "I remember you once told me about that. He does meet all your needs, doesn't he?"

"I do my best," Hu Chang said. "Catherine?"

"No." She thought about it. "Yes, the heat polish you made for me for that job in Iran. I'll check with Venable, but we may need it. Deliver both of them to the Andrews ranch when you bring Luke. I'll find a secure place for you to land. Helicopter?"

"That seems the most practical."

"I'll call Sam O'Neill and ask him to hop on a plane and get here in time to take custody of Luke." She added with sudden fierceness, "You're being very cooperative, Hu Chang. But if anything goes wrong with our getting Nardik because you're holding out to snatch that blasted Pondera, I'm going to strangle you."

"My, my, such violence. But I know something that will soothe you. Would you like to talk to Luke?"

"What else have I been asking to do?"

"Catherine?" Luke came on the line. "Hu Chang told me you'd be angry, but you shouldn't be. What else could he do? Jordack was dead, and we had to get out of there."

"You could have gone to Sam and told him. Why did you just go along with Hu

Chang as if he was some kind of Pied Piper?"

"Because I trusted him," he said simply. "It seemed to be the thing to do."

"Kelly told me about that book on hypnosis."

"Hu Chang explained. He said he wouldn't have made me do anything I didn't want to do. And now that I know it happened once, he said he couldn't hypnotize me again."

He was defending Hu Chang. It was too familiar. Like mother, like son. No matter what Hu Chang did, she had always defended him, even when she had known he was wrong. Now Luke was caught in that same net.

"I'm sorry I got you into this, Luke," she said unevenly. "I thought I could keep you safe."

"It wasn't your fault. Hu Chang said it was the nature of your relationship that you would try to save him. And that nature must always be accepted."

"Bull, you don't have to accept that I'd sacrifice you for Hu Chang. That's not happening."

"But it somehow made sense to me that

you have to take chances if you don't want to lose somebody."

"Maybe. But Hu Chang can make black look white."

"But he tells the truth, doesn't he?"

"Yes, but sometimes it gets a little twisted."

He chuckled. "But that's interesting. It's like reading a mystery and not knowing until the last page how it's going to turn out."

She sighed. "He's got you." Again, it was almost like listening to herself. "Listen, I've told him that you're the one who is important. You're the one who has to be safe. Don't let him tell you anything else, okay?"

He was silent a moment. "I know what you're saying. I don't believe . . . I'll have to think about it. I'm a little confused right now. Some things feel right. Some things feel wrong."

"What feels right?"

"Hu Chang. The moment he walked into the library, I knew that it was right he was there." He paused. "And I think it's wrong that I worry about myself and not you."

"Luke, I'm not the one who—"

"I think it's wrong." Before she could answer, he said, "Good-bye. I'm handing the phone back to Hu Chang now."

"Wait. We should talk about—"

"It seems he doesn't want to talk any longer," Hu Chang said. "So I believe we should hang up now and get to the business at hand. After you've supposedly received the call from Townberg and Luke, you'll get another call from Nardik, wanting to set up the deal. You must be very convincing, Catherine. He's no fool. Everything must seem reasonable."

"As reasonable as anything else about this nightmare," she said. "You take care of my son, Hu Chang."

"As if he were my own," he said gently.

"That's what scares me. If he were your own, you'd probably be dragging him all over the world and teaching him how to make poisons like Pondera."

He chuckled. "It would not be a bad life for him if he had the aptitude. Not with me to shoulder the—"

"Take care of him."

"Will it make you feel better to know that in my heart of hearts, I feel as if he could be my own? I didn't feel like that at our first meeting in Hong Kong, but there has been something growing . . ."

She didn't know whether those words reassured her or not. She knew from experience how demanding Hu Chang could be, particularly from those he cared about. "I'll call you as soon as the deal is set."

She hung up and looked at Gallo. "Well, what do you think?"

"Why ask me?" There was a distinct edge to his voice. "You and Hu Chang seem to have set up everything to your satisfaction."

"It's not to my satisfaction. I want this over and my son home." Her lips tightened. "But he won't be safe, even if he's home, as long as Nardik is alive. Thanks to Hu Chang's sleight of hand with Luke, we have a chance of reeling that bastard in, and I'm going to take it." She frowned. "And you're not being reasonable. This is the direction you were goading me toward, isn't it?"

"Yes, and I don't have to be reasonable. I didn't want you to be under Hu Chang's thumb, but I forgot how reckless and single-minded you could be." He smiled sardonically. "I guess I was hoping that you'd just walk away from Hu Chang and rely on me."

She shook her head. "I rely on myself, Gallo. I'm grateful for your help, but I'm not going to depend on you."

"But you're willing to trust Hu Chang even when it comes to protecting your son."

"We've been together a long time. Yes, I'm angry with him, but I trust Hu Chang when he said he'd protect Luke. I guess you don't understand my doing that."

He didn't answer for a moment. "Oddly enough, I do understand it. I don't know what makes him tick, and he probably has a dozen reasons for every agenda, but he did save Luke. I believe the principal reason he did it was that he wouldn't allow anything to hurt someone connected to you. It's taken me a long time, but I'm beginning to see what holds the two of you together. Do I resent it? Yes, but that's purely personal, and it's not going to change anything. As long as he doesn't do anything to hurt you, I'll play the game." He shrugged. "But I'll play it my way. You want your son to be safe and Nardik to be taken out, Hu Chang wants his drug, I want Andrews to live and you to survive. We've just got to hope that one of us won't be disappointed." He turned toward the door. "I'm going to go down and look around and learn every inch of this place. Then I'm going to Google all the area around here for a hundred miles and see if I can guess where Nardik will choose to meet you. Then I'll call Venable and arrange to have a Special Ops team available if we need them." He glanced at her. "I don't suppose I can talk you out of walking into the lion's den?"

"No. If I let Venable handle it when all hell broke loose, what would stop Nardik from making a call to tell his men not to wait to kill Andrews? He'd do it. You know he would. He wouldn't accept being beaten."

"And if you're there, you'd be close enough to stop him?"

"He wouldn't make that call," she said flatly. "I'll do my part. You just get busy doing yours."

"It will be my pleasure. I'll get right on it." He smiled crookedly over his shoulder. "You'll notice, I'm not arguing about your decision? It's taking great restraint, but I'm working on keeping myself from being protective and on leaving you on your own."

"Thank you."

But the door had already closed behind him.

Loneliness.

Push it away. She couldn't have it all ways. Gallo had been comforting, and she had taken from his strength, but in the end she was always alone. Even Hu Chang moved in and out of her life like a shadow.

Luke.

He was no shadow. He might not love her, but as long as she loved him, and he lived, there would never really be loneliness.

She sat down on the couch to wait for the call from Nardik and the time to set the plan in motion.

"You were not courteous to Catherine," Hu Chang said as he hung up the phone and turned to Luke. "That is not a good thing. She wishes only the best for you."

"I know." Luke frowned. "But there's something wrong . . ."

Hu Chang's gaze narrowed on his face. "You will work it out. I believe you're coming close. Perhaps I should help a little." He shrugged. "Though Catherine would object if I damage your tender feelings. Do you have tender feelings, Luke? I think not. I believe you're like my Catherine. Strong and bold, and your feelings are as strong as your heart."

"You talk like one of my books."

"But you like and enjoy books. I am flattered."

Luke looked at the adjoining door. "Why wouldn't you let me stay in the room when you were forcing Townberg to do what you wanted?"

"I knew Catherine wouldn't approve."

"What did you do?" he asked curiously. "He didn't scream or anything, and it didn't take long."

"I'm a physician. I know how to accomplish what I need to do without clumsiness. Next time, he won't even argue with me."

"What are you going to do with Townberg when you're done with him? Will you kill him?"

"Would it bother you if I did?"

He shook his head. "He killed Jordack. He probably would have killed Sam, too. He doesn't matter to me." He made a face. "But it would matter to Catherine if you did it. Not because of him but because of me. She'd worry about its being too much like what I went through before she came to get me in Russia. She worries a lot about that."

"And your 'tender' feelings?"

He looked away. "Maybe."

"Do you resent it?"

"No, she just doesn't understand. She wants me to be what I'm not. I try to be what she wants me to be, but I can't do it."

"Then why bother to try?"

He frowned. "That's a stupid question. Because she wants it."

"And Catherine has to have what she wants even though it's not logical, and she doesn't understand. Why go to all the trouble of pretending? Why should you care?" He took another verbal step forward. "Catherine could die tomorrow, you know."

Luke quickly shook his head. "She's good. She's like a soldier. She's been trained. She won't get hurt."

"She could die."

"No!"

"She's CIA, and she's good. But even the best operatives can be taken down."

"Not her. Not Catherine." His eyes were suddenly glittering with anger. "And if you thought she could get hurt, you shouldn't have told her to go after Nardik. If you knew she could get killed, you shouldn't have done that."

"It's within her capability, and it needed to be done. I will never tell her to hold back because of my fear for her. She would not thank me for it."

"Catherine's strong and smart. Nothing's going to happen to her."

"Don't get emotional. I just want you to be prepared. You're very sharp, Luke. Yet your feelings for Catherine are much too vague. I find that annoys me. I'm not like Catherine, who can't help but think of you as a child, her child. We both know you're not a child. That was burned out of you a long time ago. But the feeling wasn't burned out, and it should belong to her. I don't know if there's some buried resentment or if you're just fighting feeling too much. I don't know, and I don't care. It's time you came into focus. So think about what Catherine is to you and how you'd feel if she ended up having her head blown off by Nardik tomorrow." He smiled cheerfully.

"Oh, that did give you a jolt, didn't it? And now that I've disturbed you enough to deserve Catherine's anger about damaging your tender feelings, I'll go and untie Townberg and have him place another call." He moved toward the door. "And I won't kill him. Because, like you, I'm sensitive to how Catherine feels about such things. I'll either take him with us if he proves himself meek and pliable enough, or just make sure he won't be found until I want him to be found." He paused at the door, and said softly, "You're upset. Good. It will clear your head." He opened the door. "A clear head can be of great benefit in a relationship. You can't hide away any longer. I won't permit it. The walls are down, and they'll stay down. Just keep thinking what a terrible world this would be without our Catherine . . ."

"I might agree to substituting the drug for the boy," Nardik said warily to Catherine. "But I want the formula, too."

"You won't get it," Catherine said flatly. "Hu Chang didn't even want to give up another vial of Pondera. I had to persuade him. He certainly won't give you the formula. Don't be greedy, Nardik."

"You could be lying to me. I might not have to have a second dose."

"But you're worried and want reassurance. This would give it to you. And do you think that Hu Chang would be willing to give that second dose if he didn't think you'd use it? He said that he'd learned his lesson with Ali Gazaran when you got your hands on the extra dose he gave to him."

Silence. "He can't get it to you before eight tomorrow evening? That's too close."

"Do you think making a dose of that drug is easy? I've seen him work two days on one of his poisons. And then he has to deliver it to me after it's ready. The debate isn't until ten. He said he'd try to deliver the drug to me by eight here at the Andrews ranch. Set up a meeting anytime after that, and I'll put it in your hands." She paused. "Or you could let me meet with the person you've got here who's supposed to administer the drug . . . after you release my son."

"No, do you think I'd be fool enough to do that? Besides, I'll have to test it to make sure that you're not lying to me."

"And you want to have your chance at me."

"You don't believe I'd keep our bargain?" he asked mockingly.

"No, and I want my chance to live. I want my boy to live. You meet me somewhere out in the open and leave your goons at home. If I see anyone with you, I won't stop. When you give the order to release Luke, I'll give you the drug."

He was silent. "I'll consider it."

"I'm going to live through this, Nardik. It's the best deal you're going to get."

"Actually, I want you to live for a while. I have plans for you." He paused. "But I can wait. If I don't get you this time, I'll pluck you up when you least expect it. Bring me that drug, Catherine."

"Where?"

"When you have the Pondera, get in the car and drive away from the ranch. I'll call you and give you directions." He hung up.

Yes.

She drew a deep breath and pressed the disconnect. Up to the last minute, she hadn't been certain that he'd go along with her. There would still be hazards and traps all along the way, but at least they had a plan that might work.

Or might not.

Think positive. They were going to get that son of a bitch before he could butcher anyone else.

She took out her phone again to call Gallo and Hu Chang and tell them that Nardik had taken the bait.

Sugarland, Texas
July 3
7:40 P.M.

Catherine met Sam in the driveway of the ranch when he got out of his rental car. "Thanks for coming, Sam. You're the only one I could think of to keep Luke safe while all of this goes down."

He grimaced. "I'm surprised you'll trust him with me after I screwed up. I don't think I would."

"It would have been different if you hadn't had to deal with Hu Chang and Luke working against you from the inside. Hell, Luke unlocked the door and let Hu Chang walk in. It was something you couldn't expect. You'd have handled Nardik's men." She met his gaze. "If I didn't believe that was true, I wouldn't only not trust you with Luke,

I'd be coming after you for letting anyone take him."

He nodded. "And it will never happen again." He looked around the grounds and gave a low whistle. "Good God, it's like a giant carnival."

She could see what he meant. A giant outdoor barbecue kitchen and buffet. A band was blaring a tune from the musical *1776* in the gazebo, and the tables were already filled to overflowing with dozens of guests. "I'm leaning toward a rock-concert comparison. Wait until it gets a little darker, and the fireworks begin. Those are supposed to be nonstop until the debate starts."

Sam's gaze traveled to the hills, where hundreds of cars were already pouring through the north gates. "Holy smoke. I hope Andrews has good crowd control."

"He does. Pat Gower wouldn't have it any other way."

"When do Hu Chang and Luke get here?"

She checked her watch. "Fifteen minutes. Hu Chang will be arriving by helicopter in a field about five minutes' drive from the ranch. It was the only place that we could be assured a little privacy from the mob. John Gallo should already be there waiting." She got into the Jeep parked down the driveway. "Come on, you can go with me."

Sam got into the Jeep, but his gaze was on the stage across the grounds. "With so many people here, it's going to be a nightmare trying to find out which of Nardik's men is actually going to slip Andrews the drug."

"Tell me about it," she said as she backed out of the driveway. "And most of the hiring was done and the credentials issued before we even knew it was Andrews who was the target. I checked over Pat Gower's list and reference file, but it was impossible to spot anyone suspicious in such a short time. We'll just have to get the information from Nardik."

Sam grimaced. "Piece of cake, right?"

"No, but we've got a shot." She turned left as they left the ranch. "That's more than we had a few days ago." Her lips tightened. "And, dammit, we'll make it work for us."

Gallo was waiting by the fence bordering the field when Catherine pulled up. He was dressed in jeans, boots, and a denim shirt and looked very casual. But his expression was far from casual. He nodded toward the west. "I heard rotors. Hu Chang is right on time."

"When he wants to be." She got out of the car. "Sam O'Neill. John Gallo." She looked up at the sky. "You've always had better hearing than I do, Gallo. I don't— Yes, I hear them, too." She watched as the large helicopter came into view. She started across the field as the helicopter began to descend. "Let's go."

CHAPTER
19

Hu Chang gave Gallo a glance as he jumped out of the helicopter. "How absurd you look in that Western garb. Are you supposed to be in disguise?"

"I was supposed to blend into my surroundings at the barbecue. This isn't Hong Kong, Hu Chang. Besides, I like the West. I have a place of my own in Utah." He looked beyond him to Luke and a beefy man huddled on a seat in the corner. "Hello, Luke, I'm John Gallo. I work with your mother."

"How do you do," Luke said politely. "Where's Catherine?"

"Right here." She pushed forward and smiled. Lord, she was glad to see him. She had known he was safe, but there was still a lingering anxiety that wouldn't be dismissed. "And here's Sam. You and he are going to hang out together."

"Hi, Sam." Luke didn't look at him as he jumped out of the helicopter. "Are you okay, Catherine?"

"Of course I am."

He frowned. "But you may not stay that way. Hu Chang said you could get your head blown off."

"Hu Chang!" She shot him a furious glance. "What were you thinking?"

"Only a possibility," Hu Chang said.

"I'm not going to get my head blown off, Luke. Hu Chang was being . . . Hu Chang. Getting Nardik is just a job like any other I've done."

"I want to go with you."

"You can't do it. If I were worried about you, I wouldn't be able to concentrate. That's dangerous, Luke. You don't want me making any mistakes."

"Because then you could get your head blown off." Luke's dark eyes were suddenly glittering fiercely. "Just like Hu Chang said."

"With total inaccuracy," Gallo said. "As soon as we get you settled with Sam, I'm going to hijack this helicopter from the pilot, and Hu Chang and I are going to be on Catherine's tail. There's no way we're going to let anything happen to her." He glanced at Hu Chang. "Isn't that right?"

"With me accompanying Gallo, the chances of anything dire occurring is down to almost zero," Hu Chang said. "And since you're part of the bargaining process, we can't risk your falling into Nardik's hand, Luke." He suddenly beamed. "Much better that we risk Gallo. He's of no importance to anyone."

Luke was obviously not convinced. "What are you going to do, Catherine?"

"I go and meet Nardik by myself as agreed. Hu Chang and Gallo will be following, but they can't be too close, and Nardik would be able to tell if the Jeep is bugged. So I've asked Venable to send one of the drone planes he borrowed from the border patrol to locate and send pictures to Gallo's phone as soon as he can tell where I'm heading. By the time I meet with Nardik, they should have been able to take out any of Nardik's men that he has planted." She repeated Sam's words to her, "Piece of cake."

He shook his head. "Don't tell me that. It won't be easy."

This was proving more painful than she had thought. "Let Sam take you to the car. I have to go, Luke."

"I know that. But if I didn't think that you were telling the truth about my distracting you, I'd be going with you." He suddenly turned to Gallo, and said fiercely, "Don't you let anything happen to her. Do you hear me?" He strode toward Gallo's car. "And no one has to take me anywhere. Come on, Sam." He looked back over his shoulder. "Hu Chang, I didn't think I'd feel like this. I don't like it."

"You're not supposed to like it," Hu Chang said. "It's a crisis. You're supposed to deal with it."

"But you're not letting me. So you'd better do it for me." The door of the car slammed behind him.

Gallo grimaced. "That sounded threatening."

"And promising," Hu Chang said.

"You shouldn't have worried him," Catherine said. But she couldn't think of Luke now. As she'd told him, he was a distraction she couldn't afford. She gazed at the beefy man huddled in the corner, who must be Townberg. He was distinctly glassy-eyed. "He looks almost comatose. Is he able to function?"

"Yes." Hu Chang took out his syringe. "As soon as I give him his shot. This drug allows him to think with a certain clarity but not quickly. I may have to coach him. I'll have him call Nardik and tell him that he's landed at this field near the ranch and that O'Neill is here waiting to take the boy if he gives the word."

"And then Nardik will call me and tell me where I'm to meet him." She nodded. "I'll get on the road. Give me the Pondera."

He reached into his pocket, drew out a vial and handed it to her. "Keep it corked tightly."

"Don't worry, I will."

"And here's the heat nail polish." He handed her another vial containing a dark red liquid. "It has quick dry. You'll be able to function in one minute after applying. Get rid of the vial immediately." He smiled. "It's your color. I wouldn't want you to make a fashion faux pas."

"Heaven forbid." She turned and headed for her Jeep. "No slipups. Protect my back."

Gallo caught up with her as she reached the Jeep. "Don't take chances. If we see you're in trouble, we'll move in to help."

"Why would I take unnecessary chances?" She started the Jeep. "I have a son. But even Luke realized that I have to do my job."

"And the pressure is on to keep Andrews alive." His lips were tight. "So don't tell me that you'll play it entirely safe."

"I've got to go. We've said what we had to say."

"No, I have one more thing to say. Do what you have to do. Run your own show. But I've no intention of letting Nardik kill you either." He turned on his heel and strode back toward the helicopter. "We have too much unfinished business."

Her hands tightened on the steering wheel. Keep calm and unemotional. She had a job to do. But it was difficult to be unemotional when she was around Gallo. Even when there was no sensuality, he managed to stir her to feeling.

Nardik.

Concentrate.

Get the job done.

Gallo watched her drive away before turning to Hu Chang. "Let's get moving."

"In a moment, this drug has to take effect." He studied his face. "You're very tense. Why don't you go up to the cockpit and look over the controls. Are you sure you can fly it? I took you at your word and sent the pilot with Luke and O'Neill, but I don't wish to risk my life. I'm too valuable."

"That's debatable. Yes, I can fly it."

"Good." He turned to Townberg and took out his phone before asking him, "You're eager to have this over, aren't you, Townberg? Be very convincing, and I'll let you rest."

"You know you don't have to go along, Hu Chang," Gallo said curtly. "I can do this alone. You'll probably get in my way. You're the prize in this game, not a participant."

"It's always pleasant to be desired, but I have to disagree. I'm of great value in any engagement. I always intended to be with Catherine. And I may be needed to get information out of Nardik about the assassination. Catherine has the capability to cause great pain. But pain doesn't always have a great effect on Lucifer."

Gallo watched as Townberg's zombielike demeanor was altering by the moment as the drug took effect. The man straightened only seconds later, his cheeks flushing and his eyes taking on an eager alertness. Amazing. "That's incredible stuff. Is it dangerous?"

"Yes. Too many times, and it could kill him. I may be able to do it two more times, if necessary, without permanent damage. But if all goes well, we're through with him, and it doesn't really matter, does it?" He smiled at Townberg and handed him the telephone. "Now listen closely, Townberg, and I'll tell you exactly what to say to Nardik. If he asks you questions, stop and pretend to have cell trouble until I tell you how to answer." He was dialing the phone. "Tell him you're ready to turn the boy over to O'Neill when he tells you to do it. Everything is going well. Do you understand? Good, then here's the rest of it . . ."

Gallo had no desire to see Townberg perform like a mindless puppet. He had seen too much of that mind control when he was a prisoner of war in Korea. He turned, went into the cockpit, and settled himself into the pilot's seat.

He called Venable. "She's on the move. Have you picked up anything in the area?"

"Other than thousands of people at the Andrews ranch?" Venable asked dryly.

"How sensitive are those drones?"

"Very. If you give me a defined area, we'll be able to zero in and give you targets. But she won't have her phone so that we can track her. He'll make her discard it before she gets to him."

"She says that she has a gift from Hu Chang that will do the job. Something to do with a liquid polish that emits a powerful heat signal. She said you'll be able to find her."

"Then I'll trust her. She's never let me down. Anything else?"

Yeah, a guarantee that Catherine would come out of this alive. "No, nothing else." He hung up.

Fireworks.

It was fully dark now, and a brilliant display of fireworks lit the night sky over the Andrews ranch.

Beautiful and splendid and flamboyant.

Like Catherine.

"Townberg performed well. Everything is in place." Hu Chang slipped into the seat next to him. "Ready?"

He started the rotors. "Ready."

Nardik called when Catherine was twenty miles away from the ranch. "On your way, bitch?"

"I'm sure you know I am. You've probably been monitoring the GPS on my phone."

"Yes, and I've blocked the signal for any of your friends. Isn't technology a wonderful thing? If your car has been bugged, I'll be able to tell miles away. And you know what will happen."

"I know." She paused. "And I just got a call from Sam O'Neill, and he said that your man Townberg had promised to turn Luke over to him the minute you give the word. Where am I going, Nardik?"

"Turn west on the next road and go ten miles, then turn at the gas station and go into the hills another fifteen miles. I'll give you other directions once you reach there." He paused. "I can't tell you how eager I am to see you. Do you want me to describe the first thing I'm going to do to you?"

"No."

"I'll tell you anyway. I've thought a lot about it. I can see by your dossier that your mother was a whore. I think you need to learn the same lessons in humility that she did. When I get you to Acapulco, I'll set you up in a room and rent you by the hour. I have many friends with the drug cartels in Mexico, and I'll allow them access to you. I believe a week of that treatment will soften that bitchy arrogance. Then we'll proceed to the next lesson."

"Dream on, Nardik. You only get your chance at me. You're talking as if it's a done deal."

"It is a done deal. You're desperate, and that means you're already a loser. I can almost feel you under me, Catherine. I'll be the first to ride you before they break you. I'm waiting for you." He hung up.

Bastard.

She drew a deep breath. She couldn't let him shake her. He did have the instincts of Lucifer to have chosen to taunt her with that form of torture. There couldn't be anything in that dossier about the rape she'd suffered when she was a child, but he'd still zeroed in on that feeling of helplessness and pain. She had crushed it down and emerged stronger for it, but the memory would never entirely go away.

Okay, let it go. Call Venable and tell him where to send that drone. The meeting place had to be somewhere close to that last direction he'd given her.

She turned left into the next road and started to dial Venable.

Nardik called her one last time as she reached the end of the directions he'd given her. "Okay, turn right and go south toward the mountains. Toward me, bitch. I'll meet you to guide you the rest of the way. Turn off your phone and throw it out the window. And throw any weapons after them."

"No way, that will leave me defenseless."

"I wish it did. But you're a lethal little snake, and weapons are only an additional complement to your arsenal." His tone hardened. "Toss them away, Catherine. I'll know if you don't."

She had known it would be a futile protest. And she had to drop the argument immediately, as she would have done if Luke had really been in the bastard's hands.

She threw her knife and Glock out the window. "I've tossed out my knife and gun. Anything else?"

"Yes, throw out the phone. I'll see you soon." He hung up.

She turned off her phone and tossed it out the window.

She drew a deep breath as she looked out the windshield at the bumpy road ahead. Nardik was right, she had tried to make weapons unimportant in any conflict. Her body was a weapon, her mind was a weapon. But it still would have been comforting to have been able to at least keep the knife.

But Gallo and Hu Chang would have weapons.

The foothills were barren except for an occasional pine or fir tree, and it was totally dark except for the constant burst of fireworks in the eastern sky. The glittering explosion lit the interior of the Jeep and lit her nails resting on the steering wheel. She brushed the pad of her index figure on her thumbnail.

Heat.

The polish reacted something like an infrared beacon but was more complicated.

The polish was not casting out tremendous heat due to the compound Hu Change added or it would have burned her nails off, but she could detect a noticeable warmth. And he always made sure that the polish interacted to give off a blue glow rather than the usual illumination so that the drone could identify her.

Was it hot and strong enough to be picked up by the drone?

She had to trust Hu Chang.

"Where the hell is she, Venable?" Gallo asked harshly. "You said that drone was a damn miracle. If you've left her stranded out there, I'll—"

"Shut up, Gallo. It takes time. The drone has to make several passes while it sorts out information. Do you think I'm not worried?"

"All I'm thinking is that Nardik would like nothing better than to cut her throat, and I'm flying around here and don't even know where she is."

"Be calm, Gallo," Hu Chang said. "If that drone has any capability at all, it will be able to pick up that heat signal in the polish. It's the equivalent of ten tiny searchlight beams. The drone's computer is probably trying to analyze and identify it." He paused. "My only concern is that it will get involved in trying to identify that new source and not report it. That will not happen, will it, Venable?"

"How the hell do I know?" Venable said roughly. "It shouldn't." He hung up.

"I did not like that answer," Hu Chang said. "We depended on Venable. I hope he does not fail us."

"What would you do if he does?" Gallo asked.

"That would mean that Catherine would die." Hu Chang glanced at the exploding fireworks in the distance. "I could not bear that happening. I would take many lives, and I fear Venable's would be one of them. Mistakes are inexcusable if it causes Catherine harm."

"For once I agree with you." Gallo's gaze was searching the mountains in the distance. "And that means we'd better not make any."

Headlights.

Catherine tensed as she saw the van

driving toward her. A white van and on the side, Bonifeld Security was inscribed in bold red letters.

Bonifeld Security. She had seen trucks with that sign at the ranch, and there were hundreds of security officers with that name on the pockets of their uniforms milling around the property.

Of course, she thought. If you can't beat them, join them. Who else would merge with scarcely a ripple among the guests at the debate?

The van pulled in front of her, blocking the road. A uniformed man jumped out of the driver's seat and crossed in front of the headlights. He was familiar . . . Fair wavy hair, classically handsome features, a golden tan . . .

The photo on his phone that Gallo had shown her that day in Hong Kong. Ken Fowler. What did she know about him? Vicious. Devoted to Nardik and delighted in torture. Nardik had even said Fowler wanted to work on Luke.

No way, you son of a bitch.

"Get out." He opened her door. "My van, whore." He didn't wait for her to get out but pulled her from the seat. "Get fancy, and you'll never see your kid again. I'm going to search you. Don't move."

His hands were on her. Her breasts, between her legs, probing, painful, intimate.

Kill him?

No, take it. She had to get to Nardik.

"I'll let you have thirty more seconds," she said softly. "But you're enjoying this too much. When I think that you've had enough fun to realize I don't have a weapon, I'm going to step back, and you'll take your hands away. If you don't, I'll break your neck."

He froze. Then his hands tightened bruisingly on her breasts.

Don't show him pain or weakness. He'd like it too much. "Fifteen seconds."

"Bluff. I'm the one who has a gun." He slapped her so hard her head snapped back. "You're helpless. Can't you see that?"

"Five seconds."

He met her gaze. He faltered, then his hands fell to his sides. "I'm not afraid of you, bitch." His lips curled viciously. "Nardik promised me a long time with you in Acapulco. You'll be begging me to kill you." His hand closed on her arm, and he jerked her toward the truck. "Have you got that drug? He said to make sure you have it."

"I have it." She got into the passenger seat of the security van. "But I'm not giving it to you."

"I searched you. I didn't find it."

"I have it," she repeated. "Nardik gets it when he gives the word to release Luke."

"If he does." His smile was twisted as he got into the driver's seat. "Nardik wants you, too. Maybe too much. I don't like it, but it's better than have you walk away."

"Just take me to Nardik. I don't deal with errand boys."

He muttered a curse as he started the car. "I'm not an errand boy. I'm important to him. I'm the one he's trusting to give the drug to Andrews. He wouldn't do that if he didn't think I could do it. It means a lot of money to him . . . to us."

"Unless he didn't care if you lived or died."

"He *does* care."

"Think about it."

"I won't think about it. You're a liar." His cheeks were burning with color as his foot stomped on the accelerator. "He knows how smart I am. He knows I'll do anything to please him. Why would he want to get rid of me?"

She had touched a nerve. Good. She might need a disruption in the ranks. She repeated, "Think about it."

"We've got it," Venable's voice was tense. "The report just came in. About forty miles south of where you are. I'll send you the coordinates. She's in a white van with another person moving due north toward the foothills and that heat source Hu Chang gave her is making her glow like a meteorite."

"Destination?"

"It looks like she's heading in the direction of another vehicle on a flat plain just below the foothills."

"How many men does Nardik have there?"

"Only one man on the plain. But there are trees and boulders all around that plain. I ordered an in-depth scan of the area by the drone. I'm sending the results to your iPad." He hung up.

Gallo flipped open his iPad and brought up the picture.

"Shit."

He could immediately see the van with the heat spiking from it like blue sun rays traveling toward a single man standing alone beside a vehicle in the middle of the plain. Nardik.

But he could also see three heat-illuminated figures who were visible at some distance from Nardik.

"They're positioned to take her down the minute Nardik lifts his finger. One man behind that boulder, another in those bushes about thirty yards up the hill." He pointed to a figure behind a pine in the stand of trees closest to the vehicle. "This one is going to be the hardest to take out. There's no cover anywhere around him."

"Then you will take care of disposing of him," Hu Chang said. "I will remove the other two. But since you'll be closer, you'll have to take out Nardik and the man who is bringing Catherine to him."

"Fowler. It's probably Fowler." He was shifting directions toward the north. "I'm not going to argue with you. There isn't any time. I have to take your word that you can take out those goons. But you'd better be damn quiet, or Catherine will be in trouble."

"Oh, they will die very quietly and quickly.

I am very practiced at silent death." Hu Chang was looking down at the lapis star ring on his finger. "How far are we from Nardik?"

"Fifteen minutes. We're not really that far, but I'll have to cut the engines and land some distance away. We'll have to hike the rest of the way." He glanced at the fireworks exploding and lighting the night sky. "Thank God for those firecrackers going off nonstop. We've got to hope we get lucky, and no one hears the rotors."

"Fireworks . . . It's entirely fitting that Andrews have a hand in saving his own life, don't you think?"

"All I'm thinking is that Catherine is getting closer to Nardik every minute," Gallo said grimly, his gaze on the computer screen as he watched the van approaching the plain. "And I'm hoping like hell she'll be able to stall long enough for us to get to her."

"Welcome, Catherine." Nardik stepped forward as the van came to a stop. "I can't tell you how eager I've been to see you. Fowler, leave the headlights on while we do our negotiating. I want to see her expressions."

Catherine jumped out of the van. "By all means, let's have a little light on the subject. It will be different from your usual modus operandi. I hear you skulk in the shadows and hide behind your bodyguards." Her gaze wandered around the area. "Where are they? You can't have suddenly whipped up enough courage to face me with only this weasel Fowler as a backup."

"I'm not afraid of you." His lips curled. "You're only a woman. Women can be broken so easily." His gaze was on her face. "You have a bruise on your cheek. It seems Fowler has already started the process. I was wondering if he would be able to resist."

"He's as much of a coward as you." She was glancing around the plain, calculating the possible positioning of Nardik's men. On the way here with Fowler, she had been picking likely ambush sites. The stand of trees? The foothills? The boulders? She had demanded that there be no more than two present when she turned over the drug, but there was no doubt in her mind that Nardik had loaded the dice against her. When the action started, she had to be prepared to dodge attack from any angle.

Unless Gallo and Hu Chang came through for her.

Don't count on them. Count on the worst-possible scenario and be grateful for anything less.

"The drug," Nardik said. "Give me the drug."

Stall. Give Gallo and Hu Chang a chance to get here. Thank God Nardik still thought he had a bargaining chip in Luke. And thank Hu Chang for manipulating Townberg with such deftness to give her this opportunity. Every moment of the drive from the ranch, she had been afraid that Nardik would find out what they were doing.

She stared him in the eye. "Screw you. I'll show it to you. I won't give it to you until you make the call." She brought her long hair over her shoulder and slowly unbraided the strand underneath the heavy fall and closest to her nape, where she'd placed the tiny vial. She gave Fowler a fierce glance as he took a step toward her. "You get near me, and I'll drop this vial and smash it. You not only wouldn't get your hands on the Pondera, but you'll risk getting a whiff of it.

How do you know it's not an airborne as well as an ingested poison?"

"You wouldn't do that," Fowler said. "You could die, too, bitch."

"But Nardik's counting on my willingness to sacrifice everything because I'm a mother. I don't know about that, but I'll sure take you to hell with me if I think I'm going to lose this game."

"Back off, Fowler," Nardik said coldly. "And keep out of this. It's not your business."

Fowler flushed. "I'm the one who has to give Andrews that drug." His voice was slightly shrill. "So it's my business, too."

"You're afraid, aren't you?" Catherine asked. "You should be afraid. Everyone at the ranch will be waiting to take you down. And Nardik doesn't care."

"I care very much," Nardik said. "Stop trying to manipulate Fowler."

"You care about getting the drug into Andrews. But what about afterward? And how are you going to do it that will keep this poor asshole safe?"

"He's going to put it in the pitcher of water that's placed on the debate table in front of Andrews," Nardik said. "There will be a dozen people on that stage checking sound and video and making sure that it's secure for Andrews. It should be no problem for Fowler to slip the drug into the drinking water. It's colorless and tasteless." He smiled. "And it's a hot night, and the debate will be just as hot and vigorous. I've watched films of him at other debates and speeches. He gets thirsty. At some point during every one of them, he's had a few sips of water."

"And I don't have to stay around until he drinks it," Fowler said. "I can leave as soon as I do it and get out of there." He looked at Nardik. "Isn't that right?"

"Of course. Would I put you in any danger?" He held out his hand. "The drug."

"The phone call."

"I need to test the drug first. I can't be sure that you're not trying to fool me."

It would look suspicious if she gave in now. "Call, first. You can call Townberg back if it's not the real thing. He'll still be close enough to move on Sam and Luke."

He gazed at her for a moment, then dialed a number. "Release the boy." He hung up. "Now give it to me."

Don't give up too easily. "How do I know who you were—"

"Give it to me, or I'll call Townberg back and tell him to break the boy's neck."

She hesitated, then handed him the vial.

Nardik smiled. "Ah, a mother's desperation always carries the day. Isn't it touching, Fowler?"

Fowler stepped forward and slapped her across the mouth.

"Restrain yourself," Nardik said absently as he took out a leather kit and unzipped it. The next moment he was uncorking the vial and inserting a plastic tab into the liquid. "Now we give it a moment and see if it tests positive . . ."

"He slapped her," Hu Chang murmured, his gaze on the three figures spotlighted by the headlights. They had just reached the plain in time to see Catherine give the vial to Nardik. "We have to move quickly. She took the punishment, but it will anger her. It may precipitate matters."

"We are moving quickly," Gallo said. "I'm heading for the trees."

"No cover there," Hu Chang said.

"There's cover. In the branches of those trees. I'll climb that tree closest to us, then work my way across toward the shooter."

"Like Tarzan."

"Like me, trying to take a shooter out. Get moving, Hu Chang."

"I am moving." Hu Chang was gliding silently toward the boulder. "I will be done before you."

He might be right, Gallo thought as he faded toward the stand of trees. It was going to be hard as hell to move through those branches without sound. He had done similar actions on intelligence operations before, but this wasn't the same.

One sound that alerted that shooter in the trees could be deadly for Catherine.

Catherine made all the difference.

"It's positive." Nardik was smiling as he corked the vial. "No trickery, Catherine. I'm amazed. You must really love that boy."

"You gave me no choice. Now call Townberg and tell him that he's to come here and leave Luke and Sam alone."

"I'll call Townberg." He turned to Fowler and handed him the vial. "You have the other dose. Be sure to use both of them. Get on your way. Be careful."

Fowler nodded and shoved the vial in his pocket. "I'll do a good job. You'll be happy." He glanced at Catherine. "Do you want me to tie her up and put her in your car before I go?"

Nardik smiled. "That would be kind. Be sure to keep your gun handy. I wouldn't want you stung by the little scorpion."

Catherine tensed. It was beginning. They were going to go on the move.

Where are Gallo and Hu Chang? Don't think of them. Assume that you're alone and act accordingly.

Delay a minute or so more while I decide my next move. "You were supposed to call Townberg."

"I will call him," Nardik said. "After Fowler has you tied, I'll phone him and tell him to kill the little bastard. Did you really think that was Townberg I called before? But I'll call now, and I'll let you listen to your Luke scream." His gaze was searching her expression for any hint of pain. "You always knew that was a possibility, didn't you? You always thought I'd hurt you any way I could. You were just desperate enough to go for it."

"You have what you want, let him go." She watched Fowler coming toward her. He had his gun out as Nardik had suggested, but his expression was smugly confident. He was relying on the gun and her help-lessness before it. That was a mistake.

Use Fowler.

"We made a deal." She was looking at Nardik pleadingly as Fowler got closer to her. "You can't kill him."

"Watch me." He chuckled. "No, listen to him."

Fowler was almost close enough.

"Don't do this. I'll do—" She stabbed her knee up into Fowler's crotch as the edge of her hand came down on the wrist of his gun hand. His gun went flying as he doubled over in pain.

She could hear Nardik cursing as she dragged Fowler to the side of the van and opened the door.

It was just in time. A ping of bullets rat-tled the metal of the makeshift shield formed by the van door.

Fowler was struggling, reaching for her throat.

Get rid of him.

The ball of her hand drove upward un-der his nose, breaking it and shoving splin-ters into his brain. He went limp.

Dead.

More bullets shelling the van. But they all seemed to be coming from one direction. Nardik. He was shouting names, calling for help.

Had Gallo taken out the other men Nardik had planted?

Then move on Nardik. She had no gun, and Nardik was smarter than Fowler. But she might have another weapon. She reached in Fowler's pocket and drew out the vial of Pondera. Then she crouched and ran around the van to the other side. Nardik was still firing at the open passenger door.

She could see him crouched beside the front bumper of the car. He was cursing, his face flushed with rage as he fired.

Move fast. Hard. While he was focused on the open van door.

She uncorked the vial, gathered her muscles and sprang forward in a crouch.

But he must have seen her from the corner of his eye because he swung his gun toward her as she tackled him. He was too close to aim the weapon, but he hit her in the temple with it.

Pain.

Darkness.

He hit her again.

Fight the dizziness. Keep conscious.

"Whore. Bitch." He was lifting the gun again, this time aiming at her. "Go to hell."

She lunged forward and brought him down.

He was screaming, cursing.

His mouth . . .

Open it wider.

She jerked down his bottom lip and jammed the vial in his mouth. She saw the Pondera pouring out on his tongue as he gasped and choked to expel the vial.

His eyes widened in terror. "No!"

Too late. The vial was empty, and he was trying desperately to spit out glass and liquid.

She was so dizzy, she was seeing him only through a blur. She couldn't hold on much longer.

"Die, damn you," she whispered. "Just die."

"He'll kill the kid—anyway." His eyes were burning with malice even as he struggled for breath. "Townberg knew the boy was to die no matter . . . what happened. I beat you."

"You're dead, and he's going to live. He

was always going to live," she said unsteadily. "You're a fool. You've been had, Nardik."

His eyes widened in panic and horror. "No. It's not true. I won't—" A shudder convulsed his body, and he arched upward as his heart failed. His expression of horror froze on his face.

Dead.

Lucifer was dead, she thought hazily. Go back to your demons and brimstone.

"Catherine." Gallo was standing in front of her, his expression twisted, his voice harsh. "For God's sake, look at you. What the hell did he do to you? Why couldn't you wait to jump him? I would have been with you if you'd given me a minute."

"Alone. Never sure if I'm . . . not alone. Stop yelling . . . my head hurts." She tried to get up and would have fallen if Gallo hadn't caught her. "Andrews is safe. It was Fowler who was going to— Andrews is safe."

"Shut up." He picked her up and was carrying her toward the van. "I don't give a damn about Andrews."

She saw Hu Chang coming toward them. "Fowler has the other dose. Take it from—"

"Hush, I will attend to everything," Hu Chang said. "You were most clumsy and let Nardik hurt you. As punishment, you must be still until we make sure that you've not broken that stubborn head."

"Fine. I'm not . . ." The darkness again. "And I wasn't . . . clumsy." Push the dizziness away. Fireworks in the darkness . . . but this time she didn't know if the explosions were in the sky or in her head. Keep your eyes open. Hold on.

But she didn't have to hold on any longer, she realized. Gallo was here. Hu Chang was here.

She could let go . . .

The scent of spice and lemon . . .

Gallo.

Her eyes flew open to see him standing in a pool of brilliant morning sunlight, looking out the window across the room.

What room? Where was she?

Antiseptic green walls, crisp white linens on a narrow bed . . .

"This is a damn hospital. What am I doing here?"

He turned with a smile. "Healing, evidently. You've been in and out for the last two days. You got one helluva hit on the head, and the doctors have been keeping an eye on you."

"Two days?"

"Concussion is nothing to fool around with." His lips tightened. "Though you deserve it. Hu Chang and I took out Nardik's men and were coming in to help you. I told you not to try to do everything yourself. Why didn't you listen?"

"It was moving fast. I had to move fast, too." She touched her temple, then flinched. "I guess I didn't move fast enough."

"Oh, I don't know. You held on and managed to take Nardik down when you were barely able to function." He added, "Pat Gower has been trying to get in to see you. That mountain of flowers over there are from her and Andrews."

"How did the debate go?"

"A smash. They'll be quoting Andrews for generations. One for the history books."

"That's what Pat wanted. I'm glad . . ." She was getting drowsy again, and she shook her head to clear it. "Go get someone to check me out of here."

"No way. They said they may let you out of here tomorrow."

"I have to get back to Luke."

"I'll call him. He's in the waiting room."

She frowned. "What? You shouldn't be letting him hang around a hospital."

"Don't blame me. Hu Chang spent the night in that chair over there, and Luke decided that he should be here, too." He paused. "I stepped aside as soon as I knew you weren't in danger. I wasn't family." He came over to the bed and stared down at her. "Though I wanted like hell to stick around. I'm getting very tired of stepping aside." He bent down and gave her a quick, hard kiss. "Don't try to get out of that bed until tomorrow. It would just scare the kid if you weren't up to par. Everyone knows you're Wonder Woman. You don't have to prove it." He headed for the door. "I'll send Luke in."

The minute the door shut, she started to sit up.

She made it, but there was definitely weakness.

And drowsiness. Had they given her something?

"Hi, Catherine." Luke was standing in the doorway. "You look pale. Are you sure you should be sitting up?"

"I'm fine. I just got a bop on the head."
She smiled. "And we got the bad guy. Come
over here and let me look at you."

"Why?" He came over to the bed. "Nothing's wrong with me." He smiled back at
her. "I didn't get a bop on the head."

"I just want to look at you." She stared at
him for a long moment. "Everything okay?
I told them they shouldn't have let you stay
here. Hospitals can be depressing."

"Yeah, particularly when you're here."
He was silent a moment. "You should have
let me go with you, Catherine."

She shook her head.

"I was . . . worried. I don't like to feel like
that. I could have done something."

"Everything is fine now. Has Sam been
with you?"

He nodded. "And Hu Chang. He's outside. He said to tell you to rest and he'd see
you later." He stood looking at her, a mixture of emotions flitting across his face.
"I have to go now. He said you have to
rest."

"I'm fine. I was thinking about getting up
and checking out of this place."

He shook his head. "You have to rest."
He slowly reached out and touched her

hand, then jerked it away as if she had burned him. "You get well," he said fiercely.

Before she could answer, he had left the room.

She stared after him, then slowly settled back down in bed. She didn't understand what had happened in those moments, but she was filled with bewilderment . . . and hope.

But she couldn't process it all right now. She would lie here and rest as they were all nagging her to do. Tomorrow would do as well . . .

The next morning, her phone rang immediately after she had been served breakfast and was arguing with the nurse to bring her clothes.

Venable.

"Venable, I can't talk now. I have to get out of this place. This nurse won't bring me my clothes."

"They'll let you go. I've talked to your doctor, and he gave you an all clear." He paused. "I told him you'd have another long rest after you leave there."

"What are you talking about? I'm perfectly normal. I'm not about to rest."

"You'll rest. It's a very long flight to Hong Kong."

She stiffened. "What are you talking about? I'm going home. I'm not going to Hong Kong."

"It's your choice, but I believe you'll change your mind. Luke is in Hong Kong, Catherine."

Shock. She couldn't speak for an instant. "Explain, dammit."

"He and Hu Chang flew out shortly after he spoke to you yesterday." He paused. "I arranged for a military flight to ferry the three of us to Hong Kong."

"*You* arranged. How could you arrange to take my son out of the country without my consent?" Her voice was trembling with rage. "How would you dare, Venable?"

"Hu Chang was insistent. He wanted the boy to go with him." He added simply, "And he offered me a deal. He wouldn't give me the formula, but he promised he would never sell it to an enemy of the U.S. I did what I had to do. The boy is fine, Catherine. He wanted to go."

And that hurt even more than any other words he'd said to her.

"I may kill you, Venable."

"Then you'll have to come to Hong Kong to do it. I'm still here. We're staying at the Golden Palace. Let me know your flight, and I'll meet you at the airport." He hung up.

Her hand was shaking as she hung up the cell.

Pain and bewilderment and terrible loss.

And loneliness. Dear God, the loneliness.

What the hell was Hu Chang up to?

He was luring Luke away from her, showing him worlds of adventure and mystery that Luke would find as fascinating as he did Hu Chang. But she also knew that Hu Chang traveled dark as well as bright paths, and Luke had already been forced to negotiate tragic paths in his young life.

In my heart of hearts, I feel as if he could be my son.

No way. He's *mine.* You can't have him, Hu Chang.

She glared at the nurse as she jumped out of bed. "You go get my clothes, and if they're not here in two minutes, I'll walk out of here naked."

EPILOGUE

Hong Kong
Golden Palace

Luke was waiting for Catherine when Venable drew the speedboat up to the dock. He was wearing jeans, and a loose white shirt that was stained with dirt. His face had a smear of dirt on his cheek as well, but he was smiling.

"Hi, Catherine." He took her hand to help her from the boat. "Oops." He made a face. "I've gotten you all dirty. I ran here from the garden, and I didn't stop to wash."

"It doesn't matter." Her hand tightened on his. She didn't want to let him go. She reluctantly released him. "What were you doing in the garden?"

"Planting." He took the tail of his shirt and was wiping the dirt off her hand. "There's an entire army of gardeners re-planting Chen Lu's trees and flowers, and she said I could help. It's kind of fun."

"Chen Lu is here?"

He nodded. "She was here when we got here. She's sitting on a bench in the garden ordering everyone around." He glanced at Venable, who had not gotten out of the boat. "Hu Chang said that you didn't have to stay unless you wanted to."

"I must thank him for permission," Venable said ironically. "No, I don't want to stay. Hu Chang very kindly put me first on the firing line. I've gone through enough of a dressing-down to last me for a while." He glanced at Catherine. "I'm sorry I had to do it, Catherine. But it was imperative I deal with Hu Chang on the drug. It's my job. And now it's your job to try to get the formula from him if there's any way possible."

He put the boat in gear and roared away from the dock.

"I don't think Hu Chang will give you the formula, Catherine." Luke was gazing at Venable speeding across the water. "He won't give it to anyone."

"I don't care about the formula. I care about you." She paused, trying to frame her words. "And I want to know why you went off with Hu Chang without telling me. Didn't you know it would hurt me?"

He nodded. "I thought maybe—but Hu Chang said that it would be all right. That it was better that we brought you here." He added soberly, "I wasn't sure, but Hu Chang is very smart about most things. He said that a little hurt now, and it would all come right later."

"Hu Chang doesn't know everything." Her lips tightened. "And he doesn't think and feel like everyone either. He's different, Luke. You should have come to me and told me."

He gazed thoughtfully at her. "Are you angry with me?"

"I didn't say—" She suddenly lost control. All the pain and worry and self-imposed restraint that had been tearing at her during the long journey exploded within her. "Hell, yes, I'm angry with you. Hu Chang and you just flew off to Hong Kong and left me to trail behind you. I felt like a piece of lost luggage or something. I didn't deserve that, Luke. Not from either one of you."

His eyes widened. "You are angry. You've never talked to me like that before."

"Yes, I'm angry. I'm sorry if you don't like it, but I— Why are you smiling? This isn't funny."

"No." Luke's eyes were bright. "But it's interesting. I've always wondered if you'd ever be angry with me. You always treated me as if I—" He stopped, searching for words. "As if I were sick or dying or something."

She stared at him, stunned. "I did not."

He frowned. "Yes, you did. Like I had a terrible disease, and you had to very careful, or I'd break apart."

"I did have to be careful, dammit. I was scared to death you'd hate me, that you'd run away from me. You're a smart boy, Luke. You should have figured that out." Her voice was unsteady. "But it doesn't matter now. It happened, didn't it? You did run away from me. You and Hu Chang hopped on a plane and left me in that hospital." She drew a deep breath. "And I'm the one who feels like I'm breaking apart. But I can take it if I know you're going to be happy. That's all I ever wanted. I'm not sure Hu Chang will make you happy, but I can see how you'd want to stay with him. I did when I was just a little older than you. Sometimes, I still do."

He was still frowning. "I didn't say I wanted to stay with Hu Chang."

"Then why the devil did you go with him?" she asked fiercely.

"He said that there was a star he wanted to give you, and he had to give it to you here."

"Which makes no sense at all. Why didn't you call him on it?"

"Because I didn't see how anyone could give someone else a star, and I wanted to see how he would do it."

Luke and his boundless curiosity. "But you thought he'd be able to do it."

He nodded slowly. "I thought it would be a kind of neat present if he could pull it off."

"And a big headache if he couldn't. You shouldn't have left me like that. It wasn't fair, and it hurt me."

He didn't speak for a moment. "It hurt you? I didn't mean to do that. I don't want you to ever be hurt again." He paused, then added haltingly, "When I came to your room at the hospital, it scared me. You looked . . .

sick. Hu Chang said that you weren't going to die, but it didn't matter. He'd told me before that even though you were a good soldier, it could still happen."

"He shouldn't have talked to you about anything like that."

He shook his head. "But it was true. I knew it was true. I just didn't want to think about it."

"You shouldn't have had to think about it. You're just a boy."

"I have to think about stuff like that. I can't take care of you if I don't. And if I don't take care of you, something bad might happen." He added jerkily, "Like it did when you got hurt." His legs were parted in a belligerent stance, and he stared her in the eye. "So when I was sitting there in the hospital, I got to thinking, and here's how it should be. I know you're CIA and can't change that, but you'll have to be more careful. And I want to know what's happening. I don't want you to coddle me. If it's your problem, it should be mine, too."

She suddenly lost her breath. Had she misunderstood? Don't hope for too much. Yet how the hell could she keep from hoping when it meant everything? "And why is that, Luke?"

He didn't answer, and she could tell he was struggling for words. "I . . . care whether you live or die. It would hurt me if you were hurt or sad. I feel . . . warm when you're here and a little lonely when you're not. I think . . . we have to be together. Kelly says that I should love you, but I'm still confused about what that means. People who write about it in books seem to be confused, too. They're all over the place."

"Yeah, I've noticed." She cleared her throat. "I think we all have to work it out for ourselves."

"But I'm close?"

She nodded emphatically. "Yes, you're very close."

Thank God. Oh, thank God.

She reached out her hand and gently touched his cheek. Not too much. Go slowly. She'd won a huge victory today, and she was passionately grateful. "And I won't coddle you and try to keep you from being hurt . . . maybe."

"It's okay. I think it's all part of it." He smiled and added awkwardly, "I felt a little like that at the hospital." He stepped back and took her hand and pulled her toward the palace. "Come on. I have to get back to the garden. You can see what we're doing. I never planted anything before."

"You can have a garden at our place in Louisville." She had to hurry to keep up with him. "You never seemed interested."

"I was too busy with the books."

She suddenly stopped short. "Look, I have to see Hu Chang, Luke."

He chuckled. "Are you going to yell at him like you did me?"

"Yes."

"Then I want to see it." His smile was slyly impish. "But he's busy with Chen Lu's security team now. He said he'd see us at dinner."

"I'll go find him."

"There's Chen Lu." He waved at the woman, who was sitting on a bench by one of the fountains, and he pulled Catherine toward her. The fountain was scorched and blackened, but the water was spraying a sparkling stream into the air. "I've brought her, Chen Lu," he called. "She wants to go find Hu Chang. She's going to yell at him."

"Good. He deserves it," Chen Lu said.

"And so do you, Luke. The two of you were very naughty to Catherine." She waved her hand at a plot of earth some distance away. "Now get back to work. You have to earn your keep here."

"I will. I've decided my rose bed will be the best in your garden." He turned and trotted down the path toward the bed. "Bye, Catherine."

Chen Lu watched him affectionately before giving Catherine a brilliant smile. "It's good to see you, Catherine. I heard you were in hospital. You look well."

"I'm fine." She sat down beside Chen Lu, who was dressed in a brocade sky blue caftan and looked beautiful but terribly out of place in the scorched garden. Catherine had a sudden memory of how thin and fragile she had appeared in her black dress on the day she had left to take Rory back to Ireland. But now her smile was bright though her manner subdued. "Luke said that you had an army of gardeners planting, and he didn't exaggerate." Her gaze went to the scores of men and women in the acres of planting beds. "You should have a new growth in no time."

Chen Lu nodded. "Gallo set up the initial

work schedule before he left with you."
She looked out at the garden. "By the time
I came back, they had the charred plants
removed, new topsoil down, and were beginning to plant. I was very grateful. The
dead have to be honored, but it's good to
see rebirth. It tends to heal the heart."

"How did Rory's funeral go?"

"Sad." She made a face. "Though I threw
him the finest wake a man could ever hope
to have. It lasted three days. The pub was
full, and we drank and told great stories
about my Rory."

"As I remember, Hu Chang told you to
get your rest. It doesn't sound as if you did
that. How are you?"

"Better now. I only burned the candle
at both ends for a day or so, but it put me
down. But Rory deserved it, so I took a
chance on Hu Chang's being angry with
me. I collapsed and had to take the next
flight here and call Hu Chang and tell him
I needed him." She smiled. "He wasn't
pleased, but he came anyway. He knew
I'd probably go too far when I left. That's
why he diluted my dose when he gave it to
me. But what's life if you don't live it to the
fullest? That's what my Donal used to say.

He said, 'Chen Lu, life is the ultimate gift. Live every moment. Live for both of us.'"

"And you do," Catherine said softly.

"Every minute, just as he told me." Chen Lu gazed at Luke, who was now on his knees in the bed of roses and frowning with concentration as he dug in the earth. "I'm glad Hu Chang brought the boy here. It was not right the way he did it, but I wanted to meet your son. I have no children, but I wanted to see the boy that Hu Chang cared about."

"He's *my* son."

Chen Lu threw back her head and laughed. "And you have a right to be possessive. You'll have to keep Hu Chang from luring him into his web." Her laughter faded. "But it's a beautiful golden web that he weaves with superb skill and great thoughtfulness." She glanced away from Luke to the roses he was planting. "And he would not take Luke without you, so you're safe, Catherine."

"Am I supposed to be relieved?"

"Yes, I would be. Luke is a fine boy. Clever, curious, interesting. He needs to smile more, but I could take care of that if you care to leave him here."

"Hell, no. What is this? First Hu Chang and now you. Luke goes home with me."

"If you choose, but you're welcome to stay here. You'd fill a place. I'll be missing my Rory, and it takes time to welcome someone else after you've said good-bye."

"You have a beautiful life. But it isn't the life I'd choose."

"Think about it. Luke would be safer here." She wrinkled her nose. "I know, after everything that happened in this garden, that sounds strange. But I would see that he came to no harm. He's too important to risk."

"Of course he's too important to risk. He's my son and I love him and there's no way that—" She stopped and her eyes narrowed on Chen Lu's face. "But that isn't what you mean by that, is it? Why is he too important, Chen Lu?"

"Talk to Hu Chang." She rose to her feet. "But know that I would give you and your son a good life." She smiled as she started down the path toward the palace. "I would teach you both to laugh. It would be a hard task, but I could do it. Try me."

"Don't you dare run away." Catherine

got to her feet. "Where's Hu Chang? And where are you going?"

"I have to change for dinner. It's a little early, but I feel the need to escape. You have the same room you had before, Catherine. You have a few hours if you wish to sit here and watch Luke do his planting."

"What did you mean, Chen Lu?" she called after her with frustration. "I could shake you."

"That's why I'm running away. I'm not discreet. I'd probably tell you, and have Hu Chang angry at me." She left a trail of laughter behind her as she went into the house.

"Catherine?" Luke was looking at her inquiringly.

She probably looked as angry and frustrated as she felt. Except for those few precious moments when she realized all was going right for her relationship with Luke, all he had seen was her on the attack since he'd met her at the dock.

But as she stared at him, the anger was slipping away. Lord, he was beautiful. The sun was shining on his tousled dark hair, and his head tilted to one side as he stared

at her. It was such a familiar pose, full of
curiosity and intentness, that she felt a
melting within her. What difference did it
make if Hu Chang had schemes concerning Luke that she'd probably have to
squash at the outset? It wasn't as if she
wouldn't be able to do it. As soon as she
saw Hu Chang, the attack could begin.

But the anger and outrage could wait.
Now she was going to enjoy this moment
with Luke.

"Is there something wrong?" he asked.
"What is it? Do you need me to help you,
Catherine?"

"No." She got to her feet and strode
toward the rose bed. "But I can help you."
She dropped to her knees beside him in
the bed. "You're the boss. Give me something to do."

"Are you sure?" He skeptically studied
her sleek black slacks and tan shirt as he
handed her a trowel. "You'll get dirty."

"Probably. Ask me if I care." She smiled
and reached for one of the buckets of rose-
bushes beside him. She could smell the
damp earth and the scent of roses and felt
the warm sun on her cheeks. Her son was
beside her and they would do this task

together. Together. What a beautiful word. Her trowel dug into the earth. "We'll both have sore knees and be muddy and scratched by thorns before we finish planting the most beautiful bed in Chen Lu's garden. But it will be worth it, won't it?"

He sat back on his heels and studied her face as if she were some strange exotic puzzle he had to solve. Then he nodded slowly. "It will be worth it."

It was almost dusk when they finished planting the bed and cleaning their tools. And by the time Catherine had gone to her room, showered, and changed to the tangerine-colored silk caftan Chen Lu's maid had laid out on the bed, it was fully dark.

"You look very exotic." Chen Lu smiled as Catherine came out onto the veranda. She was dressed in a cream-colored caftan that glowed under the candles of the tiered chandeliers and made her appear almost bridal. "I've always wanted to be exotic, but I never quite made it. I can dress like an empress, but this mug of mine looks like the Mick I am." She tilted her head. "One would never believe you were the same person who came trailing up the stairs looking like a muddy ragamuffin an hour ago. But you did look like a happy ragamuffin. Where's Luke?"

"He should be down soon. I wanted to talk to Hu Chang before dinner. Where is he?"

"In the garden. He said he wanted to inspect the rose bed you and Luke created for me." She arched a mischievous brow. "He wasn't sure that you two were capable enough. He said that when you worked in his herb garden when you were in your teens, you were woefully inadequate."

"Ungrateful bastard."

"I can't argue with you. I've always been so grateful to him that it never occurred to me to question him."

"And that's why he has an ego as big as your palace." She headed for the steps leading to the garden. "But, believe me, I have enough questions for all of us."

"I thought there was a good chance that you'd abandon me to go after Hu Chang. I'll hold dinner and entertain Luke until you're ready to come back." She called after her, "Unless you're insecure about me stealing Luke away from you? I can be completely fascinating, you know."

"By all means fascinate him. He'll find it an interesting experience. Though he may look at you as if you're some kind of peculiar bug. And I'm *not* insecure."

"No, you're not, are you?" Chen Lu's tone was thoughtful. "Things change . . ."

Yes, things did change, Catherine thought as she hurried down the path. There was still fear and anxiety in her attitude toward Luke, and she now realized that it was one of the biggest barriers between them. It would take a long time for her to rid herself of that apprehension and the flashes of panic, but she was on her way.

Because Luke was on his way toward her. They were both taking small steps, but the steps were leading them closer to each other. This afternoon they had joked and worked companionably, and there had been an easiness between them that had never existed before. She didn't know if he could ever fully accept her as his mother, but this friendship and affection was a prize in itself.

"You're smiling." Hu Chang was coming

down the path toward her. "You must be happy at the prospect of seeing me. And Chen Lu told me that you were so displeased."

"You bastard." She stopped on the path, glaring at him. "You had no right to steal my son and take him to the other side of the world. I will *not* forgive you for this Hu Chang."

"I did not steal, I only borrowed him."

"And you lied to him. You told him that you wanted him to come here because you wanted to give me a present, some foolishness about a star."

"A shooting star, Catherine," he said softly.

"What is that supp—" She stopped as she remembered Hu Chang's words on the plane that had brought them to San Francisco.

Some of my drugs are like shooting stars, others are like suns.

"The Pondera," she whispered. "Venable said you wouldn't turn the drug over to him. You're going to give the drug to me and let me destroy it?"

He shook his head. "Though I know

that's what you wanted me to do. Remember, I did compromise and tell you I'd let you have right of refusal of any victim."

"That's not good enough. There shouldn't be any more victims. That drug is too dangerous. What if it somehow got on the black market?"

"I made one mistake. I'll not make another." His lips quirked. "One mistake in a lifetime is quite enough for a unique man like me."

"You want to give me something to make up for kidnapping my son? That damn Pondera is the only thing I want. Even then, I don't know if I'm going to forgive you."

"But I can't do that. I've already given it to someone else."

"Oh, *shit.* Who?"

"Luke."

She stared at him in shock. "What the hell?"

"If I'd been there for you when he was that two-year-old child, I would have kept your Luke from being kidnapped and suffering all those years. I would have kept you from suffering, Catherine. I've decided I have to provide compensation."

"I told you that was bullshit," she said impatiently. "Though it's just like you to think the greatest compensation would be in the form of a deadly poison. I won't let Luke accept a crazy gift like that. Give it to me. I'll know what to do with it."

"But I've already told you, the gift has already been given." He shook his head. "I thought it best not to give you a choice. You would only have worried. In fact, I was debating whether to tell you at all. But that would have been neither fair nor honorable."

Her hands clenched at her sides. "What do you mean? Luke only mentioned a gift for me."

"He does not know he has it. I gave it to him when the two of you visited me several weeks ago."

"The book about Chinese chemistry?"

He nodded. "The book was a trigger to reinforce the posthypnotic suggestion. I didn't want to overload him. I knew how he loved his books, and there was no question he would read it. I set a time in the future for the suggestion to take effect. I figured we'd need a little preparation time."

She stared at him in disbelief. "You gave him the formula when you hypnotized him? Dammit, then find a way to undo it and debrief him or whatever."

He shook his head.

"I won't let him walk around with that ugliness in his head. If you won't help me, I'll find someone who will."

"Pondera is a very special shooting star, Catherine. I had to put in safeguards. You could kill him, and you wouldn't kill the effect of that suggestion."

This was a nightmare. "Are you crazy?" she asked unsteadily. "You knew how I'd feel about what you did. If you care anything about me, you'll stop this horror."

"It would only be a horror in the wrong hands. I studied Luke before I gave the formula to him. He's complicated, but that's not a bad thing, and he has magnificent potential."

"As a master poisoner?" she asked bitterly.

"No, one always wants a better life for the generation that comes after. He can be what he wishes to be. It will be up to him." He tilted his head. "I'll be curious to see what he does with my gift."

"I don't want Luke to have the power to murder, Hu Chang."

"I'm sorry." His tone was regretful. "I told you there were side effects to Pondera when I created it. I can't take that power away. It's part of the balance."

"Balance? It's the whole damn shooting match."

"Not quite."

"It's the only thing I've seen."

"No, you're wrong." He paused. "You've seen Chen Lu."

"And what's that got to—" She stopped, her mind connecting, sorting possibilities. "That stuff you gave her to get her through Rory's funeral. Is that what you're talking about? You said it was something like that medicine you gave to Carmody to save his life."

"Something like. But not the same. Carmody's drug was a first generation of Pondera."

"What are you saying?"

"How old do you think Chen Lu is?"

"Late forties, early fifties. It's hard to tell."

"She's eighty-two."

"No way," she said flatly.

He nodded. "I realized that it's hard to accept. But it's true, Catherine. When she came to me to save her husband, she did not appear as she does now. She was full of vitality, but age had taken its toll." He smiled. "But even as heartbroken as she was due to her Donal's illness, I'd never seen anyone so vibrantly alive. While I treated her husband, I grew to care for both of them. They loved every second, every minute of life. It was truly remarkable."

"She said something about that to me."

"I don't doubt it. I'm surprised she didn't say more since she knew how close we are. Even though I've forbidden her to discuss Pondera, Chen Lu has to be closely monitored. Donal knew he was dying, but he didn't want her to die with him. He wanted her to keep that love of life that was so much a part of her. He wanted her to go on. Before he died, he asked me to help him, help her." He added simply, "So I did."

She asked carefully, "And just what did you do, Hu Chang?"

"I'd completed the lab experiments on Pondera a few months before, and I'd been searching for a subject who would be a good test case. Chen Lu's temperament and physical condition seemed ideal. After Donal Moriarty died, I gave Chen Lu a choice."

"What choice?"

"To keep on living physically and mentally with keenness and vigor and almost certainly to have a renewal of stem cells to a great degree." He shrugged. "Or to die because she'd lost the great love of her life. I would have accommodated her whichever she'd decided to do. It wasn't as easy a choice as you would think, and I wouldn't allow her to make that decision until I went over all the pros and cons of both choices. It took over six months until she chose Pondera."

She grabbed desperately at the two words that offered a glimmer of clarity in this bewildering fog. "Stem cells?"

"But of course. What else are we talking about? Pay attention, Catherine."

"Be quiet. I have to understand this. Are you talking about a fountain of youth?"

He gave her a look of disgust. "I don't deal in legends. Stem cell research is medically sound. Although my application is a little unorthodox."

"Unorthodox," she repeated weakly. "How long has Chen Lu been taking the drug?"

"A little over four years. Chen Lu believes it's been a great success. There's been an astonishing amount of muscle regeneration. She's very healthy, and her energy level is tremendously high."

"I noticed."

"I examine her every year and compare notes, but I've seen no ill effects." He made a face. "Chen Lu disagrees. She says if her face and body looks so young, why couldn't I get rid of that white hair."

"It's beautiful . . ."

"And if I added anything to the formula that would cause that particular change, it would send up a red flare. She mustn't look too young. It would be difficult for her . . . and for me."

"And we wouldn't want that." She moistened her lips. "No fountain of youth. How long?"

"I have no idea. It would depend on the physical condition of the person. That didn't change on the plus side of the balance sheet."

"Guess."

"Chen Lu, at least another fifty or sixty years if I keep her on Pondera." He paused. "A young, strong male with only the slightest cell deterioration." He met her gaze. "You'll have to be the one to guess. A long, long time. There aren't any guidelines."

She closed her eyes. She had no breath. She felt as if she'd been socked in the stomach.

"Shh." Hu Chang was suddenly close to her, his hand on her cheek. "It's going to be fine, Catherine."

"Is it?" She opened her eyes. "Let me get this straight. You haven't given Luke this drug, have you?"

He shook his head. "Only the choice. He'll have the knowledge and the capability to re-create Pondera when he reaches his thirtieth birthday. I figured by that time he would have had the opportunity to work through any psychological problems and be mature enough to make a decision." He smiled down into her eyes. "That's almost twenty years for us to guide him in the way we want him to go. I can see no problem."

"Us?"

"Do you think I would give a gift without

making sure that he would not suffer from it? Right now, Luke is a shooting star, but we will make sure he turns into a sun. I left you alone before. I will not do it again." He paused. "Unless you wish it."

She looked at him with frustration and extreme irritation. "That's right, back me in a corner where I don't know what in hell is going to happen with Luke, then you give me a choice."

He chuckled. "But is that not clever? How can you refuse me?"

"I intend to make a valiant attempt."

"It will do no good. We were meant to be together. Don't worry, I will make sure that you have whatever you wish. Sometimes it will be painful for me, but I realize that the only way to hold on is to let go . . . for a while." He took her hand. "Come, we will go join Chen Lu and Luke on the veranda, and over dinner, you can take the time to think and become accustomed to the idea."

For a moment she didn't move. Then she fell into step with him. "I think it will take longer than any dinner."

"Perhaps, but I've noticed you adjust beautifully to any situation. Admit it. Is this not a magnificent gift that I've given you? Luke lost years when he was in captivity, he can take them back now."

How could she deny the splendor even if fraught with risks and gigantic problems? But he'd had no right to do what he'd done without discussing it with her. Because he knew her so well, he'd realized that she would have trouble with even a hint of danger to Luke, and he'd breezed right by any possible objections. "It's a damn two-headed coin."

"Lightning bolts and the gods of Mount Olympus. It's not a bad combination. I believe I did very well with Pondera." He waved at Luke, who had come to the balustrade of the veranda and was watching them approach. "A few glitches, but it definitely has potential to become a sun."

"What doesn't kill you, makes you strong?"

"Exactly. You can see why I couldn't let it be destroyed."

"But you're not going to go public with it?"

"No, I've been dribbling out bits of my stem cell research to responsible organizations, but I can't release Pondera. What you call a two-headed coin could become a two-headed dragon breathing fire and brimstone. It's like trying to separate Siamese twins. One almost always dies or becomes much weaker. In the case of Pondera, it's the poison that usually survives. I can strike the balance and get what I need, but I wouldn't entrust it to anyone else."

She had a sudden thought. "Did you take it yourself?"

"Not yet. I haven't come to terms with the same decision I gave to Chen Lu. I find it easier to go the selfish route and give my gifts to the ones I wish to keep with me."

She stiffened, and her gaze flew to his face. "That was plural. I'm not going to be covered by that umbrella, Hu Chang. I make my own decisions. Back off."

"As you wish."

He was smiling.

"Hu Chang."

"How do you know that I didn't already give you the drug?" he asked softly. "I was with you in the hospital for many hours."

"Did you do it?"

He was silent.

"Answer me, Hu Chang."

"What is life without mystery?"

"Real and worthwhile."

"I beg to differ. Perhaps we'll discuss this at another time." He started up the stone steps to the veranda. "I've brought her back to you, Luke. And I'm wounded but still able to function."

"Did you give her your present?" Luke asked. "Did she like it?"

Hu Chang looked at Catherine. "Shall we ask her? Did you like your present, Catherine?"

"I'm not certain." The two-headed coin. Hu Chang's gift was not without the potential for awesome headaches, even tragedy, as well as a treasure sought by man through the centuries. She gazed at Luke, who was standing there strong and full of life, his eyes bright and curious, ready to take on the next challenge, ready to take on the world. She had been like that when she was his age, she remembered. No challenge too big, no goal impossible to reach.

And when had she become afraid to face those challenges, she suddenly thought impatiently. She'd just grab the treasure, fight off the dragons, and carve out a golden life for this son she loved more than life itself. "I've changed my mind. Yes, I am certain." She smiled confidently as she took Luke's hand and strolled with him toward the dinner table, where Chen Lu waited. "I like my gift very much and you're going to like it, too, Luke. Hu Chang and I will see that you do."

"Good night, Catherine." Luke yawned as he stopped at the head of the stairs. "I'll see you at breakfast. Are you going to plant with me tomorrow?"

"I wouldn't miss it."

"Good." She watched him turn and go down the hall to his room, then stop to look over his shoulder. "You're not mad at Hu Chang any longer?"

"Yes, I am. This time he did something that will take a little time for me to get over."

He frowned as he opened the door. "But you didn't act mad at dinner. Why?"

She shrugged. "Because with Hu Chang, there are always mixed feelings. You accept that if you want him to stay in your life."

"And you want him to stay?"

"Yes, no, most of the time. Mixed feelings." She paused. "But it always ends with yes, Luke. For me, it's always yes."

He nodded gravely as the door closed behind him. "For me, too."

She smiled ruefully as she went down the hall to her own room.

Hu Chang, you've got both of us, but don't get too complacent. Neither one of us is going to let you trample over us and change our lives to suit you.

Except he had done just that when he had given Luke that posthypnotic suggestion that could change all their lives in the future.

But that was twenty years in the future, and it was difficult to be afraid of something that far away. All her life she had lived in the present, and her present with Luke was looking bright enough to blur everything else beyond tomorrow. Accept Chen Lu's philosophy and enjoy every moment of the day.

She went into her suite and forced herself to cross to the French doors and go out on the balcony. She had to erase that last horrible memory of gazing down at the burning garden and watching Nardik kill Rory Benedict.

Rebirth, Chen Lu had said. There always has to be rebirth.

The moonlight was silver-bright, and from here she could see the extent of that rebirth. Hundreds of trees and bushes and earth that had been turned and made ready for seed.

Hu Chang.

He was on the path nearest to the veranda and was staring out at the plantings.

No doubt critiquing the work of the landscapers, she thought ruefully. He'd probably be out there at dawn telling them how they should have done it.

He must have sensed her eyes on him because he suddenly turned and looked up at the balcony. His expression wasn't what she had expected. It was sober, and there was a hint of pain. Was he finding this rebirth as sad as she?

Then he smiled and bowed mockingly to her.

Who knows what he was thinking? Just once she'd like to pierce that—

"Catherine."

She stiffened in shock at the voice in the room behind her.

Gallo.

"I knocked, but I didn't get an answer." He was coming across the room toward her. "Not that I wouldn't have come in anyway. I didn't fly all those hours to stand waiting in that damn hall. I'm mad as hell, and I want answers."

She whirled and left the balcony to stand before him. "What are you doing here?"

"I believe the term is showdown." His hands grasped her shoulders. "You walk out of that hospital and don't even leave me a message to tell me where you were going."

"I had something to do. I had to go get my son."

"So I heard from Hu Chang. But you couldn't let me come with you? You couldn't let me help?"

"It wasn't your business. Any debt you might have owed me you paid in full."

"Another reason why I'm here. The decks are clear. And *you're* my business." His hands were opening and closing on her shoulders in a motion that was purely sensual. "And you know damn well I'm right. What's between us isn't finished, and I'm not going to let you walk away until you tell me that you don't want it, you don't want me. But you're not going to tell me from half a world away." He pulled her close, and his lips were suddenly on her throat. Her heart leaped as his tongue touched the pulse in the hollow. "Tell me now, Catherine. Tell me how you want to walk away."

Walk? Her knees were so weak, she could hardly stand. The scent of him. The *feel* of him.

His tongue was outlining the fullness of her lower lip. "Tell me."

"You know damn well that I don't want to do anything but go to bed with you right now," she said unevenly. "But my life is complicated, and it's getting more complicated by the minute. You're a . . . distraction."

"You bet I am." His hands slid down to rub her breasts through the silk of the caftan. "And I've no objection to taking that role in your life for a while. I'll work very hard, and before we're through, I promise I'll be perfect at it."

"You're already pretty damn good." Her breasts were becoming taut under the warmth of his palms. "But I don't need . . . distractions."

"Yes, you do. You need this." He slipped the caftan off one shoulder, and his lips pressed on the hollow. "You need me. Even Hu Chang said that you did."

"What?" She was starting to shake, and all she wanted was for him to stop talking and start moving. But he had said something to which she had to pay attention. Something that had struck a chord . . .

Then it struck her.

Hu Chang.

"Dammit." She pushed Gallo away and stepped back. "What the hell do you mean that Hu Chang said that I needed you?"

"Shit." His voice was thick with self-disgust. "Wrong thing to say. But it could have gone either way."

"What does Hu Chang have to do with your being here?" She was thinking back to what he'd said earlier when she'd been too shocked at his appearance to take notice. "You said he'd told you I'd gone after my son. You didn't track him down, did you? He called you and told you where I was and why I was here."

"Yes; I'm not trying to hide anything from you, Catherine." His smile was twisted. "It's not as if Hu Chang and I are coconspirators. We're definitely not that close. He called and filled me in on why you'd left the hospital and told me that there was a possibility that you might need me here."

"I don't need you. I don't need anyone."

"Not at the moment," he said resignedly. "I blew it." His expression suddenly hardened. "Or maybe I was set up by that wily bastard."

"Not you. I'm the one he's trying to manipulate."

"I will make sure you have everything you wish. Sometimes it will be painful for me, but I realize that the only way to hold on is to let go . . . for a while."

"What?" Gallo's eyes were narrowed on her face. "Explain."

"You're a distraction? He doesn't mind a distraction for me. Well, he may mind it, but it's okay as long as it comes from him. He has to be in control." Her eyes were glittering with anger. "He is *not* in control."

She turned and strode out onto the balcony.

Hu Chang was standing where she had left him.

Alone.

Loneliness. The bond that had held them together through the years. Loneliness and an affection that was stronger than the bond itself.

Don't remember those years. Hold on to the anger.

She glared down at him. "Why the hell did you think you could act as my pimp, Hu Chang?"

"I only offered you the opportunity. You were obviously beguiled by Gallo. I thought you might enjoy him." He shrugged. "If I was wrong, send him away."

And that might be what he wanted her to do. With Hu Chang, it was difficult to tell what his purpose was at any given time.

"No, I'm not going to send him away." She gestured to Gallo, who had come out to stand beside her. "Because he's more than the chess piece you want to make him. He's one hell of a man, and I respect his mind and his courage as well as the fact that I want to go to bed with him. There's a good chance I will enjoy him if he wants me. But it's not because you want it to happen or don't want it to happen. And it won't be on your timetable. It will be because we want it. Do you understand?"

He inclined his head. "Perfectly."

"Good." She whirled and stalked back

into the bedroom and slammed the door. "Did you hear him, Gallo? He admitted it. He's outrageous."

"Oh, I heard him." Gallo leaned back against the French doors. "And I didn't like him trying to use me. If you didn't love the son of a bitch so much, I'd probably kill him. But that would be cutting off my nose to spite my face."

"I may kill him myself. You have no idea what else he's done."

"And you may or may not decide to tell me. So much of what's between you stays between you." He held up his hand as she started to speak. "And I've accepted that's the way it's going to be. I'm not interfering in your relationship, I'm going to build one of my own. All I want to know is if you meant what you told him out there."

She stared him in the eye. "I meant every word." She went to him and slid her arms around his neck. "Every syllable." She kissed him long, hard, and with passion. "Any questions?"

"No." He drew a deep breath, then stepped back. "I'll see you in the morning. I've got to get out of here."

She frowned. "Why?"

"Because I won't be able to go if I don't. I'm already cursing myself as a complete ass for doing it." He brushed his lips across her forehead. "But I'm not going to start building our relationship on the defiance you're feeling toward Hu Chang. I won't let him intrude one breath into it."

"That's not why I—"

"Tomorrow." He kissed her quickly, then was gone.

She stared blankly at the closed door. Everything had happened so quickly and none of it as she'd thought it would. Passion, bewilderment, anger, passion again. Gallo had probably been right to leave, but it was difficult to sort out her feelings at the moment. She was the one who had hurled those words of defiance at Hu Chang, but Gallo had been the one to follow through. Perhaps because Gallo had realized that her anger and hurt with Hu Chang had made her behave impulsively. She should have felt only anger, but with Hu Chang she could never feel the anger without the hurt.

And if she felt hurt, had her words also hurt Hu Chang?

She remembered that glimpse of pain

she'd thought she'd seen on his face. Hu Chang, who was always enigmatic and never revealed vulnerability.

Imagination.

No, not imagination.

And no matter how angry and indignant she was toward him, she couldn't bear that thought.

She opened the French doors and went out on the balcony.

He was no longer standing on the path.

"Here, Catherine." Hu Chang was sitting at a table on the veranda to the left of the path. "Don't worry, I'm fine."

"I wasn't worried."

He smiled. "Liar. We always worry about each other."

"You were wrong, Hu Chang."

"I did what I thought was best. Has he gone?"

"Yes, did you plan that to happen, too?"

"No, not this time," he said wearily. "I thought no further than getting him here for you. I knew you'd be angry and fretting about Luke, and I wanted to give you a gift that would take your mind off what I'd done."

"Oh, Gallo did that all right. He'll be back, Hu Chang. It was his decision."

He nodded. "Very wise. I always knew Gallo was a dangerous choice."

"It wasn't your choice to make. Tell me you won't do anything like this again."

He shook his head. "I would never lie to you. I do what I must." He smiled faintly. "But I promise that you will never be bored by anything I do. That's why you always come back to me."

"That's not why I come back."

His smile faded. "No, that is true, and I realize my good fortune." He suddenly straightened in his chair, and his smile returned. "So why do you not come down off that balcony and join me? You're not the Juliet type, and your Romeo has temporarily deserted you. I'll go raid the wine cellar for one of Chen Lu's best vintages, and we'll sit here and watch the moon travel across the night sky. You'll have the opportunity to curse and lecture me, and when you tire of that, we'll talk of other things. Or just be silent. Silence is good, too."

Watch the moon travel across the night sky . . .

The words invoked a picture too tempting to resist.

Serenity that soothed. Friendship that banished all loneliness. A closeness that needed no words.

"Yes, silence can be good, too." She turned and headed for the French doors. "But not until we have a few more words about what you did. Go get that wine, Hu Chang. I'll be right down."